Also by Georgette Heyer

The Black Moth
Simon the Coldheart
These Old Shades
The Masqueraders
Beauvallet
Powder and Patch
The Conqueror
Devil's Cub
The Convenient Marriage
Regency Buck
The Talisman Ring
An Infamous Army
Royal Escape
The Spanish Bride
The Corinthian
Faro's Daughter
Friday's Child
The Reluctant Widow
The Foundling
Arabella
The Grand Sophy
The Quiet Gentleman
Cotillion
The Toll Gate
Bath Tangle
Sprig Muslin
April Lady
Sylvester

Venetia
The Unknown Ajax
Pistols for Two
A Civil Contract
The Nonesuch
False Colours
Frederica
Black Sheep
Cousin Kate
Charity Girl
Lady of Quality
My Lord John

Mystery
Footsteps in the Dark
Why Shoot a Butler?
The Unfinished Clue
Death in the Stocks
Behold, Here's Poison
They Found Him Dead
A Blunt Instrument
No Wind of Blame
Envious Casca
Penhallow
Duplicate Death
Detection Unlimited

"Nobody does it better."

—Meredith Duran, *New York Times* bestselling author

"**Utterly timeless charm**... The dialogue sparkles with wit... And beneath that period speech, the ring of truth, the human flaws and virtues, speaks just as perfectly to today's reader."

—Nora Roberts, #1 *New York Times* bestselling author

"Georgette Heyer was **a masterful writer**: the impeccable research, the bone-dry wit, the twists and turns of plot—as complex and neatly balanced as a Regency country dance."

—Loretta Chase, *New York Times* bestselling author

"If I had to choose just one word with which to describe Georgette Heyer's books, I would say that they *sparkle*."

—Mary Balogh, *New York Times* bestselling author

"If you want **a great story**, if you want to laugh until your sides ache, if you want to know characters so well you will scratch when they itch, then Georgette Heyer is the novelist for you."

—Catherine Coulter, *New York Times* bestselling author

"Every delightful quality of Regencies—humor, charm, elegance, derring-do—was written first and brilliantly by Georgette Heyer. She is the giant upon whose shoulders the entire romance genre stands—**the first, best, and brightest** of historical romance."

—Grace Burrowes, *New York Times* bestselling author

"Georgette Heyer's Regency romances are **delightful**."

—Philippa Gregory, *New York Times* bestselling author

"Heyer's women were **spunky, daring, and outrageous**...her heroes the stuff of dreams."

—Diana Palmer, *New York Times* bestselling author

"One never forgets one's first Heyer."

—Mary Jo Putney, *New York Times* bestselling author

"Romance, adventure, **side-splitting humor**—no one writes like Georgette Heyer!"

—Lauren Willig, *New York Times* bestselling author

These Old
Shades

Georgette Heyer.

SIGNATURE COLLECTION

Includes Glossary of Regency Slang and Afterword by
Jennifer Kloester, Georgette Heyer's official biographer

sourcebooks
casablanca

Published by Sourcebooks Casablanca, an imprint of Sourcebooks, Inc.
P.O. Box 4410, Naperville, Illinois 60567-4410
(630) 961-3900
Fax: (630) 961-2168
sourcebooks.com

Originally published in 1926 in Great Britain by Heinemann, London. This edition issued based on the paperback edition published in 2009 in the United States by Sourcebooks Casablanca, an imprint of Sourcebooks, Inc.

Library of Congress Cataloging-in-Publication Data

Heyer, Georgette.
    These old shades / Georgette Heyer.
        p. cm.
    1. England--Social life and customs--18th century--Fiction. I. Title.
PR6015.E795T47 2009
823'.914--dc22
                                        2009029781

Printed and bound in Canada.
MBP 10 9 8 7 6 5 4 3 2 1

Contents

One: His Grace of Avon Buys a Soul 1

Two: Introducing the Comte de Saint-Vire........................ 13

Three: Which Tells of a Debt Unpaid.................................... 27

Four: His Grace of Avon Becomes Further Acquainted
with His Page 33

Five: His Grace of Avon Visits Versailles 48

Six: His Grace of Avon Refuses to Sell His Page 63

Seven: Satan and Priest at One.. 77

Eight: Hugh Davenant Is Amazed 91

Nine: Léon and Léonie..101

Ten: Lady Fanny's Virtue Is Outraged..................................111

Eleven: Mr Marling's Heart Is Won 127

Twelve: His Grace of Avon's Ward 132

Thirteen: The Education of Léonie 140

Fourteen: The Appearance on the Scene of
Lord Rupert Alastair...147

Fifteen: Lord Rupert Makes the Acquaintance of Léonie 158

Sixteen: The Coming of the Comte de Saint-Vire.................166

Seventeen: Of a Capture, a Chase, and Confusion.................172

Eighteen: The Indignation of Mr Manvers....................182

Nineteen: Lord Rupert Wins the Second Trick.....................194

Twenty: His Grace of Avon Takes Command
  of the Game...210

Twenty-One: The Discomfiture of the Comte
  de Saint-Vire 220

Twenty-Two: The Arrival of Another Player in
  the Game...234

Twenty-Three: Mr Marling Allows Himself to
  Be Persuaded 244

Twenty-Four: Hugh Davenant Is Agreeably Surprised.........255

Twenty-Five: Léonie Curtsies to the Polite World..............267

Twenty-Six: The Presentation of Léonie.............................282

Twenty-Seven: The Hand of Madame de Verchoureux 297

Twenty-Eight: The Comte de Saint-Vire Discovers
  an Ace in His Hand...310

Twenty-Nine: The Disappearance of Léonie.......................318

Thirty: His Grace of Avon Trumps the Comte's Ace 331

Thirty-One: His Grace of Avon Wins All 349

Thirty-Two: His Grace of Avon Astonishes Everyone
  for the Last Time..359

Afterword...369

Glossary of Regency Slang 372

Reading Group Guide..384

About the Author..386

This Age I grant (and grant with pride),
    Is varied, rich, eventful;
But if you touch its weaker side,
    Deplorably resentful;

Belaud it, and it takes your praise
    With an air of calm conviction:
Condemn it, and at once you raise
    A storm of contradiction.

Whereas with these old Shades of mine,
    Their ways and dress delight me;
And should I trip by word or line,
    They cannot well indict me.

—From "Epilogue" to *Eighteenth Century Vignettes* by Austin Dobson

One

His Grace of Avon Buys a Soul

A GENTLEMAN WAS STROLLING DOWN A SIDE STREET IN PARIS, ON his way back from the house of one Madame de Verchoureux. He walked mincingly, for the red heels of his shoes were very high. A long purple cloak, rose-lined, hung from his shoulders and was allowed to fall carelessly back from his dress, revealing a full-skirted coat of purple satin, heavily laced with gold; a waistcoat of flowered silk; faultless smallclothes; and a lavish sprinkling of jewels on his cravat and breast. A three-cornered hat, point-edged, was set upon his powdered wig, and in his hand he carried a long beribboned cane. It was little enough protection against footpads, and although a light dress sword hung at the gentleman's side its hilt was lost in the folds of his cloak, not quickly to be found. At this late hour, and in this deserted street, it was the height of foolhardiness to walk unattended and flaunting jewels, but the gentleman seemed unaware of his recklessness. He proceeded languidly on his way, glancing neither to left nor to right, apparently heedless of possible danger.

But as he walked down the street, idly twirling his cane, a body hurled itself upon him, shot like a cannon-ball from a dark alley that yawned to the right of the magnificent gentleman. The figure clutched at the elegant cloak, cried out in a startled voice, and tried to regain his balance.

His Grace of Avon swirled about, gripping his assailant's wrists and bearing them downwards with a merciless strength belied by his foppish appearance. His victim gave a whimper of pain and sank quivering to his knees.

'M'sieur! Ah, let me go! I did not mean – I did not know – I would not – Ah, m'sieur, let me go!'

His Grace bent over the boy, standing a little to one side so that the light of an adjacent street lamp fell on that white, agonised countenance. Great violet-blue eyes gazed wildly up at him, terror in their depths.

'Surely you are a little young for this game?' drawled the Duke. 'Or did you think to take me unawares?'

The boy flushed, and his eyes grew dark with indignation.

'I did not seek to rob you! Indeed, indeed I did not! I – I was running away! I – oh, m'sieur, let me go!'

'In good time, my child. From what were you running, may I ask? From another victim?'

'No! Oh, please let me go! You – you do not understand! He will have started in pursuit! Ah, please, please, milor'!'

The Duke's curious, heavy-lidded eyes never wavered from the boy's face. They had widened suddenly, and become intent.

'And who, child, is "he"?'

'My – my brother. Oh, please –'

Round the corner of the alley came a man, full-tilt. At sight of Avon he checked. The boy shuddered, and now clung to Avon's arm.

'Ah!' exploded the newcomer. 'Now, by God, if the whelp has sought to rob you, milor', he shall pay for it! You scoundrel! Ungrateful brat! You shall be sorry, I promise you! Milor', a thousand apologies! The lad is my young brother. I was beating him for his laziness when he slipped from me –'

The Duke raised a scented handkerchief to his thin nostrils.

'Keep your distance, fellow,' he said haughtily. 'Doubtless beating is good for the young.'

The boy shrank closer to him. He made no attempt to escape, but his hands twitched convulsively. Once again the Duke's strange eyes ran over him, resting for a moment on the copper-red curls that were cut short and ruffled into wild disorder.

'As I remarked, beating is good for the young. Your brother, you said?' He glanced now at the swarthy, coarse-featured young man.

'Yes, noble sir, my brother. I have cared for him since our parents died, and he repays me with ingratitude. He is a curse, noble sir, a curse!'

The Duke seemed to reflect.

'How old is he, fellow?'

'He is nineteen, milor'.'

The Duke surveyed the boy.

'Nineteen. Is he not a little small for his age?'

'Why, milor', if – if he is it is no fault of mine! I – I have fed him well. I pray you, do not heed what he says! He is a viper, a wild-cat, a veritable curse!'

'I will relieve you of the curse,' said his Grace calmly.

The man stared, uncomprehending.

'Milor' – ?'

'I suppose he is for sale?'

A cold hand stole into the Duke's, and clutched it.

'Sale, milor'? You – ?'

'I believe I will buy him to be my page. What is his worth? A louis? Or are curses worthless? An interesting problem.'

The man's eyes gleamed suddenly with avaricious cunning.

'He is a good boy, noble sir. He can work. Indeed, he is worth much to me. And I have an affection for him. I –'

'I will give a guinea for your curse.'

'Ah, but no, milor'! He is worth more! Much, much more!'

'Then keep him,' said Avon, and moved on.

The boy ran to him, clinging to his arm.

'Milor', take me! Oh, please take me! I will work well for you! I swear it! Oh, I beg of you, take me!'

His Grace paused.

'I wonder if I am a fool?' he said in English. He drew the diamond pin from his cravat, and held it so that it winked and sparkled in the light of the lamp. 'Well, fellow? Will this suffice?'

The man gazed at the jewel as though he could hardly believe his eyes. He rubbed them, and drew nearer, staring.

'For this,' Avon said, 'I purchase your brother, body and soul. Well?'

'Give it me!' whispered the man, and stretched out his hand. 'The boy is yours, milor'.'

Avon tossed the pin to him.

'I believe I requested you to keep your distance,' he said. 'You offend my nostrils. Child, follow me.' On he went, down the street, with the boy at a respectful distance behind him.

They came at last to the Rue St-Honoré, and to Avon's house. He passed in with never a glance behind him to see whether his new possession followed or not, and walked across the courtyard to the great nail-studded door. Bowing lackeys admitted him, looking in surprise at the shabby figure who came in his wake.

The Duke let fall his cloak, and handed his hat to one of the footmen.

'Mr Davenant?' he said.

'In the library, your Grace.'

Avon sauntered across the hall to the library door. It was opened for him, and he went in, nodding to the boy to follow.

Hugh Davenant sat by the fire, reading a book of poems. He glanced up as his host came in, and smiled.

'Well, Justin?' Then he saw the shrinking child by the door. 'Faith, what have we here?'

'You may well ask,' said the Duke. He came to the fire, and stretched one elegantly shod foot to the blaze. 'A whim. That dirty and starved scrap of humanity is mine.' He spoke in English, but it was evident that the boy understood, for he flushed, and hung his curly head.

'Yours?' Davenant looked from him to the boy. 'What mean you, Alastair? Surely – you cannot mean – your son?'

'Oh, no!' His Grace smiled in some amusement. 'Not this time, my dear Hugh. I bought this little rat for the sum of one diamond.'

'But – but why, in heaven's name?'

'I have no idea,' said his Grace placidly. 'Come here, rat.'

The boy came to him timidly, and allowed Justin to turn his face to the light.

'Quite a pretty child,' the Duke remarked. 'I shall make him my page. So entertaining to possess a page, body and soul.'

Davenant rose, and took one of the boy's hands in his.

'I suppose you will explain, some time or another,' he said. 'For the present, why not feed the poor child?'

'You are always so efficient,' sighed the Duke. He turned to the table, on which a cold supper was laid, awaiting him. 'Wonderful. You might almost have known that I should bring home a guest. You may eat, little rat.'

The boy looked up at him shyly.

'Please, milor', I can wait. I – I would not eat your supper. I would rather wait, if – if you please.'

'I do not please, my child. Go and eat.' He sat down as he spoke, twirling his quizzing-glass. After a moment's hesitation the boy went to the table and waited for Hugh to carve him a leg of chicken. Having supplied his wants, Hugh came back to the fire.

'Are you mad, Justin?' he asked, faintly smiling.

'I believe not.'

'Then why have you done this? What do you, of all men, want with a child of his age?'

'I thought it might be an amusement. As you doubtless know, I am suffering from *ennui*. Louise wearies me. This' – he waved one white hand towards the famished boy – 'is a heaven-sent diversion.'

Davenant frowned.

'You surely do not intend to adopt the child?'

'He – er – adopted me.'

'You are going to make him as your son?' persisted Hugh incredulously.

The Duke's eyebrows rose, rather superciliously.

'My dear Hugh! A child from the gutter? He shall be my page.'

'And what interest will that afford you?'

Justin smiled, and his glance travelled to the boy.

'I wonder?' he said softly.

'You have some special reason?'

'As you so sapiently remark, my dear Hugh, I have some special reason.'

Davenant shrugged his shoulders, and allowed the subject to drop. He sat watching the child at the table, who presently finished his repast, and came to the Duke's side.

'If you please, sir, I have finished.'

Avon put up his eyeglass.

'Have you?' he said.

The boy knelt suddenly, and to Davenant's surprise, kissed the Duke's hand.

'Yes, sir. Thank you.'

Avon disengaged himself, but the boy knelt still, looking up into the handsome face with humble eyes. The Duke took a pinch of snuff.

'My esteemed child, there sits the man you had best thank.' He waved his hand towards Davenant. 'I should never have thought of feeding you.'

'I – I thanked you for saving me from Jean, milor',' the boy answered.

'You are reserved for a worse fate,' said the Duke sardonically. 'You now belong to me – body and soul.'

'Yes, sir. If you please,' murmured the boy, and sent him a swift glance of admiration from beneath his long lashes.

The thin lips curled a little.

'The prospect is no doubt pleasing?'

'Yes, sir. I – I would like to serve you.'

'But then, you do not know me very well,' said Justin, with a slight chuckle. 'I am an inhuman taskmaster, eh, Hugh?'

'You are not the man to care for a child of his age,' said Hugh quietly.

'True, very true. Shall I give him to you?'

A trembling hand touched his great cuff.

'Please, sir – '

Justin looked across at his friend.

'I do not think I shall, Hugh. It is so entertaining, and so – er – novel, to be a gilded saint in the eyes of – er – unfledged innocence. I shall keep the boy for just so long as he continues to amuse me. What is your name, my child?'

'Léon, sir.'

'How delightfully brief!' Always a faint undercurrent of sarcasm ran beneath the surface of the Duke's smooth voice. 'Léon. No more, no less. The question is – Hugh will of course have the answer ready – what next to do with Léon?'

'Put him to bed,' said Davenant.

'Naturally – And do you think – a bath?'

'By all means.'

'Ah yes!' sighed the Duke, and struck a hand-bell at his side.

A lackey came in answer to the summons, bowing deeply.

'Your Grace desires?'

'Send me Walker,' said Justin.

The lackey effaced himself, and presently a neat individual came in, gray-haired and prim.

'Walker! I have something to say to you. Yes, I remember. Walker, do you observe this child?'

Walker glanced at the kneeling boy.

'Ay, your Grace.'

'He does. Marvellous,' murmured the Duke. 'His name, Walker, is Léon. Strive to bear it in mind.'

'Certainly, your Grace.'

'He requires several things, but first a bath.'

'Ay, your Grace.'

'Secondly, a bed.'

'Yes, your Grace.'

'Thirdly, a nightgown.'

'Yes, your Grace.'

'Fourthly, and lastly, a suit of clothes. Black.'

'Black, your Grace.'

'Severe and funereal black, as shall befit my page. You will procure them. No doubt you will prove yourself equal to this occasion. Take the child away, and show him the bath, the bed, and the nightgown. And then leave him alone.'

'Very good, your Grace.'

'And you, Léon, rise. Go with the estimable Walker. I shall see you tomorrow.'

Léon came to his feet, and bowed.

'Yes, Monseigneur. Thank you.'

'Pray, do not thank me again,' yawned the Duke. 'It fatigues me.' He watched Léon go out, and turned to survey Davenant.

Hugh looked full into his eyes.

'What does this mean, Alastair?'

The Duke crossed his legs, and swung one foot.

'I wonder?' he said pleasantly. 'I thought that you would be able to tell me. You are always so omniscient, my dear.'

'Some scheme you have in mind, I know,' Hugh said positively. 'I have known you long enough to be sure of that. What do you want with that child?'

'You are sometimes most importunate,' complained Justin. 'Never more so than when you become virtuously severe. Pray spare me a homily.'

'I have no intention of lecturing you. All I would say is that it is impossible for you to take that child as your page.'

'Dear me!' said Justin, and gazed pensively into the fire.

'For one thing he is of gentle birth. One can tell that from his speech, and his delicate hands and face. For another – his innocence shines out of his eyes.'

'How very distressing!'

'It would be very distressing if that innocence left him – because of you,' Hugh said, a hint of grimness in his rather dreamy voice.

'Always so polite,' murmured the Duke.

'If you wish to be kind to him –'

'My dear Hugh! I thought you said you knew me?'

Davenant smiled at that.

'Well, Justin, as a favour to me, will you give me Léon, and seek a page elsewhere?'

'I am always sorry to disappoint you, Hugh. I desire to act up to your expectations on all possible occasions. So I shall keep Léon. Innocence shall walk behind Evil – you see, I forestall you – clad in sober black.'

'Why do you want him? At least tell me that?'

'He has Titian hair,' said Justin blandly. 'Titian hair has ever been one of – my – ruling – passions.' The hazel eyes glinted for a moment, and were swiftly veiled. 'I am sure you will sympathise with me.'

Hugh rose and walked to the table. He poured himself out a glass of burgundy, and sipped it for a time in silence.

'Where have you been this evening?' he asked at length.

'I really forget. I believe I went first to De Touronne's house. Yes, I remember now. I won. Strange.'

'Why strange?' inquired Hugh.

Justin flicked a grain of snuff from his great cuff.

'Because, Hugh, in the days, not so long since, when it was – ah – common knowledge that the noble family of Alastair was on the verge of ruin – yes, Hugh, even when I was mad enough to contemplate marriage with the present – er – Lady Merivale – I could only lose.'

'I've seen you win thousands in a night, Justin.'

'And lose them the following night. Then, if you remember, I went away with you to – now, where did we go? Rome! Of course!'

'I remember.'

The thin lips sneered a little.

'Yes. I was the – ah – rejected and heart-broken suitor. I should have blown my brains out to be quite correct. But I was past the age of drama. Instead I proceeded – in due course – to Vienna. And I won. The reward, my dear Hugh, of vice.'

Hugh tilted his glass, watching the candle-light play on the dark wine.

'I heard,' he said slowly, 'that the man from whom you won that fortune – a young man, Justin –'

'– with a blameless character.'

'Yes. That young man – so I heard – *did* blow his brains out.'

'You were misinformed, my dear. He was shot in a duel. The reward of virtue. The moral is sufficiently pointed, I think?'

'And you came to Paris with a fortune.'

'Quite a considerable one. I bought this house.'

'Yes. I wonder how you reconcile it with your soul?'

'I haven't one, Hugh. I thought you knew that.'

'When Jennifer Beauchamp married Anthony Merivale you had something approaching a soul.'

'Had I?' Justin regarded him with amusement.

Hugh met his look.

'And I wonder too what Jennifer Beauchamp is to you now?'

Justin held up one beautiful white hand.

'Jennifer Merivale, Hugh. She is the memory of a failure, and of a spell of madness.'

'And yet you have never been quite the same since.'

Justin rose, and now the sneer was marked.

'I told you half an hour ago, my dear, that it was my endeavour to act up to your expectations. Three years ago – in fact, when I heard from my sister Fanny of Jennifer's marriage – you said with your customary simplicity that although she would not accept my suit, she had made me. *Voilà tout.*'

'No.' Hugh looked thoughtfully across at him. 'I was wrong, but –'

'My dear Hugh, pray do not destroy my faith in you!'

'I was wrong, but not so much wrong. I should have said that Jennifer prepared the way for another woman to make you.'

Justin closed his eyes.

'When you become profound, Hugh, you cause me to regret the day that saw me admit you into the select ranks of my friends.'

'You have so many, have you not?' said Hugh, flushing.

'*Parfaitement.*' Justin walked to the door. 'Where there is money there are also – friends.'

Davenant set down his glass.

'Is that meant for an insult?' he said quietly.

Justin paused, his hand on the door-knob.

'Strange to say it was not. But by all means call me out.'

Hugh laughed suddenly.

'Oh, go to bed, Justin! You are quite impossible!'

'So you have often told me. Good night, my dear.' He went out, but before he had shut the door bethought himself of something, and looked back, smiling. '*A propos*, Hugh, I have got a soul. It has just had a bath, and is now asleep.'

'God help it!' Hugh said gravely.

'I am not sure of my cue. Do I say amen, or retire cursing?' His eyes mocked, but the smile in them was not unpleasant. He did not wait for an answer, but shut the door, and went slowly up to bed.

Two

Introducing the Comte de Saint-Vire

SHORTLY AFTER NOON ON THE FOLLOWING DAY AVON SENT FOR HIS page. Léon came promptly, and knelt to kiss the Duke's hand. Walker had obeyed his master's commands implicitly, and in place of the shabby, grimy child of the evening before was a scrupulously neat boy, whose red curls had been swept severely back from his brow, and whose slim person was clad in plain black raiment, with a starched muslin cravat about his neck.

Avon surveyed him for a moment.

'Yes. You may rise, Léon. I am going to ask you some questions. I desire you will answer them truthfully. You understand?'

Léon put his hands behind him.

'Yes, Monseigneur.'

'You may first tell me how you come to know my language.'

Léon shot him a surprised glance.

'Monseigneur?'

'Pray do not be guileless. I dislike fools.'

'Yes, Monseigneur. I was only surprised that you knew. It was at the inn, you see.'

'I do not think I am obtuse,' said Avon coldly, 'but I see naught.'

'Pardon, Monseigneur. Jean keeps an inn, and very often English travellers come. Not – not noble English, of course.'

'I see. Now you may relate your history. Begin with your name.'

'I am Léon Bonnard, Monseigneur. My mother was the Mère Bonnard, and my father –'

'– was the Père Bonnard. It is not inconceivable. Where were you born, and when did your worthy parents die?'

'I – I do not know where I was born, Monseigneur. It was not in Anjou, I think.'

'That is of course interesting,' remarked the Duke. 'Spare me a list of the places where you were not born, I beg of you.'

Léon coloured.

'You do not understand, Monseigneur. My parents went to live in Anjou when I was a baby. We had a farm at Bassincourt, *auprès de Saumur*. And – and we lived there until my parents died.'

'Did they die simultaneously?' inquired Justin.

Léon's straight little nose wrinkled in perplexity.

'Monseigneur?'

'At one and the same time.'

'It was the plague,' explained Léon. 'I was sent to Monsieur le Curé. I was twelve then, and Jean was twenty.'

'How came you to be so much younger than this Jean?' asked Justin, and opened his eyes rather wide, so that Léon looked full into them.

A mischievous chuckle escaped Léon; he returned the piercing stare frankly.

'Monseigneur, my parents are dead, so I cannot ask them.'

'My friend –' Justin spoke softly. 'Do you know what I do to impertinent pages?'

Léon shook his head apprehensively.

'I have them whipped. I advise you to have a care.'

Léon paled, and the laugh died out of his eyes.

'Pardon, Monseigneur. I – I did not mean to be impertinent,' he said contritely. 'My mother had once a daughter who died. Then – then I came.'

'Thank you. Where did you learn to speak as a gentleman?'

'With M. le Curé, Monseigneur. He taught me to read and to write and to know Latin a little, and – and many other things.'

Justin raised his eyebrows.

'And your father was a farmer? Why did you receive this extensive education?'

'I do not know, Monseigneur. I was the baby, you see, and the favourite. My mother would not have me work on the farm. That is why Jean hates me, I think.'

'Possibly. Give me your hand.'

Léon extended one slender hand for inspection. Justin took it in his, and surveyed it through his eyeglass. It was small, and finely made, with tapering fingers roughened by toil.

'Yes,' said the Duke. 'Quite a pretty member.'

Léon smiled engagingly.

'*Quant à ça*, you have very beautiful hands, Monseigneur, I think.'

The Duke's lips quivered.

'You overwhelm me, my child. As you were saying, your parents died. What then?'

'Oh, then Jean sold the farm! He said he was made for greater things. But I do not know.' Léon tilted his head to one side, considering the point. The irrepressible dimple appeared, and was swiftly banished. Léon eyed his master solemnly, and a little nervously withal.

'We will leave Jean's capabilities out of the discussion,' said Justin smoothly. 'Continue your story.'

'Yes, Monseigneur. Jean sold the farm, and took me away from M. le Curé.' Léon's face clouded over. 'Monsieur wanted to keep me, but Jean would not have it so. He thought I should be useful.

So of course Monsieur could do naught. Jean brought me to Paris. That was when he made me –' Léon stopped.

'Go on!' said Justin sharply. 'That was when he made you – ?'

'Work for him,' said Léon lamely. He encountered a searching glance, and his big eyes fell before it.

'Very well,' said Justin at last. 'We will leave it at that. *Et puis?*'

'Then Jean bought the inn in the Rue Sainte-Marie, and – and after a time he met Charlotte, and – and married her. Then it was worse, because Charlotte hated me.' The blue eyes flashed. 'I tried to kill her once,' said Léon naïvely. 'With the big carving-knife.'

'Her hatred is not incomprehensible,' said Justin dryly.

'N-no,' replied Léon doubtfully. 'I was only fifteen then. I remember I did not have anything to eat all day – besides the beating. And – and that is all, Monseigneur, till you came, and took me away.'

Justin picked up a quill and passed it through his fingers.

'May I ask why you tried to kill this Charlotte – er – with the carving-knife?'

Léon flushed, and looked away.

'There – there was a reason, Monseigneur.'

'I do not doubt it.'

'I – oh, I think she was very unkind and cruel and she – she made me angry. That was all.'

'I am both cruel and unkind, but I do not advise you to try and kill me. Or any of my servants. You see, I know what the colour of your hair denotes.'

The long dark lashes lifted again, and the dimple showed.

'*Colère de diable,*' Léon said.

'Precisely. You will do well to hide it with me, my child.'

'Yes, Monseigneur. I do not seek to kill those whom I love.'

Justin's lips curled rather sardonically.

'I am relieved. Now listen to me. You will henceforth be my

page; you will be clothed and fed, and well provided for, but in return I will have obedience from you. You understand?'

'But yes, Monseigneur.'

'You will learn that my word is law with my servants. And this is my first command: if anyone should question you as to who you are, or from where you come, you will answer only that you are Avon's page. You will forget your past until I give you leave to remember it. You see?'

'Yes, Monseigneur.'

'And you will obey Walker as you would myself.'

The firm chin was tilted at that; Léon looked speculatively at the Duke.

'If you do not' — the soft voice grew softer still — 'you will find that I too know how to punish.'

'If it is your will that I obey this Walker,' said Léon with dignity, 'I will do it, *y-your-r-r Gr-r-race!*'

Justin looked him over.

'Certainly you will do so. And I prefer that you call me Monseigneur.'

The blue eyes twinkled wickedly.

'This Walker, he has told me that when I speak to you, Monseigneur, I must say "your-r-r" ah, bah! I cannot, *enfin!*'

For one moment Justin stared haughtily at his page. Instantly the twinkle disappeared. Léon stared back gravely.

'Be very careful,' Justin warned him.

'Yes, Monseigneur,' Léon said meekly.

'You may go now. This evening you will accompany me out.' The Duke dipped his quill in the inkhorn, and started to write.

'Where, Monseigneur?' inquired the page with great interest.

'Is that your affair? I dismissed you. Go.'

'Yes, Monseigneur. Pardon!' Léon departed, carefully closing the door behind him. Outside he met Davenant, coming slowly down the stairs. Hugh smiled.

'Well, Léon? Where have you been all the morning?'

'Dressing myself, in these new clothes, m'sieu'. I think I look nice, *n'est-ce pas?*'

'Very nice. Where are you going now?'

'I do not know, m'sieu'. Perhaps there is something I may do for Monseigneur?'

'If he gave you no orders there is nothing. Can you read?'

'But yes! I was taught. Ah, I have forgotten, m'sieu'!'

'Have you?' Hugh was amused. 'If you come with me, child, I'll find you a book.'

Twenty minutes later Hugh entered the library to find the Duke still writing, as Léon had left him.

'Justin, who and what is Léon? He is a delightful child; certainly no peasant!'

'He is a very impertinent child,' said Justin, with the ghost of a smile. 'He is the first page I have had who ever dared to laugh at me.'

'Did he laugh at you? A very wholesome experience for you, Alastair. How old is the child?'

'I have reason to believe that he is nineteen,' said Justin placidly.

'Nineteen! Faith, it's not possible! He is a babe!'

'Not entirely. Do you come with me to Vassaud's tonight?'

'I suppose so. I've no money to lose, but what matter?'

'You need not play,' said Justin.

'If one does not play, why visit a gaming-house?'

'To talk to the *monde*. I go to Vassaud's to see Paris.' He resumed his writing, and presently Hugh strolled away.

At dinner that evening Léon stood behind the Duke's chair, and waited upon him. Justin seemed hardly to notice him, but Hugh could not take his eyes from that piquant little face. Indeed, he stared so hard that at last Léon stared back, with great dignity, and some reproach. Observing his friend's fixed regard, Justin turned, and put up his glass to look at Léon.

'What are you doing?' he asked.

'Monseigneur, only looking at M. Davenant.'

'Then do not.'

'But he looks at me, Monseigneur!'

'That is another matter.'

'I do not see that that is fair,' remarked Léon, *sotto voce*.

Some time after dinner the two men set out for Vassaud's. When Hugh realised that Léon was to accompany them he frowned, and took Avon aside.

'Justin, have done with this affectation! You can have no need of a page at Vassaud's, and it's no place for such a child!'

'My very dear Hugh, I do wish you would allow me to know my own mind,' answered Justin sweetly. 'The page goes with me. Another whim.'

'But why? The child should be in bed!'

Justin flicked a speck of snuff from his coat.

'You force me to remind you, Hugh, that the page is mine.'

Davenant compressed his lips, and swung out of the door. Nonchalantly, his Grace followed.

Vassaud's was crowded, early in the evening though it was. The two men left their cloaks with the lackey in the vestibule, and proceeded, with Léon in their wake, across the hall to the broad stairway which led to the gaming-rooms on the first floor. Hugh saw a friend standing at the foot of the stairs, and paused to exchange a greeting, but Avon swept on, bowing slightly to right and left as some chance acquaintance hailed him. He did not stop to speak to anyone, although several called to him as he passed, but went on his regal way with just a faint smile on his lips.

Léon followed him close, his blue eyes wide with interest. He attracted some attention, and many were the curious glances cast from him to the Duke. He flushed delicately when he encountered such a glance, but his Grace appeared to be quite unaware of the surprise he had created.

'What ails Alastair now?' inquired the Chevalier d'Anvau, who was standing with one De Salmy in a recess on the staircase.

'Who knows?' De Salmy shrugged elegantly. 'He must ever be unusual. Good evening, Alastair.'

The Duke nodded to him. 'I rejoice to see you, De Salmy. A hand of piquet later?'

De Salmy bowed. 'I shall be delighted.' He watched Avon pass on, and shrugged again. 'He bears himself as though he were the king of France. I mislike those strange eyes. Ah, Davenant, well met!'

Davenant smiled pleasantly. 'You here? A crowd, is it not?'

'All Paris,' agreed the Chevalier. 'Why has Alastair brought his page?'

'I have no idea, Justin is never communicative. I see Destourville is back.'

'Ah yes, he arrived last night. You have no doubt heard the scandal?'

'Oh, my dear Chevalier, I never listen to scandal!' Hugh laughed, and went on up the stairs.

'*Je me demande*,' remarked the Chevalier, watching Hugh's progress through his eyeglass, 'why it is that the good Davenant is a friend of the bad Alastair?'

The salon on the first floor was brilliantly lighted, and humming with gay, inconsequent conversation. Some were already at play, others were gathered about the buffet, sipping their wine. Hugh saw Avon through the folding doors that led into a smaller salon, the centre of a group, his page standing at a discreet distance behind him.

A muttered exclamation near him made him turn his head. A tall, rather carelessly dressed man was standing beside him, looking across the room at Léon. He was frowning, and his heavy mouth was shut hard. Through the powder his hair glinted red, but his arched brows were black, and very thick.

'Saint-Vire?' Hugh bowed to him. 'You are wondering at Alastair's page? A freak, is it not?'

'Your servant, Davenant. A freak, yes. Who is the boy?'

'I do not know. Alastair found him yesterday. He is called Léon. I trust Madame your wife is well?'

'I thank you, yes. Alastair found him, you say? What does that mean?'

'Here he comes,' answered Hugh. 'You had best ask him.'

Avon came up with a swish of silken skirts, and bowed low to the Comte de Saint-Vire.

'My dear Comte!' The hazel eyes mocked. 'My very dear Comte!' Saint-Vire returned the bow abruptly. 'M. le Duc!'

Justin drew forth his jewelled snuff-box, and presented it. Tall as he was, Saint-Vire was made to look insignificant beside this man of splendid height and haughty bearing.

'A little snuff, dear Comte? No?' He shook the foaming ruffles back from his white hand, and very daintily took a pinch of snuff. His thin lips were smiling, but not pleasantly.

'Saint-Vire was admiring your page, Justin,' Davenant said. 'He is exciting no little attention.'

'No doubt.' Avon snapped his fingers imperiously and Léon came forward. 'He is almost unique, my dear Comte. Pray look your fill.'

'Your page is of no interest to me, m'sieur,' Saint-Vire answered shortly, and turned aside.

'Behind me.' The command was given coldly, and at once Léon stepped back. 'The so worthy Comte! Comfort him, Hugh.' Avon passed on again, and in a little while was seated at a card table, playing lansquenet.

Davenant was called to another table presently, and proceeded to play at faro, with Saint-Vire as his partner. A foppish gentleman sat opposite him, and started to deal.

'*Mon cher*, your friend is always so amusing. Why the page?' he glanced towards Avon's table.

Hugh gathered up his cards.

'How should I know, Lavoulère? Doubtless he has a reason. And – forgive me – I am weary of the subject.'

'He is so – so arresting,' apologised Lavoulère. 'The page. Red hair – oh, but of a radiance! – and blue, blue eyes. Or are they purple-black? The little oval face, and the patrician nose – ! Justin is wonderful. You do not think so, Henri?'

'Oh, without doubt!' Saint-Vire answered. 'He should have been an actor. *Quant à moi*, I would humbly suggest that enough notice has been taken of the Duc and his page. Your play, Marchérand.'

At Avon's table one of the gamblers yawned, pushing back his chair.

'*Mille pardons*, but I thirst! I go in search of refreshment.'

The game had come to an end, and Justin was toying with his dice-box. He glanced up now, and waved to Château-Mornay to keep his seat.

'My page will fetch wine, Louis. He is not only to be gazed upon. Léon!'

Léon slipped from behind Avon's chair, from where he had been an intent spectator of the game.

'Monseigneur?'

'Canary and burgundy, at once.'

Léon withdrew, and nervously threaded his way between the tables to the buffet. He returned presently with a tray, which he presented to Justin, on one knee. Justin pointed silently to where Château-Mornay sat, and blushing for his mistake, Léon went to him, and again presented the tray. When he had served each one in turn he looked inquiringly up at his master.

'Go to M. Davenant, and ask him if he has commands for you,' said Justin languidly. 'Will you hazard a throw with me, Cornalle?'

'Ay, what you will.' Cornalle pulled a dice-box from his pocket. 'Two ponies? Will you throw?'

Justin cast his dice carelessly on the table, and turned his head to watch Léon. The page was at Davenant's elbow. Davenant looked up.

'Well, Léon? What is it?'

'Monseigneur sent me, m'sieur, to see if you had commands for me.'

Saint-Vire shot him a quick look, leaning back in his chair, one hand lying lightly clenched on the table.

'Thank you, no,' Hugh replied. 'Unless – Saint-Vire, will you drink with me? And you, messieurs?'

'I thank you, Davenant,' said the Comte. 'You have no thirst, Lavoulère?'

'At the moment, no. Oh, if you all must drink, then so will I!'

'Léon, will you fetch burgundy, please?'

'Yes, m'sieur,' bowed Léon. He was beginning to enjoy himself. He walked away again, looking about him appreciatively. When he returned he made use of the lesson just learned at Avon's table, and presented the silver tray first to Saint-Vire.

The Comte turned in his chair, and picking up the decanter, slowly poured out a glassful, and handed it to Davenant. He poured out another, his eyes on Léon's face. Conscious of the steady regard, Léon looked up, and met Saint-Vire's eyes frankly. The Comte held the decanter poised, but poured no more for a long minute.

'What is your name, boy?'

'Léon, m'sieur.'

Saint-Vire smiled. 'No more?'

The curly head was shaken. '*Je ne sais plus rien, m'sieur.*'

'So ignorant?' Saint-Vire went on with his work. As he picked up the last glass he spoke again. 'Methinks you have not been long with M. le Duc?'

'No, m'sieur. As m'sieur says.' Léon rose, and looked across at Davenant. 'M'sieur?'

'That is all, Léon, thank you.'

'So you have found a use for him, Hugh? Was I not wise to bring him? Your servant, Lavoulère.'

The soft voice startled Saint-Vire, and his hand shook, so that a little liquid was spilled from his glass. Avon stood at his side, quizzing-glass raised.

'A very prince of pages,' smiled Lavoulère. 'How is your luck tonight, Justin?'

'Wearisome,' sighed the Duke. 'For a week it has been impossible to lose. From the dreamy expression on Hugh's face I infer that it is not so with him.' He went to stand behind Hugh's chair, laying a hand on his shoulder. 'Belike, my dear Hugh, I shall bring you better luck.'

'I have never known you do that yet,' retorted Davenant. He set down his emptied glass. 'Shall we play again?'

'By all means,' nodded Saint-Vire. 'You and I are in a sad way, Davenant.'

'And shall soon be in a sadder,' remarked Hugh, shuffling the pack. 'Remind me, Lavoulère, that in future I only play with you as my partner.' He dealt the cards round, and as he did so, spoke quietly to the Duke, in English. 'Send the child downstairs, Alastair. You have no need of him.'

'I am as wax in your hands,' replied his Grace. 'He has served his turn. Léon, you will await me in the hall.' He stretched out his hand to pick up Hugh's cards. 'Dear me!' He laid them down again, and watched the play in silence for a while.

At the end of the round Lavoulère spoke to him.

'Where is your brother, Alastair? The so charming youth! He is quite, quite mad!'

'Lamentably so. Rupert, for all I know, is either languishing in an English sponging house, or living upon my hapless brother-in-law's bounty.'

'That is Miladi Fanny's husband, yes? Edward Marling, n'est-ce pas? You have only the one brother and sister?'

'They more than suffice me,' said his Grace.

Lavoulère laughed. '*Voyons*, it amuses me, your family! Is there no love between you at all?'

'Very little.'

'And yet I have heard that you reared them, those two!'

'I have no recollection of it,' said Justin.

'Come now, Justin, when your mother died you kept a hand on the reins!' expostulated Davenant.

'But lightly, my dear. Enough only to make both a little afraid of me; no more.'

'Lady Fanny is very fond of you.'

'Yes, I believe she is occasionally,' agreed Justin calmly.

'Ah, Miladi Fanny!' Lavoulère kissed his finger-tips. 'Behold! How she is *ravissante!*'

'Also behold that Hugh wins,' drawled his Grace. 'My compliments, Davenant.' He shifted his position slightly, so that he faced Saint-Vire. 'Pray how is Madame, your charming wife, dear Comte?'

'Madame is well, I thank you, m'sieur.'

'And the Vicomte, your so enchanting son?'

'Also.'

'Not here tonight, I think?' Avon raised his glass, and through it surveyed the room. 'I am desolated. No doubt you deem him too young for these delights? He is but nineteen, I believe?'

Saint-Vire laid his cards face downwards on the table, and looked angrily up at that handsome, enigmatic countenance.

'You are most interested in my son, M. le Duc!'

The hazel eyes widened and narrowed again.

'But how could it be otherwise?' asked the Duke politely.

Saint-Vire picked up his cards again.

'He is at Versailles, with his mother,' he said curtly. 'My play, Lavoulère?'

Three

Which Tells of a Debt Unpaid

WHEN DAVENANT RETURNED TO THE HOUSE IN THE RUE ST-Honoré, he found that although Léon had long since come in, and was now in bed, his Grace was still out. Guessing that Avon had gone from Vassaud's to visit his latest light o' love, Hugh went into the library to await him. Soon the Duke sauntered in, poured himself out a glass of canary wine, and came to the fire.

'A most instructive evening. I hope my very dear friend Saint-Vire recovered from the sorrow my early departure must have occasioned him?'

'I think so,' smiled Hugh. He rested his head back against the cushions of his chair, and looked at the Duke with rather a puzzled expression on his face. 'Why do you so hate one another, Justin?'

The straight brows rose.

'Hate? I? My dear Hugh!'

'Very well, if you like it better I will say why does Saint-Vire hate you?'

'It is a very old tale, Hugh; almost a forgotten tale. The – er – *contretemps* between the amiable Comte and myself took place in the days before I had the advantage of possessing your friendship, you see.'

'So there was a *contretemps*? I suppose you behaved abominably?'

'What I admire in you, my dear, is your charming candour,' remarked his Grace. 'But in this instance I did not behave abominably. Amazing, is it not?'

'What happened?'

'Very little. It was really quite trivial. So trivial that nearly everyone has forgotten it.'

'It was a woman, of course?'

'Even so. No less a personage than the present Duchesse de Belcour.'

'Duchesse de Belcour?' Hugh sat upright in surprise. 'Saint-Vire's sister. That red-haired shrew?'

'Yes, that red-haired shrew. As far as I remember, I admired her – er – shrewishness – twenty years ago. She was really very lovely.'

'Twenty years ago! So long! Justin, surely you did not –'

'I wanted to wed her,' said Avon pensively. 'Being young and foolish. It seems incredible now; yet so it was. I applied for permission to woo her – yes, is it not amusing? – to her worthy father.' He paused, looking into the fire. 'I was – let me see! Twenty – a little more; I forget. My father and her father had not been the best of friends. Again a woman; I believe my sire won the encounter. I suppose it rankled. And on my side there were, even at that age, my dear, some trifling intrigues.' His shoulders shook. 'There always are – in my family. The old Comte refused to give me leave to woo his daughter. Not altogether surprising, you think? No, I did not elope with her. Instead I received a visit from Saint-Vire. He was then Vicomte de Valmé. That visit was almost humiliating.' The lines about Justin's mouth were grim. 'Al-most hu-miliating.'

'For you?'

Avon smiled.

'For me. The noble Henri came to my lodging with a large

and heavy whip.' He looked down as Hugh gasped, and the smile
grew. 'No, my dear, I was not thrashed. To resume: Henri was
enraged; there was a something between us, maybe a woman – I
forget. He was very much enraged. It should afford me some
consolation, that I had dared to raise my profligate eyes to the
daughter of that most austere family of Saint-Vire. Have you ever
noticed the austerity? It lies in the fact that the Saint-Vire amours
are carried on in secrecy. Mine, as you know, are quite open.
You perceive the nice distinction? *Bon!*' Avon had seated himself
on the arm of a chair, legs crossed. He started to twirl his wine-
glass, holding the narrow stem between thumb and finger. 'My
licentious – I quote his very words, Hugh – behaviour; my entire
lack of morals; my soiled reputation; my vicious mind; my – but I
forget the rest. It was epic – all these made my perfectly honour-
able proposal an insult. I was to understand that I was as the dirt
beneath the Saint-Vire feet. There was much more, but at length
the noble Henri came to his peroration. For my impudence I was
to receive a thrashing at his hands. I! Alastair of Avon!'

'But Justin, he must have been mad! It was not as though you
were low-born! The Alastairs –'

'Precisely. He was mad. These red-haired people, my dear
Hugh! And there was something between us. No doubt I had at
some time or other behaved abominably to him. There followed,
as you may imagine, a short argument. It did not take me long
to come to my peroration. In short, I had the pleasure of cutting
his face open with his own whip. Out came his sword.' Avon
stretched out his arm, and the muscles rippled beneath the satin of
his coat sleeve. 'I was young, but I knew a little of the art of the
duello, even in those days. I pinked him so well that he had to be
carried home in my coach, by my lackeys. When he had departed
I gave myself up to thought. You see, my dear, I was, or fancied
that I was, very much in love with that – er – red-haired shrew.

The noble Henri had told me that his sister had deemed herself insulted by my court. It occurred to me that perhaps the lady had mistaken my suit for a casual intrigue. I visited the Hôtel Saint-Vire to make known mine intentions. I was received not by her father, but by the noble Henri, reclining upon a couch. There were also some friends of his. I forget. Before them, before his lackeys, he informed me that he stood in – er – *loco parentis*, and that his sister's hand was denied me. Further that if I so much as dared to accost her his servants would whip me from her presence.'

'Good God!' cried Hugh.

'So I thought. I retired. What would you? I could not touch the man; I had well nigh killed him already. When next I appeared in public I found that my visit to the Hôtel Saint-Vire had become the talk of Paris. I was compelled to leave France for a time. Happily another scandal arose which cast mine into the shade, so Paris was once more open to me. It is an old, old story, Hugh, but I have not forgotten.'

'And he?'

'He has not forgotten either. He was half mad at the time, but he would not apologise when he came to his senses; I don't think I expected him to do so. We meet now as distant acquaintances; we are polite – oh, scrupulously! – but he knows that I am still waiting.'

'Waiting…?'

Justin walked to the table and set down his glass.

'For an opportunity to pay that debt in full,' he said softly.

'Vengeance?' Hugh leaned forward. 'I thought you disliked melodrama, my friend?'

'I do; but I have a veritable passion for – justice.'

'You've nourished thoughts of – vengeance – for twenty years?'

'My dear Hugh, if you imagine that the lust for vengeance has been my dominating emotion for twenty years, permit me to correct the illusion.'

'Has it not grown cold?' Hugh asked, disregarding.

'Very cold, my dear, but none the less dangerous.'

'And all this time not one opportunity has presented itself?'

'You see, I wish it to be thorough,' apologised the Duke.

'Are you nearer success now than you were – twenty years ago?'

A soundless laugh shook Justin.

'We shall see. Rest assured that when it comes it will be – so!'
Very slowly he clenched his hand on his snuff-box, and opened
his fingers to show the thin gold crushed.

Hugh gave a little shiver.

'My God, Justin, do you know just how vile you can be?'

'Naturally: Do they not call me – Satanas?' The mocking smile
came; the eyes glittered.

'I hope to heaven Saint-Vire never puts himself in your power!
It seems they were right who named you Satanas!'

'Quite right, my poor Hugh.'

'Does Saint-Vire's brother know?'

'Armand? No one knows save you, and I, and Saint-Vire.
Armand may guess, of course.'

'And yet you and he are friends!'

'Oh, Armand's hatred for the noble Henri is more violent than
ever mine could be.'

In spite of himself Hugh smiled.

'It is a race betwixt you, then?'

'Not a whit. I should have said that Armand's is a sullen detesta-
tion. Unlike me, he is content to hate.'

'He, I suppose, would sell his soul for Saint-Vire's shoes.'

'And Saint-Vire,' said Avon gently, 'would sell his soul to keep
those shoes from Armand.'

'Yes, one knows that. It was common gossip at the time that
that was his reason for marrying. One could not accuse him of
loving his wife!'

'No,' said Justin, and chuckled as though at some secret thought.

'Well,' Hugh went on, 'Armand's hopes of the title were very surely dashed when Madame presented Saint-Vire with a son!'

'Precisely,' said Justin.

'A triumph for Saint-Vire, that!'

'A triumph indeed,' suavely agreed his Grace.

Four

His Grace of Avon Becomes Further
Acquainted with His Page

FOR LÉON THE DAYS PASSED SWIFTLY, EACH ONE TEEMING WITH some new excitement. Never in his life had he seen such sights as now met his eyes. He was dazzled by the new life spread before him; from living in a humble, dirty tavern, he was transported suddenly into gorgeous surroundings, fed with strange foods, clad in fine clothes, and taken into the midst of aristocratic Paris. All at once life seemed to consist of silks and diamonds, bright lights, and awe-inspiring figures. Ladies, whose fingers were covered with rings, and whose costly brocades held an elusive perfume, would stop to smile at him sometimes; great gentlemen with powdered wigs and high heels would flip his head with careless fingers as they passed. Even Monseigneur sometimes spoke to him.

Fashionable Paris grew accustomed to see him long before he became accustomed to his new existence. After a while people ceased to stare at him when he came in Avon's wake, but it was some time before he ceased to gaze on all that met his eyes, in wondering appreciation.

To the amazement of Avon's household, he still persisted in his worship of the Duke. Nothing could shake him from his standpoint, and if one of the lackeys vented his outraged feelings below-stairs in a tirade against Avon, Léon was up in arms at once, blind rage taking possession of him. Since the Duke had ordained that none should lay violent hands on his page, save at his express command, the lackeys curbed their tongues in Léon's presence, for he was over-ready with his dagger, and they dare not disobey the Duke's orders. Gaston, the valet, felt that this hot partisanship was sadly wrong; that any should defend the Duke struck forcibly at his sense of propriety, and more than once he tried to convince the page that it was the duty of any self-respecting menial to loathe the Duke.

'*Mon petit*,' he said firmly, 'it is ridiculous. It is unthinkable. *Même*, it is outrageous. It is against all custom. The Duke, he is not human. Some call him Satanas, and *mon Dieu*, they have reason!'

'I have never seen Satan,' answered Léon, from a large chair where he sat with his feet tucked under him. 'But I do not think that Monseigneur is like him.' He reflected. 'But if he is like the devil no doubt I should like the devil very much. My brother says I am a child of the devil.'

'That is shame!' said fat Madame Dubois, the housekeeper, shocked.

'Faith, he has the devil's own temper!' chuckled Gregory, a footman.

'But listen to me, you!' insisted Gaston. 'M. le Duc is of a hardness! Ah, but who should know better than I? I tell you, *moi qui vous parle*, if he would but be enraged all would go well. If he would throw his mirror at my head I would say naught! That is a gentleman, a noble! But the Duc! Bah! He speaks softly – oh, so softly! – and his eyes they are al-most shut, while his voice – *voilà*, I shudder!' He did shudder, but revived at the murmur of applause. 'And you, *petit*! When has he spoken to you as a boy? He speaks to you as his dog! Ah, but it is *imbécile* to admire such a man! It is not to be believed!'

'I am his dog. He is kind to me, and I love him,' said Léon firmly.

'Kind! Madame, you hear?' Gaston appealed to the house-keeper, who sighed, and folded her hands.

'He is very young,' she said.

'Now I will tell you of a thing!' Gaston exclaimed. 'This Duc, what did he do, think you, three years ago? You see this *hôtel*? It is fine, it is costly! *Eh bien!* Me, I have served the Duke for six years, so you may know that I speak truth. Three years ago he was poor! There were debts and mortgages. Oh, we lived the same, *bien sûr*; the Alastairs are always thus. We had always the same mag-nificence, but there were only debts behind the splendour Me, I know. Then we go to Vienna. As ever the Duc he play for great stakes: that is the way of his house. At first he loses. You would not say he cared, for still he smiles. That too is his way. Then there comes a young nobleman, very rich, very joyous. He plays with the Duc. He loses, he suggests a higher stake; the Duc, he agrees. What would you? Still that young noble loses. On and on, until at last – pouf! It is over! That fortune, it has changed hands. The young man, he is ruined – *absolument!* The Duc, he goes away. He smiles – ah, that smile! The young man fights a duel with pistols a little later, and he fires wide, wide! Because he was ruined he chose Death! And the Duc' – Gaston waved his hands – 'he comes to Paris and buys this *hôtel* with that young noble's fortune!'

'Ah!' sighed Madame, and shook her head.

Léon tilted his chin a little.

'It is no such great matter. Monseigneur would always play fair. That young man was a fool. *Voilà tout!*'

'*Mon Dieu*, is it thus you speak of the wickedness? Ah, but I could tell of things! If you knew the women that the Duc has courted! If you knew –'

'Monsieur!' Madame Dubois raised protesting hands. 'Before me?'

'I ask pardon, madame. No, I say nothing. Nothing! But what I know!'

'Some men,' said Léon gravely, 'are like that, I think. I have seen many.'

'*Fi donc!*' Madame cried. 'So young, too!'

Léon disregarded the interruption, and looked at Gaston with a worldly wisdom that sat quaintly on his young face.

'And when I have seen these things I have thought that it is always the woman's fault.'

'Hear the child!' exclaimed Madame. 'What do you know, *petit*, at your age?'

Léon shrugged one shoulder, and bent again over his book.

'Perhaps naught,' he answered.

Gaston frowned upon him, and would have continued the discussion had not Gregory forestalled him.

'Tell me, Léon, do you accompany the Duke tonight?'

'I always go with him.'

'Poor, poor child!' Madame Dubois sighed gustily. 'Indeed, it is not fitting.'

'Why is it not fitting? I like to go.'

'I doubt it not, *mon enfant*. But to take a child to Vassaud's, and to Torquillier's – *voyons*, it is not *convenable!*'

Léon's eyes sparkled mischievously.

'Last night I went with Monseigneur to the Maison Chourval,' he said demurely.

'What!' Madame sank back in her chair. 'It passes all bounds!'

'Have you been there, Madame?'

'I? *Nom de Dieu*, what next will you ask? Is it likely that I should go to such a place?'

'No, Madame. It is for the nobles, is it not?'

Madame snorted.

'And for every pretty slut who walks the streets!' she retorted.

Léon tilted his head to one side.

'Me, I did not think them pretty. Painted, and vulgar, with loud voices, and common tricks. But I did not see much.' His brow wrinkled. 'I do not know – I *think* perhaps I had offended Monseigneur, for of a sudden he swept round, and said, "Await me below!" He said it as though he were angered.'

'Tell us, Léon, what is it like, the Maison Chourval?' asked Gaston, unable to conceal his curiosity.

'Oh, it is a big *hôtel*, all gold and dirty white, and smelling of some scent that suffocates one. There is a card-room, and other rooms; I forget. There was much wine, and some were drunk. Others, like Monseigneur, were just bored. The women – ah, they are just nothing!'

Gaston was rather disappointed; he opened his mouth to question Léon further, but Madame's eye was upon him, and he shut it again. A bell was heard in the distance, and at the sound of it Léon shut his book, and untucked his legs, waiting expectantly. A few minutes later a footman appeared with a summons for him. The page sprang up delightedly, and ran to where a cracked mirror hung. Madame Dubois watched him smooth his copper curls, and smiled indulgently.

'*Voyons, petit*, you are as conceited as a girl,' she remarked.

Léon flushed, and left the mirror.

'Would you have me present myself to Monseigneur in disorder? I suppose he is going out. Where is my hat? Gaston, you have sat upon it!' He snatched it from the valet, and hurriedly twitching it into shape, went out in the wake of the footman.

Avon was standing in the hall, talking to Hugh Davenant. He twirled a pair of soft gloves by their tassels, and his three-cornered hat was under one arm. Léon sank down on to one knee.

The hard eyes travelled over him indifferently.

'Well?'

'Monseigneur sent for me?'

'Did I? Yes, I believe you are right. I am going out. Do you come with me, Hugh?'

'Where?' asked Davenant. He bent over the fire, warming his hands.

'I thought it might be amusing to visit La Fournoise.'

Hugh made a grimace of distaste.

'I like actresses on the stage, Justin, but not off it. La Fournoise is too opulent.'

'So she is. You may go, Léon. Take my gloves.' He tossed them to the page, and his hat after them. 'Come and play at piquet, Hugh.' He strolled away to the salon, yawning, and with a tiny shrug of his shoulders Hugh followed.

At the Comtesse de Marguéry's ball that night Léon was left to await his master in the hall. He found a chair in a secluded corner, and settled down quite contentedly to watch the arrival of the guests. As it was the Duke's custom to make his appearance as late as possible, he was not very hopeful of seeing many arrivals. He pulled a book out of his capacious pocket, and started to read.

For a while only the desultory conversation of the lackeys came to his ears, as they lounged against the stair-rail. Then suddenly they sprang to attention, and the idle chatter stopped. One flung open the door, while another stood ready to relieve this late-comer of his hat and cloak.

Léon raised his eyes from his book in time to see the Comte de Saint-Vire enter. He was becoming familiar with the notables of town, but even had this not been so Saint-Vire would have been hard to mistake. In these days of fastidiousness in all matters of dress, the Comte was conspicuous for the carelessness with which he bore himself, and the slight disorder of his clothes. He was tall, and loose-limbed, with a heavy face, and beak-like nose. His mouth had a sullen curve, and his eyes a latent fierceness in their dark pupils. As usual his thick hair, rather grizzled now, was inadequately powdered, so that here and there a gleam of red showed. He wore many jewels, seemingly chosen at random, and with no regard to the colour of his coat.

His coat was revealed now, as he allowed the attendant lackey to take his long cloak. Purple velvet met Léon's critical eye; a salmon-pink vest with embroidering in gold and silver; purple smallclothes with white stockings loosely rolled above the knee; and red-heeled shoes with large jewelled buckles. The Comte shook out his ruffles, and put up one hand to straighten his tumbled cravat. As he did so he cast a quick glance about him, and saw the page. A frown came, and the heavy mouth pouted a little. The Comte gave the lace at his throat an impatient twist and walked slowly towards the stairs. With his hand on the rail he paused, and half-turning, jerked his head as a sign that he wished to speak to Léon.

The page rose at once, and went to him.

'M'sieur?'

The spatulate fingers on the rail drummed methodically; Saint-Vire looked the page over broodingly, and for a moment did not speak.

'Your master is here?' he said at last, and the very lameness of the question seemed to indicate that it was but an excuse to call Léon to him.

'Yes, m'sieur.'

The Comte hesitated still, tapping his foot on the polished floor.

'You accompany him everywhere, I believe?'

'When Monseigneur wishes it, m'sieur.'

'From where do you come?' Then, as Léon looked puzzled, he changed the question, speaking sharply. 'Where were you born?'

Léon let fall the long lashes over his eyes.

'In the country, m'sieur,' he said.

The Comte's thick brows drew together.

'What part of the country?'

'I do not know, m'sieur.'

'You are strangely ignorant,' said Saint-Vire sarcastically.

'Yes, m'sieur.' Léon glanced up, chin firmly set. 'I do not know why m'sieur should take so great an interest in me.'

'You are impertinent. I have no interest in peasant-children.' The Comte went on up the staircase, to the ballroom.

In a group by the door stood his Grace of Avon, clad in shades of blue, with his star on his breast, a cluster of blazing diamonds. Saint-Vire paused for a moment before he tapped that straight shoulder.

'If you please, m'sieur…!'

The Duke turned to see who accosted him, eyebrows raised. When his eyes alighted on Saint-Vire the haughty look faded, and he smiled, bowing with the exaggerated flourish that made a veiled insult of the courtesy.

'My dear Comte! I had almost begun to fear that I should not have the felicity of meeting you here tonight. I trust I see you well?'

'I thank you, yes.' Saint-Vire would have passed on, but again his Grace stood in the way.

'Strange to say, dear Comte, Florimond and I were but this instant speaking of you – your brother, rather. Where is the good Armand?'

'My brother, m'sieur, is this month in attendance at Versailles.'

'Ah? Quite a family gathering at Versailles,' smiled the Duke. 'I trust the Vicomte, your so charming son, finds court life to his taste?'

The man who stood at the Duke's elbow laughed a little at this, and addressed Saint-Vire.

'The Vicomte is quite an original, is he not, Henri?'

'Oh, the boy is young yet!' Saint-Vire answered. 'He likes court well enough.'

Florimond de Chantourelle tittered amiably.

'He so amused me with his megrims and his sighs! He told me once that he liked best to be in the country, and that 'twas his ambition to have a farm under his own management at Saint-Vire!'

A shadow crossed the Comte's face.

'A boy's fancy. When at Saint-Vire he pines for Paris. Your pardon, messieurs – I see Madame de Marguéry.' He brushed past Avon as he spoke, making his way towards his hostess.

'Our friend is always so delightfully brusque,' remarked the Duke. 'One wonders why he is tolerated.'

'He has moods,' answered Chantourelle. 'Sometimes he is very agreeable, but he is not much liked. Now Armand is another matter. Of a gaiety – ! You know that there is enmity between them?' He lowered his voice mysteriously, agog to relate the tale.

'The dear Comte is at pains to show us that it is so,' said Avon. 'My esteemed friend!' He waved one languid hand to a lavishly powdered and painted individual. 'Did I see you with Mademoiselle de Sonnebrune? Now that is a taste I find hard to cultivate.'

The painted gentleman paused, simpering.

'Oh, my dear Duc, she is the *dernier cri*! One must worship at her feet; it is *de rigueur*, I assure you.'

Avon put up his glass the better to observe Mademoiselle.

'H'm! Is Paris so devoid of beauties, then?'

'You do not admire her, no? It is a stately beauty, of course.' He was silent for a while, watching the dancers; then he turned again to Avon. '*A propos*, Duc, is it true that you have acquired a most striking page? I have been out of Paris this fortnight, but I hear now that a red-haired boy goes everywhere in your wake.'

'Quite true,' said Justin. 'I thought that the violent but fleeting interest of the world had died?'

'No, oh no! It was Saint-Vire who spoke of the boy. It seems there is some mystery attached to him, is it not so? A nameless page!'

Justin turned his rings round, smiling faintly.

'You may tell Saint-Vire, my friend, that there is no mystery. The page has a very good name.'

'I may tell him?' The Vicomte was puzzled. 'But why, Duc? 'Twas but an idle conversation.'

'Naturally.' The enigmatical smile grew. 'I should have said that you may tell him if he asks again.'

'Certainly, but I do not suppose – Ah, there is Davenant! *Mille pardons, Duc!*' He minced away to meet Davenant.

Avon smothered a yawn in his scented handkerchief, and proceeded in his leisurely fashion to the card-room, where he remained for perhaps an hour. Then he sought out his hostess, complimented her in his soft voice, and departed.

Léon was half asleep downstairs, but he opened his eyes as the Duke's footfall sounded, and jumped up. He assisted the Duke into his cloak, handed him his hat and gloves, and asked whether he was to summon a chair. But the Duke elected to walk, and further commanded his page to keep step beside him. They walked slowly down the street and had turned the corner before Avon spoke.

'My child, when the Comte de Saint-Vire questioned you this evening, what did you answer?'

Léon gave a little skip of surprise, looking up at his master in frank wonderment.

'How did you know, Monseigneur? I did not see you.'

'Possibly not. No doubt you will answer my question in your own good time.'

'Pardon, Monseigneur! M. le Comte asked me where I was born. I do not understand why he should wish to know.'

'I suppose you told him so?'

'Yes, Monseigneur,' nodded Léon. He looked up, twinkling. 'I thought you would not be angered if I spoke just a little rudely to that one?' He saw Avon's lips curl, and flushed in triumph at having made the Duke smile.

'Very shrewd,' remarked Justin. 'And then you said – ?'

'I said I did not know, Monseigneur. It is true.'

'A comforting thought.'

'Yes,' agreed the page. 'I do not like to tell lies.'

'No?' For once Avon seemed disposed to encourage his page to talk. Nothing loth, Léon continued.

'No, Monseigneur. Of course it is sometimes necessary, but I do not like it. Once or twice I lied to Jean because I was afraid to tell the truth, but that is cowardly, *n'est-ce pas*? I think it is not so wicked to lie to your enemy, but one could not lie – to a friend, or – or to somebody one loved. That would be a black sin, would it not?'

'As I cannot remember ever having loved anyone, I am hardly fitted to answer that question, my child.'

Léon considered him gravely.

'No one?' he asked. 'Me, I do not love often, but when I do it is for ever. I loved my mother, and the Curé, and – and I love you, Monseigneur.'

'I beg your pardon?' Avon was a little startled.

'I – I only said that I loved you, Monseigneur.'

'I thought that I could not have heard aright. It is, of course, gratifying, but I do not think you have chosen too wisely. I am sure they will seek to reform you, below-stairs.'

The big eyes flashed.

'They dare not!'

The quizzing-glass was raised.

'Indeed? Are you so formidable?'

'I have a very bad temper, Monseigneur.'

'And you use it in my defence. It is most amusing. Do you fly out upon – my valet, for instance?'

Léon gave a tiny sniff of scorn.

'Oh, he is just a fool, Monseigneur!'

'Lamentably a fool. I have often remarked it.'

They had come to Avon's *hôtel* by now, and the waiting lackeys held the door for them to pass through. In the hall Avon paused, while Léon stood expectantly before him.

'You may bring wine to the library,' said the Duke, and went in.

When Léon appeared with a heavy silver tray Justin was seated by the fire, his feet upon the hearth. Beneath drooping lids he watched his page pour out a glass of burgundy. Léon brought it to him.

'Thank you.' Avon smiled at Léon's evident surprise at the unusual courtesy. 'No doubt you imagined that I was sadly lacking in manners? You may sit down. At my feet.'

Léon promptly curled up on the rug, cross-legged, and sat looking at the Duke, rather bewildered, but palpably pleased.

Justin drank a little wine, still watching the page, and then set the glass down on a small table at his elbow.

'You find me a trifle unexpected? I desire to be entertained.'

Léon looked at him seriously.

'What shall I do, Monseigneur?'

'You may talk,' Avon said. 'Your youthful views on life are most amusing. Pray continue.'

Léon laughed suddenly.

'I do not know what to say, Monseigneur! I do not think I have anything interesting to talk about. I chatter and chatter, they tell me, but it is all nothing. Madame Dubois lets me talk, but Walker — ah, Walker is dull and strict!'

'Who is Madame — er — Dubois?'

Léon opened his eyes very wide.

'But she is your housekeeper, Monseigneur!'

'Really? I have never seen her. Is she a stimulating auditor?'

'Monseigneur?'

'No matter. Tell me of your life in Anjou. Before Jean brought you to Paris.'

Léon settled himself more comfortably, and as the arm of Avon's chair was near enough to be an inviting prop, he leaned against it, unaware that he was committing a breach of etiquette. Avon said nothing, but picked up his glass and started to sip the wine it held.

'In Anjou – it is all so very far away,' sighed Léon. 'We lived in a little house, and there were horses and cows and pigs – oh, many animals! And my father did not like it that I would not touch the cows or the pigs. They were dirty, you understand. Maman said I should not work on the farm, but she made me care for the fowls. I did not mind that so much. There was one speckled hen, all mine. Jean stole it to tease me. Jean is like that, you know. Then there was M. le Curé. He lived a little way from our farm, in a tiny house next the church. And he was very, very good and kind. He gave me sweetmeats when I learned my lessons well, and sometimes he told stories oh, wonderful stories of fairies and knights! I was only a baby then, but I can still remember them. And my father said it was not seemly that a priest should tell of things that are not, like fairies. I was not very fond of my father. He was like Jean, a little… Then there was the plague, and people died. I went to the Curé, and – but Monseigneur knows all this.'

'Tell me of your life in Paris, then,' said Justin.

Léon nested his head against the arm of the chair, looking dreamily into the fire. The cluster of candles at Avon's elbow played softly over the copper curls so that they seemed alive and on fire in the golden light. Léon's delicate profile was turned towards the Duke, and he watched it inscrutably; each quiver of the fine lips, each flicker of the dark lashes. And so Léon told his tale, haltingly at first, and shyly, hesitating over the more sordid parts, his voice fluctuating with each changing emotion until he seemed to forget to whom he spoke, and lost himself in his narration. Avon listened in silence, sometimes smiling at the quaint philosophy the boy unfolded, but more often expressionless, always watching Léon's face with narrowed keen eyes. The hardships and endurances of those years in Paris were revealed more by what was left unsaid than by any complaint or direct allusion to the petty tyrannies and cruelties of Jean and his wife. At times the recital was that of a child, but every now and then a note of age and experience crept into the little deep voice, lending a strange whimsicality to the story, which seemed to invest the teller with a Puck-like quality of old and young wisdom. When at last the rambling tale was finished Léon moved slightly, and put up a timid hand to touch the Duke's sleeve.

'And then you came, Monseigneur, and you brought me here, giving me everything. I shall never forget that.'

'You have not seen the worst of me yet, my friend,' answered Justin. 'I am really not the hero you think of me. When I bought you from your estimable brother it was not, believe me, from any desire to save you from bondage. I had a use for you. If it should chance that you are after all of no use to me I am quite likely to cast you forth. I say this that you may be warned.'

'If you send me away I will drown myself!' said Léon passionately. 'When you are tired of me, Monseigneur, I will serve in your kitchen. But I will never leave you.'

'Oh, when I am tired of you I shall give you to M. Davenant!' Avon chuckled a little. 'It should be amusing – Dear me, speak of angels – !'

Hugh came quietly in, but paused on the threshold, staring at the two by the fire.

'Quite a touching picture, eh, Hugh? Satanas in a new role.' He flicked Léon's head with one careless finger. 'Bed, my child.'

Léon rose at once, and reverently kissed the Duke's hand. With a little bow to Davenant he went out.

Hugh waited until he had closed the door; then he strode forward to the fire, frowning. Resting his elbow on the mantelpiece, his other hand thrust deep into his pocket, he stood looking down at his friend with a good deal of severity in his glance.

'When are you going to end this folly?' he demanded.

Justin tilted his head back, returning the angry stare with one of amused cynicism.

'What ails you now, my good Hugh?'

'Seeing that child at your feet fills me with – disgust!'

'Yes, I thought that you seemed perturbed. It must tickle your sense of the ridiculous to observe me upon a pinnacle of heroism.'

'It sickens me! That child worshipping at your feet! I hope his admiration stings you! If it could make you realise your own unworthiness it were to some purpose!'

'Unhappily it does not. May I ask, my dear Hugh, why you take so great an interest in – a page?'

'It is his youth and innocence that command my pity.'

'Curiously enough he is by no means as innocent as you imagine.'

Davenant turned impatiently on his heel. He walked to the door, but as he opened it Avon spoke again.

'By the way, my dear, I am relieving you of my company tomorrow. Pray hold me excused from going with you to Lourdonne's card-party.'

Hugh looked back.

'Oh? Where are you going?'

'I am going to Versailles. I feel that it is time I again paid homage to King Louis. I suppose it is useless to ask your company?'

'Quite, I thank you. I've no love for Versailles. Is Léon to go with you?'

'I have really not given the matter a thought. It seems probable. Unless you wish to take him to Lourdonne's?'

Hugh left the room without a word.

Five

His Grace of Avon Visits Versailles

THE DUKE'S LIGHT TOWN COACH, WITH ITS FOUR GRAY HORSES, stood at the door of his house shortly before six on the following evening. The horses champed at their bits and tossed their beautiful heads in impatience, and the paved courtyard rang with the sound of their stamping. The postilions, liveried in black and gold, stood to their heads, for the Duke's horses were not chosen for their docility.

In the hall Léon awaited his master, aglow with excitement. His Grace had issued certain orders earlier in the day; in accordance with them the page was dressed in black velvet, with real lace at his throat and wrists. He carried his tricorne beneath his arm, and in his other hand he held his master's beribboned cane.

Avon came slowly down the stairs, and seeing him Léon drew in a quick breath of wonderment. The Duke was always magnificent, but tonight he had surpassed himself. His coat was made of cloth-of-gold, and on it the blue ribbon of the Garter lay, and three orders blazed in the light of the candles. Diamonds nestled in the lace of his cravat, and formed a solid bar above the riband that tied back his powdered hair. His shoes had jewelled heels and buckles, and below his knee he wore the Garter. Over his arm he carried a

long black cloak, lined with gold, which he handed to Léon; and
in his hand was his snuff-box, and scented handkerchief. He looked
his page over in silence, and frowned at last, and turned to his valet.

'You may perhaps call to mind, my good Gaston, a golden
chain studded with sapphires, presented to me by I forget whom.
Also a sapphire clasp in the shape of a circle.'

'Y-yes, Monseigneur?'

'Fetch them.'

Gaston hurried away, presently to reappear with the required
ornaments. Avon took the heavy sapphire chain and threw it over
Léon's head so that it lay across his breast, glowing with an inward
fire, yet no brighter or more liquid than the boy's eyes.

'Monseigneur!' gasped Léon. He put up his hand to feel the
precious chain.

'Give me your hat. The clasp, Gaston.' Unhurriedly he fixed
the diamond and sapphire circle on the upturned brim of the
page's hat. Then he gave it to Léon, and stepped back to observe
the effect of his handiwork. 'Yes, I wonder why I never thought
of sapphires before? The door, my infant.'

Still dazed by his master's unexpected action, Léon flew to open
the door for him. Avon passed out, and climbed into the waiting
coach. Léon looked up at him inquiringly, wondering whether he
was to mount the box or enter with his master.

'Yes, you may come with me,' said Avon, answering the
unspoken question. 'Tell them to let go the horses.'

Léon delivered the order, and sprang hurriedly into the coach,
for he knew the ways of Avon's horses. The postilions mounted
quickly, and in a trice the fretting horses leaped forward in their
collars, and the coach swerved round towards the wrought-iron
gates. Out they swept, and down the narrow street as swiftly as
was possible. But the very narrowness of the street, the slippery
cobblestones, and the many twists and turns, made their progress

necessarily slow, so that it was not until they came out on the
road to Versailles that the speed and power of the horses could be
demonstrated. Then they seemed to spring forward as one, and
the coach bowled along at a furious pace, lurching a little over the
worst bumps in the road, but so well sprung that for the most part
the surface of the road might have been of glass for all the jolting
or inconvenience that the occupants felt.

It was some time before Léon could find words to thank the
Duke for his chain. He sat on the edge of the seat beside the Duke,
fingering the polished stones in awe, and trying to squint down at
his breast to see how the chain looked. At length he drew a deep
breath and turned to gaze at his master, who lay back against the
velvet cushions idly surveying the flying landscape.

'Monseigneur – this is – too precious for – *me* to wear,' he said
in a hushed voice.

'Do you think so?' Avon regarded his page with an amused
smile.

'I – I would rather not wear it, Monseigneur. Suppose – suppose I were to lose it?'

'I should then be compelled to buy you another. You may lose
it an you will. It is yours.'

'Mine?' Léon twisted his fingers together. '*Mine*, Monseigneur?
You cannot mean that! I – I have done nothing – I could do
nothing to deserve such a present.'

'I suppose it had not occurred to you that I pay you no
wage? Somewhere in the Bible – I don't know where – it
says that the labourer is worthy of his hire. A manifestly false
observation for the most part, of course, but I choose to give
you that chain as – er – hire.'

Léon pulled his hat off at that, and slipped the chain over his
head, almost throwing it at the Duke. His eyes burned dark in a
very pale face.

'I do not want payment! I would work myself to death for you, but payment – no! A thousand times no! You make me angry!'

'Evidently,' murmured his Grace. He picked up the chain, and began to play with it. 'Now I had imagined you would be pleased.'

Léon brushed his hand across his eyes. His voice shook a little as he answered.

'How could you think that? I – I never looked for payment! I served you for love, and – and out of gratitude, and – you give me a chain! As if – as if you thought I should not continue to work well for you without payment!'

'If I had thought that I should not have given it to you,' yawned his Grace. 'It may interest you to know that I am not accustomed to being spoken to in this fashion by my pages.'

'I – I am sorry, Monseigneur,' whispered Léon. He turned his face away, biting his lips.

Avon watched him for a time in silence, but presently the mixture of forlornness and hurt dignity in his page drew a soft laugh from him, and he pulled one of the bright curls admonishingly.

'Do you expect me to apologise, my good child?'

Léon jerked his head away, and still stared out of the window.

'You are very haughty.' The mocking note in that gentle voice brought a wave of colour to Léon's cheeks.

'I – you are not – kind!'

'So you have just discovered that? But I do not see why I should be called unkind for rewarding you.'

'You do not understand!' said Léon fiercely.

'I understand that you deem yourself insulted, infant. It is most entertaining.'

A tiny sniff, which was also a sob, answered him. Again he laughed, and this time laid a hand on Léon's shoulder. Under the steely pressure Léon came to his knees, and stayed there, eyes downcast. The chain was flung over his head.

'My Léon, you will wear this because it is my pleasure.'

'Yes, Monseigneur,' said Léon stiffly.

The Duke took the pointed chin in his hand, and forced it up.

'I wonder why I bear with you?' he said. 'The chain is a gift. Are you satisfied?'

Léon pressed his chin down quickly to kiss the Duke's wrist.

'Yes, Monseigneur. Thank you. Indeed I am sorry.'

'Then you may sit down again.'

Léon picked up his hat, gave a shaky laugh, and settled himself on the wide seat beside the Duke.

'I think I have a very bad temper,' he remarked naïvely. 'M. le Curé would have made me do penance for it. He used to say that temper is a black sin. He talked to me about it – oh, often!'

'You do not appear to have profited unduly from his discourse,' replied Avon dryly.

'No, Monseigneur. But it is difficult, you understand. My temper is too quick for me. In a minute it is up, and I cannot stop it. But I am nearly always sorry afterwards. Shall I see the King tonight?'

'Quite possibly. You will follow me close. And do not stare.'

'No, Monseigneur. I will try not to. But that is difficult too.' He looked round confidently as he spoke, but the Duke, to all outward appearance, was asleep. So Léon snuggled into one corner of the coach, and prepared to enjoy the drive in silence. Occasionally they passed other vehicles, all bound for Versailles, but not once did a coach pass them. The four English thorough-breds swept by their French brethren time and again, and those within the coaches that were left behind leaned out to see who it was that drove at such a pace. The crest on the door of Avon's coach, seen in the light of their own lanterns, told them surely enough, and the black and gold livery was unmistakable.

'One might have known,' said the Marquis de Chourvanne, drawing in his head. 'Who else would drive at such a pace?'

'The English Duc?' asked his wife.

'Of course. Now I met him last night and he spoke no word of coming to the levee tonight.'

'Theodore de Ventour told me that no one knows from one moment to the next where the Duc will be.'

'*Poseur!*' snorted the Marquis, and put up the window.

The black and gold coach rolled on its way, scarcely checking till Versailles was reached. Then it slowed to enter the gates, and Léon sat forward to peer interestedly out into the gloom. Very little met his eyes, save when the coach passed under a lamp, until they entered the Cour Royale. Léon stared first this way and then that. The three-sided court was a blaze of light, shining from every unshuttered window that gave on to it, and further supplemented by great flambeaux. Coaches were streaming in a long line to the entrance, pausing there to allow their burdens to alight, then passing on to allow others to take their place.

Not until they finally drew up at the door did the Duke open his eyes. He looked out, dispassionately surveying the brilliant court, and yawned.

'I suppose I must alight,' he remarked, and waited for his footman to let down the steps. Léon climbed down first, and turned to assist his Grace. The Duke stepped slowly out, paused for a moment to look at the waiting coaches, and strolled past the palace lackeys with Léon at his heels, still holding the cloak and cane. Avon nodded to him to relinquish both to an expectant servant, and proceeded through various antechambers to the Marble Court, where he was soon lost in the crowd. Léon followed as best he might while Avon greeted his friends. He had ample opportunity for taking stock of his surroundings, but the vast dimensions of the court, and its magnificence, dazzled him. After what seemed to be an interminable time, he found that they were no longer in the Marble Court, having moved slowly but surely to the left.

They stood now before a great marble staircase, heavily encrusted with gold, up which a stream of people were wending their way. Avon fell in with a very much painted lady, and offered his arm. Together they mounted the broad stairs, crossed the hall at the top, and traversed various chambers until they came to the old Œil de Bœuf. Restraining an impulse to clutch the whaleboned skirts of Avon's coat, Léon followed him as closely as he dared into a room beside which all the others through which he had passed faded to nothingness. Someone had said downstairs that the levee was being held in the Galerie des Glaces; Léon realised that this was it. It seemed to him that the huge gallery was even double its real size, filled with a myriad candles in scintillating chandeliers, peopled by thousands of silk-clad ladies and gentlemen, until he discovered that one entire side was covered by gigantic mirrors. Opposite were as many windows; he tried to count them but ceased presently in despair, for groups of people from time to time obscured his view. The room was stuffy, yet cold, covered by two great Aubusson carpets. There were very few chairs, he thought, for this multitude of people. Again the Duke was bowing to right and left, sometimes stopping to exchange a few words with a friend, but always working his way to one end of the gallery. As they neared the fireplace the crowd became less dense, and Léon was able to see more than the shoulders of the man in front of him. A stout gentleman in full court dress and many orders sat in a gilded chair by the fire, with various gentlemen standing about him, and a fair lady in a chair by his side. The wig of this gentleman was almost grotesque, so large were the rolling curls that adorned it. He wore pink satin with gold lacing; he was bejewelled and painted, with black patches on his florid face, and a diamond-hilted sword at his side.

Avon turned his head to speak to Léon, and smiled faintly at the look of astonishment on the page's face.

'You have seen the King. Await me now over there.' He waved his hand towards an embrasure, and Léon started to retrace his steps, feeling very much as though his one support and guide in this vast place had deserted him.

The Duke paid homage to King Louis the Fifteenth, and to the pale Queen beside him, stayed for a few minutes to speak to the Dauphin, and proceeded in a leisurely fashion to where stood Armand de Saint-Vire, in attendance on the King.

Armand clasped his hands in warm welcome.

'*Mon Dieu*, but it is refreshing to see your face, Justin! I did not know even that you were in Paris. Since when have you returned, *mon cher?*'

'Nearly two months ago. Really, this is most fatiguing. I am thirsty already, but I suppose it is quite impossible to obtain any burgundy?'

Armand's eyes sparkled in sympathy.

'In the Salle de Guerre!' he whispered. 'We will go together. No, wait, *mon ami*, La Pompadour has seen you. Ah, she smiles! You have all the luck, Justin.'

'I could find another name for it,' said Avon, but he went to the King's mistress, and bowed exceedingly low as he kissed her hand. He remained at her side until the Comte de Stainville came to claim her attention, and then made good his escape to the Salle de Guerre. There he found Armand, with one or two others, partaking of light French wines, and sugared sweetmeats.

Someone handed the Duke a glass of burgundy; one of the footmen presented a plate of cakes, which he waved aside.

'A welcome interlude,' he remarked. '*A ta santé*, Joinlisse! Your servant, Tourdeville. A word in your ear, Armand.' He took Saint-Vire aside to where a couch stood. They sat down, and for a time talked of Paris, court-life, and the trials of a gentleman-in-waiting. Avon allowed his friend to ramble on, but at the first pause in Armand's rather amusing discourse, he turned the subject.

'I must make my bow to your charming sister-in-law,' he said. 'I trust she is present tonight?'

Armand's round good-humoured face became marred all at once by a gloomy scowl.

'Oh yes. Seated behind the Queen, in an obscure corner. If you are *épris* in that direction, Justin, your taste has deteriorated.' He snorted disdainfully. 'Curds and whey! How Henri could have chosen her passes my comprehension!'

'I never credited the worthy Henri with much sense,' answered the Duke. 'Why is he in Paris and not here?'

'Is he in Paris? He was in Champagne. He fell into slight disfavour here.' Armand grinned. 'That damnable temper, you understand. He left Madame, and that clodhopping son.'

Avon put up his eyeglass.

'Clodhopping?'

'What, have you not seen him, then? A boorish cub, Justin, with the soul of a farmer. And that is the boy who is to be Comte de Saint-Vire! *Mon Dieu*, but there must be bad blood in Marie! My beautiful nephew did not get his boorishness from us. Well, I never thought that Marie was of the real nobility.'

The Duke looked down at his wine.

'I must certainly see the young Henri,' he said. 'They tell me that he is not very like his father or his mother.'

'Not a whit. He has black hair, a bad nose, and square hands. It is a judgment on Henri! First he weds a puling, sighing woman with no charm and less beauty, and then he produces – that!'

'One would almost infer that you are not enamoured of your nephew,' murmured his Grace.

'No, I am not! I tell you, Justin, if it had been a true Saint-Vire I could have borne it better. But this – this half-witted bumpkin! It would enrage a saint!' He set down his glass on a small table with a force that nearly smashed the frail vessel. 'You may say that

I am a fool to brood over it, Alastair, but I cannot forget! To spite me Henri marries this Marie de Lespinasse, who presents him with a son after three fruitless years! First it was a still-born child, and then, when I had begun to think myself safe, she astonishes us all with a boy! Heaven knows what I have done to deserve it!'

'She astonished you with a boy. I think he was born in Champagne, was he not?'

'Ay, at Saint-Vire. Plague take him. I never set eyes on the brat until three months later when they brought him to Paris. Then I was well-nigh sick with disgust at Henri's fatuous triumph.'

'Well, I must see him,' repeated the Duke. 'How old is he?'

'I neither know nor care. He is nineteen,' snapped Armand. He watched the Duke rise, and smiled in spite of himself. 'Where's the good of growling, eh? It's the fault of this damned life I lead, Justin. It's all very well for you who come on a visit to this place. You think it very fine and splendid, but you've not seen the apartments they give to the gentlemen-in-waiting. Airless holes, Justin, I give you my word! Well, let's go back into the gallery.'

They went out, and paused for a moment just within the gallery.

'Yes, there she is,' said Armand. 'With Julie de Cornalle over there. Why do you want her?'

Justin smiled. 'You see, *mon cher*,' he explained sweetly, 'it will afford me such a satisfaction to be able to tell the dear Henri that I spent a pleasant half-hour with his fascinating wife.'

Armand chuckled. 'Oh, if that is your will – ! You so love the dear Henri, do you not?'

'But of course,' smiled the Duke. He waited until Armand had melted into the crowd before he beckoned to Léon, who, in obedience to his commands, still stood in the embrasure. The page came to him, slipping between two groups of chattering ladies, and followed him across the gallery to the couch on which sat Madame de Saint-Vire.

Avon swept the lady a magnificent leg.

'My dear Comtesse!' He took her thin hand, and holding it with the tips of his fingers just brushed it with his lips. 'I had hardly dared hope for this joy.'

She inclined her head, but out of the corner of her eye she was watching Léon. Mademoiselle de Cornalle had moved away, and Avon seated himself in her place. Léon went to stand behind him.

'Believe me, Comtesse,' continued the Duke, 'I was desolated not to see you in Paris. How is your delightful son?'

She answered nervously, and under pretence of arranging her skirt changed her position on the couch, so that she almost faced Avon, and thus was able to see the page behind him. Her eyes fluttered up to the boy's face, and widened for an instant before they fell. She became aware of Avon's smiling scrutiny, and coloured deeply, unfurling her fan with fingers that trembled slightly.

'My – my son? Oh, Henri is well, I thank you! You see him over there, m'sieur, with Mademoiselle de Lachère.'

Justin's gaze followed the direction of her pointing fan. He beheld a short, rather stocky youth, dressed in the height of fashion and seated mumchance beside a sprightly lady who was with difficulty restraining a yawn. The Vicomte de Valmé was very dark, with brown eyes heavy lidded now from weariness and boredom. His mouth was a trifle wide, but well-curved; his nose, so far from following the Saint-Vire aquiline trend, showed a tendency to turn up.

'Ah, yes!' said Justin. 'I should hardly have recognised him, madame. One looks usually for red hair and blue eyes in a Saint-Vire, does not one?' He laughed gently.

'My son wears a wig,' answered Madame rather quickly. Again she sent a fleeting glance towards Léon. Her mouth twitched slightly, uncontrollably. 'He – he has black hair. It often happens so, I believe.'

'Ah, no doubt,' agreed Justin. 'You are looking at my page, madame? A curious combination, is it not? – his copper hair and black brows.'

'I? No, why should I – ?' With an effort she collected her wits. 'It is an unusual combination, as you say. Who – who is the child?'

'I have no idea,' said his Grace blandly. 'I found him one evening in Paris, and bought him for the sum of a jewel. Quite a pretty boy, is he not? He attracts no little attention, I assure you.'

'Yes – I suppose so. It seems hard to believe that – that hair is – is natural.' Her eyes challenged him, but again he laughed.

'It must seem quite incredible,' he said. 'It is so seldom that one sees that – particular – combination.' Then, as the Comtesse stirred restlessly, opening and shutting her fan, he deftly turned the subject. 'Ah, behold the Vicomte!' he remarked. 'His fair companion has deserted him.'

The Comtesse looked across at her son, who was standing irresolute a few paces away. He saw his mother's eyes upon him, and came to her, heavy footed and deliberate, glancing curiously at the Duke.

'My – my son, m'sieur. Henri, the Duc of Avon.'

The Vicomte bowed, but although his bow was of just the required depth, and the wave of his hat in exact accordance with the decrees of fashion, the whole courtesy lacked spontaneity and grace. He bowed as one who had been laboriously coached in the art. Polish was lacking, and in its place was a faint suggestion of clumsiness.

'Your servant, m'sieur.' The voice was pleasant enough if not enthusiastic.

'My dear Vicomte!' Avon flourished his handkerchief. 'I am charmed to make your acquaintance. I remember you when you were still with your tutor, but of late years I have been denied the pleasure of meeting you. Léon, a chair for m'sieur.'

The page slipped from his place behind the couch, and went to fetch a low chair which stood against the wall, some few paces away. He set it down for the Vicomte, bowing as he did so.

'If m'sieur will be seated?'

The Vicomte looked him over in surprise. For a moment they stood shoulder to shoulder, the one slim and delicate, with eyes that matched the sapphires about his neck; and glowing curls swept back from a white brow beneath whose skin the veins showed faintly blue. The other was thick-set and dark, with square hands and short neck; powdered, perfumed, and patched, dressed in rich silks and velvet, but in spite of all rather uncouth and awkward. Avon heard Madame draw in her breath swiftly, and his smile grew. Then Léon went back to his original place, and the Vicomte sat down.

'Your page, m'sieur?' he asked. 'You were saying that you had not met me, I think? You see, I do not love Paris, and when my father permits I stay in Champagne, at Saint-Vire.' He smiled, casting a rueful glance at his mother. 'My parents do not like me to be in the country, m'sieur. I am a great trial to them.'

'The country…' The Duke unfobbed his snuff-box. 'It is pleasing to the eye, no doubt, but it is irrevocably associated in my mind with cows and pigs – even sheep. Necessary but distressing evils.'

'Evils, m'sieur? Why –'

'Henri, the Duc is not interested in such matters!' interposed the Comtesse. 'One – does not talk of – of cows and pigs at a levee.' She turned to Avon, smiling mechanically. 'The boy has an absurd whim, m'sieur: he would like to be a farmer! I tell him that he would very soon tire of it.' She started to fan herself, laughing.

'Yet another necessary evil,' drawled his Grace. 'Farmers. You take snuff, Vicomte?'

The Vicomte helped himself to a pinch.

'I thank you, m'sieur. You have come from Paris? Perhaps you have seen my father?'

'I had that felicity yesterday,' replied Avon. 'At a ball. The Comte remains the same as ever, madame.' The sneer was thinly veiled. Madame flushed scarlet.

'I trust you found my husband in good health, m'sieur?'

'Excellent, I believe. May I be the bearer of any message you may wish to send, madame?'

'I thank you, m'sieur, but I am writing to him – tomorrow,' she answered. 'Henri, will you fetch me some negus? Ah, madame!' She beckoned to a lady who stood in a group before them.

The Duke rose. 'I see my good Armand yonder. Pray give me leave, madame. The Comte will be overjoyed to hear that I found you well – and your son.' He bowed, and left her, walking away into the dwindling crowd. He sent Léon to await him in the Œil de Bœuf, and remained for perhaps an hour in the gallery.

When he joined Léon in the Œil de Bœuf he found him almost asleep, but making valiant efforts to keep himself awake. He followed the Duke downstairs, and was sent to retrieve Avon's cloak and cane. By the time he had succeeded in obtaining these articles the black and gold coach was at the door.

Avon swung the cloak over his shoulders and sauntered out. He and Léon entered the luxurious vehicle, and with a sigh of content Léon nestled back against the soft cushions.

'It is all very wonderful,' he remarked, 'but very bewildering. Do you mind if I fall asleep, Monseigneur?'

'Not at all,' said his Grace politely. 'I trust you were satisfied with the King's appearance?'

'Oh yes, he is just like the coins!' said Léon drowsily. 'Do you suppose he likes to live in such a great palace, Monseigneur?'

'I have never asked him,' replied the Duke. 'Versailles does not please you?'

'It is so very large,' explained the page. 'I feared I had lost you.'

'What an alarming thought!' remarked his Grace.

'Yes, but you came after all.' The deep little voice was getting sleepier and sleepier. 'It was all glass and candles, and ladies, and – *Bonne nuit*, Monseigneur,' he sighed. 'I am sorry, but everything is muddled, and I am so very tired. I do not think I snore when I sleep, but if I do, then of course you must wake me. And I might slip, but I hope I shall not. I am right in the corner, so perhaps I shall remain here. But if I slip on to the floor –'

'Then I suppose I am to pick you up?' said Avon sweetly.

'Yes,' agreed Léon, already on the borderland of sleep. 'I won't talk any more now. Monseigneur does not mind?'

'Pray do not consider me in the slightest,' answered Avon. 'I am here merely to accommodate you. If I disturb you I beg you will not hesitate to mention it. I will then ride on the box.'

A very sleepy chuckle greeted this sally, and a small hand tucked itself into the Duke's.

'I wanted to hold your coat because I thought I should lose you,' murmured Léon.

'I presume that is why you are holding my hand now?' inquired his Grace. 'You are perhaps afraid lest I should hide myself under the seat?'

'That is silly,' replied Léon. 'Very silly. *Bonne nuit*, Monseigneur.'

'*Bonne nuit, mon enfant*. You will not lose me – or I you – very easily, I think.'

There was no answer, but Léon's head sank against his Grace's shoulder, and remained there.

'I am undoubtedly a fool,' remarked the Duke. He pushed a cushion under Léon's relaxed arm. 'But if I wake him he will begin to talk again. What a pity Hugh is not here to see!… I beg your pardon, my infant?' But Léon had muttered only in his sleep. 'If you are going to converse in your sleep I shall be compelled to take strong measures of prevention,' said his Grace. He leaned his head back against the padded seat, and smiling, closed his eyes.

Six

His Grace of Avon Refuses to Sell His Page

WHEN DAVENANT MET HIS GRACE AT BREAKFAST NEXT MORNING he found that the Duke was in excellent spirits. He was more than usually urbane, and whenever his eye alighted on Léon he smiled, as if at some pleasant thought.

'Was the levee well attended?' asked Hugh, attacking a red sirloin. Unlike the Duke, who never ate more than a roll for breakfast, he made a hearty meal of eggs and bacon, and cold meats, washed down by English ale, especially imported by the Duke for his delectation.

The Duke poured himself out a second cup of coffee.

'Crowded, my dear Hugh. It was in honour of some birthday, or saint's day, or something of the sort.'

'Did you see Armand?' Hugh reached out his hand for the mustard.

'I saw Armand, and the Comtesse, and the Vicomte, and everybody I least wished to meet.'

'One always does. I suppose La Pompadour was delighted to see you?'

'Oppressively so. The King sat on his throne and smiled benignantly. Just like a coin.'

Hugh suspended his fork in mid-air.

'Just like a what?'

'A coin. Léon will explain. Or possibly he has forgotten.'

Hugh looked inquiringly at the page.

'What is the joke, Léon? Do you know?'

Léon shook his head.

'No, m'sieur.'

'Ah, I thought perhaps you would not remember,' said his Grace. 'Léon was quite satisfied with the King, Hugh. He confided to me that he was just like the coins.'

Léon blushed.

'I – I am afraid I was asleep, Monseigneur.'

'Very nearly so. Do you always sleep as one dead?'

'N-no. That is – I do not know, Monseigneur. I was put to bed in all my clothes.'

'Yes, I did that. Having wasted ten minutes in endeavouring to rouse you, I thought that the simplest plan would be to carry you up to bed. You are not all joy, my infant.'

'I am very sorry, Monseigneur; you should have made me wake up.'

'If you would tell me how that may be done I shall do so on the next occasion. Hugh, if you must eat beef, pray do not brandish it in my face at this hour.'

Davenant, whose fork was still suspended midway between his plate and mouth, laughed, and went on eating.

Justin began to sort the letters that lay beside his plate. Some he threw away, others he slipped into his pocket. One had come from England, and spread over several sheets. He opened them and started to decipher the scrawl.

'From Fanny,' he said. 'Rupert is still at large, it seems. At Mistress Carsby's feet. When I saw him last he was madly in love with Julia Falkner. From one extreme to another.' He turned over the page. 'Now, how interesting! Dear Edward has given Fanny a chocolate-coloured coach with pale-blue cushions. The wheels are picked out in blue.' He held the sheet at arm's length. 'It seems strange, but no doubt Fanny is right. I have not been in England for such a time – Ah, I beg her pardon! You will be relieved to hear, my dear Hugh, that the wheat in England still grows as ever it did. Ballentor has fought another duel, and Fanny won fifty guineas at play the other night. John is in the country because town air does not suit him. Now, is John her lap-dog or her parrot?'

'Her son,' said Davenant.

'Is he? Yes, I believe you are right. What next? If I can find her a French cook she vows she will love me more than ever. Léon, tell Walker to find me a French cook. – She wishes she could visit me as I suggested some time ago – how rash of me! – but it is quite impossible as she cannot leave her darling Edward alone, and she fears he would not accompany her to my hovel. Hovel. Not very polite of Fanny. I must remember to speak to her about it.'

'*Hôtel*,' suggested Hugh.

'Once more you are right. *Hôtel* it is. The rest of this enthralling communication concerns Fanny's toilettes. I will reserve it. Oh, have you finished?'

'Finished and gone,' answered Davenant, rising. 'I am riding out with D'Anvau. I shall see you later.' He went out.

Avon leaned his arms on the table, resting his chin on the back of his clasped hands.

'Léon, where does your remarkable brother live?'

Léon started, and fell back a pace.

'Mon – Monseigneur?'

'Where is his inn?'

Suddenly Léon fell on his knees beside Avon's chair, and clutched the Duke's sleeve with desperate fingers. His face was upturned, pale and agonised, the great eyes swimming in tears.

'Oh no, no, no, Monseigneur! You would not – Oh, please not

that! I – I will never go to sleep again! Please, please forgive me! Monseigneur! Monseigneur!'

Avon looked down at him with upraised brows. Léon had pressed his forehead against his master's arm, and was shaking with suppressed sobs.

'You bewilder me,' complained the Duke. 'What is it that I am not to do, and why will you never sleep again?'

'Don't – don't give me back to Jean!' implored Léon, clinging tighter still. 'Promise, promise!'

Avon loosened the clasp on his sleeve.

'My dear Léon, I beg you will not weep over this coat. I have no intention of giving you to Jean, or to anyone else. Stand up, and do not be ridiculous.'

'You must promise! You shall promise!' Léon shook the arm he held almost fiercely.

The Duke sighed. 'Very well: I promise. Now tell me where I may find your brother, my child.'

'I won't! I won't! You – he – I won't tell you!'

The hazel eyes became hard.

'I have borne much from you in patience, Léon, but I will not brook your defiance. Answer me at once.'

'I dare not! Oh, please, please do not make me tell! I – I do not mean to be defiant! But perhaps Jean is sorry now that – that he let me go, and – and will try to m-make you give me back!' He was plucking at the Duke's sleeve now, and again Avon removed the frenzied fingers.

'Do you think Jean could make me give you back?' he asked.

'N-no – I don't know. I thought perhaps because I went to sleep you were angered, and – and –'

'I have already told you that it is not so. Strive to have a little sense. And answer my question.'

'Yes, Monseigneur. I – I am sorry. Jean – Jean lives in the Rue

Sainte-Marie. There is only one inn – the Crossbow. Oh, what are you going to do, Monseigneur?'

'Nothing at all alarming, I assure you. Dry your tears.'

Léon hunted through his various pockets.

'I – I have lost my handkerchief,' he apologised.

'Yes, you are very young, are you not?' commented his Grace. 'I suppose I must give you mine.'

Léon took the fine lace handkerchief which the Duke held out, wiped his eyes, blew his nose, and gave it back again. The Duke received it gingerly, and eyed the crumpled ball through his quizzing-glass.

'Thank you,' he said. 'You are nothing if not thorough. I think you had better keep it now.'

Léon pocketed it cheerfully.

'Yes, Monseigneur,' he said. 'Now I am happy again.'

'I am relieved,' said the Duke, and rose. 'I shall not want you this morning.' He strolled out, and in half an hour's time was in his coach, driving towards the Rue Sainte-Marie.

The street was very narrow, with refuse in the kennels on either side of the road; the houses were mostly tumbledown, projecting outward from the first storey. Hardly one had all its windows intact; there were cracked and missing panes on all sides, and where curtains hung they were ragged and dirty. Half a dozen partly clothed children were playing in the road, and scattered to right and left as the coach drove up, standing on the footway, and watched the progress of this fine equipage with astonished eyes, and many startled comments.

The tavern of the Crossbow was situated midway down the squalid street, and from its open door issued a smell of cooking, and of cabbage water, thrown carelessly out into the kennel. The coach drew up outside the inn, and one of the footmen sprang down to open the door for his Grace to alight. His countenance

was quite impassive, and only by the lofty tilt of his chin did he
betray his emotions.

His Grace came slowly down from the coach, his handkerchief
held to his nose. He picked his way across the filth and garbage to
the inn door, and entered what appeared to be the taproom and
the kitchen. A greasy woman was bending over the fire at one end,
a cooking-pot in her hand, and behind the counter opposite the
door stood the man who had sold Léon to the Duke a month ago.

He gaped when he saw Avon enter, and for a moment did not
recognise him. He came forward cringingly, rubbing his hands
together, and desired to know Monseigneur's pleasure.

'I think you know me,' said his Grace gently.

Bonnard stared, and suddenly his eyes dilated, and his full-
blooded countenance turned a sickly gray.

'Léon! Milor' – I –'

'Precisely. I want two words with you in private.'

The man looked at him fearfully, passing his tongue between
his lips. 'I swear by God –'

'Thank you. In private I said.'

The woman, who had watched the encounter open-mouthed,
came forward now, arms akimbo. Her soiled dress was in disorder,
cut low across her scraggy bosom, and there was a smudge of dirt
on her cheek.

'Now, if the little viper has said aught against us,' she began
shrilly, but was cut short by Avon's lifted hand.

'My good woman, I have no desire to speak with you. You
may return to your stew-pots. Bonnard, in private!'

Charlotte would have interrupted again, but her husband hus-
tled her back to the stove, whispering to her to hold her tongue.

'Yes, milor', indeed yes! If milor' will follow me?' He pushed
open the crazy, rat-eaten door at the other end of the room, and
ushered his Grace into the parlour. The room was scantily furnished,

but it was not so dirty as the taproom. Avon went to the table that stood by the window, flicked the dust from its surface with a corner of his cloak, and sat down on the edge of the rickety structure.

'Now, my friend. That you may not misunderstand me, or seek to evade me, let me tell you that I am the Duke of Avon. Yes, I thought that you would be surprised. You realise, I am sure, that it would be very dangerous to play with me. I am going to ask you one or two questions about my page. I wish to know first where he was born.'

'I – I think in the north, Monseigneur. In – Champagne, but I am not sure. Our – our parents never spoke of that time, and I can scarce remember – I –'

'No? It seems strange that you do not know why your worthy parents went so suddenly to live in Anjou.'

Bonnard looked at him helplessly.

'My – my father told me that he had come into money! Indeed, I know no more, Monseigneur! I would not lie. I swear I would not!'

The fine lips curled sardonically.

'We will pass over that. How comes it that Léon is so unlike you in face and form?'

Bonnard rubbed his forehead. There was no mistaking the perplexity in his eyes.

'I do not know, Monseigneur. I have often wondered. He was ever a weakly child, petted and cosseted when I was made to work on the farm. My mother cared nothing for me beside him. It was all Léon, Léon, Léon! Léon must learn to read and write, but I – the eldest – must tend the pigs! A sickly, pert lad he was ever, Monseigneur! A viper, a –'

Avon tapped the lid of his snuff-box with one very white finger.

'Do not let us misunderstand one another, my friend. There never was a Léon. A Léonie, perhaps. I want that explained.'

The man shrank.

'Ah, Monseigneur! Indeed, indeed I did it for the best! It was impossible to have a girl of that age here, and there was work to be done. It was better to dress her as a boy. My wife – Monseigneur will understand – women are jealous, milor'. She would not have a girl here. Indeed, indeed, if the boy – girl – has said aught against us, he lies! I could have turned him out into the streets, for he had no claim on me. Instead, I kept him, clothed him, fed him, and if he says he was ill-treated it is a lie! He is a wicked brat with a vicious temper. You could not blame me for hiding his sex, Monseigneur! It was for his sake, I swear! He liked it well enough. Never did he demand to be a girl!'

'No doubt he had forgotten,' said Avon dryly. 'Seven years a boy... Now –' He held up a louis. 'Mayhap this will refresh your memory. What do you know of Léon?'

The man looked at him in a puzzled way.

'I – do not understand, Monseigneur. What do I know of him?'

Avon leaned forward slightly, and his voice became menacing.

'It will not serve you to feign ignorance, Bonnard. I am very powerful.'

Bonnard's knees shook.

'Indeed, Monseigneur, I do not understand! I cannot tell you what I do not know! Is – is aught amiss with Léon?'

'You never thought that he was, perhaps, not your parents' child?'

Bonnard's jaw dropped.

'Not – Why, Monseigneur, what do you mean? Not my parents' child. But –'

Avon sat back.

'Does the name Saint-Vire convey aught to you?'

'Saint-Vire... Saint-Vire... no. Stay, the name has a familiar ring! But – Saint-Vire – I do not know.' He shook his head hopelessly. 'It may be that I have heard my father speak the name, but I cannot remember.'

'A pity. And when your parents died was there no document found belonging to them which concerned Léon?'

'If there was, milor', I never saw it. There were old accounts and letters – I cannot read, Monseigneur, but I have them all.' He looked at the louis, and licked his lips. 'If Monseigneur would care to see for himself? They are here, in that chest.'

Avon nodded. 'Yes. All of them.'

Bonnard went to the chest and opened it. After some search he found a sheaf of papers, which he brought to the Duke. Avon went through them quickly. For the most part they were, as Bonnard had said, farm accounts, with one or two letters amongst them. But at the bottom of the pile was a folded slip of paper, addressed to Jean Bonnard, on the estate of M. le Comte de Saint-Vire, in Champagne. It was only a letter from some friend, or relation, and it held nothing of importance, save the address. The Duke held it up.

'This I will take.' He tossed the louis to Bonnard. 'If you have lied to me, or deceived me, you will be sorry. At present I am willing to believe that you know nothing.'

'I have spoken naught but the truth, Monseigneur, I swear!'

'Let us hope that it is so. One thing, however' – he produced another louis – 'you can tell me. Where shall I find the Curé at Bassincourt, and what is his name?'

'M. de Beaupré, Monseigneur, but he may be dead now, for aught I know. He was an old man when we left Bassincourt. He used to live in a little house beside the church. You cannot mistake it.'

Avon threw the louis into his eager hand.

'Very well.' He went to the door. 'Be advised by me, my friend, and strive to forget that you ever had a sister. For you had not, and it might be that if you remember a Léonie there would be a reckoning to be paid for your treatment of her. I shall not forget you, I assure you.' He swept out, and through the taproom to his coach.

***

That afternoon, when Avon sat in the library of his house, writing to his sister, a footman came to him and announced that M. de Faugenac wished to see him.

The Duke raised his head.

'M. de Faugenac? Admit him.'

In a few minutes' time there entered a tubby little gentleman with whom his Grace was but slightly acquainted. Avon rose as he came in and bowed.

'Monsieur!'

'Monsieur!' De Faugenac returned the bow. 'Pardon the unseemly hour of this intrusion, I beg!'

'Not at all,' answered the Duke. 'Fetch wine, Jules. Pray be seated, m'sieur.'

'No wine for me, I thank you! The gout, you understand. A sad affliction!'

'Very,' agreed his Grace. 'Is there something I can do for you, I wonder?'

De Faugenac stretched his hands to the fire.

'Yes, I come on business, m'sieur. Bah, the ugly word! M'sieur will pardon the interruption, I am sure! A splendid fire, Duc!'

Avon bowed. He had seated himself on the arm of a chair, and was looking at his visitor in mild surprise. He drew out his snuff-box and offered it to De Faugenac, who helped himself to a liberal pinch and sneezed violently.

'Exquisite!' he said enthusiastically. 'Ah, the business! M'sieur, you will think I come upon a strange errand, but I have a wife!' He beamed at Avon, and nodded several times.

'I felicitate you, m'sieur,' said Avon gravely.

'Yes, yes! A wife! It will explain all.'

'It always does,' answered his Grace.

'Aha, the pleasantry!' De Faugenac broke into delighted laughter. 'We know, we husbands, we know!'

'As I am not a husband I may be excused my ignorance. I am sure you are about to enlighten me.' His Grace was becoming bored, for he had remembered that De Faugenac was an impoverished gentleman usually to be found at the heels of Saint-Vire.

'Indeed yes. Yes, indeed. My wife. The explanation! She has seen your page, m'sieur!'

'Wonderful!' said the Duke. 'We progress.'

'We – ? You said progress? We? Progress?'

'It seems I erred,' Avon sighed. 'We remain at the same place.'

De Faugenac was puzzled for a moment, but all at once his face broke into fresh smiles.

'Another pleasantry! Yes, yes, I see!'

'I doubt it,' murmured Avon. 'You were saying, m'sieur, that your wife had seen my page.'

De Faugenac clasped his hands to his breast. 'She is ravished! She is envious! She pines!'

'Dear me!'

'She gives me no peace!'

'They never do.'

'Aha! No, never, never! But you do not take my meaning, m'sieur, you do not take my meaning!'

'But then, that is hardly my fault,' said Avon wearily. 'We have arrived at the point at which your wife gives you no peace.'

'That is the matter in a nutshell! She eats out her heart for your so lovely, your so enchanting, your so elegant –'

Avon held up his hand. 'M'sieur, my policy has ever been to eschew married women.'

De Faugenac stared. 'But – but – what do you mean, m'sieur? Is it another pleasantry? My wife pines for your page.'

'How very disappointing!'

'Your page, your so elegant page! She plagues me day and night to come to you. And I am here! Behold me!'

'I have beheld you for the past twenty minutes, m'sieur,' said Avon rather tartly.

'She begs me to come to you, to ask you if you would part with your page! She cannot rest until she has him to hold her train for her, to carry her gloves and fan. She cannot sleep at night until she knows that he is hers!'

'It seems that madame is destined to spend many sleepless nights,' said Avon.

'Ah no, m'sieur! Consider! It is said that you bought your page. Now, is it not truly said that what may be bought may be sold?'

'Possibly.'

'Yes, yes! Possibly! M'sieur, I am as a slave to my wife.' He kissed the tips of his fingers. 'I am as the dirt beneath her feet.' He clasped his hands. 'I must bestow on her all that she desires, or die!'

'Pray make use of my sword,' invited his Grace. 'It is in the corner behind you.'

'Ah no! M'sieur cannot mean that he refuses! It is impossible! M'sieur, you may name your own price and I will give it!'

Avon stood up. He picked up a silver hand-bell, and rang it.

'M'sieur,' he said silkily, 'you may bear my compliments to the Comte de Saint-Vire, and tell him that Léon, my page, is not for sale. Jules, the door.'

De Faugenac rose, very crestfallen. 'M'sieur?'

Avon bowed.

'M'sieur. You mistake! You do not understand!'

'Believe me, I understand perfectly.'

'Ah, but you have no soul thus to thwart a lady's wish!'

'My misfortune entirely, m'sieur. I am desolated that you are unable to stay longer. M'sieur, your very obedient!' So he bowed De Faugenac out.

No sooner had the door closed behind the little man than it opened again to admit Davenant.

'Who in the name of all that's marvellous was that?' he asked.

'A creature of no account,' replied his Grace. 'He wished to buy Léon. An impertinence. I am going into the country, Hugh.'

'Into the country? Why?'

'I forget. No doubt I shall call the reason to mind some time. Bear with me, my dear; I am still moderately sane.'

Hugh sat down.

'You never were sane. 'Pon rep, you're a casual host!'

'Ah Hugh, I crave your pardon on my knees! I encroach on your good nature.'

'Damme, you're very polite! Is Léon to accompany you?'

'No, I leave him in your charge, Hugh, and I counsel you to have a care for him. While I am away he will not leave the house.'

'I thought there was some mystery. Is he in danger?'

'N-no. I can hardly say. But keep him close, and say naught, my dear. I should not be pleased if harm came to him. Incredible as it may seem, I am becoming fond of the child. I must be entering upon my dotage.'

'We are all fond of him,' said Hugh. 'But he is an imp.'

'Undoubtedly. Do not allow him to tease you; he is an impertinent child. Unhappily he cannot be brought to realise that fact. And here he is.'

Léon came in and smiled confidingly as he met the Duke's eyes.

'Monseigneur, you told me to be ready to accompany you out at three, and it is now half-past the hour,' he said.

Hugh's shoulders shook with suppressed laughter; he turned away, coughing.

'It would appear that I owe you an apology,' said his Grace. 'Pray hold me excused for once. I am not going out after all. Come here.'

Léon approached.

'Yes, Monseigneur?'

'I am going into the country for a few days, my infant, from tomorrow. Oblige me by looking on M. Davenant as master in mine absence, and do not, on any account, leave the house until I return.'

'Oh!' Léon's face fell. 'Am I not to come with you?'

'I am denying myself that honour. Please do not argue with me. That is all that I wished to say.'

Léon turned away and went with lagging steps to the door. A small sniff escaped him, and at the sound of it Avon smiled.

'Infant, the end of the world has not come. I shall return, I hope, within the week.'

'I wish – oh, I wish that you would take me!'

'That is hardly polite to M. Davenant. I do not think he is likely to ill-use you. I am not going out tonight, by the way.'

Léon came back.

'You – you won't go tomorrow without saying goodbye, will you, Monseigneur?'

'You shall hand me into my coach,' promised the Duke, and gave him his hand to kiss.

Seven

Satan and Priest at One

THE VILLAGE OF BASSINCOURT, WHICH LAY SOME SIX OR SEVEN miles to the west of Saumur, in Anjou, was a neat and compact place whose white houses were for the most part gathered about its hub, a square market-place paved by cobblestones as large as a man's fist. On the north the square was flanked by various houses of the more well-to-do inhabitants; on the west by smaller cottages, and by a lane that led into the square at right angles to this side, and which stretched out into the open country, winding this way and that to touch each of the three farms that lay to the west of Bassincourt. On the south side was the small gray church, within whose square tower a cracked bell was wont to ring out its summons to the villagers. The church stood back from the market-place with its burial ground all about it and beyond, on one side, the Curé's modest house, squatting in its own garden, and seeming to smile across the square in gentle rulership.

The east side of the square was close-packed by shops, a black smith's yard, and a white inn, over whose open door hung a gay green shield, with a painting of the Rising Sun thereon. The sign swung to and fro with every wind that blew, creaking a little if the gale were fierce, but more often sighing only on its rusted chains.

On this particular day of November the square was a-hum with voices, and echoing occasionally to a child's shrill laugh, or to the stamp of a horse's hoofs on the cobbles. Old Farmer Mauvoisin had driven into Bassincourt with three pigs for sale in his cart, and had drawn up at the inn to exchange the time of day with the landlord, and to quaff a tankard of thin French ale while his pigs grunted and snuffled behind him. Close by, gathered about a stall where La Mère Gognard was selling vegetables, was a group of women, alternately haggling and conversing. Several girls in stiff gowns kilted high above their ankles, their feet in clumsy wooden sabots, stood chattering beside the ancient porch which led into the graveyard; in the centre of the square, near to the fountain, some sheep were herded, while a party of possible buyers picked their way amongst them, prodding and inspecting at will. From the blacksmith's yard came the ring of hammer on anvil, mingled with spasmodic snatches of song.

Into this busy, contented scene rode his Grace of Avon, upon a hired horse. He came trotting into the market-place from the eastern road that led to Saumur, dressed all in sombre black, with lacing of gold. As soon as his horse's hoofs struck the uneven cobblestones he reined in, and sitting gracefully at ease in the saddle, one gloved hand resting lightly on his hip, cast a languid glance round.

He attracted no little attention. The villagers stared at him from his point-edged hat to his spurred boots, and back again. One tittering girl, remarking those cold eyes and the thin, curling lips, whispered that it was the devil himself come amongst them. Although her companion scoffed at her for a foolish maid, she crossed herself surreptitiously, and drew back into the shelter of the porch.

The Duke's glance swept all round the square, and came to rest at last on a small boy, who watched him with goggling eyes, and his thumb in his mouth. One hand in its embroidered gauntlet beckoned imperiously, and the small boy took a hesitating step forward in answer to the Duke's summons.

His Grace looked down at him, faintly smiling. He pointed to the house beside the church.

'Am I right in thinking that that is the abode of your Curé?'

The boy nodded.

'Yes, milor'.'

'Do you think that I shall find him within?'

'Yes, milor'. He came back from the house of Madame Tournaud an hour since, if you please, milor'.'

Avon swung himself lightly down from the saddle, and twitched the bridle over his horse's head.

'Very well, child. Be so good as to hold this animal for me until I return. You will thus earn a louis.'

The boy took the bridle willingly.

'A whole louis, milor?' For holding your horse?' he said breathlessly.

'Is it a horse?' The Duke eyed the animal through his quizzing-glass. 'Perhaps you are right. I thought it was a camel. Take it away and water it.' He turned on his heel, and sauntered up to the Curé's house. The wondering villagers saw M. de Beaupré's housekeeper admit him, and started to propound their views on this strange visitation, one to the other.

His Grace of Avon was led through a tiny spotless hall to the Curé's sanctum, a sunny room at the back of the house. The rosy-cheeked housekeeper ushered him into her master's presence with unruffled placidity.

'Here, *mon père*, is a gentleman who desires speech with you,' she said, and then withdrew, without another glance at the Duke.

The Curé was seated at a table by the window, writing on a sheet of paper. He looked up to see who was his visitor, and perceiving a stranger, laid down his quill and rose. He was slight, with thin, beautiful hands, calm blue eyes, and aristocratic features. He wore a long soutane, and his head was uncovered. For an instant Avon thought that the milky-white hair was a wig, so ordered were the soft waves, and then he saw that it was natural, brushed smoothly back from a broad low brow.

'M. de Beaupré, I believe?' His Grace bowed deeply.

'Yes, m'sieur, but you have the advantage of me.'

'I am one Justin Alastair,' said the Duke, and laid his hat and gloves on the table.

'Yes? You will pardon me, monsieur, if I do not at once recognise you. I have been out of the world for many years, and for the moment I cannot call to mind whether you are of the Alastairs of Auvergne, or of the English family.' De Beaupré cast him an appraising look, and put forward a chair.

Justin sat down.

'The English family, monsieur. You perhaps knew my father?'

'Slightly, very slightly,' answered De Beaupré. 'You are the Duc of Avon, I think? What may I have the honour of doing for you?'

'I am the Duke of Avon, m'sieur, as you say. Am I right in thinking that I address a relative of the Marquis de Beaupré?'

'His uncle, m'sieur.'

'Ah!' Justin bowed. 'You are the Vicomte de Marrillon, then.'

The Curé seated himself at the table again.

'I renounced that title years ago, m'sieur, deeming it empty. My family will tell you that I am mad. They do not mention my name.' He smiled. 'Naturally, I have disgraced them. I chose to work amongst my people here when I might have worn a cardinal's hat. But I suppose you did not come all the way to Anjou to hear that. What is it I may do for you?'

Justin offered his host some snuff.

'I hope, m'sieur, that you may be able to enlighten me,' he said.

De Beaupré took a pinch of snuff, holding it delicately to one nostril.

'It is hardly probable, m'sieur. As I said, I have long since withdrawn from the world, and what I knew of it I have well-nigh forgotten.'

'This, *mon père*, has naught to do with the world,' replied his Grace. 'I want you to cast your mind back seven years.'

'Well?' De Beaupré picked up his quill and passed it through his fingers. 'Having done that, *mon fils*, what then?'

'Having done that, m'sieur, you may perhaps recall a family living here of the name of Bonnard.'

The Curé nodded. His eyes never wavered from Avon's face.

'More particularly the child – Léonie.'

'One wonders what the Duc of Avon knows of Léonie. I am not likely to forget.' The blue eyes were quite inscrutable.

His Grace swung one booted leg gently to and fro.

'Before I go further, *mon père*, I would have you know that I speak in confidence.'

The Curé brushed his quill lightly across the table.

'And before I consent to respect the confidence, my son, I will learn what it is you want of a peasant girl, and what that peasant girl is to you,' he answered.

'At the moment she is my page,' said Avon blandly.

The Curé raised his brows.

'So? Do you usually employ a girl as your page, M. le Duc?'

'It is not one of my most common practices, *mon père*. This girl does not know that I have discovered her sex.'

The quill brushed the table again, rhythmically.

'No, my son? And what comes to her?'

Avon looked haughtily across at him.

'M. de Beaupré, you will pardon me, I am sure, for pointing out to you that my morals are not your concern.'

The Curé met his look unflinchingly.

'They are your own, my son, but you have seen fit to make them all the world's. I might retort: Léonie's welfare is not your concern.'

'She would not agree with you, *mon père*. Let us understand one another. Body and soul she is mine. I bought her from the ruffian who called himself her brother.'

'He had reason,' said De Beaupré calmly.

'Do you think so? Rest assured, m'sieur, that Léonie is safer with me than with Jean Bonnard. I have come to ask your help for her.'

'I have never before heard that – Satanas – chose a priest for his ally, m'sieur.'

Avon's teeth showed white for a moment in a smile.

'Withdrawn as you are from the world, *mon père*, you yet have heard that?'

'Yes, m'sieur. Your reputation is well known.'

'I am flattered. In this case my reputation lies. Léonie is safe with me.'

'Why?' asked De Beaupré serenely.

'Because, my father, there is a mystery attached to her.'

'It seems an insufficient reason.'

'Nevertheless it must suffice. My word, when I give it, is surety enough.'

The Curé folded his hands before him, and looked quietly into Avon's eyes. Then he nodded.

'It is very well, *mon fils*. Tell me what became of *la petite*. That Jean was worthless, but he would not leave Léonie with me. Where did he take her?'

'To Paris, where he bought a tavern. He dressed Léonie as a boy, and a boy she has been for seven years. She is my page now, until I end that comedy.'

'And when you end it, what then?'

Justin tapped one polished finger-nail against the lid of his snuff-box.

'I take her to England – to my sister. I have some vague notion of ah – adopting her. As my ward, you understand. Oh, she will be chaperoned, of course!'

'Why, my son? If you desire to do good to *la petite* send her to me.'

'My dear father, I have never desired to do good to anyone. I have a reason for keeping this child. And, strange to say, I have developed quite a keen affection for her. A fatherly emotion, believe me.'

The housekeeper entered at this moment, bearing a tray with wine and glasses upon it. She arranged the refreshment at her master's elbow, and withdrew.

De Beaupré poured his visitor out a glass of canary.

'Proceed, my son. I do not yet see how I can aid you, or why you have journeyed all this way to see me.'

The Duke raised the glass to his lips.

'A most tedious journey,' he agreed. 'But your main roads are good. Unlike ours in England. I came, my father, to ask you to tell me all that you know of Léonie.'

'I know very little, m'sieur. She came to this place as a babe, and left it when she was scarce twelve years old.'

Justin leaned forward, resting one arm on the table.

'From where did she come, *mon père*?'

'It was always kept secret. I believe they came from Champagne. They never told me.'

'Not even – under the seal of the confessional?'

'No. That were of no use to you, my son. From chance words that the Mère Bonnard from time to time let fall I gathered that Champagne was their native country.'

'M'sieur,' Justin's eyes widened a little, 'I want you to speak plainly. Did you think when you saw Léonie grow from babyhood into girlhood that she was a daughter of the Bonnards?'

The Curé looked out of the window. For a moment he did not answer.

'I wondered, monsieur...'

'No more? Was there nothing to show that she was not a Bonnard?'

'Nothing but her face.'

'And her hair, and her hands. Did she remind you of no one, my father?'

'It is difficult to tell at that age. The features are still unformed. When the Mère Bonnard was dying she tried to say something. That it concerned Léonie I know, but she died before she could tell me.'

His Grace frowned quickly. 'How inconvenient!'

The Curé's lips tightened. 'What of *la petite*, sir? What became of her when she left this place?'

'She was, as I told you, compelled to change her sex. Bonnard married some shrewish slut, and bought a tavern in Paris. Faugh!' His Grace took snuff.

'It was perhaps as well then that Léonie was a boy,' said De Beaupré quietly.

'Without doubt. I found her one evening when she was flying from punishment. I bought her, and she mistook me for a hero.'

'I trust, *mon fils*, that she will never have cause to change her opinion.'

Again the Duke smiled.

'It is a hard rôle to maintain, my father. Let us pass over that. When first I set eyes on her it flashed across my brain that she was related to – someone I know.' He shot the Curé a swift glance, but De Beaupré's face was impassive. 'Someone I know. Yes. On the fleeting conviction I acted. The conviction has grown, *mon père*, but I have no proof. That is why I come to you.'

'You come in vain, monsieur. There is nothing to tell whether Léonie be a Bonnard or not. I too suspected, and because of that I took pains with *la petite*, and taught her to the best of mine ability.

I tried to keep her here when the Bonnards died, but Jean would not have it so. You say he ill-treated her? Had I thought that I would have done more to retain the child. I did not think it. True I had never an affection for Jean, but he was kind enough to *la petite* in those days. He promised to write to me from Paris, but he never did so, and I lost trace of him. Now it seems that Chance has led you to Léonie, and you suspect what I suspected.'

Justin set down his wine-glass.

'Your suspicion, *mon père?*' It was spoken compellingly.

De Beaupré rose, and went to the window.

'When I saw the child grow up in a delicate mould; when I saw those blue eyes, and those black brows, coupled with hair of flame, I was puzzled. I am an old man, and that was fifteen or more years ago. Yet even then I had been out of the world for many years, and I had seen no one of that world since the days of my youth. Very little news reaches us here, monsieur; you will find me strangely ignorant. As I say, I watched Léonie grow up, and every day I saw her become more and more like to a family I had known before I was a priest. It is not easy to mistake a descendant of the Saint-Vires, m'sieur.' He turned, looking at Avon.

The Duke lay back in his chair. Beneath his heavy lids his eyes glittered coldly.

'And thinking that – suspecting that, my father – you yet let Léonie slip through your fingers? You knew also that the Bonnards came from Champagne. It is to be supposed that you remembered where the Saint-Vire estate lay.'

The Curé looked down at him in surprised hauteur.

'I fail to understand you, m'sieur. It is true that I thought Léonie a daughter of Saint-Vire, but what could that knowledge avail her? If Madame Bonnard wished her to know, she could have told her. But Bonnard himself recognised the child as his. It was better that Léonie should not know.'

The hazel eyes opened wide.

'*Mon père*, I think we are at cross–purposes. In plain words, what do you think Léonie?'

'The inference is sufficiently obvious, I think,' said the Curè, flushing.

Avon shut his snuff-box with a click.

'We will have it in plain words, nevertheless, my father. You deemed Léonie a base-born child of the Comte de Saint-Vire. It is possible that you have never appreciated the situation between the Comte and his brother Armand.'

'I have no knowledge of either, m'sieur.'

'It is manifest, *mon père*. Listen to me a while. When I found Léonie that night in Paris a dozen thoughts came into my head. The likeness to Saint-Vire is prodigious, I assure you. At first I thought as you. Then there flashed before mine eyes a picture of Saint-Vire's son as last I had seen him. A raw clod, my father. A clumsy, thick-set yokel. I remembered that between Saint-Vire and his brother had ever been a most deadly hatred. You perceive the trend of the matter? Saint-Vire's wife is a sickly creature; it was common knowledge that he married her simply to spite Armand. Now behold the irony of fate. Three years pass. Madame fails to present her lord with anything but a still-born child. Then – miraculously a son is born, in Champagne. A son who is now nineteen years old. I counsel you, my father, to put yourself in Saint-Vire's place for one moment, not forgetting that the flame of the Saint-Vire hair is apt to enter the Saint-Vire head. He is determined that there shall be no mistake this time. He carries Madame into the country, where she is brought to bed, and delivered of – let us say – a girl. Conceive the chagrin of Saint-Vire! But, my father, we will suppose that he had prepared for this possibility. On his estate was a family of the name of Bonnard. We will say that Bonnard was in his employ. Madame Bonnard gives birth to a son some few days before the birth of – Léonie. In a fit of Saint-Vire madness the Comte exchanged the children. Evidently he bribed Bonnard very heavily, for we know that the Bonnard family came here and bought a farm, bringing with them Léonie de Saint-Vire, and leaving their son to become – Vicomte de Valmé. *Eh bien?*'

'Impossible!' said De Beaupré sharply. 'A fairy tale!'

'Nay, but listen,' purred his Grace. 'I find Léonie in the streets of Paris. *Bien.* I take her to my *hôtel*, I clothe her as my page. She accompanies me everywhere, and thus I flaunt her under the nose of Saint-Vire. That same nose quivers with apprehension, *mon père.* That is nothing, you say? Wait! I take Léon – I call her Léon – to Versailles, where Madame de Saint-Vire is in attendance. One may always trust a woman to betray a secret, monsieur. Madame was agitated beyond all words. She could not drag her eyes from Léon's face. A day later I receive an offer from one of Saint-Vire's satellites to buy Léon. You see? Saint-Vire dare not show his hand in the matter. He sends a friend to work for him. Why? If Léon is a base-born child of his, what is simpler – if he wants to rescue her from my clutches – than to approach me, telling me all? He does not do that. Léonie is his legitimate daughter, and he is afraid. For aught he knows I may have proof of that fact. I should tell you, *mon père*, that he and I are not the closest of friends. He fears me, and he dare not move one way or the other lest I should suddenly disclose some proof of which he knows nothing. It may also be that he is not sure that I know, or even suspect, the truth. I do not quite think that. I have something of a reputation, my father, for – uncanny omniscience. Whence, in part, my *sobriquet.*' He smiled. 'It is my business to know everything, father. I am thus a personality in polite circles. An amusing pose. To return: You perceive that M. le Comte de Saint-Vire finds himself in something of a quandary?'

The Curé came slowly to his chair, and sat down.

'But, m'sieur – what you suggest is infamous!'

'Of course it is. Now I had hoped, *mon père*, that you would know of some document to prove the truth of my conviction.'

De Beaupré shook his head.

'There was none. I went through all the papers with Jean, after the plague.'

'Saint-Vire is more clever than I had imagined, then. Nothing, you say? It seems that this game must be carefully played.'

De Beaupré was hardly listening.

'Then – at her death, when Madame Bonnard tried so hard to speak to me, it must have been that!'

'What did she say, *mon père*?'

'So little! "*Mon père – écoutez donc – Léonie n'est pas – je ne peux plus – !*" No more. She died with those words on her lips.'

'A pity. But Saint-Vire shall think that she made confession – in writing. I wonder if he knows that the Bonnards are dead? M. de Beaupré, if he should come here, on this same errand, allow him to think that I bore away with me – a document. I do not think he will come. It is probable that he purposely lost trace of the Bonnards.' Justin rose, and bowed. 'My apologies for wasting your time in this fashion, my father.'

The Curé laid a hand on his arm.

'What are you going to do, my son?'

'If she is indeed what I think her I am going to restore Léonie to her family. How grateful they will be! If not –' He paused. 'Well, I have not considered that possibility. Rest assured that I shall provide for her. For the present she must learn to be a girl again. After that we shall see.'

The Curé looked full into his eyes for a moment.

'My son, I trust you.'

'You overwhelm me, father. As it chances, I am to be trusted this time. One day I will bring Léonie to see you.'

The Curé walked with him to the door, and together they passed out into the little hall.

'Does she know, m'sieur?'

Justin smiled

'My dear father, I am far too old to place my secrets in a woman's keeping. She knows nothing.'

'The poor little one! Of what like is she now?'

Avon's eyes gleamed.

'She is something of an imp, *mon père*, with all the Saint-Vire spirit, and much impudence of which she is unaware. She has seen much, as I judge, and at times I espy a cynicism in her that is most entertaining. For the rest she is wise and innocent by turn. An hundred years old one minute, a babe the next. As are all women!'

They had come to the garden gate now, and Avon beckoned to the boy who held his horse.

Some of the anxious lines were smoothed from De Beaupré's face.

'My son, you have described the little one with feeling. You speak as one who understands her.'

'I have reason to know her sex, my father.'

'That may be. But have you ever felt towards a woman as you feel towards this – imp?'

'She is more a boy to me than a girl. I admit I am fond of her. You see, it is so refreshing to have a child of her age – and sex – in one's power, who thinks no ill of one, nor tries to escape. I am a hero to her.'

'I hope that you will ever be that. Be very good to her, I pray you.'

Avon bowed to him, kissing his hand with a gesture of half-ironical respect.

'When I feel that I can no longer maintain the heroic pose I will send Léonie – by the way, I am adopting her – back to you.'

'*C'est entendu*,' nodded De Beaupré. 'For the present I am with you. You will take care of the little one, and perhaps restore her to her own. *Adieu, mon fils.*'

Avon mounted, tossed the small boy a louis, and bowed again, low over his horse's withers.

'I thank you, father. It seems that we understand one another very well – Satan and priest.'

'Perhaps you have been misnamed, my son,' said De Beaupré, smiling a little.

'Oh, I think not! My friends know me rather well, you see. *Adieu, mon père!*' He put on his hat, and rode forward across the square, towards Saumur.

The small boy, clutching his louis, raced to his mother's side.

'*Maman, Maman!* It was the Devil! He said so himself!'

Eight

Hugh Davenant Is Amazed

A WEEK AFTER AVON'S DEPARTURE FOR SAUMUR, HUGH DAVENANT sat in the library, endeavouring to amuse the very disconsolate Léon with a game of chess.

'I would like to play cards, if you please, m'sieur,' said Léon politely, on being asked his pleasure.

'Cards?' repeated Hugh.

'Or dice, m'sieur. Only I have no money.'

'We will play chess,' said Hugh firmly, and set out the ivory men.

'Very well, m'sieur.' Léon privately thought Hugh a little mad, but if he wished to play chess with his friend's page he must of course be humoured.

'Do you think Monseigneur will return soon, m'sieur?' he asked presently. 'I remove your bishop.' He did so, to Hugh's surprise. 'It was a little trap,' he explained. 'Now it is check.'

'So I see. I grow careless. Yes, I expect Monseigneur will return quite soon. Farewell to your rook, my child.'

'I thought you would do that. Now I move a pawn forward, so!'

'Much ado about nothing, petit. Where did you learn to play this game? Check.'

Léon interposed one of his knights. He was not taking a very keen interest in the game.

'I forget, m'sieur.'

Hugh looked across at him shrewdly.

'You've a surprisingly short memory, have you not, my friend?'

Léon peeped at him through his lashes.

'Yes, m'sieur. It – it is very sad. And away goes your queen. You do not attend.'

'Do I not? Your knight is forfeit, Léon. You play a monstrous reckless game.'

'Yes, that is because I like to gamble. Is it true, m'sieur, that you leave us next week?'

Hugh hid a smile at the proprietary 'us.'

'Quite true. I am bound for Lyons.'

Léon's hand hovered uncertainly over the board.

'I have never been there,' he said.

'No? There is time yet.'

'Oh, but I do not wish to go!' Léon swooped down upon a hapless pawn, and took it. 'I have heard that Lyons is a place of many smells, and not very nice people.'

'So you won't go there? Well, perhaps you're wise. What's toward?' Hugh raised his head, listening.

There was some slight commotion without; the next moment a footman flung open the library door, and the Duke came slowly in.

Table, chessboard, and men went flying. Léon had sprung impetuously out of his chair, and had almost flung himself at Avon's feet, all etiquette and decorum forgotten.

'Monseigneur, Monseigneur!'

Over his head Avon met Davenant's eyes.

'He is mad, of course. I beg you will calm yourself, my Léon.'

Léon gave his hand a last kiss, and rose to his feet.

'Oh, Monseigneur, I have been miserable!'

'Now, I should never have suspected Mr Davenant of cruelty to infants,' remarked his Grace. 'How are you, Hugh?' He strolled forward, and just touched Hugh's outstretched hands with his finger-tips. 'Léon, signify your delight at seeing me by picking up the chessmen.' He went to the fire, and stood with his back to it, Hugh beside him.

'Have you had a pleasant time?' Hugh asked.

'A most instructive week. The roads here are remarkable. Allow me to point out to your notice, Léon, that an insignificant pawn lies under that chair. It is never wise to disregard the pawns.'

Hugh looked at him. 'What may that mean?' he inquired.

'It is merely advice, my dear. I should have made an excellent father. My philosophy is almost equal to Chesterfield's.'

Hugh chuckled. 'Chesterfield's conversation is marvellous.'

'A little tedious. Yes, Léon, what now?'

'Shall I bring wine, Monseigneur?'

'Mr Davenant has certainly trained you well. No, Léon, you shall not bring wine. I trust he has been no trouble, Hugh?'

Léon cast Davenant an anxious glance. There had been one or two slight battles of will between them. Hugh smiled at him.

'His behaviour has been admirable,' he said.

His Grace had seen the anxious look, and the reassuring smile. 'I am relieved. May I now have the truth?'

Léon looked up at him gravely, but volunteered no word. Hugh laid his hand on Avon's shoulder.

'We have had a few small disputes, Alastair. That is all.'

'Who won?' inquired his Grace.

'We reached the end by a compromise,' said Hugh solemnly.

'Very unwise. You should have insisted on utter capitulation.' He took Léon's chin in his hand, and looked into the twinkling blue eyes. 'Even as I should have done.' He pinched the chin. 'Should I not, infant?'

'Perhaps, Monseigneur.'

The hazel eyes narrowed.

'Perhaps? What is this? Are you so demoralised during this one short week?'

'No, oh no!' Léon's dimples quivered. 'But I am very obstinate, Monseigneur, sometimes. Of course I will always try to make myself do as you wish.'

Avon released him.

'I believe you will,' he said unexpectedly, and waved one white hand to the door.

'I suppose it is useless to ask where you have been?' said Hugh, when Léon had gone.

'Quite.'

'Or where you intend to go next?'

'No, I believe I can answer that. I am going to London.'

'London?' Hugh was surprised. 'I thought you intended to remain here some months?'

'Did you, Hugh? I never have intentions. That is why mothers of lovely daughters eye me askance. I am constrained to return to England.' He drew from his pocket a fan of dainty chicken-skin, and spread it open.

'What constrains you?' Hugh frowned upon the Duke's fan. 'Why that new affectation?'

Avon held the fan at arm's length.

'Exactly what I ask myself, dear Hugh. I found it awaiting me here. It comes from March, who begs –' He searched in his pocket for a folded sheet of paper, and putting up his glass, read the scrawled lines aloud. 'Begs – yes, here we are. "I send you this pretty trifle, which I give you my word is now become the rage here, all men who aspire to be beaux using them both in warm weather and cold, so that we rival the ladies now in this matter. I beg you will make use of it, my dear Justin; it is cunningly painted, you will agree, and was procured by me from Geronimo, expressly for you. The golden sticks should please you, as I hope they will do.'" Avon raised his eyes from the letter to observe the fan, which was painted black, with a gold design, and gold sticks and tassels. 'I wonder if I do like it?' he said.

'Foppery!' answered Hugh shortly.

'Undoubtedly. Natheless it will give Paris something fresh to talk about. I shall purchase a muff for March. Of miniver, I think. You perceive that I must return to England forthwith.'

'To give March a muff?'

'Precisely.'

'I perceive that you will make that an excuse. Léon goes with you?'

'As you say, Léon goes with me.'

'I had meant to ask you once again to give him to me.'

The Duke fanned himself with an air, handling the chicken-skin like a woman.

'I really could not permit it, my dear; it would be most improper.'

Hugh looked sharply up at him.

'Now, what mean you by that, Justin?'

'Is it possible that you have been hoodwinked? Dear, dear!'

'You'll explain, if you please!'

'I had come to think you omniscient,' sighed his Grace. 'You have had Léon in your care for eight days, and you are as innocent of his deception as you were when I first introduced him to your notice.'

'You mean?'

'I mean, my dear, that Léon is Léonie.'

Davenant threw up his hands. 'You knew, then!'

His Grace stopped fanning himself. 'I knew? I knew from the first. But you?'

'Perhaps a week after he came here. I hoped that you knew nothing.'

'Oh, my dear Hugh!' Avon shook with gentle laughter. 'You thought me guileless! I forgive you only because you have restored my faith in your omniscience.'

'I never dreamed that you suspected!' Hugh took a few quick steps across the room and back again. 'You've hidden it well!'

'So also have you, my dear.' Avon resumed his fanning. 'What was your object in allowing the deception to go on?'

'What was yours, oh worthy Hugh?'

'I dreaded lest you should discover the truth! I wanted to take the child away from you.'

His Grace smiled slowly, eyes nearly shut.

'The fan expresses my emotions. I must kiss March's hands and feet. Metaphorically speaking.' He waved the fan gently to and fro.

Davenant glared at him for a moment, annoyed at his nonchalance. Then an unwilling laugh broke from him.

'Justin, pray put that fan away! If you know that Léon is a girl what will you do? I beg that you will give her to me –'

'My dear Hugh! Bethink you, you are but thirty-five – quite a child still. It would be most improper. Now, I – I am over forty. A veteran, and therefore harmless.'

'Justin –' Hugh came to him, and laid a hand on his arm. 'Will you sit down, and talk this over – quietly and reasonably?'

The fan paused.

'Quietly? But did you imagine that I wished to bawl at you?'

'No. Don't be flippant, Justin. Sit down.'

Avon went to a chair, and sat upon its arm.

'When you become excited, my dear, you remind me of an agitated sheep. Quite irresistible, believe me.'

Hugh controlled a quivering lip, and seated himself opposite the Duke. Avon stretched out his hand to where a small spindle-legged table stood and pulled it into place between himself and Davenant.

'So. I am now reasonably safe. Continue, Hugh.'

'Justin, I am not jesting –'

'Oh, my dear Hugh!'

'– and I want you also to be serious. Put away that damned fan!'

'It incites you to wrath? If you assault me I shall summon assistance.' But he shut the fan, and held it so, between his hands. 'I am all attention, beloved.'

'Justin, you and I are friends, are we not? Let us for once have plain speaking!'

'But you always speak plainly, dear Hugh,' murmured his Grace.

'You've been kind – ay, I admit that – to little Léon; you've permitted him to take many liberties with you. At times I've hardly recognised you with him. I thought – well, never mind that. And all the while you knew he was a girl.'

'You are becoming rather involved,' remarked Avon.

'She, then. You knew she was a girl. Why have you allowed her to keep up the pretence? What do you mean by her?'

'Hugh –' Avon tapped the table with his fan. 'Your painful anxiety impels me to inquire – what do *you* mean by her?'

Davenant looked his disgust.

'My God, do you think you are amusing? I mean this: That I will have her away from you if it costs me my life.'

'This becomes interesting,' said Avon. 'How will you have her away from me, and why?'

'You can ask that? I never thought you were a hypocrite, Justin.'

Avon unfurled his fan.

'If you were to ask me, Hugh, why I permit myself to bear with you I could not tell you.'

'My manners are atrocious. I know it. But I've an affection for Léon, and if I allowed you to take her, innocent as he is –'

'Careful, Hugh, careful!'

'Oh, *she*, then! If I allowed that – I –'

'Calm yourself, my dear. If I did not fear that you would mutilate it I would lend you my fan. May I make known mine intentions?'

'It's what I want!'

'I should not have guessed that, somehow. Strange how one may be mistaken. Or even how two may be mistaken. It will surprise you to hear that I am fond of Léon.'

'No. She will make a beautiful girl.'

'Remind me one day to teach you how to achieve a sneer, Hugh. Yours is too pronounced, and thus is but a grimace. It should be but a faint curl of the lips. So. But to resume. You will at least be surprised to hear that I had not thought of Léonie in the light of a beautiful girl.'

'It amazes me.'

'That is much better, my dear. You are an apt pupil.'

'Justin, you are impossible. This is no laughing matter!'

'Certainly not. You see in me – a strict guardian.'

'I don't understand.'

'I am taking Léonie to England, where I shall place her 'neath my sister's wing until I have found some discreet lady who will act the part of duenna to my ward, Mademoiselle Léonie de Bonnard. Again the fan expresses my emotions.' He performed a sweep in the air with it, but Hugh was staring in open-mouthed wonderment.

'You – your ward! But – why?'

'Oh, my reputation!' mourned his Grace. 'A whim, Hugh, a whim!'

'You'll adopt her as your daughter?'

'As my daughter.'

'For how long? If it be a whim only –'

'It is not. I have a reason. Léonie will not leave me until – let us say until she finds a more fitting home.'

'Until she marries, you mean?'

The thin black brows twitched suddenly together.

'I did not mean that, but let it stand. All that signifies is that
Léonie is as safe in my care as she would be in – I will say yours,
for want of a better simile.'

Hugh rose. 'I – you – Good God, Justin, are you jesting?'

'I believe not.'

'You seriously mean what you say?'

'You seem dazed, my dear.'

'More like a sheep, than ever, then,' retorted Hugh, with a
quick smile, and held out his hand. 'If you are honest now – and
I think you are –'

'You overwhelm me,' murmured his Grace.

'– you are doing something that is –'

'– quite unlike anything I have ever done before.'

'Something that is damned good!'

'But then you do not know my motives.'

'I wonder if you yourself know your motives?' Hugh said
quietly.

'Very obscure, Hugh. I flatter myself that I do know – full
well.'

'I am not so certain.' Hugh sat down again. 'Ay, you've
amazed me. What now? Does Léon know that you have
discovered his – her – fiend seize it, I am becoming involved
again! – sex?'

'She does not.'

Hugh was silent for a few moments.

'Perhaps she will not wish to remain with you when you tell
her,' he said at last.

'It is possible, but she is mine, and she must do as I bid her.'

Suddenly Hugh rose again, and went to the window.

'Justin, I don't like it.'

'May I ask why you do not like it?'

'She – she is too fond of you.'

'Well?'

'Would it not be kinder to make some arrangement – send her away?'

'Whither, my conscientious one?'

'I don't know.'

'How helpful! As I do not know either, I think we may safely banish that notion.'

Hugh turned, and came back to the table.

'Very well. I trust no harm will come of this, Justin. When shall you – put an end to her boyhood?'

'When we arrive in England. You see, I am deferring that moment as long as may be.'

'Why?'

'One reason, my dear, is that she might feel shy of me in her boy's raiment when once I knew the secret. The other – the other –' He paused, and studied his fan, frowning. 'Well, let us be honest. I have grown fond of Léon, and I do not want to exchange him for Léonie.'

'I thought so,' Hugh nodded. 'Be kind to Léonie, Justin.'

'It is my intention,' bowed the Duke.

Nine

Léon and Léonie

EARLY IN THE NEXT WEEK DAVENANT LEFT PARIS FOR LYONS. ON the same day Avon summoned his *maître d'hôtel*, Walker, to his presence, and informed him that he was leaving France on the morrow. Well accustomed to his master's sudden decisions, Walker felt no surprise. He was a discreet personage with an unyielding countenance. For many years he had been in the Avon employ, and as he had proved himself to be scrupulously honest and trustworthy, the Duke had placed him in charge of his Paris establishment. As his Grace owned another establishment in St James's Square, London, and kept both open and staffed with servants, this post was one of considerable importance. It was Walker's duty to keep the Hôtel Avon in such strictness and order that it should always be ready for the Duke or for his brother.

When Walker left the library he went below-stairs to inform Gaston, the valet, Meekin, the groom, and Léon, the page, that they must hold themselves in readiness to depart from Paris tomorrow morning. He found Léon seated on the table in the housekeeper's room, swinging his legs and munching a slice of cake. Madame Dubois was sitting in a large chair before the fire, dolefully regarding him. She welcomed Walker with a coy smile, for she was a comely woman, but Léon, having cast one glance towards the prim figure in the doorway, tilted his head a little, and went on eating.

'*Eh bien, m'sieur!*' Madame smoothed her gown, smiling upon the *maître d'hôtel.*

'I crave pardon thus to have disturbed you, madame.' Walker bowed. 'I came but to find Léon.'

Léon wriggled round to face him.

'You perceive me, Walker,' he said.

A slight spasm contracted Walker's features. Alone amongst the staff Léon never gave him a prefix to his name.

'His Grace sent for me a few moments back to tell me that he is leaving for London tomorrow. I come to warn you, Léon, that you must be ready to accompany him.'

'Bah! He had told me that this morning,' said Léon scornfully.

Madame nodded.

'Yes, and he comes to eat a last cake with me, *le petit.*' She sighed gustily. 'Indeed, my heart is heavy to think I must lose thee, Léon. But thou – thou art glad, little ingrate!'

'I have never been to England, you see,' apologised Léon. 'I am so excited, *ma mère.*'

'*Ah, c'est cela!* So excited that you will forget fat old Madame Dubois.'

'No, I swear I will not! Walker, will you have some of Madame's cake?'

Walker drew himself up.

'No, I thank you.'

'*Voyons*, he insults your skill, *ma mère!*' chuckled Léon.

'I assure you, madame, it's no such thing.' Walker bowed to her and withdrew.

'He is like a camel,' remarked the page placidly.

He repeated this observation to the Duke next day, as they sat
in the coach, bound for Calais.

'A camel?' said his Grace. 'Why?'

'We-ll...' Léon wrinkled his nose. 'I saw one once, a long time
ago, and I remember it walked along with its head very high,
and a smile on its face, just like Walker. It was so full of dignity,
Monseigneur. You see?'

'Perfectly,' yawned his Grace, leaning farther back into the corner.

'Do you think that I shall like England, Monseigneur?' asked
Léon presently.

'It is to be hoped that you will, my infant.'

'And – and do you think that I shall feel sick upon the ship?'

'I trust not.'

'So do I,' said Léon devoutly.

As it chanced the journey was quite uneventful. They spent one
night on the road to Calais, and embarked next day on a night
boat. Much to Léon's disgust, the Duke sent him into his cabin,
with orders to remain there. For perhaps the first time in all his
Channel crossings Avon remained on deck. Once he went down
to the tiny cabin, and finding Léon fast asleep in a chair, lifted
him, and put him gently into a bunk, covering him with a fur rug.
Then he went out again to pace the deck until morning.

When Léon appeared on deck next morning he was shocked
to find that his master had remained there all night, and said so.
Avon pulled one of his curls and, having breakfasted, went below
to sleep until Dover was reached. Then he emerged, and with
becoming languor went ashore, Léon at his heels. Gaston had
disembarked one of the first, and by the time the Duke arrived at
the inn on the quay had roused the landlord to activity. A private
parlour awaited them, with lunch set out on the table.

Léon eyed the meal with some disapproval and not a little
surprise. A sirloin of English beef stood at one end of the table,

flanked by a ham and some capons. A fat duck was at the other
end, with pasties and puddings. There was also a flagon of burgundy, and a jug of foaming ale.

'Well, my Léon?'

Léon turned. His Grace had entered the room, and stood
behind him, fanning himself. Léon looked sternly at the fan, and
seeing the condemnation in his eyes, Avon smiled.

'The fan does not find favour with you, infant?'

'I do not like it at all, Monseigneur.'

'You distress me. What think you of our English meats?'

Léon shook his head.

'Terrible, Monseigneur. It is – it is *barbare!*'

The Duke laughed, and came to the table. At once Léon went
to him, intending to stand behind his chair.

'Child, you will observe that two places are laid. Seat yourself.'
He shook out his napkin, and picked up the carving-knife and
fork. 'Will you essay the duck?'

Léon sat down shyly.

'Yes, please, Monseigneur.' He was served, and began to eat,
rather nervously, but daintily, as Avon saw.

'So – so this is Dover,' remarked Léon presently, in a politely
conversational tone.

'You are right, infant,' replied his Grace. 'This is Dover. You
are pleased to approve?'

'Yes, Monseigneur. It is queer to see everything English, but I
like it. I should not like it if you were not here, of course.'

Avon poured some burgundy into his glass.

'I fear you are a flatterer,' he said severely.

Léon smiled.

'No, Monseigneur. Did you remark the landlord?'

'I know him well. What of him?'

'He is so little, and so fat, with such a bright, bright nose! When he bowed to you, Monseigneur, I thought he would burst! It looked so droll!' His eyes twinkled.

'A horrible thought, my child. You would appear to have a slightly gruesome sense of humour.'

Léon gave a delighted chuckle.

'Do you know, Monseigneur,' he said, wrestling with a stubborn joint, 'I had never seen the sea until yesterday! It is very wonderful, but just for a little while it made the inside of me go up and down. Like that.' He described the motion with his hand.

'My dear Léon! Really, I cannot have that topic discussed at meal time. You make me feel quite ill.'

'Well, it made me feel ill, Monseigneur. But I was not sick. I shut my mouth very tightly —'

Avon picked up his fan and dealt Léon a smart rap with it across the knuckles.

'Continue to keep it shut, infant, I beg of you.'

Léon rubbed his hand, looking at the Duke in aggrieved wonderment.

'Yes, Monseigneur, but —'

'And do not argue.'

'No, Monseigneur. I was not going to argue. I only —'

'My dear Léon, you are arguing now. I find you most wearisome.'

'I was trying to explain, Monseigneur,' said Léon, with great dignity.

'Then please do not. Confine your energy to the duck.'

'Yes, Monseigneur.' Léon continued eating in silence for perhaps three minutes. Then he looked up again. 'When do we begin to go to London, Monseigneur?'

'What an original way of putting it!' remarked his Grace. 'We begin in about an hour's time.'

'Then when I have finished my *déjeuner* may I go for a walk?'

'I am desolated to have to refuse my permission. I want to talk to you.'

'To talk to me?' echoed Léon.

'Madness, you think? I have something of import to say. What is the matter now?'

Léon was examining a black pudding with an expression akin to loathing on his face.

'Monseigneur, this' – he pointed disdainfully at the pudding – 'this is not for *people* to eat! Bah!'

'Is aught amiss with it?' inquired his Grace.

'Everything!' said Léon crushingly. 'First I am made to feel sick upon that ship, and then I am made to feel sick again by an evil – pudding, you call it? *Voyons*, it is a good name! Pig-pudding! Monseigneur, you must not eat it! It will make you –'

'Pray do not describe my probable symptoms as well as your own, infant. You have certainly been prodigiously ill-used, but endeavour to forget it! Eat one of those sweetmeats.'

Léon selected one of the little cakes, and started to nibble it.

'Do you always eat these things in England, Monseigneur?' he asked, pointing to the beef and the puddings.

'Invariably, my infant.'

'I think it would be better if we did not stay very long here,' said Léon firmly. 'I have finished now.'

'Then come here.' His Grace had moved to the fire, and was sitting on the oaken settle. Léon sat beside him obediently.

'Yes, Monseigneur?'

Avon started to play with his fan, and his mouth was rather grim. He was frowning slightly, and Léon racked his brains to think how he could have offended his master. Suddenly Avon laid his hand on Léon's and held it in a cool strong clasp.

'My infant, it has become necessary for me to put an end to the little comedy you and I have been playing.' He paused, and saw the big eyes grow apprehensive. 'I am very fond of Léon, my child, but it is time he was Léonie.'

The little hand in his quivered.

'Monseigneur!'

'Yes, my child. You see, I have known from the very first.'

Léonie sat rigid, staring up into his face with the look of a stricken creature in her eyes. Avon put up his free hand to pat her white cheek.

'It is no such great matter after all, infant,' he said gently.

'You – you won't send me – away?'

'I will not. Have I not bought you?'

'I – I may still be your page?'

'Not my page, child. I am sorry, but it is not possible.'

All the rigidity went out of the slight frame. Léonie gave one great sob, and buried her face in his coat sleeve.

'Oh please! Oh please!'

'Infant, sit up! Come, I object to having my coat ruined. You have not heard all yet.'

'I won't, I won't!' came the muffled voice. 'Let me be Léon! Please let me be Léon!'

His Grace lifted her.

'Instead of my page you shall be my ward. My daughter. Is it so terrible?'

'I do not want to be a girl! Oh please, Monseigneur, please.' Léonie slipped from the settle to the floor, and knelt at his feet, gripping his hand. 'Say yes, Monseigneur! Say yes!'

'No, my babe. Dry your tears and listen to me. Don't tell me you have lost your handkerchief.'

Léonie drew it from her pocket, and mopped her eyes.

'I don't w-want to be – a girl!'

'Nonsense, my dear. It will be far more pleasant to be my ward than my page.'

'No!'

'You forget yourself,' said his Grace sternly. 'I will not be contradicted.'

Léonie gulped down another sob.

'I — I am sorry, Monseigneur.'

'It's very well. As soon as we have come to London I am going to take you to my sister — no, do not speak — my sister, Lady Fanny Marling. You see, infant, you cannot live with me until I have found some lady to act as — ah — duenna.'

'I will not! I will not!'

'You will do as I say, my good child. My sister with clothe you as befits your new position, and teach you to be — a girl. You will learn these things —'

'I will not! Never, never!'

'— because I command it. Then, when you are ready, you shall come back to me, and I will present you to Society.'

Léonie tugged at his hand.

'I won't go to your sister! I will be just Léon! You cannot make me do as you say, Monseigneur; I will *not*!'

His Grace looked down at her in some exasperation.

'If you were still my page I should know how to deal with you,' he said.

'Yes, yes! Beat me, if you like, and let me still be your page! Ah, please, Monseigneur!'

'Unhappily it is impossible. Recollect, my infant, that you are mine, and must do as I say.'

Léonie promptly collapsed into a crumpled heap beside the settle, and sobbed into the hand she held. Avon allowed her to weep unrestrainedly for perhaps three minutes. Then he drew his hand away.

'You want me to send you away altogether?'

'Oh!' Léonie started up. 'Monseigneur, you would not! You — oh no, no!'

'Then you will obey me. It is understood?'

There was a long pause. Léonie stared hopelessly into the cold hazel eyes. Her lip trembled, and a large tear rolled down her cheek.

'Yes, Monseigneur,' she whispered, and drooped her curly head.

Avon leaned forward, and put his arm about the childish figure, drawing it close.

'A very good infant,' he said lightly. 'You will learn to be a girl to please me, Léonie.'

She clung to him, her curls tickling his chin.

'Will – will it please you, Monseigneur?'

'Above all things, child.'

'Then – I'll try,' said Léonie, a heartbroken catch in her voice. 'You won't l leave me with y-your sister for l-long, will you?'

'Only until I can find someone to take care of you. Then you shall go to my house in the country, and learn to curtsy, to flirt with your fan, to simper, to have the vapours –'

'I – won't!'

'I hope not,' said his Grace, smiling faintly. 'My dear child, there is no need for such misery.'

'I have been Léon for so – so long! It will be so very, very hard!'

'I think it will,' said Avon, and took the crumpled handkerchief from her. 'But you will try to learn all that you are taught, that I may be proud of my ward.'

'Could you be, Monseigneur? Of – of *me*?'

'It is quite possible, my infant.'

'I should like that,' said Léonie, more happily. 'I will be very good.'

The Duke's fine lips twitched.

'So you may be worthy of me? I wish Hugh could hear.'

'Does – does he know?'

'It transpired, my child, that he always knew. Allow me to suggest that you rise from your knees. So. Sit down.'

Léonie resumed her place on the settle, and gave a doleful sniff.

'I must wear petticoats, and not say bad words, and always be with a woman. It is very hard, Monseigneur. I do not like women. I wish to be with you.'

'And I wonder what Fanny will say to you?' remarked his Grace. 'My sister, Léonie, is all a woman.'

'Is she like you?' asked Léonie.

'Now, how am I to take that?' inquired his Grace. 'She is not like me, infant. She is golden-haired and blue-eyed. I beg your pardon?'

'I said Bah!'

'You seem partial to that observation. It is not at all ladylike, my dear. You will obey Lady Fanny, and you will not flout and scorn her because of her golden hair.'

'Of course I shall not. She is your sister, Monseigneur,' answered Léonie. 'Will she like me, do you think?' She looked up at him with a troubled gleam in her eyes.

'Why not?' said his Grace flippantly.

A little smile flitted across Léonie's mouth.

'Oh – oh, I do not know, Monseigneur!'

'She will be kind to you for my sake.'

'Thank you,' said Léonie meekly, and with eyes downcast. Then, as Avon said nothing, she peeped up, and the roguish dimple appeared. Seeing it, Avon ruffled her curls as though she still had been a boy.

'You are refreshing,' he said. 'Fanny will try and make you like the rest of her sex. I believe that I do not want that.'

'No, Monseigneur. I will be just myself.' She kissed his hand, and her lip trembled. She controlled it, and smiled through her tears. 'You have taken my handkerchief, Monseigneur.'

Ten

Lady Fanny's Virtue Is Outraged

LADY FANNY MARLING, REPOSING ON A SETTEE, FOUND LIFE monotonous. She pushed away the book of poems, over which she had been yawning, and started to play with one golden curl that had strayed over her shoulder and lay glistening on the lace of her wrapper. She was *en déshabillé*, her fair hair unpowdered, and loosely dressed beneath a Mechlin cap whose blue ribands were tied under her chin in a coquettish bow. She wore a blue taffeta gown, with a broad fichu about her perfect shoulders, and as the room in which she sat was furnished in gold and blue and white, she had reason to be pleased with herself and her setting. She was pleased, but she would have liked it better had there been some-one with her to share the aesthetic pleasure. So when she heard the clang of her front-door bell her china-blue eyes brightened, and she stretched out her hand for her mirror.

In a few minutes her black page tapped upon the door. She put the mirror down, and turned her head to look at him.

Pompey grinned and bobbed his woolly head.

'Genelman to see ma'am!'

'His name?' she asked.

A soft voice spoke from behind the page.

'His name, my dear Fanny, is Avon. I am fortunate to find you at home.'

Fanny shrieked, clapped her hands, and flew up to greet him.

'Justin! You! Oh, how prodigiously delightful!' She would not permit him to kiss her finger-tips, but flung her arms about his neck, and embraced him. 'I declare, 'tis an age since I have seen you! The cook you sent is a marvel! Edward will be so pleased to see you! Such dishes! And a sauce at my last party which I positively cannot describe!'

The Duke disengaged himself, shaking out his ruffles.

'Edward and the cook would appear to have become entangled,' he remarked. 'I trust I find you well, Fanny?'

'Yes, oh yes! And you? Justin, you cannot imagine how glad I am that you have come back! I vow I have missed you quite too dreadfully! Why what is this?' Her eyes had alighted on Léonie, wrapped in a long cloak, her tricorne in one hand, a fold of the Duke's coat in the other.

His Grace loosened the tight hold on his garment, and allowed Léonie to clutch his hand.

'This, my dear, was, until yesterday, my page. It is now my ward.'

Fanny gasped, and fell back a pace.

'Your – your ward! This boy? Justin, have you taken leave of your senses?'

'No, my dear, I have not. I solicit your kindness for Mademoiselle Léonie de Bonnard.'

Fanny's cheeks grew crimson. She drew her small figure up, and her eyes became haughtily indignant.

'Indeed, sir? May I ask why you bring your – your ward here?'

Léonie shrank a little, but spoke never a word. Very silky became Avon's voice.

'I bring her to you, Fanny, because she is my ward, and because I have no duenna for her. She will be glad of you, I think.'

Fanny's delicate nostrils quivered.

'You think so? Justin, how dare you! How dare you bring her here!' She stamped her foot at him. 'You have spoiled everything now! I hate you!'

'You will perhaps accord me a few minutes' private conversation?' said his Grace. 'My infant, you will await me in this room.' He went to one end of the room and opened a door, disclosing an antechamber. 'Come, child.'

Léonie looked up at him suspiciously. 'You'll not go?'

'I will not.'

'Promise! Please, you must promise!'

'This passion for oaths and promises!' sighed Avon. 'I promise, my infant.'

Léonie released his hand then, and went into the adjoining room. Avon shut the door behind her, and turned to face his wrathful sister. From his pocket he drew his fan, and spread it open.

'You are really very foolish, my dear,' he said, and came to the fire.

'I am at least respectable! I think it very unkind and insulting of you to bring your – your –'

'Yes, Fanny? My – ?'

'Oh, your *ward*! It's not decent! Edward will be very, very angry, and I hate you!'

'Now that you have unburdened yourself of that sentiment no doubt you will allow me to explain.' His Grace's eyes were nearly shut, and his thin lips sneered.

'I do not want an explanation! I want you to take that creature away!'

'When I have told my story, and if you still wish it, I will take her away. Sit down, Fanny. The expression of outraged virtue is entirely wasted on me.'

She flounced into a chair.

'I think you are very unkind! If Edward comes in he will be furious.'

'Then let us hope that he will not come in. Your profile is enchanting, my dear, but I would sooner see both your eyes.'

'Oh, Justin!' She clasped her hands, anger forgotten. 'You think it enchanting still? I vow, I thought I looked a positive fright when I looked in the mirror this morning! 'Tis age, I suppose. Oh, I am forgetting to be angry with you! Indeed, I am so thankful to see you again I cannot be cross! But you must explain, Justin.'

'I will start mine explanation, Fanny, with an announcement. I am not in love with Léonie. If you will believe that it will make matters more simple.' He tossed the fan on the couch, and drew out his snuff-box.

'But − but if you are not in love with her, why − what − Justin, I don't understand! You are most provoking!'

'Pray accept my most humble apologies. I have a reason for adopting the child.'

'Is she French? Where did she learn to speak English? I wish you would explain!'

'I am endeavouring to do so, my dear. Allow me to say that you give me very little opportunity.'

She pouted. 'Now you are cross. Well, start, Justin! The child is pretty enough, I grant you.'

'Thank you. I found her in Paris one evening, clad as a boy, and fleeing from her unpleasant − er − brother. It transpired that this brother and his inestimable wife had made the child masquerade as a boy ever since her twelfth year. She was thus of more use to them. They kept a low tavern, you see.'

Fanny cast up her eyes.

'A tavern-wench!' She shuddered, and raised her scented hand-kerchief to her nose.

'Precisely. In a fit of − let us say − quixotic madness, I bought

Léonie, or Léon, as she called herself, and took her home with
me. She became my page. I assure you she created no little interest
in polite circles. It pleased me to keep her a boy for a time. She
imagined that I was in ignorance of her sex. I became a hero to
her. Yes, is it not amusing?'

'It is horrid! Of course the girl hopes to intrigue you. La, Justin,
how can you be such a fool?'

'My dear Fanny, when you know Léonie a little better you will
not accuse her of having designs upon me. She is in very truth the
infant I call her. A gay, impertinent, and trusting infant. I have a
notion that she regards me in the light of a grandparent. To resume:
as soon as we arrived at Dover I told her that I knew her secret. It
may surprise you to hear, Fanny, that the task was damnably hard.'

'It does,' said Fanny frankly.

'I was sure it would. However, I did it. She neither shrank from
me nor tried to coquette. You can have no idea how refreshing
I found it.'

'Oh, I make no doubt you found it so!' retorted Fanny.

'I am glad that we understand one another so well,' bowed his
Grace. 'For reasons of mine own I am adopting Léonie, and because
I will have no breath of scandal concerning her I bring her to you.'

'You overwhelm me, Justin.'

'Oh, I trust not! I believe you told me some months ago that
our cousin by marriage, the unspeakable Field, had died?'

'What has that to do with it?'

'It follows, my dear, that our respected cousin, his wife, whose
name I forget, is free. I have a mind to make her Léonie's chaperon.'

'Lud!'

'And as soon as may be I will send her and Léonie down to
Avon. The infant must learn to be a girl again. Poor infant!'

'That is all very well, Justin, but you cannot expect me to house
the girl! I vow 'tis preposterous! Think of Edward!'

'Pray hold me excused. I never think of Edward unless I can help it.'

'Justin, if you are minded to be disagreeable –'

'Not at all, my dear.' The smile faded from his lips. Fanny saw that his eyes were unwontedly stern. 'We will be serious for once, Fanny. Your conviction that I had brought my mistress to your house –'

'Justin!'

'I am sure you will forgive my plain speaking. That conviction, I say, was pure folly. It has never been my custom to compromise others in my numerous affairs, and you should know that I am sufficiently strict where you are concerned.' There was peculiar meaning in his voice, and Fanny, who had once been famed for her indiscretions, dabbed at her eyes.

'How c-can you be *s-so* unkind! I do not think you are at all nice to-day!'

'But I trust I have made myself plain? You realise that the child I have brought you is but a child? – an innocent child?'

'I am sorry for her if she is!' said her ladyship spitefully.

'You need not be sorry. For once I mean no harm.'

'If you mean her no harm how can you think to adopt her?' Fanny tittered angrily. 'What do you suppose the world will say?'

'It will be surprised, no doubt, but when it sees that my ward is presented by the Lady Fanny Marling its tongue will cease to wag.'

Fanny stared at him.

'I present her? You're raving! Why should I?'

'Because, my dear, you have a kindness for me. You will do as I ask. Also, though you are thoughtless, and occasionally exceedingly tiresome, I never found you cruel. 'Twere cruelty to turn my infant away. She is a very lonely, frightened infant, you see.'

Fanny rose, twisting her handkerchief between her hands. She glanced undecidedly at her brother.

'A girl from the back streets of Paris, of low birth –'

'No, my dear. More I cannot say, but she is not born of the *canaille*. You have but to look at her to see that.'

'Well, a girl of whom I know naught – foisted on me! I declare 'tis monstrous! I could not possibly do it! What would Edward say?'

'I am confident that you could, if you would, cajole the worthy Edward.'

Fanny smiled. 'Yes, I could, but I do not want the girl.'

'She will not tease you, my dear. I wish you to keep her close, to dress her as befits my ward, and to be gentle with her. Is it so much to ask?'

'How do I know that she will not ogle Edward, this innocent maid?'

'She is too much the boy. Of course, if you are uncertain of Edward –'

She tossed her head.

'Indeed, 'tis no such thing! 'Tis merely that I've no wish to house a pert, red-headed girl.'

His Grace bent to pick up his fan.

'I crave your pardon, Fanny. I'll take the child elsewhere.'

Fanny ran to him, penitent all at once.

'Indeed and you shall not! Oh, Justin, I am sorry to be so disobliging!'

'You'll take her?'

'I – yes, I'll take her. But I don't believe all you say of her. I'll wager my best necklet she's not so artless as she would have you think.'

'You would lose, my dear.' His Grace moved to the door into the antechamber, and opened it. 'Infant, come forth!'

Léonie came, her cloak over her arm. At sight of her boy's raiment Fanny closed her eyes as though in acute pain.

Avon patted Léonie's cheek.

'My sister has promised to care for you until I can take you myself,' he said. 'Remember, you will do as she bids you.'

Léonie looked shyly across at Fanny, who stood with primly set lips and head held high. The big eyes noted the unyielding pose, and fluttered up to Avon's face.

'Monseigneur – please do not – leave me!' It was a despairing whisper, and it amazed Fanny.

'I shall come to see you very soon, my babe. You are quite safe with Lady Fanny.'

'I don't – want you to go away! Monseigneur, you – you do not understand!'

'Infant, I do understand. Have no fear; I shall come back again!' He turned to Fanny, and bowed over her hand. 'I have to thank you, my dear. Pray convey my greetings to the excellent Edward. Léonie, how often have I forbidden you to clutch the skirts of my coat?'

'I – I am sorry, Monseigneur.'

'You always say that. Be a good child, and strive to bear with your petticoats.' He held out his hand, and Léonie dropped on one knee to kiss it. Something sparkling fell on to those white fingers, but Léonie turned her head away, surreptitiously wiping her eyes.

'F-Farewell, Mon-monseigneur.'

'Farewell, my infant. Fanny, your devoted servant!' He made a profound leg, and went out, shutting the door behind him.

Left alone with the small but forbidding Lady Fanny, Léonie stood as though rooted to the ground, looking hopelessly towards the shut door, and twisting her hat in her hands.

'Mademoiselle,' said Fanny coldly, 'if you will follow me I will show you your apartment. Have the goodness to wrap your cloak about you.'

'Yes, madame.' Léonie's lip trembled. 'I am – very sorry, madame,' she said brokenly. A tiny sob escaped her, valiantly suppressed, and suddenly the icy dignity fell from Fanny. She ran forward, her skirts rustling prodigiously, and put her arms about her visitor.

'Oh, my dear, I am a shrew!' she said. 'Never fret, child! Indeed, I am ashamed of myself. There, there!' She led Léonie to the sofa, and made her sit down, petting and soothing until the choked sobs died away.

'You see, madame,' Léonie explained, rubbing her eyes with her handkerchief. 'I felt so – very lonely. I did not mean to cry, but when – Monseigneur – went away – it was so very dreadful!'

'I wish I understood!' sighed Fanny. 'Are you fond of my brother, child?'

'I would die for Monseigneur,' said Léonie simply. 'I am here only because he wished it.'

'Oh, my goodness gracious me!' said Fanny. 'Here's a pretty coil! My dear, be warned by me, who knows him! Have naught to do with Avon: he was not called Satanas for no reason.'

'He is not a devil to me. And I do not care.'

Fanny cast up her eyes.

'Everything is upside down!' she complained. Then she jumped up. 'Oh, you must come up to my chamber, child. 'Twill be so droll to clothe you! See!' She measured herself against Léonie. 'We are very much of a height, my love. Perhaps you are a little taller. Not enough to signify.' She fluttered to where Léonie's cloak had fallen, caught it up, and wrapped it about her charge. 'For fear lest the servants should see and chatter,' she explained. 'Now come with me.' She swept out, one arm about Léonie's waist, and, meeting her butler on the stairs, nodded condescendingly to him. 'Parker, I have my brother's ward come unexpectedly to visit me. Be good enough to bid them prepare the guest-chamber. And send my tirewoman to me.' She turned to whisper in Léonie's ear. 'A most faithful, discreet creature, I give you my word.' She led the girl into her bedroom, and closed

the door. 'Now we shall see! Oh, 'twill be most entertaining, I
dare swear!' She kissed Léonie again, and was wreathed in smiles.
'To think I was so dull! 'Pon rep, I owe my darling Justin a debt
of gratitude. I shall call you Léonie.'

'Yes, madame.' Léonie recoiled slightly, fearing another embrace.
Fanny tripped to her wardrobe.

'And you must call me Fanny, my dear. Off with those – those
dreadful clothes!'

Léonie glanced down her slim figure.

'But, madame, they are very fine clothes! Monseigneur gave
them to me.'

'Indelicate creature! Off with them, I say! They must be burned.'

Léonie sat down plump upon the bed.

'Then I will not take them off.'

Fanny turned, and for a moment they stared at one another.
Léonie's chin was tilted, her dark eyes flashed.

'You are very tiresome,' pouted Fanny. 'What can you want
with man's attire?'

'I will not have them burned!'

'Oh, 'tis very well, my dear! Keep them if you will!' said
Fanny hastily, and wheeled about as the door opened. 'Here is
Rachel! Rachel, this is Mademoiselle de Bonnard, my brother's
ward. She – she wants some clothes.'

The tirewoman gazed at Léonie in horrified wonder.

'So I should think, my lady,' she said austerely.

Lady Fanny stamped her foot.

'Wicked, insolent woman! Don't dare to sniff! And if you say a
word below-stairs, Rachel –'

'I would not so demean myself, your ladyship.'

'Mademoiselle – has come from France. She – she was compelled to wear those garments. It does not matter why. But – but
now she wants to change them.'

'No, I do not,' said Léonie truthfully.

'Yes, yes, you do! Léonie, if you are disagreeable, I shall lose my temper!'

Léonie looked at her in some surprise.

'But I am not disagreeable. I only said –'

'I know, I know! Rachel, if you look like that, I vow I will box your ears!'

Léonie crossed one leg under her.

'I think I will tell Rachel everything,' she said.

'My dear! Oh, as you please!' Fanny flounced to a chair, and sat down.

'You see,' said Léonie gravely, 'I have been a boy for seven years.'

'Lawks, miss!' breathed Rachel.

'What is that?' inquired Léonie, interested.

'It is nothing!' said Fanny sharply. 'Go on, child.'

'I have been a page, Rachel, but now Monseign – I mean, the Duc of Avon wants to make me his – his ward, so I have to learn to be a girl. I do not want to, you understand, but I must. So please will you help me?'

'Yes, miss. Of course I will!' said Rachel, whereupon her mistress flew up out of her chair.

'Admirable creature! Rachel, find linen! Léonie, I implore you, take off those breeches!'

'Don't you like them?' inquired Léonie.

'Like them!' Fanny waved agitated hands. 'They are monstrous improper! Take them off!'

'But they are of an excellent cut, madame.' Léonie proceeded to wriggle out of her coat.

'You must not – you positively must not speak of such things!' said Fanny earnestly. ''Tis most unseemly.'

'But madame, one cannot help seeing them. If men did not wear them –'

'*Oh!*' Fanny broke into scandalised laughter. 'Not another word!'

For the next hour Léonie was bundled in and out of garments, while Fanny and Rachel twisted and turned her, laced and unlaced her, and pushed her this way and that. To all their ministrations she submitted patiently, but she displayed no interest in the proceedings.

'Rachel, my green silk!' commanded her ladyship, and held out a flowered petticoat to Léonie.

'The green, my lady?'

'The green silk that became me not, stupid girl! Quickly! 'Twill be ravishing with your red hair, my love!' She seized a brush, and proceeded to arrange the tumbled curls. 'How could you cut it? 'Tis impossible to dress your hair now. No matter. You shall wear a green riband threaded through, and – oh, hasten, Rachel!'

Léonie was put into the green silk. It was cut low across the chest, to her evident confusion, and spread over a great hoop below the waist.

'Oh, said I not that 'twould be ravishing?' cried Fanny, stepping back to look at her handiwork. 'I cannot bear it! Thank goodness Justin is to take you into the country! You are far, far too lovely! Look in the mirror, ridiculous child!'

Léonie turned to see herself in the long glass behind her. She seemed taller, all at once, and infinitely more beautiful, with her curls clustering about her little pointed face, and her big eyes grave and awed. Her skin showed very white against the apple-green silk. She regarded herself in wonder, and between her brows was a troubled crease. Fanny saw it.

'What! Not satisfied?'

'It is very splendid, madame, and – and I look nice, I think, but –' she cast a longing glance to where her discarded raiment lay. 'I want my breeches!'

Fanny flung up her hands.

'Another word about those breeches, and I burn them! You make me shudder, child!'

Léonie looked at her solemnly.

'I do not at all understand why you do not like −'

'Provoking creature! I insist on your silence! Rachel, take those − those garments away this instant! I declare I will not have them in my room.'

'They shall not be burned!' said Léonie challengingly.

Fanny encountered the fierce glance and gave vent to a little titter.

'Oh, as you will, my love! Put them in a box, Rachel, and convey them to Mistress Léonie's apartment. Léonie, I will have you look at yourself! Tell me, is it not a modish creation?' She went to the girl and twitched the heavy folds of silk into position.

Léonie regarded her reflection again.

'I think I have grown,' she said. 'What will happen if I move, madame?'

'Why, what should happen?' asked Fanny, staring.

Léonie shook her head dubiously.

'I think something will burst, madame. Me perhaps.'

Fanny laughed.

'What nonsense! Why, 'tis laced so loosely that it might almost fall off you! Nay, never pick your skirts up so! Oh, heaven, child, you must not show your legs! 'Tis positively indecent!'

'Bah!' said Léonie, and gathering up her skirts, walked carefully across the room. 'Certainly I shall burst,' she sighed. 'I shall tell Monseigneur that I cannot wear women's clothes. It is as though I were in a cage.'

'Don't say you'll − burst − again!' implored Fanny. ''Tis a most unladylike expression.'

Léonie paused in her perambulations to and fro.

'Am I a lady?' she inquired.

'Of course you are! What else?'

The roguish dimple peeped out for the first time, and the blue eyes danced.

'Well, what now? Is it so funny?' asked Fanny, a trifle peevishly.

Léonie nodded. 'But yes, madame. And – and very perplexing.' She came back to the mirror, and bowed to her own reflection. '*Bonjour, Mademoiselle de Bonnard! Peste, qu'elle est ridicule!*'

'Who?' demanded Fanny.

Léonie pointed a scornful finger at herself. 'That silly creature.'

''Tis yourself.'

'*No!*' said Léonie with conviction. 'Never!'

'You are most provoking!' cried Fanny. 'I have been at pains to dress you in my prettiest gown – yes, the very prettiest, though to be sure it became me not – and you say 'tis silly!'

'But no, madame. It is I who am silly. Could I not keep my breeches just for tonight?'

Fanny clapped her hands to her ears.

'I positively will not listen. Don't dare to mention that word to Edward, I implore you!'

'Edward? Bah, what a name! Who is it?'

'My husband. A dear creature, I give you my word, but I faint to think of what he would feel an you spoke of breeches in his hearing!' Fanny gave a little gurgle of laughter. 'Oh, how entertaining 'twill be to buy clothes for you! I quite love Justin for bringing you to me! And whatever will Rupert say?'

Léonie withdrew her gaze from the mirror.

'That is Monseigneur's brother, *ne'est-ce pas?*'

'The most provoking creature,' nodded Fanny. 'Quite mad, you know. But then we Alastairs are all of us that. No doubt you have observed it?'

The big eyes twinkled.

'No, madame.'

'What! And you have – have lived with Avon for three

months?' Fanny cast up her eyes. The sound of a shutting door somewhere below roused her to sudden activity. 'There! That is Edward returned from White's already! I think I will go down and – and talk to him while you rest. Poor child, I dare swear you are dreadfully fatigued?'

'N-no,' said Léonie. 'But you will tell Mr Marling that I have come, is it not so? And if he does not like it – and I do not think that he will – I can –'

'Fiddle!' said Fanny, blushing faintly. 'No such thing, my love, I assure you. Edward will be enchanted! Of course he will, stupid child! A pretty thing 'twould be an I could not twist him round my finger. 'Twas only that I wanted you to rest, and indeed you shall! I vow you are nigh dropping with fatigue! Don't try to argue with me, Léonie!'

'I am not arguing,' Léonie pointed out.

'No – well, I thought you might, and it makes me so cross! Come with me, and I will take you to your chamber.' She led Léonie to a blue guest-chamber, and sighed. 'Ravishing!' she said. 'I wish you were not quite so lovely. Your eyes are like those velvet curtains. I got them in Paris, my dear. Are they not exquisite? I forbid you to touch your dress while I am gone, mind!' She frowned direfully, patted Léonie's hand, and was gone in a whirl of silks and laces, leaving Léonie alone in the middle of the room.

Léonie walked to a chair, and sat down carefully, heels together, and hands demurely clasped in her lap.

'This,' she told herself, 'is not very nice, I think. Monseigneur has gone away, and I could never find him in this great, horrible London. That Fanny is a fool, I think. Or perhaps she is mad, as she said.' Léonie paused to consider the point. 'Well, perhaps she is just English. And Edward will *not* like me to be here. *Mon Dieu*, I suppose he will think I am just *une fille de joie*. That is very possible. I wish Monseigneur had not gone.' This thought occupied her mind for some moments, and led to another. 'I wonder what he will think of me when he sees me? That Fanny said I was lovely. Of course that is just silly, but I think I look a little pretty.' She rose, and planted her chair down before the mirror. She frowned upon her reflection and shook her head. 'You are not Léon: that is very certain. Only one little bit of you is Léon.' She bent forward to look at her feet, shod still in Léon's shoes. '*Hélas!* Only yesterday I was Léon the page, and now I am Mademoiselle de Bonnard. And I am very uncomfortable in these clothes. I think too that I am a *little* frightened. There is not even M. Davenant left. I shall be forced to eat pudding, and that woman will kiss me.' She heaved a large sigh. 'Life is very hard,' she remarked sadly.

Eleven

Mr Marling's Heart Is Won

LADY FANNY FOUND HER HUSBAND IN THE LIBRARY, STANDING before the fire and warming his hands. He was a medium-sized man, with regular features and steady gray eyes. He turned as she entered the room, and held out his arms to her. Lady Fanny tripped towards him.

'Pray have a care for my gown, Edward. 'Tis new come from Cerisette. Is it not elegant?'

'Prodigious elegant,' agreed Marling. 'But if it means that I must not kiss you I shall think it hideous.'

She raised china-blue eyes to his face.

'Just one then, Edward. Oh, you are greedy, sir! No, Edward, I'll not be held. I've a monstrous exciting thing to tell you.' She shot him a sidelong glance, wondering how he would take her news. 'Do you remember, my love, that I was so *ennuyée* to-day that I could almost have cried?'

'Do I not!' smiled Marling. 'You were very cruel to me, sweet.'

'Oh no, Edward! I was not cruel! 'Twas you who were so very provoking. And then you went away, and I was so dull! But now it is all over, and I have something wonderful to do!'

Edward slipped an arm about her trim waist.

'Faith, what is it?'

"Tis a girl,' she answered. 'The most beautiful girl, Edward!'

'A girl?' he repeated. 'What new whim is this? What do you want with a girl, my dear?'

'Oh, I didn't want her! I never thought about her at all. How could I, when I'd not set eyes on her? Justin brought her.'

The clasp about her waist slackened.

'Justin?' said Marling. 'Oh!' His voice was polite, but not enthusiastic. 'I thought he was in Paris.'

'So he was, until a day or two ago, and if you are minded to be disagreeable, Edward, I shall cry. I am very *fond* of Justin!'

'Ay, dear. Go on with your tale. What has the girl, whoever she is, to do with Avon?'

'That is just the astonishing part of it!' said Fanny, her brow clearing as if by magic. 'She is Justin's adopted daughter! Is it not interesting, Edward?'

'*What?*' Marling's arm fell away from her. 'Justin's what?'

'Adopted daughter,' she answered airily. 'The sweetest child, my dear, and so devoted to him! I declare I quite love her already, although she is so lovely, and – oh, Edward, don't be cross!'

Edward took her by the shoulders, and made her look up at him.

'Fanny, do you mean to tell me that Alastair had the effrontery to bring the girl here? And you were mad enough to take her in?'

'Indeed, sir, and why not?' she demanded. 'A pretty thing 'twould be an I turned away my brother's ward!'

'Ward!' Marling almost snorted.

'Yes, sir, his ward. Oh, I'll not deny I thought the same as you when first I saw her, but Justin swore 'twas not so. And Edward, you know how strict Justin is with me. You can't be cross! Why, 'tis but a child, and half a boy at that!'

'Half a boy, Fanny? What mean you?'

'She has been a boy for seven years,' said Fanny triumphantly.

Then, as the lines about his mouth hardened, she stamped her foot angrily. 'You're very unkind, Edward! How dare you suppose that darling Justin would bring his light o' love to my house? 'Tis the stupidest notion I ever heard! He wants me to chaperon the child until he can prevail upon Madam Field to come. What if she has been a boy? Pray what has that to say to anything?'

Marling smiled unwillingly.

'You must admit that for Justin to adopt a girl —'

'Edward, I truly believe that he means no ill! Léonie has been his page — Oh, now you are shocked again!'

'Well, but —'

'I won't hear a word!' Fanny put up her hands to his mouth. 'Edward, you'll not be angry, and hard?' she coaxed. 'There's some mystery about Léonie, I feel sure, but — oh, my dear, you have only to look in her eyes! Now listen to me, dear Edward!'

He imprisoned her hands in his, drawing her to the couch.

'Very well, my dear, I'll listen.'

Fanny seated herself.

'Dearest Edward! I knew you'd be kind! You see, Justin came here to-day with Léonie dressed as a boy. I was so enchanted! I never imagined that Justin was in England! Oh, and he has a fan! You cannot conceive anything so absurd, dear! Though indeed I believe they are become quite the most fashion —'

'Ay, Fanny, but you were to explain about this girl – Léonie.'

'I was explaining,' she protested, pouting. 'Well, he sent Léonie into another room — my dear, I think she positively worships him, poor child — and he begged me to keep her with me for a few days because he does not want there to be a shadow of scandal attached to her. And I am to clothe her, and oh, Edward, will it not be entertaining? She has red hair, and black eyebrows, and I have given her my green silk. You cannot imagine how quite too tiresomely lovely she is, though perhaps she would look better in white.'

'Never mind that, Fanny. Go on with your story.'

'To be sure. It seems that Justin found her in Paris – only then he thought she was a boy – and she was being ill-treated by some tavern-keeper. So Justin bought her and made her his page. And he says that he has a fondness for her, and will make her his ward. And oh, Edward, I have just thought how wonderfully romantic 'twould be an he married her! But she is only a child, and dreadfully boyish. Only fancy! – she insisted on keeping her breeches! Now, Edward, say that you will be nice to her, and that I may keep her! Say it, Edward, say it!'

'I suppose you must keep her,' he said reluctantly. 'I cannot turn her out. But I do not like it.'

Fanny embraced him.

'It doesn't signify in the least, Edward. You will fall in love with her, and I shall be jealous.'

'There's no fear of that, you little rogue,' he said, and gave her hand a quick squeeze.

'No, and I am so glad. And now go and put on that new puce coat. 'Tis prodigious modish, and I want you to look very nice tonight.'

'Are we not dining out?' he asked. 'I thought –'

'Dining out! Good gracious, Edward, and that child a visitor, and only just arrived! No indeed!' With that she rustled out of the room, full of a new importance.

An hour later, when Marling sat in the withdrawing-room awaiting his wife, the door was flung open, and Fanny sailed in. Behind her came Léonie, hesitantly. Edward rose quickly, staring.

'My love,' said Fanny, 'this is my husband, Mr Marling. Edward, Mademoiselle de Bonnard.'

Marling bowed; so also did Léonie, but paused in the act of doing so.

'I must curtsy, is it not so? Bah, what skirts!' She smiled shyly up at Edward. 'Please pardon me, m'sieur. I have not learned to curtsy yet.'

'Give him your hand, child,' commanded Fanny.

The small hand was extended.

'Please, why?' asked Léonie.

Marling kissed her finger-tips punctiliously, and released them. Léonie's cheeks were tinged with colour, and she looked doubtfully up at him.

'*Mais, m'sieur –*' she began.

'Mademoiselle?' In spite of himself Marling smiled.

'*C'est peu convenable,*' explained Léonie.

'No such thing,' said Fanny briskly. 'Gentlemen do always kiss the lady's hands. Remember that, my love. And now my husband will give you his arm to the dining-room. Lay but the tips of your fingers on it, like that. What ails you now, child?'

'It is nothing, madame. Only that I am not at all myself. I think that I look very strange.'

'Tell the silly child that it is not so, Edward,' sighed her ladyship.

Edward found that he was patting Léonie's hand.

'My dear, 'tis as my lady says. You look very proper and charming.'

'Ah bah!' said Léonie.

Twelve

His Grace of Avon's Ward

A FORTNIGHT LATER, WHEN LÉONIE WAS PRACTISING A COURT curtsy before the mirror in her room, Fanny entered with the announcement that Avon had come at last. Léonie arose from her curtsy with more haste than grace.

'Monseigneur!' she cried, and would have flown from the room, had it not been for Fanny, who resolutely barred her passage. 'Let me go! Let me go! Where is he?'

''Pon rep, Léonie, that is no way to receive a gentleman!' said her ladyship. 'To run downstairs like a hoydenish miss, with your hair in a tangle, and your gown caught up! Come back to the mirror.'

'Oh, but –'

'I insist!'

Léonie came reluctantly and was passive while Fanny arranged her gown of primrose silk, and combed out the unruly curls.

'Léonie, you tiresome creature, where is your riband?'

Léonie fetched it meekly.

'I do not like to feel a riband in my hair,' she complained. 'I would rather –'

'It is of no consequence at all,' said Fanny severely. 'I am determined you shall look your best. Shake out your petticoat, and pick up your fan. And if you dare to run forward in an unmaidenly way I shall be so mortified –'

'Let me go now! Please, I am ready!'

'Then follow me, child, so!' Out swept Fanny, and down the stairs. 'Remember! A decorous curtsy, my love, and give him your hand to kiss.' As she spoke she opened the door into the withdrawing-room.

'Bah!' said Léonie.

His Grace was standing by the window, looking out.

'So my sister has not induced you to stop saying "bah"?' he said, and turned. For a moment he said nothing, but stood looking at his ward. 'Infant, it is very well,' he said at last, slowly.

Léonie sank into a curtsy, talking all the time.

'I must do this because madame says so, and you bade me do as she told me, Monseigneur, but oh, I would rather bow to you!' She rose gracefully, and danced forward. 'Monseigneur, Monseigneur, I thought that you would never come! I am so very pleased to see you!' She caught his hand to her lips. 'I have been good and patient, and now will you take me, please?'

'Léonie!'

'Well, but madame, I want so much for him to take me.'

Avon raised his eyeglass.

'Stand still, child. Fanny, I kiss your hands and feet. I am almost surprised at the miracle you have wrought.'

'Monseigneur, do you think that I am nice?' asked Léonie, tiptoeing before him.

'It's an inadequate word, child. You are no longer Léon.'

She sighed, shaking her head.

'I wish I were Léon still. Monseigneur, do *you* understand what it is to be put into petticoats?'

Fanny started, and frowned direfully.

'Naturally I do not, my beautiful ward,' Justin answered

gravely. 'I can imagine that after the freedom of your breeches, petticoats are a little cramping.'

Léonie turned triumphantly to Fanny.

'Madame, he said it! You heard him! He spoke of breeches!'

'Léonie – Justin, I'll not have you let her bewail her – her breeches – as she is for ever doing! And don't, don't say "bah," Léonie!'

'She has fatigued you, my dear? I believe I warned you that she was something of a rogue.'

Fanny relented.

'Indeed, and we love her dearly! I could wish that you would leave her with us longer.'

Léonie took a firm hold on Avon's coat sleeve.

'You won't, will you, Monseigneur?'

He disengaged himself.

'My infant, you must strive to be more polite. One would infer that you had been unhappy with Lady Fanny.'

'Yes, Monseigneur, very unhappy. It is not because she is not kind, for she has been very kind to me, but I belong to you.'

Over her head Justin looked mockingly at his sister.

'It distresses you, my dear? I believe you are right, Léonie. I have come to fetch you.'

She was all smiles at once.

'Voyons, now I am happy! Where will you take me, Monseigneur?'

'Into the country, child. Ah, the worthy Edward! Your devoted servant, Edward.'

Marling had entered quietly. Stiffly he returned Avon's bow.

'I would have a word with you an it please you, Alastair,' he said.

'But does it please me?' wondered his Grace. 'No doubt you wish to speak concerning my ward?'

Edward looked annoyed.

'In private, sir.'

'Quite unnecessary, my dear Edward, I assure you.' He flicked Léonie's cheek with one careless finger. 'Mr Marling has no doubt warned you that I am no fit companion for the young and – ah – innocent, infant?'

'No-no.' Léonie tilted her head. 'I know all about that, you see. Me, I am not very innocent, do you think?'

'That will do, Léonie!' hastily interposed Fanny. 'You'll drink a dish of Bohea with me, Justin? Léonie shall be ready to accompany you tomorrow. Léonie, my love, I have left my handkerchief in your room. Be so good as to fetch it for me. And Edward may go too. Yes, Edward, please!' So she drove them out, and turned again to her brother. 'Well, Justin, I've done as you desired me.'

'Admirably, my dear.'

Her eyes twinkled.

'At no small cost, Justin.'

'It is no matter, Fanny.'

She eyed him irresolutely.

'What now, Justin?'

'Now I take her to Avon.'

'With Cousin Field?'

'But could you doubt it?' he bowed.

'Easily.' She curled her lip. 'Justin, what is it you intend? You've some scheme, I know. I'll believe you mean no ill by Léonie.'

'It is always wise to believe the worst of me, Fanny.'

'I confess I don't understand you, Justin. 'Tis most provoking.'

'It must be,' he agreed.

She drew nearer, coaxing him.

'Justin, I do wish that you would tell me what is in your mind!'

He took a pinch of snuff, and shut the box with a snap.

'You must learn, my dear Fanny, to curb your curiosity. Suffice it that I am as a grandfather to that child. It should suffice.'

'It does, in part, but I do so want to know what scheme you have in your head!'

'I am sure you do, Fanny,' he said sympathetically.

'You are very horrid,' she pouted. A sudden smile came. 'Justin, what new whim is this? Léonie speaks of you as of a strict governor. 'Tis for ever "Monseigneur would not like me to do that," or "Do you think that Monseigneur would mind?" It's not like you, my dear.'

'An I knew less of the world's ways I should no doubt be a more lenient guardian,' he said. 'As it is, Fanny –' He shrugged, and drew his fan from one of his great pockets.

Léonie came back into the room, holding up her gown with one little hand.

'I could not find your handkerchief, madame,' she began, and then saw Avon's fan. A look of disapproval came over her face; there was a measure of reproof in the candid blue eyes. Avon smiled.

'You will grow accustomed to it, my child.'

'Never,' said Léonie positively. 'It does not please me at all.'

'But then,' murmured his Grace, 'I do not use it to please you.'

'*Pardon,* Monseigneur!' she answered contritely, and peeped at him through her lashes. The irresistible dimple quivered.

'She'll snare him,' thought Fanny. 'She is all too fascinating.'

***

Justin took his ward down to Avon by coach the following day, in company with Madam Field, on whose amiable vapidity Léonie looked with scant respect. Justin was quick to read her opinion of the lady, and when they arrived at Avon, took her aside.

'This,' said Léonie buoyantly, 'is a nice house. I like it.'

'I am rejoiced to hear you say so,' replied his Grace ironically.

Léonie looked round the panelled hall, with its carven chairs, its paintings, and tapestry, and the gallery above.

'Perhaps it is a little sombre,' she said. 'Who is this gentleman?' She went to a suit of armour, and regarded it with interest.

'It is not a gentleman at all, my infant. It is the armour one of my ancestors wore.'

'*Vraiment?*' She wandered away to the foot of the stairs, and inspected an ancient portrait. 'Is this another ancestor, this foolish woman?'

'A very famous one, my dear.'

'She has a stupid smile,' Léonie remarked. 'Why was she famous? What for?'

'Principally for her indiscretions. Which reminds me, child, that I want to speak to you.'

'Yes, Monseigneur?' Léonie was staring now at a shield which hung above the fireplace. '"*J'y serai.*" That is French.'

'Your intelligence is remarkable. I wish to speak to you of my cousin, Madam Field.'

Léonie looked at him over her shoulder, grimacing.

'May I say what I think, Monseigneur?'

He sat down on the great carved table, swinging his eyeglass.

'To me, yes.'

'She is just a fool, Monseigneur.'

'Indubitably. And therefore, my infant, you must not only bear with her folly, but you must be at pains to cause her no trouble.'

Léonie seemed to debate within herself.

'Must I, Monseigneur?'

Justin looked at her, and recognised the naughty twinkle in her eye.

'Because I will it so, my child.'

The little straight nose wrinkled.

'Oh, *eh bien!*'

'I thought so,' remarked Avon beneath his breath. 'It is a promise, Léonie?'

'I do not think that I will promise,' Léonie temporised. 'I will *try*.' She came and stood before him. 'Monseigneur, it is very kind of you to bring me to this beautiful place, and to give me everything just as though I were not the sister of an innkeeper. Thank you very much.'

Justin looked at her for a moment, and his lips twisted in a curious smile.

'You think me a paragon of all the virtues, don't you, *ma fille*?'

'Oh no!' she answered candidly. 'I think it is only to me that you are kind. With some women you are not good at all. I cannot help knowing these things, Monseigneur!'

'And yet, child, you are content to remain with me?'

'But of course!' she answered in some surprise.

'You are full of trust,' he remarked.

'Of course,' she said again.

'This,' said Avon, looking at the rings on his hand, 'is a new experience. I wonder what Hugh would say?'

'Oh, he would pull down his mouth, so! And shake his head. I think he is sometimes not very wise.'

He laughed, and laid a hand on her shoulder.

'I never thought, *ma fille*, to take unto me a ward so much after mine own heart. I beg you will be careful not to shock Madam Field.'

'But with you I may say what I please?'

'You always do,' he replied.

'And you will stay here?'

'For the present. I have to attend to your education, you see. There are things you have to learn that I can best teach you.'

'What, *par example*?'

'To ride?'

'On a horse? *Vraiment?*'

'The prospect pleases you?'

'Yes, oh yes! And will you teach me to fight with a sword, Monseigneur?'

'It's not a ladylike occupation, *ma fille*'

'But I do not always want to be a lady, Monseigneur! If I may learn to fight with a sword I will try very hard to learn the other silly things.'

He looked down at her, smiling.

'I believe you are trying to drive a bargain with me! What if I will not teach you to fence?'

She dimpled.

'Why, then I fear I shall be very stupid when you teach me to curtsy, Monseigneur. Oh, Monseigneur, say you will! Please say it quickly! Madame is coming.'

'You force my hand,' he bowed. 'I will teach you, imp.'

Madam Field entered the hall in time to see her charge execute a neat step-dance. She murmured expostulations.

Thirteen

The Education of Léonie

THE DUKE REMAINED AT AVON FOR OVER A MONTH, DURING WHICH time Léonie applied herself energetically to the task of becoming a lady. Madam Field's ideal of this estate was luckily not Avon's. He had no wish to see his ward sitting primly over her stitchery, which was just as well, perhaps, for after the first attempt Léonie declared that nothing would induce her to ply a needle. Madam Field was a little flustered by this defection, and by Léonie's taste for sword-play, but she was far too good-natured and indefinite to do more than murmur nervous remonstrances. She stood very much in awe of her cousin, and although she was by birth an Alastair she felt her-self to be a wholly inferior creature. She had been happy enough with her husband, an obscure gentleman with a taste for farming, but she knew that in the eyes of her family she had disgraced herself by marrying him. This had not troubled her much while he lived, but now that he was dead, and she had returned to what had once been her own *milieu*, she was uncomfortably conscious of the step downwards that she had taken in her foolish youth. She was rather frightened of Avon, but she liked to live in his house. When she looked about her, at faded tapestries, at stretches of velvet lawns, at portraits innumerable, and crossed swords above the doorway, she remembered anew the glory of past Alastairs, and some almost forgotten chord stirred within her.

Léonie was enchanted by Avon Court, and demanded to know its history. She walked with Justin in the grounds, and learned how Hugo Alastair, coming with the Conqueror, settled there, and built himself a fair dwelling, which was destroyed in the troublesome times of King Stephen; how it was built again by Sir Roderick Alastair; how he was given a barony, and prospered; and how the first Earl, under Queen Mary, pulled down the old building and erected the present house. And she learned of the bombardment that partially destroyed the West Wing, when Earl Henry held all for the King against the usurper Cromwell, and was rewarded for it at the Restoration by a dukedom. She saw the sword of the last Duke, the same that he had used in tragic '15, for King James III, and heard a small part of Justin's own adventures, ten years ago, for King Charles III. Justin touched but lightly on this period of his life; his work in that attempt, Léonie guessed, had been secret and tortuous, but she learned that the true King was Charles Edward Stuart, and learned to speak of the little war-like man on the throne as Elector George.

Her education at Justin's hands was a source of interest and amusement to her. Up in the long picture gallery he taught her to dance, with an eagle eye for the smallest fault, or the least hint of awkwardness in her bearing. Madam Field came to play on the spinet for them, and watched with an indulgent smile while they trod each stately measure. She reflected that she had never seen her unapproachable cousin so human, as with this laughing sprite of a girl. They danced the minuet, and the long lines of ancestors gazed down upon them indulgently.

Avon made Léonie practise her curtsy, and made her combine her pretty roguishness with some of the haughtiness that character-ised my Lady Fanny. He showed her how to extend her hand for a man to kiss, how to use her fan, and how to place her patches. He would walk with her in the pleasaunce, teaching every rule of deportment until she was word perfect. He insisted that she should cultivate certain queenliness of bearing. She soon learned, and would rehearse her newest lesson before him, enjoying herself hugely, radiant if she earned a word of praise.

She could already ride, but astride only. She was disgusted with the side-saddle, and for a while rebelled against it. For the space of two days her will held fast against Avon's, but his frigid politeness disarmed her, and on the third day she came to him with head hanging, and faltered:

'I am sorry, Monseigneur. I – I will ride as you wish.'

So they rode together in the grounds until she had mastered this new art, and then they went out over the countryside, and those who saw the Duke beside this beautiful girl cast knowing glances at each other, and shook their heads wisely, for they had seen other beautiful girls with Avon.

Bit by bit the Court, so long bereft of a mistress, began to wear a more cheerful air. Léonie's glad young spirit pervaded it; she flung back heavy curtains, and consigned ponderous screens to the lumber room. Windows were opened to let in the wintry sun, and bit by bit the oppressive solemnity of the place disappeared. Léonie would have none of the stern neatness that was wont to reign there. She tumbled prim cushions, pushed chairs out of place, and left books lying on odd tables, caring nothing for Madam Field's shocked protests. Justin permitted her to do as she pleased; it amused him to watch her gyrations, and he liked to hear her give orders to his expressionless lackeys. Clearly she had the habit of command: unusual she might be, but never did she exhibit any lack of breeding.

Her lessons were soon put to the test. On one occasion he said suddenly:

'We will suppose, Léonie, that I am the Duchess of Queensberry, and that you have just been presented to me. Show me how you would curtsy.'

'But you cannot be a duchess, Monseigneur,' she objected. 'That is ridiculous. You don't *look* like a duchess! Let us pretend you are the Duke of Queensberry.'

'The Duchess. Show me the curtsy.'

Léonie sank down and down.

'Like this: low, but not so low as to the Queen. This is a very good curtsy I am doing, *n'est-ce pas?*'

'It is to be hoped you would not talk all the time,' said his Grace. 'Spread out your skirts, and do not hold your fan like that. Show me again.'

Léonie obeyed meekly.

'It is very difficult to remember everything,' she complained. 'Now let us play at piquet, Monseigneur.'

'Presently. Curtsy now to – Mr Davenant.'

She swept her skirts right regally, and with head held high extended one small hand. Avon smiled.

'Hugh is like to be amazed,' he remarked. 'It's very well, *ma fille.* Curtsy now to me.'

At that she sank down with bent head, and raised his hand to her lips.

'No, my child.'

She rose. 'That is the way I do it, Monseigneur. I like it.'

'It is incorrect. Again, and the proper depth. You curtsied then as to the King. I am but an ordinary mortal, remember.'

Léonie searched in her mind for a fitting retort.

'Lawks!' she said vaguely.

His Grace stiffened, but his lips twitched.

'I – beg – your – pardon?'

'I said "lawks,"' said Léonie demurely.

'I heard you.' His Grace's voice was cold.

'Rachel said it,' Léonie ventured, peeping up at him. 'She is Lady Fanny's maid, you know. You do not like it?'

'I do not. I should be glad if you would refrain from modelling your conversation on that of Lady Fanny's maid.'

'Yes, Monseigneur. Please, what does it mean?'

'I have not the slightest idea. It is a vulgarity. There are many sins, *ma belle*, but only one that is unforgivable. That is vulgarity.'

'I won't say it again,' promised Léonie. 'I will say instead – *tiens*, what is it? – Tare an' ouns!'

'I beg you will do no such thing, *ma fille*. If you must indulge in forceful expressions confine them to 'pon rep, or merely Lud!'

'Lud? Yes, that is a pretty one. I like it. I like Lawks best, though. Monseigneur is not angry?'

'I am never angry,' said Avon.

At other times he fenced with her, and this she enjoyed most of all. She donned shirt and breeches for the pastime, and displayed no little aptitude for the game. She had a quick eye and a supple wrist, and she very soon mastered the rudiments of this manly art. The Duke was one of the first swordsmen of the day, but this in no wise discomposed Léonie. He taught her to fence in the Italian manner, and showed her many subtle passes which he had learned abroad. She experimented with one of them, and since his Grace's guard, at that moment, was lax, broke through. The button of her foil came to rest below his left shoulder.

'*Touché*,' said Avon. 'That was rather better, infant.'

Léonie danced in her excitement.

'Monseigneur, I have killed you! You are dead! You are dead!'

'You display an unseemly joy,' he remarked. 'I had no notion you were so bloodthirsty.'

'But it was so clever of me!' she cried. 'Was it not, Monseigneur?'

'Not at all,' he said crushingly. 'My guard was weak.'

Her mouth dropped. 'Oh, you let me do it!'

His Grace relented 'No, you broke through, *ma fille*.'

Sometimes he talked to her of personalities of the day, explaining who this was, and who that, and how they were related.

'There is March,' he said, 'who will be Duke of Queensberry. You have heard me speak of him. There is Hamilton, who is famous for his wife. She was one of the Miss Gunnings – beauties, my dear, who set London by the ears not so many years ago. Maria Gunning married Coventry. If you want wit, there is Mr Selwyn, who has quite an inimitable way with him: he would hate to be forgotten. He lives in Arlington Street, child, and wherever you go you may be sure of meeting him. In Bath I believe Nash still reigns. A parvenu, infant, but a man of some genius. Bath is his kingdom. One day I will take you there. Then we have the Cavendish – Devonshire, my dear; and the Seymours, and my Lord Chesterfield, whom you will know by his wit and his dark eyebrows. Whom else? There is my Lord of Bath, and the Bentincks, and his Grace of Newcastle, of some fame. If you want the Arts you have the tedious Johnson: a large man, with a larger head. He is not worth your consideration. He lacks polish. There is Colley Cibber, one of our poets, Mr Sheridan, who writes plays for us, and Mr Garrick, who acts them; and a score of others. In painting we have Sir Joshua Reynolds, who shall paint you, perhaps, and a great many others whose names elude me.'

Léonie nodded.

'Monseigneur, you must write their names down for me. Then I shall remember.'

'*Bien*. We come now to your own country. Of the Blood Royal we have the Prince de Condé, who is now, as I reckon, twenty years of age – *à peu près*. There is the Comte d'Eu, son of the Duc de Maine, one of the bastards, and the Duc de Penthièvre, son of yet another bastard. Let me see. Of the nobility there is M. de Richelieu, the model of true courtesy, and the Duc de Noailles, famed for the battle of Dettingen, which he lost. Then we have the brothers Lorraine-Brionne, and the Prince d'Armagnac. My memory fails me. Ah yes, there is M. de Belle-Isle, who is the grandson of the great Fouquet. He is an old man now. *Tiens*, almost I had forgot the estimable Chavignard – Comte de Chavigny, child – a friend of mine. I might go on for ever, but I will not.'

'And there is Madame de Pompadour, is there not, Monseigneur?'

'I spoke of the nobility, *ma fille*,' said his Grace gently. 'We do not count the cocotte amongst them. La Pompadour is a beauty of no birth, and wit – a little. My ward will not trouble her head with any such.'

'No, Monseigneur,' said Léonie, abashed. 'Please tell me some more.'

'You are insatiable. Well, let us essay. D'Anvau you have seen. A little man, with a love of scandal. De Salmy you have also seen. He is tall and indolent, and hath somewhat of a reputation for sword-play. Lavoulère comes of old stock, and doubtless has his virtues even though they have escaped my notice. Machérand has a wife who squints. I need say no more. Château-Mornay will amuse you for half an hour, no longer. Madame de Marguéry's salons are world-famous. Florimond de Chantourelle is like some insect. Possibly a wasp, since he is always clad in bright colours, and always plagues one.'

'And M. de Saint-Vire?'

'My very dear friend Saint-Vire. Of course. One day, infant, I will tell you all about the so dear Comte. But not to-day. I say only this, my child – you will beware of Saint-Vire. It is understood?'

'Yes, Monseigneur, but why?'

'That also I will tell you one day,' said his Grace calmly.

Fourteen

The Appearance on the Scene of Lord Rupert Alastair

WHEN AVON LEFT THE COUNTRY LÉONIE WAS AT FIRST DISCONSO-
late. Madam Field was not an exhilarating companion, as her mind
ran on illness and death, and the forward ways of the younger
generation. Fortunately the weather became warmer, and Léonie
was able to escape from the lady into the park, well-knowing that
Madam was not fond of any form of exercise.

When she rode out Léonie was supposed to have a groom in
attendance, but she very often dispensed with this formality, and
explored the countryside alone, revelling in her freedom.

Some seven miles from Avon Court lay Merivale Place, the
estate of my Lord Merivale and his beautiful wife, Jennifer. My lord
had grown indolent of late years, and my lady, for two short seasons
London's toast, had no love for town life. Nearly all the year they
lived in Hampshire, but sometimes they spent the winter in Bath,
and occasionally, my lord being smitten with a longing for the
friends of his youth, they journeyed to town. More often my lord
went alone on these expeditions, but he was never away for long.

It was not many weeks before Léonie rode out in the direction
of the Place. The woods that lay about the old white house lured
her, and she rode into them, looking round with great interest.

The trees were sprouting new leaves, and here and there early spring flowers peeped up between the blades of grass. Léonie picked her way through the undergrowth, delighting in the wood's beauty, until she came to where a stream bubbled and sang over the rounded stones on its bed. Beside this stream, on a fallen tree-trunk, a dark lady was seated, with a baby playing on the rug at her feet. A small boy, in a very muddied coat, was fishing hopefully in the stream.

Léonie reined in short, guiltily aware of trespass. The youthful fisherman saw her first, and called to the lady on the tree-trunk.

'Look, Mama!'

The lady looked in the direction of his pointing finger, and raised her brows in quick surprise.

'I am very sorry,' Léonie stammered. 'The wood was so pretty – I will go.'

The lady rose, and went forward across the strip of grass that separated them.

'It's very well, madam. Why should you go?' Then she saw that the little face beneath the hat's big brim was that of a child, and she smiled. 'Will you not dismount, my dear, and bear me company a while?'

The wistful, uncertain look went out of Léonie's eyes. She dimpled, nodding.

'*S'il vous plaît, madame.*'

'You're French? Are you staying here?' inquired the lady.

Léonie kicked her foot free of the stirrup, and slid to the ground.

'But yes, I am staying at Avon. I am the – bah, I have forgotten the word! – the – the ward of Monseigneur le Duc.'

A shadow crossed the lady's face. She made a movement as though to stand between Léonie and the children. Léonie's chin went up.

'I am not anything else, madame, *je vous assure*. I am in the charge of Madame Field, the cousin of Monseigneur. It is better that I go, yes?'

'I crave your pardon, my dear. I beg that you will stay. I am Lady Merivale.'

'I thought you were,' confided Léonie. 'Lady Fanny told me of you.'

'Fanny?' Jennifer's brow cleared. 'You know her?'

'I have been with her two weeks, when I came from Paris. Monseigneur thought it would not be *convenable* for me to be with him until he had found a lady suitable to be my *gouvernante*, you see.'

Jennifer, in the past, had had experience of his Grace's ideas of propriety, and thus she did not see at all, but she was too polite to say so. She and Léonie sat down on the tree-trunk while the small boy stared round-eyed.

'No one likes Monseigneur, I find,' Léonie remarked. 'Just a few, perhaps. Lady Fanny, and M. Davenant, and me, of course.'

'Oh, you like him, then?' Jennifer looked at her wonderingly.

'He is so good to me, you understand,' explained Léonie. 'That is your little son?'

'Yes, that is John. Come and make your bow, John.'

John obeyed, and ventured a remark:

'Your hair is quite short, madam.'

Léonie pulled off her hat.

'But how pretty!' exclaimed Jennifer. 'Why did you cut it?'

Léonie hesitated.

'Madame, please will you not ask me? I am not allowed to tell people. Lady Fanny said I must not.'

'I hope 'twas not an illness?' said Jennifer, with an anxious eye to her children.

'Oh no!' Léonie assured her. Again she hesitated. 'Monseigneur did not say I was not to tell. It was only Lady Fanny, and she is not always very wise, do you think? And I do not suppose that she would want me not to tell you, for you were at the convent with her, *n'est-ce pas*? I have only just begun to be a girl, you see, madame.'

Jennifer was startled.

'I beg your pardon, my dear?'

'Since I was twelve I have always been a boy. Then Monseigneur found me, and I was his page. And – and then he discovered that I was not a boy at all, and he made me his daughter. I did not like it at first, and these petticoats still bother me, but in some ways it is very pleasant. I have so many things all my own, and I am a lady now.'

Jennifer's eyes grew soft. She patted Léonie's hand.

'You quaint child! For how long do you think to stay at Avon?'

'I do not quite know, madame. It is as Monseigneur wills. And I have to learn so many things. Lady Fanny is to present me, I think. It is nice of her, is it not?'

'Prodigious amiable,' Jennifer agreed. 'Tell me your name, my dear.'

'I am Léonie de Bonnard, madame.'

'And your parents made the – the Duke your guardian?'

'N-no. They have been dead for many years, you see. Monseigneur did it all himself.' Léonie glanced down at the babe. 'Is this also your son, madame?'

'Yes, child, this is Geoffrey Molyneux Merivale. Is he not beautiful?'

'Very,' said Léonie politely. 'I do not know babies very well.' She rose, and picked up her plumed hat. 'I must go back, madame. Madame Field will have become agitated.' She smiled mischievously. 'She is very like a hen, you know.'

Jennifer laughed. 'But you'll come again? Come to the house one day, and I will present my husband.'

'Yes, if you please, madame. I should like to come. *Au revoir, Jean; au revoir, bébé!*'

The baby gurgled, and waved an aimless hand. Léonie hoisted herself into the saddle.

'One does not know what to say to a baby,' she remarked. 'He is very nice, of course,' she added. She bowed, hat in hand, and turning, made her way back along the path down which she had come, to the road.

Jennifer picked up the baby, and calling to John to follow, went through the wood and across the gardens to the house. She relinquished the children to their nurse, and went in search of her husband.

She found him in the library, turning over his accounts, a big, loose-limbed man, with humorous gray eyes, and a firm-lipped mouth. He held out his hand.

'Faith, Jenny, you grow more lovely each time I look upon you,' he said.

She laughed, and went to sit on the arm of his chair.

'Fanny thinks us unfashionable, Anthony.'

'Oh, Fanny – ! She's fond enough of Marling at heart.'

'Very fond of him, Anthony, but she is modish withal, and likes other men to whisper pretty things in her ear. I fear that I shall never have the taste for town ways.'

'My love, if I find "other men" whispering in your ear –'

'My lord!'

'My lady?'

'You are monstrous ungallant, sir! As if they – as if I would!'

His hold about her tightened.

'You might be the rage of town, Jenny, an you would.'

'Oh, is that your will, my lord?' she teased. 'Now I know that you are disappointed in your wife. I thank you, sir!' She slipped from him, and swept a mock curtsy.

My lord jumped up and caught her.

'Rogue, I am the happiest man on earth.'

'My felicitations, sir. Anthony, you have had no word from Edward, have you?'

'From Edward? Nay, why should I?'

'I met a girl to-day in the woods who has stayed with the Marlings. I wondered whether he had written to tell you.'

'A girl? Here? Who was she?'

'You'll be surprised, my lord. She is a very babe, and – and she says she is the Duke's ward.'

'Alastair?' Merivale's brow wrinkled. 'What new whim can that be?'

'I could not ask, of course. But is it not strange that – that man – should adopt her?'

'Perchance he is a reformed character, my love.'

She shivered. 'He could never be that. I feel so sorry for this child – in his power. I asked her to come and see me one day. Was it right of me?'

He frowned. 'I'll have no dealings with Alastair, Jenny. I am not like to forget that his Grace saw fit to abduct my wife.'

'I wasn't your wife then,' she protested. 'And – and this child – this Léonie – is not like that at all. I should be so pleased if you would let her come.'

He made her a magnificent leg.

'My lady, you are mistress in your own house,' he said.

So it was that when next Léonie rode over to Merivale she was received gladly both by Jennifer and her lord. She was rather shy at first, but her nervousness fled before Merivale's smile. Over a dish of Bohea she made gay conversation, and presently turned to her host.

'I wanted to meet you, milor',' she said cheerfully. 'I have heard much – oh, much – about you!'

Merivale sat bolt upright.

'Who in the world – ?' he began uneasily.

'Lady Fanny, and Monseigneur, a little. Tell me, m'sieur, did you really stop Lord Harding's coach – ?'

'For a wager, child, for a wager!'

She laughed. 'Aha, I knew! And he was very angry, was he not? And it had to be kept secret, because in – in dip-lo-mat-ic circles it –'

'For heaven's sake, child!'

'And *now* you are called The Highwayman!'

'No, no, only to my intimates!'

Jennifer shook her head at him.

'Oh, my lord! Go on, Leonie. Tell me some more. The wretch has grossly deceived me, I'll have you know.'

'Mademoiselle,' said Merivale, wiping his heated brow, 'have pity!'

'But tell me,' she insisted. 'Was it not very exciting to be a highwayman for one night?'

'Very,' he said gravely. 'But not at all respectable.'

'No,' she agreed. 'One does not always want to be respectable, I think. Me, I am a great trial to everybody, because I am not respectable at all. It seems that a lady may do many bad things and still be respectable, but if one speaks of such things as breeches then one is unladylike. I find it very hard.'

His eyes danced. He tried to suppress a laugh, and failed.

'Faith, you must come often to see us, mademoiselle! 'Tis not often we meet such a charming little lady.'

'You must come to see me next,' she answered. 'That is right, is it not?'

'I am afraid –' began Jennifer uncomfortably.

'His Grace and I do not visit,' ended Merivale.

Léonie flung up her hands.

'Oh, *parbleu!* Everyone I meet is the same! It does not surprise me that sometimes Monseigneur is wicked when everybody is so unkind to him.'

'His Grace has a way of making it difficult for one to be –
er – kind to him,' said Merivale grimly.

'M'sieur,' answered Léonie with great dignity, 'it is not wise to
speak thus of Monseigneur to me. He is the only person in the
whole world who cares what happens to me. So you see I will
not listen to people who try to warn me against him. It makes
something inside me get all hot and angry.'

'Mademoiselle,' said Merivale, 'I crave your pardon.'

'I thank you, m'sieur,' she said gravely.

She came often to Merivale after that, and once dined there
with Madam Field, who had no knowledge of the rift between
Avon and Merivale.

A fortnight passed, bringing no word from Justin, but at the end
of it a travelling coach, loaded with baggage, arrived at Merivale,
and a tall young exquisite leaped out. He was admitted into the
house and met by Jennifer, who laughed when she saw him, and
held out both her hands.

'Why, Rupert! Have you come to stay?'

He kissed her hands, and then her cheek.

'Devil take it, Jenny, you're too lovely, 'pon my soul you are!
Lord, here's Anthony! I wonder if he saw?'

Merivale gripped his hand.

'One of these days, Rupert, I'll teach you a lesson,' he threatened.
'What's to do? You've brought enough baggage for three men.'

'Baggage? Nonsense, man! Why, there's only a few things
there, I give you my word! One must dress, y'know, one must
dress. Anthony, what's this fandangle about Justin? Fanny's devilish mysterious, but the tale's all over town that he's adopted a
girl! Stap me, but that's –' He broke off, remembering Jennifer's
presence. 'I've come down to see for myself. God knows where
Justin is! I don't.' He looked sharply at Merivale, consternation in
his face. 'He's not at Avon, is he?'

'Calm yourself,' soothed Merivale. 'He is not here.'

'Praise the Lord for that. Who is the girl?'

'A pretty child,' Merivale answered guardedly.

'Ay, I'd have guessed that. Justin had ever a nice taste in —'
Again he stopped. 'Thunder an' turf, I beg your pardon, Jenny! I'd
forgot. Demmed careless of me!' He looked ruefully at Merivale.
'I must always be saying the wrong thing, Tony. It's this rattle-pate
of mine, and what with the bottle — well, well!'

Merivale led him into the library, where a lackey came to them
presently, bringing wine. Rupert settled his long length in a chair
and drank deeply.

'Truth to tell, Tony,' he said confidently, 'I'm more at ease when
the ladies are not present. My tongue runs away with me, burn it!
Not but what Jenny's a devilish fine woman,' he added hastily. 'The
wonder is that you admit me into your house. When one thinks
'twas my brother ran off with Jenny —' He shook his head comically.

'You're always welcome,' smiled Merivale. 'I've no fear that
you'll seek to abduct Jenny.'

'Lord, no! I'm not saying that I haven't trifled somewhat with
women now and then — one has to, y'know. Honour of the name,
my boy — but I've no real taste for 'em, Tony, none at all.' He
refilled his glass. ''Tis a queer thing, when you come to think on't.
Here am I, an Alastair, with never an intrigue to my name. I feel
it sometimes,' he sighed, ''tis as though I were no true Alastair.
Why, there's never been one of us —'

'I'd not crave the vice, Rupert,' said Merivale dryly.

'Oh, I don't know! There's Justin, now, and wherever he is there
is sure to be some wench. I'm not saying aught against him, mind
you, but we don't love one another overmuch. I'll say one thing
for him, though: he's not mean. I daresay you'll not believe me,
Tony, but since he came into that fortune of his I've not been in a
sponging house once.' He looked up with some pride. 'Not once.'

'It's marvellous,' Merivale agreed. 'And have you really come down here to see Léonie?'

'Is that her name? Ay, what else?'

The gray eyes began to twinkle.

'I thought mayhap 'twas to see myself and Jennifer?'

'Oh, of course, of course!' Rupert assured him, sitting up hurriedly. He saw the twinkle, and sank back again. 'Devil take you, Tony, you're laughing at me! Ay, I'd a mind to see Justin's latest. Is she alone at the Court?'

'No, with a cousin of yours. Madam Field.'

'What, not old cousin Harriet? Lud, what will Justin be at next? He's got his eye fixed to the proprieties this time, eh?'

'I believe it's true that she is no more than his ward.'

Rupert cocked one incredulous eyebrow.

'For which reason, my dear fellow, you'll either treat her with becoming respect, or journey back to town.'

'But, Tony – Damn it, you know Justin!'

'I wonder if any of us do? I know this child.'

'I'll see for myself,' said Rupert. He chuckled. 'I'd give something to see Justin's face when he finds I've been poaching on his land! Not that I want to anger him; he's devilish unpleasant when he's crossed.' He paused, frowning prodigiously. 'You know, Tony, I often wonder what he feels about me. He's fond of Fanny, I'll swear. He was devilish strict with her in the old days – never think it, would you? – But me – he gives me a handsome allowance these days, yet it's seldom he has a friendly word for me.'

'Do you want a friendly word from him?' inquired Merivale, smoothing a wrinkle from his satin sleeve.

'Oh, well! He's my brother, y'know! Queer part of it is he used to take precious good care what happened to me when I was a youngster. He was always a damned smooth-tongued icicle, of course. I don't mind telling you, Tony, I'm still something nervous of him.'

'I don't pretend to understand him, Rupert. I used to think there was good in him somewhere. The child – Léonie – worships him. Have a care to what you say in her presence!'

'My dear fellow, it's not likely I'd say aught –'

'It's more than likely,' retorted Merivale. 'Addle-pated young scamp!'

'Now stap me, that's not fair!' cried Rupert, heaving himself up. 'Scamp, did you say? What about the High Toby, my boy, eh?'

Merivale flung up his hand.

'*Touché!* For the love of heaven, Rupert, don't spread that tale about town!'

Rupert smoothed his ruffled hair, and managed to assume an expression of vast superiority.

'Oh, I'm not such a fool as you think, Tony, I assure you!'

'Well, thank God for that!' answered Merivale.

Fifteen

Lord Rupert Makes the Acquaintance of Léonie

Rupert rode over to the Court the very next day and heralded his arrival by a prolonged peal on the door-bell, accompanied by several resounding knocks. Léonie was seated by the fire in the hall, and the commotion startled her a little. When the butler came to admit the visitor she rose, and peeped round the corner of the screen to see who it was. A gay, boisterous voice met her ears.

'Hey, Johnson! Not dead yet? Where's my cousin?'

'Oh, it's you, my lord?' said the old man. ''Tis no one else would make a such a thundering on the door, to be sure. Madam's within.'

Rupert strode past him into the hall. At sight of Léonie regarding him in some trepidity from the fireplace he swept off his hat and bowed.

'Your pardon, mamzelle. Thunder an' turf, what's come over the place?' He cast an astonished glance about him. 'It's been like a tomb for centuries, and now – !'

'It's my Lord Rupert, madam,' explained Johnson apologetically. He frowned severely at his young master. 'Ye can't stay here, my lord. This is his Grace's ward. Mistress Léonie de Bonnard.'

'I'm at Merivale, old sobersides,' said the graceless Rupert. 'If you say I'm to go, mamzelle, I will.'

Léonie's nose wrinkled in perplexity.

'Rupert? Oh, you are the brother of Monseigneur!'

'Mon – ? Oh, ay, ay! That's it!'

Léonie skipped forward.

'I am very pleased to see you,' she said politely. 'Now I curtsy and you kiss my hand, n'est-ce pas?'

Rupert stared. 'Ay, but –'

'Eh bien!' Léonie sank, and rose, and held out her small hand. Rupert kissed it punctiliously.

'I never before was told by a lady to kiss her hand,' he remarked.

'I should not have said it?' she asked anxiously. 'Voyons, these things are very difficult to learn! Where is Monseigneur, please?'

'Lord, I don't now, my dear! Ours is no united household, I give you my word!'

Léonie looked at him gravely.

'You are the young Rupert. I know. I have heard tell of you.'

'Not a might of good, I'll be bound. I'm the scapegrace of the family.'

'Oh no! I have heard people speak of you in Paris, and I think they like you very much.'

'Do they, by Gad? Do you come from Paris, my dear?'

She nodded. 'I was Monseigneur's pa –' She clasped her hands over her mouth, and her eyes danced.

Rupert was greatly intrigued. He cast a shrewd glance at her short curls.

'Pa – ?'

'I must not say. Please do not ask me!'

'You were never his page?'

Léonie stared down at her toes.

'Here's a romance!' said Rupert, delighted. 'His page, by all that's marvellous!'

'You must not tell!' she said earnestly. 'Promise!'

'Mum as a corpse, my dear!' he answered promptly. 'I never thought to stumble on such a fairy tale! What are you doing cooped up here?'

'I am learning to be a lady, milor'.'

'Milor' be damned, saving your presence! My name's Rupert.'

'Is it *convenable* for me to call you that?' she inquired. 'I do not know these things, you see.'

'*Convenable*, my dear? I pledge you my word it is! Are you not my brother's ward?'

'Y-es.'

'*Eh bien*, then, as you'd say yourself! Fiend seize it, here's my cousin!'

Madam Field came down the stairs, peering out of her short-sighted eyes.

'Well, to be sure! And is it indeed you, Rupert?' she exclaimed.

Rupert went forward to meet her.

'Ay, cousin, it's myself. I hope I see you in your customary good health?'

'Save for a trifling touch of the gout. Léonie! You here?'

'I presented myself, cousin. I believe I am something in the nature of an uncle to her.'

'An uncle? Oh no, Rupert, surely not!'

'I will not have you for an uncle,' said Léonie with her nose in the air. 'You are not enough respectable.'

'My love!'

Rupert burst out laughing.

'Faith, I'll none of you for a niece, child. You are too saucy.'

'Oh no, Rupert!' Madam assured him. 'Indeed, she is very good!' She looked at him doubtfully. 'But, Rupert, do you think you should be here?'

'Turning me from mine own roof, cousin?'

'I protest, I did not mean –'

'I am come to make the acquaintance of my brother's ward, cousin, as is fitting.' His voice was convincing. Madam's brow cleared.

'If you say so, Rupert – pray where are you staying?'

'At Merivale, cousin, by night, but here, an it please you, by day.'

'Does – does Justin know?' ventured Madam.

'Do you suggest that Alastair would object to my presence, cousin?' demanded Rupert in righteous indignation.

'Oh no, indeed! You misunderstand me! I make no doubt 'tis monstrous dull for Léonie to have only me to bear her company. Perhaps you will sometimes ride out with her? The child will leave her groom at home, which is vastly improper, as I have told her many times.'

'I'll ride with her all day!' promised Rupert jovially. 'That is if she will have me.'

'I should like it, I think,' said Léonie. 'I have never met anyone *tout comme vous.*'

'If it comes to that,' said Rupert, 'I've never met a girl like you.'

Madam Field sighed, and shook her head.

'I fear she will never become quite as I should wish,' she said sadly.

'She'll be the rage of town,' Rupert prophesied. 'Will you walk with me to the stables, Léonie?'

'I will get a cloak,' she nodded, and ran lightly upstairs.

When she returned Madam Field had delivered a short lecture to Rupert, and had extracted a promise from him that he would behave with suitable decorum towards Léonie.

As soon as they had left the house, Léonie, dancing along beside Rupert with little excited steps, looked up at him with her confiding smile.

'I have thought of a plan,' she announced. 'Suddenly it came to me! Will you please fight me with a sword?'

'Will I do what?' ejaculated Rupert, stopping short

She stamped an impatient foot. 'Fight with swords! Fence!'

'Thunder an' turf, what next? Ay, I'll fence with you, rogue.'

'Thank you *very* much! You see, Monseigneur began to teach me, but then he went away, and Madam Field does not fence at all. I asked her.'

'You should ask Anthony Merivale to teach you, my dear. Justin's good, I'll admit, but Anthony nearly worsted him once.'

'Aha! I knew there was a mystery! Tell me, did Monseigneur intrigue himself with miladi Jennifer?'

'Ran off with her in Anthony's teeth, my dear!'

'*Vraiment?* She would not like that, I think.'

'Lord no! But what woman would?'

'I should not mind,' said Léonie calmly. 'But Lady Merivale – ah, that is another thing! Was she married then?'

'Devil a bit. Justin's not often in an affair with a married woman. He wanted to marry her.'

'It would not have done,' she said wisely. 'She would have wearied him. Milor' then came to the rescue?'

'Ay, and tried to fight Justin *à outrance*. Marling stopped it. Never was there such a scene! They don't speak now, y'know. Damned awkward, seeing that we've known Merivale since we were children. Marling don't love Justin overmuch either.'

'Oh!' Léonie was scornful. 'He is a kind man, that one, but of a dullness!'

'Ay, but 'tis enough to make a man sober to be wedded to Fanny, I can tell you.'

'I think your family is very strange,' she remarked. 'Everyone in it hates everyone else. Oh no, Lady Fanny sometimes loves Monseigneur!'

'Well, you see, we'd a spitfire for Mother,' Rupert explained. 'And the old Duke was no saint, the Lord knows! 'Tis no wonder we grew up like snarling dogs.'

They had arrived at the stables, where Rupert's horse had been taken. He spoke to one of the grooms, hailing him good-naturedly, and went to inspect the few horses that were there. By the time they returned to the house he and Léonie might have known one another for years. Rupert was delighted with his brother's ward, and had already decided to remain some time at Merivale. A girl who was as outspoken as a boy, and who evidently did not expect him to make love to her, was something quite new to Rupert. A month ago he had danced attendance on Mistress Julia Falkner; he was weary of the pastime, and had determined to eschew feminine company. But Leonie, with her friendliness and her quaint ways, would be a pleasant amusement, he thought. She was very young, too, and his loves had hitherto been older than himself. He promised himself a few week's gaiety unspoiled by any fear that he would be entrapped into marriage.

He came again next day, and was informed by the lackey who admitted him that Léonie awaited him in the picture-gallery. Thither went he, and found her wandering round in coat and breeches, inspecting his ancestors.

'By Gad!' he exclaimed. 'You – you rogue!'

She turned quickly, and laid a finger on her lips. 'Where is madame?'

'Cousin Harriet? I've not seen her. Léonie, you should always wear those clothes. They suit you, 'pon my soul they do!'

'I think so too,' she sighed. 'But if you tell madame she will be agitated, and she will say that it is unmaidenly. I brought the foils up.'

'Oh, we're to fence, are we, Amazon?'

'You said you would!'

'As you will, as you will! Damme, I'd like to see Julia's face an she knew!' He chuckled impishly.

She nodded. He had told her of Mistress Falkner already.

'I do not suppose that she would like me,' she observed. She swept a hand round, indicating the many portraits. 'There are a great number of people in your family, are there not? This one is nice. He is like Monseigneur, a little.'

'Lord, child, that's old Hugo Alastair! Devilish rake-helly fellow! They're a damned gloomy lot, all of 'em, and everyone has a sneer on his face for all the world like Justin himself. Come and look at this one; it's my respected parent.'

Léonie looked up into Rudolph Alastair's dissipated countenance.

'He does not please me at all,' she said severely.

'Never pleased anyone, my dear. Here's her Grace. She was French like yourself. Lord, did you ever see such a mouth? Fascinating, y'know, but a temper like the fiend.'

Léonie moved on to where the last picture hung. An awed look came into her eyes.

'And this is – Monseigneur.'

'It was done a year ago. Good, eh?'

The hazel eyes under their drooping lids looked mockingly down on them.

'Yes, it is good,' said Léonie. 'He does not always smile just so. I think he was not in a nice humour when that was painted.'

'Fiendish, ain't he? Striking of course, but Lord, what a damned mask of a face! Never trust him, child, he's a devil.'

The swift colour flooded Léonie's cheeks.

'He is not. It is you who are a gr-r-reat stupid!'

'But it's true, my dear. I tell you he's Satan himself. Damme, I ought to know!' He turned just in time to see Léonie seize one of the foils. 'Here! What will you be at – ?' He got no further, but leaped with more speed than dignity behind a chair, for Léonie, her eyes flaming, was bearing down upon him with the rapier poised in a distinctly alarming manner. Rupert hoisted the chair, and held it to keep Léonie at arm's length, a look of comical dismay on his face. Then, as Léonie lunged across the chair, he took to his heels and fled down the gallery in laughing panic, Léonie close behind him. She drove him into a corner, where he had perforce to stay, using his chair as a protection.

'No, no! Léonie, I say! Hey, you nearly had me! The button'll come off for a certainty! Devil take it, it's monstrous. Put it down, you wild-cat! Put it down!'

The wrath died out of Léonie's face. She lowered the foil.

'I wanted to kill you,' she said calmly. 'I *will* if you say things to me like that of Monseigneur. Come out. You are cowardly!'

'I like that!' Rupert put the chair down cautiously. 'Put that damned foil down, and I'll come.'

Léonie looked at him, and suddenly began to laugh. Rupert came out of the corner, smoothing his ruffled hair.

'You looked so very funny!' gasped Léonie.

Rupert eyed her gloomily. Words failed him.

'I would like to do it again, just to see you run!'

Rupert edged away. A grin dawned. 'For the Lord's sake don't!' he begged.

'No, I won't,' Léonie said obligingly. 'But you are not to say those things —'

'Never again! I swear I won't! Justin's a saint!'

'We will fence now, and not talk any more,' said Léonie regally. 'I am sorry I frightened you.'

'Pooh!' said Rupert loftily.

Her eyes twinkled.

'You *were* frightened! I saw your face. It was so fun —'

'That'll do,' said Rupert. 'I was taken unawares.'

'Yes, that was not well done of me,' she said. 'I am sorry, but you understand I have a quick temper.'

'Yes, I understand that,' grimaced Rupert.

'It is very sad, *n'est-ce pas?* But I am truly sorry.'

He became her slave from that moment.

Sixteen

The Coming of the Comte de Saint-Vire

THE DAYS SPED PAST, AND STILL THE DUKE DID NOT COME. RUPERT and Léonie rode, fenced, and quarrelled together like two children while, from afar, the Merivales watched, smiling.

'My dear,' said his lordship, 'she reminds me strangely of someone, but who it is I cannot for the life of me make out.'

'I don't think I have ever seen anyone like her,' Jennifer answered. 'My lord, I have just thought that 'twould be a pretty thing if she married Rupert.'

'Oh, no!' he said quickly. 'She is a babe, for sure, but, faith, she's too old for Rupert!'

'Or not old enough. All women are older than their husbands, Anthony.'

'I protest I am a staid middle-aged man!'

She touched his cheek.

'You are just a boy. I am older by far.'

He was puzzled, and a little worried.

'I like it so,' she said.

Meanwhile at Avon Léonie and her swain made merry together. Rupert taught Léonie to fish, and they spent delightful days by the stream and returned at dusk, tired and wet, and unbelievably dirty.

Rupert treated Léonie as a boy, which pleased her, and he told her
endless tales of Society, which also pleased her. But most of all she
liked him to remember scraps of recollection of his brother. To
these she would listen for hours at a time, eyes sparkling, and lips
parted to drink in every word.

'He is – he is grand *seigneur!*' she said once, proudly.

'Oh, ay, every inch of him! I'll say that. He'll count no
cost, either. He's devilish clever, too.' Rupert shook his head
wisely. 'Sometimes I think there's nothing he don't know.
God knows how he finds things out, but he does. All pose, of
course, but it's damned awkward, I give you my word. You
can't keep a thing secret from him. And he always comes on
you when you least expect him – or want him. Oh, he's cunning, devilish cunning.'

'I think you do like him a little,' Léonie said shrewdly.

'Devil a bit. Oh, he can be pleasant enough, but it's seldom he
is! One's proud of him, y'know, but he's queer.'

'I wish he would come back,' sighed Léonie.

Two days later Merivale, on his way to Avon village, met them,
careering wildly over the country. They reined in when they saw
him and came to him. Léonie was flushed and panting, Rupert
was sulky.

'He is a great stupid, this Rupert,' Léonie announced.

'She has led me a fine dance this day,' Rupert complained.

'I do not want you with me at all,' said Léonie, nose in air.

Merivale smiled upon their quarrel.

'My lady said a while ago that I was a boy, but 'fore Gad
you make me feel a graybeard,' he said. 'Farewell to ye both!'
He rode on to the village, and there transacted his business. He
stopped for a few minutes at the Avon Arms, and went into the
coffee-room. In the doorway he ran into a tall gentleman who
was coming out.

'Your pardon, sir,' he said, and stared in amazement. 'Saint-Vire! Why, what do ye here, Comte? I'd no notion –'

Saint-Vire had started back angrily, but he bowed now, and if his tone was not cordial, at least he was polite.

'Your servant, Merivale. I had not thought to see you here.'

'Nor I you. Of all the queer places in which to meet you! What brings you here?'

Saint-Vire hesitated for a moment.

'I am on my way to visit friends,' he said, after a while. 'They live – a day's journey north of this place. My schooner is at Portsmouth.' He spread out his hands. 'I am forced to break my journey to recover from a slight indisposition which attacked me *en route*. What would you? One does not wish to arrive *souffrant* at the house of a friend?'

Merivale thought the story strange, and Saint-Vire's manner stranger still, but he was too well-bred to show incredulity.

'My dear Comte, it's most opportune. You will give me the pleasure of your company at dinner at Merivale? I must present you to my wife.'

Again it seemed that Saint-Vire hesitated.

'Monsieur, I resume my journey tomorrow.'

'Well, ride out to Merivale this evening, Comte, I beg of you.'

Almost the Comte shrugged.

'*Eh bien*, m'sieur, you are very kind. I thank you.'

He came that evening to Merivale and bowed deeply over Jennifer's hand.

'Madame, this is a great pleasure. I have long wished to meet the wife of my friend Merivale. Is it too late to felicitate, Merivale?'

Anthony laughed. 'We are four years married, Comte.'

'One has heard much of the beauty of Madame le Baronne,' Saint-Vire said.

Jennifer withdrew her hand.

'Will you be seated, monsieur? I am always glad to see my husband's friends. For where are you bound?'

Saint-Vire waved a vague hand.

'North, madame. I go to visit my friend – er – Chalmer.'

Merivale's brow creased.

'Chalmer? I don't think I know –'

'He lives very much in seclusion,' explained Saint-Vire, and turned again to Jennifer. 'Madame, I think I have never met you in Paris?'

'No, sir, I have not been outside mine own country. My husband goes there sometimes.'

'You should take madame,' Saint-Vire smiled. 'You we see often, n'est-ce pas?'

'Not so often as of yore,' Merivale answered. 'My wife has no taste for town life.'

'Ah, one understands then why you stay not long abroad these days, Merivale!'

Dinner was announced, and they went into the adjoining room. The Comte shook out his napkin.

'You live in most charming country, madame. The woods here are superb.'

'They are finer about Avon Court,' said Anthony. 'There are some splendid oaks there.'

'Ah, Avon! I am desolated to hear that the Duc is away. I hoped – but it is not to be.'

In the recesses of Merivale's brain memory stirred. Surely there had been some scandal, many years ago?

'No, Avon, I believe, is in London. Lord Rupert is staying with us – he is at the Court now, dining with Madam Field, and Mademoiselle de Bonnard, the Duke's ward.'

Saint-Vire's hand, holding the wine-glass, shook a little.

'Mademoiselle de – ?'

'Bonnard. You knew that Avon had adopted a daughter?'

'I heard some rumour,' the Comte said slowly. 'So she is here?'

'For a time only. She is to be presented soon, I think.'

'*Vraiment?*' The Comte sipped his wine. 'No doubt she is *ennuyée* here.'

'I think she is well enough,' Merivale answered. 'There is much to amuse her at Avon. She and that scamp, Rupert, have taken to playing at hide-and-seek in the woods. They are naught but a pair of children!'

'Aha?' Saint-Vire slightly inclined his head. 'And the Duc is, you say, in London?'

'I cannot say for sure. None ever knows where he will be next. Léonie expects him daily, I think.'

'I am sorry to have missed him,' said Saint-Vire mechanically.

After dinner he and Merivale played at piquet together, and soon Rupert came striding in, and stopped dead upon the threshold at sight of the visitor.

'Thun – Your very devoted, Comte,' he said stiffly, and stalked over to where Jennifer was seated. 'What's that fellow doing here?' he growled in her ear.

She laid a finger on her lips. 'The Comte was just saying that he is sorry to have missed seeing your – your brother, Rupert,' she said clearly.

Rupert stared at Saint-Vire.

'Eh? Oh, ay! My brother will be heartbroken, I assure you, sir. Did you come to pay him a visit?'

A muscle quivered beside the Comte's heavy mouth.

'No, milor'. I am on my way to visit friends. I thought maybe to see M. le Duc on my way.'

'Pray let me be the bearer of any message you may wish to send him, sir,' said Rupert.

'*Cela ne vaut pas la peine, m'sieur,*' said the Comte politely.

No sooner had he taken his leave of them than Rupert scowled upon his host.

'Devil take you, Tony, why did you ask that fellow here? What's he doing in England? 'Pon my soul, it's too bad that I should have to meet him, and be civil!'

'I noticed no civility,' remarked Merivale. 'Was there some quarrel between him and Alastair?'

'Quarrel! He's our worst enemy, my dear! He insulted the name! I give you my word he did! What, don't you know? He hates us like the devil! Tried to horse-whip Justin years ago.'

Enlightenment came to Merivale.

'Of course I remember! Why in the world did he pretend he wanted to meet Alastair?'

'I don't like him,' Jennifer said, troubled. 'His eyes make me shiver. I think he is not a good man.'

'What puzzles me,' said Rupert, 'is why he should be the living spit of Léonie.'

Merivale started up.

'That is it, then! I could not think where I had seen her like! What does it all mean?'

'Oh, but she is not like him!' protested Jennifer. ''Tis but the red hair makes you say so. Léonie has a sweet little face!'

'Red hair *and* dark eyebrows,' said Rupert. 'Damme, I believe there's more in this than we think! It's like Justin to play a deep game, stap me if it isn't!'

Merivale laughed at him. 'What game, rattle-pate?'

'I don't know, Tony. But if you'd lived with Justin for as many years as I have you wouldn't laugh. Justin hasn't forgot the quarrel, I'll swear! He never forgets. There's something afoot, I'll be bound.'

Seventeen

Of a Capture, a Chase, and Confusion

'Oh, PARBLEU!' Léonie said in disgust. 'This Rupert he is always late, the *vaurien!*'

'My dearest love,' Madam Field reproved her. 'That expression! Indeed, it is not becoming in a young lady! I must beg of you —'

'To-day I am not a lady at all,' said Léonie flatly. 'I want Monseigneur to come.'

'My dear, it is hardly proper in you to —'

'Ah, bah!' said Léonie, and walked away.

She went to her own apartment, and sat disconsolately down at the window.

'It is two weeks since Monseigneur wrote,' she reflected. 'And then he said, I come soon now. *Voyons*, this is no way to keep that promise! And Rupert is late again.' A sparkle came into her eyes. She jumped up. 'I will have a game with Rupert,' she said.

With this intention she pulled her boy's raiment out of the cupboard, and struggled out of her skirts. Her hair had grown, but it was not yet long enough to be confined in the nape of her neck by a riband. It clustered about her head still in a myriad of soft curls. She brushed it back from her forehead, dressed herself in shirt and breeches and coat, and catching up her tricorne, swaggered downstairs. Luckily Madam Field was nowhere to be seen, so she escaped without let or hindrance into the garden. It was the first time she had ventured out of doors in her boy's gear, and since it was an illicit pleasure her eyes twinkled naughtily. Rupert, with all his laxity, had in him a quaint streak of prudery, as she knew.

He would of a certainty be shocked to see her parading the grounds thus clad, and as this was precisely what she wanted she set out in the hope of meeting him, making for the woods that ran down towards the road.

Half-way across the big meadow that separated her from the woodland she espied Rupert coming from the stables, carrying his hat under his arm, and whistling jauntily. Léonie cupped her hands about her mouth.

'*Ohé*, Rupert!' she called gleefully.

Rupert saw her, stood still for a moment, and then came striding towards her.

'Fiend seize it, what will you be at next?' he shouted. ''Pon my soul, it's scandalous, stap me if it's not! Home with you, you hoyden!'

'I shall not, Milor' Rupert!' she cried tauntingly, and danced away. 'You cannot make me!'

'Can I not, then?' called Rupert and, dropping his hat, broke into a run.

Léonie straightway dived into the wood, and fled as for her life, for she knew very well that if he caught her Rupert would have no hesitation in picking her up and carrying her back to the house.

'Wait till I catch you!' threatened Rupert, crashing through the undergrowth. 'Damme, I've torn my ruffle, and the lace cost me fifteen guineas! Plague take it, where are you!'

Léonie sent a mocking cry echoing through the wood, and ran on, listening to Rupert's blundering progress behind her. She led him in and out of the trees, through bushes, round in circles, and over the stream, always keeping just out of sight, until she found herself coming out into the road. She would have turned, and doubled back, had she not chanced to see a light travelling coach standing nearby. She was surprised, and tiptoed to peep at it over a low thorn-bush. In the distance she heard Rupert's voice, half-exasperated, half-laughing. She threw back her head to call to him, and as she did so, saw to her amazement the Comte de Saint-Vire, walking quickly up on one of the paths that led through the wood. He was frowning, and his heavy mouth pouted. He looked up, and as his glance fell upon her the frown went from his face, and he came hurrying towards her.

'I give you good morrow, Léon the Page,' he said, and the words bit. 'I had hardly hoped that I should find you thus soon. The luck is with me this round, I think.'

Léonie retreated a little. Avon's warning was in her mind.

'*Bonjour, m'sieur*,' she said, and wondered what he was doing in the Duke's grounds, or why he was in England at all. 'Did you go to see Monseigneur?' she asked, with wrinkled brow. 'He is not here.'

'I am desolated,' said Saint-Vire sarcastically, and came right up to her. She shrank, and in a fit of inexplicable panic, called to Rupert.

'Rupert, Rupert, *à moi!*'

Even as she cried Saint-Vire's hand was over her mouth and his other arm about her waist. Struggling madly, she was swept from the ground and borne at a run to where the coach stood waiting. Without compunction she bit deeply into the hand over her mouth. There was a muttered oath, the hand flinched a little, and she jerked her head away to shriek again.

'Rupert, Rupert, *on m'enporte! À moi, à moi, à moi!*'

His voice came to her, nearer at hand.

'Who – what – ? What the devil – ?'

She was flung then into the coach, sprang up like a small fury, but was thrust roughly back again. She heard Saint-Vire give an order to the coachman; then he jumped in beside her, and the coach lurched forward.

Rupert came plunging out into the road, hot and dishevelled, just in time to see the coach disappear round the bend in the road, in the direction of the village.

He had suspected at first that Léonie was only teasing him, but her second cry had held a note of genuine alarm, while now there was no sign of her. With characteristic impetuosity he went headlong down the road in pursuit of the coach, never stopping to consider the wisdom of returning to the stables for his horse. Full-tilt he went, hatless, with torn ruffles, and wig askew. The coach was out of sight, but he ran on until he was blown. Then he dropped into a walk. When he had got his breath back he ran again, and had a grin for the comic figure he knew he must be cutting. He had no idea who had seized Léonie, or why, but he felt certain that she was in that coach. His fighting spirit was aroused and, incidentally, his love of adventure: he determined to catch the coach if it cost him his life. So, alternately running and walking, he came at last to the straggling village, three miles distant, and seeing the first cottage, broke once more into a weary jog-trot.

The blacksmith was working in his yard, and looked up in astonishment as Rupert's well-known figure approached.

'Hey, there!' Rupert panted. 'A coach – passed this way. Where went – it?'

The smithy rose and touched his forelock. 'Yes, my lord.'

'Devil take you! The coach!'

'Yes, my lord, yes,' said the puzzled smith.

'Did – it – pass here?' demanded Rupert in stentorian tones. Light broke upon the smith.

'Why, yes, your lordship, and stopped at the Arms. 'Tis gone this twenty minutes.'

'Curse it! Whither?'

The smith shook his head.

'Beg pardon, your lordship, but I was not watching.'

'You're a fool,' said Rupert, and plodded on.

The landlord of the Avon Arms was more communicative. He came bustling out to meet his young lordship, and threw up his hands at sight of him.

'My lord! Why, your lordship has lost his hat! Your coat, sir –'

'Never mind my coat,' said Rupert. 'Where went that coach?'

'The French gentleman's coach, sir?'

Rupert had collapsed on to the settle, but he sat bolt upright now.

'French? *French?* So that's it, is it? Oho, M. le Comte! But what the deuce does he want with Léonie?'

The landlord looked at him sympathetically, and waited for him to explain.

'Ale!' said Rupert, sinking back again. 'And a horse, and a pistol.'

The landlord was more perplexed than ever, but he went off to fetch ale in a large tankard. Rupert disposed of it speedily, and drew a deep breath.

'Did the coach stop here?' he demanded. 'Did you see my brother's ward in it?'

'Mistress Léonie, my lord? No, indeed! The French gentleman did not alight. He was in a mighty hurry, sir, seemingly.'

'Scoundrel!' Rupert shook his fist, scowling.

Mr Fletcher retreated a pace.

'Not you, fool,' said Rupert. 'What did the coach stop for?'

'Why, sir, the reckoning was not paid, and the moossoo had left his valise. The servant jumps off the box, comes running in here to settle the reckoning with me, snatches up the valise, and was out of the place before I'd time to fetch my breath. They're queer people, these Frenchies, my lord, for there was me never dreaming the gentleman proposed to leave to-day. Driving hell for leather, they was, too, and as good a team of horses as ever I see.'

'Rot his black soul!' fumed Rupert. 'The devil's in it now, and no mistake. A horse, Fletcher, a horse!'

'Horse, sir?'

'Burn it, would I want a cow? Horse, man, and quickly!'

'But, my lord —'

'Be hanged to your buts! Go find me a horse and a pistol!'

'But, my lord, I've no riding horses here! Farmer Giles hath a cob, but —'

'No horse? Damme, it's disgraceful! Go and fetch the animal the smith's shoeing now! Away with you!'

'But, my lord, that is Mr Manvers's horse, and —'

'Devil take Mr Manvers! Here, I'll go myself! No, stay! A pistol, man.'

The landlord was upset.

'My lord, it's a touch of the sun must have got into your head!'

'Sun at this time of the year?' roared Rupert, thoroughly exasperated. 'Go find me a pistol, sirrah!'

'Yes, my lord, yes!' said Fletcher, and retreated in haste.

Rupert set off down the road to the blacksmith's, and found him whistling to himself as he worked.

'Coggin! Coggin, I say!'

The blacksmith paused.

'Yes, my lord?'

'Hurry with that shoe, my man! I want the horse.'

Coggin stared, open-mouthed.

'But — but 'tis not one of his Grace's horses, sir —'

'Tare an' ouns, would his Grace own such a brute? Do ye take me for a fool?'

'But 'tis Mr Manvers's roan, your lordship!'

'I don't care if 'tis the devil's own chestnut!' cried Rupert. 'I want it, and that's enough! How long before you have that shoe on?'

'Why, sir, twenty minutes, or maybe longer.'

'A guinea for you if you hasten!' Rupert searched in his pockets and produced two crowns. 'And ask it of Fletcher,' he added, stowing the crowns away again. 'Don't sit staring at me, man! Hammer that shoe on, or I'll take the hammer to knock sense into your head withal! Stap me if I won't!'

Thus adjured, the smith set to with a will.

'The groom's walked on to Fawley Farm, my lord,' he ventured presently. 'What will your honour have me say to him when he comes back?'

'Tell him to present Lord Rupert Alastair's compliments to Mr Manvers – who the devil *is* Mr Manvers? – and thank him for the loan of his horse.' Rupert walked round the animal, inspecting its points. 'Horse, is it? Cow-hocked bag of bones! A man's no right to own a scarecrow like this! You hear me, Coggin?'

'Yes, my lord. Certainly, sir!'

'Hurry with that shoe, then, and fetch the animal up to the Arms.' Away went Rupert up the road again to the inn, where he found Fletcher awaiting him with a large pistol.

''Tis loaded, sir,' Fletcher warned him. 'Indeed, my lord, and are you sure your lordship is well?'

'Never mind! Which way did the coach go?'

'Making for Portsmouth, sir, as I judge. But surely to goodness your lordship isn't of a mind to chase it?'

'What else, fool? I want a hat. Produce me one.'

Fletcher resigned himself to the inevitable.

'If your lordship would condescend to take my Sunday beaver –'

'Ay, 'twill suffice. Make out the reckoning and I'll pay – er – when I return. Damn that fellow Coggin! Will he be all night at his work? They've nigh on an hour's start of me already!'

But Coggin came presently, leading the roan. Rupert stowed his pistol away in the saddle holster, tightened the girths, and sprang into the saddle. The smith gave vent to a last appeal.

'My lord, Mr Manvers is a testy gentleman, and indeed –'

'To hell with Mr Manvers, I'm sick of the fellow!' said Rupert, and rode off at a canter.

The borrowed horse was no fiery charger, as Rupert soon discovered. It cherished its own ideas as to a suitable pace to maintain, and managed to do so for the most part, to its own satisfaction and Rupert's disgust. Thus it was close on four in the afternoon when he came at last into Portsmouth, and both he and his mount were very weary.

He rode at once to the quay, and learned that the private schooner anchored there for the past three days had set sail not an hour ago. Rupert dashed Mr Fletcher's hat on the ground.

'Blister me, I'm too late!'

The harbour-master eyed him in polite surprise, and picked up the hat.

'Tell me now,' said Rupert, dismounting. 'Was it a French scoundrel embarking?'

'Ay, sir, 'twas a foreign gentleman with red hair, and his son.'

'Son?' ejaculated Rupert.

'Ay, sir, a sick lad it was. The moossoo said he was suffering from a fever. He carried him on board like one dead, all muffled up in a great cloak. I said to Jim here, "Jim," I said, "it's a shame to take the boy on board, ill as he is, that it is."'

'Drugged, by Gad!' exclaimed Rupert. 'I'll have his blood for this! Taken her to France, has he! Now, what in thunder does he want with her? Hi, you! When does the next packet sail for Le Havre?'

'Why, sir, there's no boat for the likes of you till Wednesday,' said the harbour-master. Rupert's ruffles might be torn, and his coat muddied, but the harbour-master knew a gentleman when he saw one.

Rupert glanced ruefully down his person

'The likes of me, eh? Well, well!' He pointed with his whip to a ramshackle vessel laden with bales of cloth. 'Where is she bound for?'

'For Le Havre, sir, but 'tis only a trading ship, as your honour sees.'

'When does she sail?'

'Tonight, sir. She's lain here two days too long already, waiting for the wind to turn, but she'll be away with the tide soon after six.'

'That's the ship for me,' said Rupert briskly. 'Where's her master?'

The harbour-master was perturbed.

''Tis but a dirty old boat, sir, and never a –'

'Dirty? So am I dirty, damn it!' said Rupert. 'Go find me the master, and tell him I want a passage to France this night.'

So off went the harbour-master, to return anon with a burly individual in homespun, with a great black beard. This gentleman eyed Rupert stolidly and, removing the long clay pipe from his mouth, rumbled forth two words.

'Twenty guineas.'

'What's that?' said Rupert. 'Not a farthing more than ten, you rogue!'

The bearded gentleman spat deliberately into the sea, but vouchsafed no word. A dangerous light came into Rupert's eyes. He tapped the man on the shoulder with his riding-whip.

'Fellow, I am Lord Rupert Alastair. You shall have ten guineas off me and for the rest I'll see you damned.'

The harbour-master pricked up his ears.

'I was hearing, my lord, that his Grace has the *Silver Queen* anchored in Southampton Water.'

'The devil fly away with Justin!' exclaimed Rupert wrathfully. 'He was always wont to have her here!'

'Maybe, sir, if you was to ride to Southampton –'

'Ride to hell! I'd find them painting her, like as not. Come now, fellow, ten guineas!'

The harbour-master took his colleague aside and whispered urgently. Presently he turned, and addressed Rupert.

'I am saying, my lord, as how fifteen guineas is a fair price.'

'Fifteen guineas it is!' said Rupert promptly, thinking of the two crowns in his pocket. 'I shall have to sell the horse.'

'Six o'clock we sets sail, and don't wait for nobbut,' growled the captain, and walked off.

Rupert rode into the town, and by good fortune was able to sell Mr Manvers's roan for the sum of twenty guineas. The sale being accomplished he went to the inn on the quayside, and refreshed himself with a wash, and a bowl of punch. Thus fortified he boarded the sailing vessel, and sat him down on a coil of rope, thoroughly enjoying the adventure, and not a little amused.

''Fore Gad, I never was in such a mad chase!' he remarked to the sky. 'Here's Léonie spirited off by Saint-Vire, the Lord knows why, or where, for that matter – and myself hot on the scent with five crowns in my pocket, and the landlord's hat on my head. And what am I going to do when I find the chit?' He pondered deeply. 'It's a plaguey queer business, so it is,' he decided. 'Justin's at the back of it, I'll be bound. And where the devil is Justin?' Suddenly he flung back his head and laughed. 'Damme, I'd give something to see old cousin Harriet's face when she finds me gone off with Léonie! Hey, hey, here's a pretty coil, to be sure, for, faith, I don't know where I am, and I don't know where Léonie is, nor she where I am, and at Avon they don't where any of us are!'

Eighteen

The Indignation of Mr Manvers

MADAM FIELD WAS WORRIED, FOR IT WAS AFTER SIX IN THE EVE-
ning and neither Léonie nor Rupert had returned. Considerably
flustered at length, Madam sent a messenger to Merivale to inquire
whether the truants were there. Half an hour later the lackey
returned, with Merivale riding beside him. Merivale went swiftly
to the withdrawing-room, and as soon as he entered Madam Field
sprang up.

'Oh, Lord Merivale! Oh, and have you brought the child
home? I have been in such a taking, for I never saw her after
eleven in the morning, or maybe 'twas later, or perhaps a little
earlier – I cannot say for sure. And never a sign of Rupert, so I
thought mayhap they were with you –'

Merivale broke into the flood of words.

'I've not seen either of them since this morning when Rupert
set out to come here,' he said.

Madam's jaw dropped. She let fall her fan, and began to cry.

'Oh dear, oh dear, and Justin telling me to have a care to her!
But how could I tell, for sure 'twas his own brother! Oh, my lord,
can they – can they have eloped?'

Merivale laid his hat and whip on the table.

'Eloped? Nonsense, madam! Impossible!'

'She was ever a wild piece,' wept Madam. 'And Rupert so scatter-brained! Oh, what shall I do, my lord? What shall I do?'

'Pray, madam, dry your tears!' begged Merivale. 'I am convinced there's naught so serious in this as an elopement. For God's sake, madam, calm yourself.'

But Madam, to his dismay, went into a fit of the vapours. My lord turned to the servant.

'Ride back to Merivale, my man, and request my lady to join me here,' he ordered, with an uneasy eye on the prostrate lady. 'And – and send madam's abigail here! Mayhap the children are playing some trick on us,' he muttered to himself. 'Madam, I beg you will not alarm yourself unduly!'

Madam Field's maid came running with salts and presently the lady recovered somewhat, and lay upon the couch calling on heaven to witness that she had done her best. To all Merivale's questions she could only reply that she had had no notion of such wickedness, and what Justin would say she dared not think. Came my Lady Merivale, in her chaise, and was ushered into the withdrawing-room.

'Madam! Why, madam, what is this? Anthony, have they not returned? Fie, they are trying to frighten us! Depend upon it, that is it! Never fret, madam, they'll return soon.' She went to the agitated chaperon, and began to chafe her hands. 'Pray, madam, hush. It's no such great matter, I am sure. Mayhap they have lost their way somewhere, for they are out riding, you may be sure.'

'My dear, Rupert knows every inch of the country,' Merivale said quietly. He turned again to the lackey. 'Be good enough to send to the stables and see whether my lord and Mistress Léonie have taken the horses.'

Ten minutes later the man returned with the news that Lord Rupert's horse was in a loose box, and had been there all day.

Whereupon Madam had a fresh attack of the vapours, and Merivale frowned.

'I don't understand this,' he said. 'If they had eloped –'

'Oh, Anthony, can they have done that?' Jennifer cried aghast. 'Oh no, surely! Why, the child can think of no one but the Duke, and as for Rupert –'

'Listen!' said my lord sharply, and raised his hand.

Outside they heard horses, and the scrunch of wheels on the gravel. Madam started up.

'Heaven be praised, they have come back!'

With one accord Anthony and Jennifer deserted the ailing lady, and hurried into the hall. The great front-door stood open, and into the house stepped his Grace of Avon, elegant in a coat of fine purple velvet, laced with gold, a many-caped greatcoat, over all, worn carelessly open, and polished top-boots on his feet. He paused on the threshold and raised his eyeglass to survey the Merivales.

'Dear me!' he said languidly. 'An unexpected honour. Your ladyship's devoted servant.'

'Oh lord!' said Merivale, for all the world like a rueful boy.

His Grace's lips quivered, but Jennifer blushed fiery red. Merivale went forward.

'You must deem this an unwarranted intrusion, Duke,' he began stiffly.

'Not at all,' bowed his Grace. 'I am charmed.'

Merivale returned the bow.

'I was summoned to Madam Field's assistance,' he said. 'Otherwise I should not be here, believe me.'

Leisurely the Duke divested himself of his greatcoat, and shook out his ruffles.

'But shall we not repair to the withdrawing-room?' he suggested. 'You are saying, I think, that you came to my cousin's assistance?' He led the way to the withdrawing-room, and bowed them in. Madam Field, seeing him, gave a shriek, and fell back upon her cushions.

'Oh, mercy, 'tis Justin!' she cried.

Jennifer went to her. 'Hush, madam! Calm yourself!'

'You appear to be strangely afflicted, cousin,' remarked his Grace.

'Oh Justin — oh cousin! I have no notion! So innocent they seemed! I can scarce believe —'

'Innocent! Of course they were!' snorted Merivale. 'Have done with this elopement foolery! It's mere child's talk!'

'Oh Anthony, do you think so indeed?' said Jennifer thankfully.

'I do not wish to seem importunate,' said the Duke, 'but I should like an explanation. Where, may I ask, is my ward?'

'That,' said Merivale, 'is the very root of the matter.'

The Duke stood very still.

'Indeed!' he said softly. 'Pray continue. Cousin, I must request you to cease your lamentations.'

Madam's noisy sobs abated. She clutched Jennifer's hand and sniffed dolefully.

'I know nothing more than this,' said Merivale. 'She and Rupert have been absent since eleven of the clock this morning.'

'Rupert?' said his Grace.

'I should have told you that Rupert has been staying with us these past three weeks.'

'You amaze me,' said Avon. His eyes were as hard as agates. He turned, and put his snuff-box down on the table. 'The mystery would seem to be solved,' he said evenly.

'Sir!' It was Jennifer who spoke. His Grace looked at her indifferently. 'If you are thinking that — that they have eloped, I am sure — oh, I am sure that 'tis not so! Such a notion was never in either of their heads!'

'So?' Avon looked from one to the other. 'Pray enlighten me!'

Merivale shook his head.

'Faith, I cannot. But I would stake mine honour that there's been no thought of love between them. They are the veriest children, and even now I suspect they may be playing a trick on us. More than that —' He paused.

'Yes?' said Avon.

Jennifer broke in. 'Sir, the child can talk of no one but yourself!' she said impetuously. 'You have all her — her adoration!'

'So I thought,' answered Avon. 'But one may be mistaken. I believe there is a saying that youth will to youth.'

'It's no such thing,' Merivale averred. 'Why, they are for ever quarrelling! Moreover they have taken no horses. Mayhap they are hiding somewhere to frighten us.'

A footman came to them.

'Well?' Avon spoke without turning his head.

'Mr Manvers, your Grace, who desires speech with my Lord Rupert.'

'I have not the pleasure of Mr Manvers's acquaintance,' said the Duke, 'but you may admit him.'

Entered a little wiry gentleman with red cheeks and bright, angry eyes. He glared at the assembled company and, singling out the Duke, rapped forth a question.

'Are you Lord Rupert Alastair, sir?'

'I am not,' said his Grace.

The irate little man rounded on Merivale.

'You, sir?'

'My name is Merivale,' Anthony replied.

'Then where is Lord Rupert Alastair?' demanded Mr Manvers, in a voice of baffled rage.

His Grace took snuff.

'That is what we should all like to know,' he said.

'Damme, sir, do you think to play with me?' fumed Mr Manvers.

'I have never played with anyone,' said the Duke.

'I am come here to find Lord Rupert Alastair! I demand speech with him! I want an explanation of him!'

'My dear sir,' said Avon. 'Pray join our ranks! We all want that.'

'Who the devil are you?' cried the exasperated little man.

'Sir,' bowed his Grace. 'I believe I *am* the devil. So they say.'

Merivale was shaken with silent laughter. Mr Manvers turned to him.

'Is this a mad-house?' he asked. 'Who is he?'

'He is the Duke of Avon,' said Merivale unsteadily.

Mr Manvers pounced on Avon again.

'Ah! Then you are Lord Rupert's brother!' he said vindictively.

'My misfortune, sir, believe me.'

'What I demand to know is this!' said Mr Manvers. '*Where is my roan?*'

'I haven't the least idea,' said his Grace placidly. 'I am not even sure that I know what you are talking about.'

'Faith, I am sure I don't!' chuckled Merivale.

'My roan horse, sir! Where is it? Answer me that!'

'I fear you will have to hold me excused,' said the Duke. 'I know nothing about your horse. In fact, I am not, at the moment, interested in your horse – roan or otherwise.'

Mr Manvers raised his fists heavenwards.

'Interested in it!' he spluttered. 'My horse has been stolen!'

'You have all my sympathy,' yawned his Grace. 'But I fail to see what concern it is of mine.'

Mr Manvers thumped the table.

'Stolen, sir, by your brother, Lord Rupert Alastair, this very day!'

His words brought about a sudden silence.

'Continue!' requested his Grace. 'You interest us now exceedingly. Where, when, how, and why did Lord Rupert steal your horse?'

'He stole it in the village, sir, this morning! And I may say, sir, that I consider it a gross impertinence! A piece of insolence that infuriates me! I am a calm man, sir, but when I receive such a message from a man of birth, of title –'

'Oh, he left a message, did he?' interposed Merivale.

'With the blacksmith, sir! My groom rode over on the roan to the village, and the horse casting a shoe, he took him to the smith, very properly! While Coggin was shoeing the animal my fellow walked on to Fawley to execute my commands.' He breathed heavily. 'When he returned, the horse was gone! The smith – damn him for a fool! – tells me that Lord Rupert insisted on taking the horse – *my* horse, sir! – and left his compliments for me, and his – his *thanks* for the loan of my horse!'

'Very proper,' said his Grace.

'Damme, sir, it's monstrous!'

A gurgling laugh came from Jennifer.

'Oh, was there ever such a boy?' she cried. 'What in the world should he want with your horse, sir?'

Mr Manvers scowled at her.

'Exactly, madam! Exactly! What did he want with my horse? The man's mad, and should be clapped up! Coggin tells me he came running into the village like one demented, with no hat on his head! And not one of those gaping fools had the sense to stop him from seizing my horse! A set of idiots, sir!'

'I can well believe it,' said Avon. 'But I do not yet see how your information can help us.'

Mr Manvers fought with himself.

'Sir, I am not come here to help you!' he raged. 'I have come to demand my horse!'

'I would give it you had I it in my possession,' said his Grace kindly. 'Unfortunately Lord Rupert has your horse.'

'Then I want its recovery!'

'Do not distress yourself!' Avon advised him. 'No doubt he will return it. What I wish to know is, why did Lord Rupert want your horse, and where did he go?'

'If that dolt of a landlord is to be believed,' said Mr Manvers, 'he has gone to Portsmouth.'

'Fleeing the country, evidently,' murmured his Grace. 'Was there a lady with Lord Rupert?'

'No, there was not! Lord Rupert went off at a disgraceful pace in pursuit of a coach, or some such nonsense.'

The Duke's eyes widened.

'Almost I begin to see daylight,' he said. 'Proceed.'

Merivale shook his head.

'I'm all at sea,' he confessed. 'The mystery grows.'

'On the contrary,' his Grace replied gently. 'The mystery is very nearly solved.'

'I don't understand you – any of you!' exploded Mr Manvers.

'That was not to be expected,' said Avon. 'Lord Rupert, you say, went to Portsmouth in pursuit of a coach. Who was in that coach?'

'Some damned Frenchman, Fletcher said.'

Merivale started; so also did Jennifer.

'Frenchman?' Merivale echoed. 'But what did Rupert –'

His Grace was smiling grimly.

'The mystery,' he said, 'is solved. Lord Rupert, Mr Manvers, borrowed your horse to go in pursuit of M. le Comte de Saint-Vire.'

Merivale gasped. 'You knew he was here, then?'

'I did not.'

'Then how a' God's name – ?'

Again the Duke took snuff.

'Shall we say – intuition, my dear Anthony?'

'But – but why did Rupert pursue Saint-Vire? And – and what was Saint-Vire doing on the road to Portsmouth? He told me he was journeying north to visit a friend! This goes beyond me!'

'What I want to know,' Jennifer said, 'is, where is Léonie?'

'Ay, that's the question,' nodded Merivale.

'Your pardon, sir,' interjected Mr Manvers, 'but the question is, where is my horse?'

They turned to the Duke for enlightenment.

'Léonie,' said the Duke, 'is by now on the way to France, in company with the Comte de Saint-Vire. Rupert, I imagine, is also on his way to France, for I do not suppose he was in time to intercept them. Mr Manvers' horse is in all probability at Portsmouth. Unless, of course, Rupert has taken it to France with him.'

Mr Manvers collapsed into the nearest chair.

'Taken – taken my horse to France, sir? Oh, it's monstrous! It's monstrous!'

'For God's sake, Avon, be more explicit!' begged Merivale. 'Why has Saint-Vire run off with Léonie? He had not even seen her!'

'On the contrary,' said Avon, 'he has seen her many times.'

Jennifer rose to her feet.

'Oh, sir, he will not harm her?'

'No, he will not harm her, my lady,' Avon replied, and there was a glint in his eyes. 'You see, there will be no time for that. He has Rupert hard on his heels – and me.'

'You'll go?'

'Of course I shall go. Follow my example, and place your trust in Rupert. It seems I shall live to be grateful to him yet.'

'Alastair, what in God's name does all this mean?' demanded Merivale. 'Rupert himself swore there was a mystery as soon as he saw Léonie's likeness to Saint-Vire.'

'So Rupert saw that? I appear to have underrated Rupert's intelligence. I believe I can satisfy your curiosity. Come with me into the library, my dear Merivale.'

Past enmity was forgotten. Anthony went to the door. Mr Manvers sprang up.

'But all this doesn't help me to my horse!' he said bitterly.

With his hand on the door Avon paused, and looked back.

'My good sir,' he said haughtily, 'I am weary of your horse. It has served its turn, and shall be restored to you.' He went out with Merivale, and shut the door behind him. 'So. One moment, Anthony. Johnson!'

The butler came forward. 'Your Grace?'

'Bid them harness Thunderbolt and Blue Peter to the curricle at once, place my large valise in it, and tell one of the women to pack some clothes for Mistress Léonie. Within half an hour, Johnson.'

'Very good, your Grace,' bowed the old man.

'And now, Merivale, this way.'

'By Gad, you're a cool devil!' exclaimed Merivale, and followed him to the library.

His Grace went to his desk and extracted from it a brace of gold-mounted pistols.

'Briefly, Anthony, the matter is this: Léonie is Saint-Vire's daughter.'

'I never knew he had a daughter!'

'No one knew. You thought he had a son, perhaps?'

'Yes. Well, naturally! I've seen the boy many times.'

'He is no more Saint-Vire's son than you are,' said his Grace, snapping the breech of one of his pistols. 'His name is Bonnard.'

'Good God, Alastair, do you mean to tell me that Saint-Vire had the audacity to exchange the children? Because of Armand?'

'I am delighted to find that you understand the situation so well,' said the Duke. 'I beg you will let it go no further, for the time is not yet.'

'Very well, but what a piece of villainy! Does he know that you know?'

'I had best tell you the whole story,' sighed Avon.

When they at length emerged from the library Merivale's face was a study of mingled emotions, and he appeared to be speechless. Jennifer met them in the hall.

'You are going, sir? You – you will bring her back?'

'That I cannot say,' Avon replied. 'She will be safe with me, my lady.'

Her eyes fell.

'Yes, sir, I feel that that is so.'

His Grace looked at her.

'You surprise me,' he said.

She put her hand out, hesitating.

'She has told me so much. I cannot but be sure of your – kindness.' She paused. 'Sir, what – what lies between you and me is past, and should be forgotten.'

His Grace bowed over her hand; his lips were smiling.

'Jenny, if I said that I had forgotten you would be offended.'

'No,' she answered, and a laugh trembled in her voice. 'I should be glad.'

'My dear, I desire nothing better than to please you.'

'I think,' she said, 'that there is one now who holds a greater place in your heart than ever I held.'

'You err, Jenny. I have no heart,' he replied.

A silence fell. It was broken by a lackey.

'Your Grace, the curricle waits.'

'How will you cross?' Merivale asked.

'In the *Silver Queen*. She lies in Southampton Water. Unless Rupert has already commandeered her. If that should chance to be so, I suppose I must hire a vessel.'

Mr Manvers came up.

'Sir, I will not stay with that woman who has the vapours,' he said. 'It is very well for you to say you are weary of my horse, but I want its instant recovery!'

The Duke had donned his great-cloak, and now he picked up his hat and gloves.

'My Lord Merivale will be charmed to assist you,' he said, with the glimmering of a smile. He bowed low to them all, and was gone.

Nineteen

Lord Rupert Wins the Second Trick

Léonie awoke, sighing. Nausea threatened to overwhelm her, and for a few minutes she lay with closed eyes, in semi-consciousness. By degrees she shook off the effects of the drug, and struggled up, a hand to her head. She looked about her in bewilderment, and found that she was on a couch in a strange apartment, alone. Bit by bit memory came, and she got up, and went to the window.

'*Tiens!*' she said, looking out. 'Where am I now? I do not know this place. It is the sea.' She stared at the harbour in bewilderment. 'That man gave me an evil drink, I remember. And I went to sleep, I suppose. Where is this wicked Comte? I think that I bit him very hard, and I know that I kicked him. And then we came to that inn – where was it? – miles and miles from Avon – and he brought me coffee.' She chuckled. 'And I threw it at him. *How* he did swear! Then he brought more coffee, and he made me drink it. Faugh! Coffee, he called it? Pig-wash! What then? *Peste*, I do not know anything more!' She turned to look at the clock on the mantelpiece, and frowned. '*Mon Dieu*, what is this?' She went to the clock, and regarded it fixedly. '*Sotte!*' she addressed it. 'How can you be noon? It was noon when he made me drink that evil pig-wash. *Tu ne marches pas.*'

The steady ticking gave her the lie. She put her head on one side. '*Comment? Voyons*, I do not understand this at all. Unless' – her eyes widened – 'am I in tomorrow?' she wondered. 'I *am* in tomorrow! That man made me go to sleep, and I have slept all day and night! *Sacré bleu*, but I am angry with that man! I am glad that I bit him. Doubtless he means to kill me, but why? Perhaps Rupert will come and save me, but I think that I will save myself, and not wait for Rupert, for I do *not* want to be killed by this Comte.' She considered. 'No, mayhap he does not want to kill me. But if he does not – *Grand Dieu*, can it be that he elopes with me? No, that is not possible, because he believes I am a boy. And I do not think that he can love me very much.' Her eyes twinkled impishly. 'Now I will go,' she said.

But the door was fast, and the windows too small to allow her to escape through them. The twinkle died, and the small mouth set mutinously.

'*Parbleu, mais c'est infame!* He locks me in, *enfin*! Oh, I am *very* angry!' She laid her finger on her lips. 'If I had a dagger I would kill him, but I have no dagger, *tant pis*. What then?' She paused. 'I am a little frightened, I think,' she confessed. 'I must escape from this wicked person. It will be better, perhaps, if I am still asleep.'

Footsteps sounded. Quick as thought Léonie returned to her couch, covered herself with her cloak, and lay down, with closed eyes. A key grated in the lock, and someone entered. Léonie heard Saint-Vire's voice.

'Bring *déjeuner* here, Victor, and do not let any enter. The child still sleeps.'

'*Bien, m'sieur.*'

'Now, who is Victor?' wondered Léonie. 'It is the servant, I suppose. *Dieu me sauve!*'

The Comte came to her side, and bent over her, listening to her breathing. Léonie tried to still the uncomfortably hard beating of her heart. Evidently the Comte noticed nothing unusual, for he moved away again. Presently Léonie heard the chink of crockery.

'It is very hard that I must listen to this pig-person eating, when I am so hungry,' she reflected. 'Oh, but I will make him very sorry!'

'When will m'sieur have the horses put to?' inquired Victor.

'Oho!' thought Léonie. 'We travel further, then!'

'There is no need for haste now,' Saint-Vire answered. 'That young fool, Alastair, would not follow us to France. We will start at two.'

Léonie's eyes nearly flew open. She restrained herself with an effort.

'*Le misérable!*' she thought savagely. 'Am I in Calais? No, for this is of a certainty not Calais. Perhaps I am at Le Havre. I do not immediately see what I am to do, but certainly I will go on being asleep. We went to Portsmouth, then. I think that Rupert *will* come, if he saw the way we went, but I must not wait for him. I would like to bite that man again. *Diable*, I am in great danger, it seems! I have a very cold feeling in my inside, and I wish that Monseigneur would come. That is foolishness, of course. He does not know that anything has happened to me. Ah, bah! Now this pig-person eats, while I starve! Certainly I will make him sorry.'

'The lad sleeps overlong, m'sieur,' Victor said. 'He should wake soon now.'

'I do not expect it,' Saint-Vire replied. 'He is young, and I gave him a strong dose. There is no cause for alarm, and it suits my purpose better if he sleeps for a while yet.'

'*Sans doute!*' thought Léonie. 'So that was it! He drugged me! He is of a wickedness! I must breathe more heavily.'

Time went lagging by, but at length there came some commotion without, and Victor entered the room again.

'The coach awaits, m'sieur. Shall I take the boy?'

'I will. You have paid the reckoning?'

'Yes, m'sieur.'

Saint-Vire went to Léonie and lifted her. She was limp in his hold.

'I must let my head fall back, so! And my mouth open a little, thus! *Voyons*, I am being very clever! But I do not in the least know what comes to me. This man is a fool.'

She was carried out, and put into the coach, and propped up with cushions.

'You will make for Rouen,' Saint-Vire said, '*En avant!*'

The door was shut, Saint-Vire settled himself beside Léonie, and the coach rolled forward.

Léonie set her wits to work.

'This becomes more and more difficult. I do not see that I can do anything but continue to sleep while this man sits beside me. Presently we shall stop to change horses, for these are not good, I think. Perhaps this pig-person will get out then. If he thinks I am asleep he will do that, for he will want to eat again. But *still* I do not see how I am to escape. I will say a prayer to the *Bon Dieu* to show me a way.'

Meanwhile the coach travelled on at a fair rate, and the Comte took a book from his pocket and began to read it, glancing occasionally at the inert figure beside him. Once he felt Léonie's pulse, and seemed to be satisfied, for he sank back into his corner and resumed his reading.

They must have been over an hour on the road when it happened. There was a terrific bump, a lurch, shouts, and the stamping of frightened horses, and the coach toppled slowly into the ditch, so that the door by Léonie was only a yard from the hedge. She was flung violently against the side of the coach, with Saint-Vire atop of her, and it was only by a supreme effort of will that she refrained from throwing out a hand to save herself.

Saint-Vire struggled up, and wrenched at the off-side door, calling to know what was the matter. Victor's voice answered.

'The near back wheel, m'sieur! We have one of the horses down, and a trace broken!'

Saint-Vire swore roundly, and hesitated, glancing at his captive. Once more he bent over her, listening to her breathing, and then jumped down into the road, shutting the door behind him. Léonie heard him join in the mêlée without, and scrambled up. Cautiously she opened the door that leaned drunkenly to the hedge, and slipped out, crouching low. The men were at the horses' heads, and Saint-Vire was hidden from her sight by one of the plunging leaders. Bent almost double she fled down the road, keeping to the ditch, and, coming presently upon a gap in the high hedge, pushed her way through it into the field beyond. She was hidden now from the road, but she knew that at any moment Saint-Vire might discover her escape, and she ran on, dizzy and trembling, back along the way they had come, looking wildly round for some hiding-place. The field stretched away on either side; the bend in the road was some hundred yards further on, and there was no sign of human habitation, or friendly woodland.

Then in the distance she heard the sound of a horse's hoofs on the hard road, galloping from the direction of Le Havre. She peeped through the hedge, wondering whether she dared call upon this furious rider to stop and assist her. The horse came round the bend. She saw a familiar blue coat, muddied over, a torn ruffle, and a dark handsome young face, flushed and excited.

She tore her way through the hedge, flew out into the road, and waved her hands.

'*Rupert, Rupert, j'y suis!*' she shrieked.

Rupert pulled up, wrenching his horse back upon its haunches, and let out a whoop of triumph.

'Quick! Oh, quick!' Léonie panted, and ran to his stirrup.

He hoisted her up before him.

'Where is he? Where's that black scoundrel?' he demanded. 'How did you —'

'Turn, turn!' she commanded. 'He is there, with that coach, and there are three others! Oh, quickly, Rupert!' She pulled the horse round, but Rupert held it in still.

'No, damme, I'll have his blood, Léonie. I've sworn —'

'Rupert, there are three with him, and you have no sword! Now he has seen! *Nom de Dieu, en avant!*'

He looked over his shoulder, undecided. Léonie saw Saint-Vire snatch a pistol from his pocket, and drove her heels into the horse's flanks with all her might. The animal leaped forward; something sang past Léonie's cheek, scorching it; there was a terrific oath from Rupert, and the horse bolted with them down the road. A second explosion came, and Léonie felt Rupert lurch in the saddle, and heard the quick intake of his breath.

'*Touché*, b'gad!' he gasped. 'On with you, you madcap!'

'*Laisse moi, laisse moi!*' she cried, and snatched the bridle from him, urging the frightened horse round the bend. 'Hold to me, Rupert, it is well now.'

Rupert could still laugh.

'Well, is it? Gad — what a — chase! Steady, steady! There's — lane — further down — turn into it — never reach — Le Havre.'

She twisted the bridle round her little hands, and pulled gallantly.

'He will mount one of those horses,' she said, thinking quickly. 'And he will ride to Le Havre. Yes, yes, we will turn down the lane; Rupert, *mon pauvre*, are you badly hurt?'

'Right shoulder — 'tis naught. There — should be   village. There's the lane! Steady him, steady him! Good girl! Hey, what an adventure!'

They swept into the lane, saw cottages ahead, and a farm. Of impulse Léonie pulled up her mount, turned aside to the hedge, and made the horse push through into the fields. Then on she drove him, cross-country, at a canter.

Rupert was swaying in the saddle.

'What – will you be at?' he said hoarsely.

'*Laisse moi!*' she repeated. 'That is too near the road. He would be sure to look for us. I go further.'

'Damme, let him look for us! I'll put a bullet through his black heart, so I will!'

Léonie paid no heed, but rode on with a wary eye on the lookout for shelter. Rupert, she knew, was losing blood fast, and could not long endure. To the right, in the distance, she saw a church spire, and made for it, a cold fear in her heart.

'Have courage, Rupert! Hold to me, and it will be very well!'

'Ay, I'm well enough,' said Rupert faintly. 'Courage be damned! It's not I who'd run away! Burn it, I can't get my hand to the hole he's made in me! Gently, gently, and 'ware rabbit-holes!'

A mile further the village was reached, a little peaceful haven, with its church sitting placidly by. Men working on the fields stared in amazement at the fleeing couple, but they rode on into the cobbled street, and up it till they came upon a tiny inn, with a swinging board over the door, and stables lying tumbledown about the yard.

Léonie reined in, and the horse stood quivering. An ostler gaped at them, mop in hand.

'You there!' Léonie called imperiously. 'Come and help m'sieur to the ground! Quickly, great fool! He is wounded by – by highwaymen!'

The man looked fearfully down the road, but seeing no dread footpad, came to do Léonie's bidding. Then the landlord bustled out to see what was toward, an enormous man with a scratch wig on his head, and a twinkle in his eye. Léonie held out her hand to him.

'Ah, *la bonne chance!*' she cried. 'Aid, m'sieur, I beg of you! We were travelling to Paris, and were set upon by a party of footpads.'

'Tare an' ouns!' said Rupert. 'Do you think I'd run from a parcel of greasy footpads? Think of another tale, for the love of God!'

The landlord slipped an arm about his lordship, and lifted him down. Léonie slid to the ground, and stood trembling.

'*Mon Dieu*, what an escape!' said the landlord. 'These footpads! You, Hector! Take m'sieur's legs, and help me bear him to a guest-chamber.'

'Devil take you, leave my legs alone!' swore Rupert. 'I can – I can walk!'

But the landlord, a practical man, saw that he was almost fainting, and bore him without more ado up the stairs to a little chamber under the eaves. He and the ostler laid his lordship on the bed, and Léonie fell on her knees beside him.

'Oh, but he is wounded to death!' she cried. 'Help me with his coat!'

Rupert opened his eyes.

'Fiddle!' he said, and sank into unconsciousness.

'Ah, an Englishman!' cried the landlord, struggling with his lordship's tight-fitting coat.

'An English milor',' nodded Léonie. 'I am his page.'

'*Tiens!* One would know it was a great gentleman. Ah, the fine coat so spoiled! The shirt we must tear.' He proceeded to do so, and turning my lord to his side, laid bare the wound. 'It needs a surgeon, *bien sûr*. Hector shall ride to Le Havre. These highwaymen!'

Léonie was busy staunching the blood.

'Yes, a surgeon!' she started. 'Ah, but Le Havre! He will be – they will pursue us there!' She turned to the landlord. 'Hector must know naught of us if he is questioned!'

The landlord was bewildered.

'No, no, they would not dare! The highwaymen keep to the open country, my child.'

'It – they were not – highwaymen,' Léonie confessed, blushing. 'And I am not really Lord Rupert's page.'

'*Hein?* What is this?' demanded the landlord.

'I – I am a girl,' said Léonie. 'I am the ward of the English Duc of Avon, and – and Lord Rupert is his brother!'

The landlord stared from one to the other, and a mighty frown came.

'Ah, I see well! It is an elopement! Now I will tell you, mademoiselle, that I do not –'

'But no!' Léonie said. 'It is that the – the man who pursues us stole me from the house of Monseigneur le Duc, and he drugged me, and brought me to France, and I think he would have killed me. But Milor' Rupert came swiftly, and our coach lost a wheel, and I slipped out, and ran and ran and ran! Then milor' came, and the man who stole me fired at him, and – and that is all!'

The landlord was incredulous.

'*Voyons*, what tale is this you tell me?'

'It is quite true,' sighed Léonie, 'and when Monseigneur comes you will see that it is as I say. Oh please, you must help us!'

The landlord was not proof against those big, beseeching eyes.

'Well, well!' he said. 'You are safe here, and Hector is discreet.'

'And you won't let – that man – take us?'

The landlord blew out his cheeks.

'I am master here,' he said. 'And I say that you are safe. Hector shall ride to Le Havre for a surgeon, but as for this talk of Ducs!' He shook his head indulgently, and sent a wide-eyed serving maid to fetch Madame and some linen.

Madame came swiftly, a woman as large about as her husband, but comely withal. Madame cast one glance at Lord Rupert, and issued sharp orders, and began to rend linen. Madame would listen to nobody until she had tightly bound my Lord Rupert.

'*Hé, le beau!*' she said. 'What wickedness! That goes better now.' She laid a plump finger to her lips, and stood billowing, her other hand on her hip. 'He must be undressed,' she decided. 'Jean, you will find a nightshirt.'

'Marthe,' interposed her husband. 'This boy is a lady!'

'*Quel horreur!*' remarked Madame placidly. 'Yes, it is best that we undress him, *le pauvre!*' She turned, and drove the peeping maid out, and Léonie with her, and shut the door on them.

Léonie wandered down the stairs and went out into the yard. Hector was already gone on his way to Le Havre; there was no one in sight, so Léonie sank wearily on a bench hard by the kitchen window, and burst into tears.

'Ah, bah!' she apostrophised herself fiercely. '*Bête! Imbécile! Lâche!*'

But the tears continued to flow. It was a damp, drooping little figure that met Madame's eye when she came sailing out into the yard.

Madame, having heard the strange story from her husband, was properly shocked and wrathful. She stood with arms akimbo, and began severely:

'This is a great wickedness, mademoiselle! I would have you know that we –' She broke off, and went forward. 'But no, but no, *ma petite!* There is nothing to cry about. *Tais-toi, mon chou!* All will go well, trust Maman Marthe!' She enfolded Léonie in a large embrace, and in a few minutes a husky voice said, muffled:

'I am *not* crying!'

Madame shook with fat chuckles.

'I am *not!*' Léonie sat up. 'But oh, I think I am very miserable, and I wish Monseigneur were here, for that man will surely find us, and Rupert is like one dead!'

'It is true then that there is a Duc?' Madame asked.

'Of course it is true!' said Léonie indignantly. 'I do not tell lies!'

'An English Duc, *alors*? Ah, but they are of a wildness, these English! But thou – thou art French, little cabbage!'

'Yes,' said Léonie. 'I am so tired I cannot tell you all now.'

'It is I who am a fool!' Madame cried. 'Thou shalt to bed, *mon ange*, with some hot *bouillon*, and the wing of a fowl. That goes well, *hein?*'

'Yes, please,' Léonie answered. 'But there is Milor' Rupert, and I fear that he will die!'

'Little foolish one!' Madame scolded. 'I tell thee – *moi qui te parle* – that it is well with him. It is naught. A little blood lost; much weakness – and that is all. It is thou who art nigh dead with fatigue. Now thou shalt come with me.'

So Léonie, worn out with the terrors and exertions of the past two days, was tucked up between cool sheets, fed, crooned over, and presently left alone to sleep.

When she awoke the morning sun streamed in at the window, and sounds of bustle came from the street below. Madame was smiling at her from the doorway.

She sat up and rubbed her eyes.

'Why – why, it is morning!' she said. 'Have I slept so long?'

'Nine of the clock, little sluggard. It is better now?'

'Oh, I am very well to-day!' Léonie said, and threw back the blankets. 'But Rupert – the doctor – ?'

'*Doucement, doucement*, said I not that it was naught? The doctor came when thou were asleep, my cabbage, and in a little minute the bullet was out, and no harm done, by the grace of the good God. Milor' lies on his pillows, and calls for food, and for thee.' Madame chuckled. 'And when I bring him good broth he snatches the wig from his head, and demands red beef, as they have it in England. *Dépêches toi, mon enfant.*'

Twenty minutes later Léonie went dancing into Rupert's chamber, and found that wounded hero propped up by pillows, rather pale, but otherwise himself. He was disgustedly spooning Madame's broth, but his face brightened at the sight of Léonie.

'Hey, you madcap! Where in thunder are we now?'

Léonie shook her head.

'That I do not know,' she confessed. 'But these people are kind, *n'est-ce pas?*'

'Deuced kind,' Rupert agreed, then scowled. 'That fat woman won't bring me food, and I'm devilish hungry. I could eat an ox, and this is what she gives me!'

'Eat it!' Léonie commanded. 'It is very good, and an ox is not good at all. Oh, Rupert, I feared you were dead!'

'Devil a bit!' said Rupert cheerfully. 'But I'm as weak as a rat, confound it. Stap me if I know what we're at, the pair of us! What happened to you? And why by all that's queer did Saint-Vire run off with you?'

'I do not know. He gave me an evil drug, and I slept for hours and hours. He is a pig-person. I hate him. I am glad that I bit him, and threw the coffee over him.'

'Did you, b'gad? Blister me if I ever met such a lass! I'll have Saint-Vire's blood for this, see if I don't!' He wagged his head solemnly, and applied himself to the broth. 'Here am I chasing you to God knows where, with never a sou in my pocket, nor a sword at my side, and the landlord's hat on my head! And what they'll be thinking at home the Lord knows! I don't!'

Léonie curled herself up on the bed, and was requested not to sit on his lordship's feet. She shifted her position a little, and related her adventures. That done, she demanded to know what had befallen Rupert.

'Blessed if I know!' said Rupert. 'I went haring after you as far as the village, and learned the way you went. So I got me a horse, and set off for Portsmouth. But the luck was against me, so it was! You'd set sail an hour since, and the only boat leaving the harbour was a greasy old tub – well, well! What did I do then? 'Pon my soul I almost forget! No, I have it! I went off to sell the horse. Twenty meagrely guineas was all he fetched, but a worse –'

'Sold one of Monseigneur's horses?' exclaimed Léonie.

'No, no, 'twas a brute I got at the blacksmith's, owned by – burn it, what's the fellow's name – Manvers!'

'Oh, I see!' said Léonie, relieved. 'Go on. You did very well, Rupert!'

'Not so bad, was it?' said Rupert modestly. 'Well, I bought a passage on the old tub, and we got in at Le Havre at one, or thereabouts.'

'We did not leave Le Havre until two! He thought you would not follow, and he said that he was safe enough now!'

'Safe, eh? I'll show him!' Rupert shook his fist. 'Where was I?'

'At Le Havre,' Léonie prompted.

'Oh, ay, that's it! Well, by the time I'd paid this fee and that my guineas were all gone, so off I went to sell my diamond pin.'

'Oh! It was such a pretty pin!'

'Never mind that. The trouble I had to get rid of the damned thing you'd scarce believe. 'Pon my soul, I believe they thought I'd stolen it!'

'But did you sell it?'

'Ay, for less than half its worth, rot it! Then I skipped off to the inn to inquire of you, and to get me something to eat. Thunder and turf, but I was hungry!'

'So was I!' sighed Léonie. 'And that pig-person ate and ate!'

'You put me out,' said Rupert severely. 'Where was I? Oh yes! Well, the landlord told me that Saint-Vire was gone off by coach to Rouen at two o'clock, so the next thing I had to do was to hire a horse to be after you again. That's all there is to it, and devilish good sport it was! But where we are now, or what we're to do, beats me!'

'The Comte will come, do you not think?' Léonie asked anxiously.

'I don't know. He can't very well snatch you when I'm here.
I wish I knew what the plague he wants with you. Y'know, this
is mighty difficult, for we haven't either of us a notion what the
game is we're playing.' He frowned, thinking. 'Of course, Saint-
Vire may come to steal you again. He'll have ridden back to Le
Havre first, depend on't, and when he finds we've not been there
he may scour the countryside, for he knows he hit me and it's
likely we'd be hiding somewhere near.'

'What are we to do?' asked Léonie, with pale cheeks.

'What, not afraid, are you? Damn it, he can't walk off with you
under my very nose!'

'Oh, he can, Rupert, he can! You are so weak you cannot
help me!'

Rupert made an effort to hoist himself up, and failed dismally.
He lay fuming.

'Well, damme, I can fire!'

'But we have no gun!' objected Léonie. 'At any moment he
may come, and these people will never be able to keep him out.'

'Pistol, child, pistol! Lord, what will you say next? Of course we
have one! D'ye take me for a fool? Feel in the pockets of my coat.'

Léonie jumped down from the bed, and dragged my lord's coat
from the chair. She produced Mr Fletcher's unwieldy pistol from
one of its pockets, and brandished it gleefully.

'Rupert, you are very clever! Now we can kill that pig-person!'

'Hi, put it down!' commanded Rupert in some alarm. 'You
know naught of pistols, and we'll have an accident if you fiddle
with it! The thing's loaded and cocked!'

'I do know about pistols!' said Léonie indignantly. 'You point
it, so! And pull this thing.'

'For God's sake, put it down!' cried Rupert. 'You're levelling
the damned thing at me, silly chit! Put it on the table beside me,
and find my purse. It's in my breeches pocket.'

Léonie laid the pistol down reluctantly, and rummaged anew for the purse.

'How much have we?' Rupert asked.

Léonie emptied the guineas on to the bed. Three rolled on to the floor, and one dropped into Rupert's broth with a splash.

''Pon my soul, you are a careless minx!' said Rupert, fishing for the coin in his bowl. 'There's another gone now, under the bed!'

Léonie dived after the errant guineas, retrieved them, and sat down on the bed to count them.

'One, two, four, six, and a louis – oh, and another guinea, and three sous, and –'

'That's not the way! Here, give 'em to me! There's another gone under the bed, burn it!'

Léonie was grovelling under the bed in search of the coin when they heard the clatter of wheels outside.

'What's that?' said Rupert sharply. 'Quick! To the window!'

Léonie extricated herself with difficulty, and ran to the window.

'Rupert, 'tis he! *Mon Dieu, mon Dieu*, what are we to do?'

'Can you see him?' Rupert demanded.

'No, but there is a coach, and the horses are steaming! Oh listen, Rupert!'

Voices were heard below, expostulating. Evidently Madame was guarding the staircase.

'Saint-Vire, I'll bet a monkey!' said Rupert. 'Where's that pistol? Plague take this broth!' He threw the bowl and the rest of its contents on to the floor, settled his wig straight, and reached out a hand for the pistol, a very grim look on his drawn young face.

Léonie darted forward and seized the weapon.

'You are not enough strong!' she said urgently. 'See, you have exhausted yourself already! Leave me! I will shoot him dead!'

'Here, no, I say!' expostulated Rupert. 'You'll blow him to smithereens! Give it to me! Fiend seize it, do as I say!'

The commotion below had subsided a little, and footsteps could be heard mounting the stairs.

'Give that pistol to me, and get you to the other side of the bed,' ordered Rupert. 'By Gad, we'll see some sport now! Come *here*!'

Léonie had backed to the window, and stood with the pistol levelled at the door, her finger crooked about the trigger. Her mouth was shut hard, and her eyes blazed. Rupert struggled impatiently to rise.

'For God's sake, give it to me! We don't want to kill the fellow!'

'Yes, we do,' said Léonie. 'He gave me an evil drug.'

The door opened.

'If you come one step into the room I will shoot you dead!' said Léonie clearly.

'And I thought that you would be pleased to see me, *ma fille*,' said a soft, drawling voice. 'I beg you will not shoot me dead.' Greatcoated, booted and spurred, not a hair of his elegant wig out of place, his Grace of Avon stood upon the threshold, quizzing-glass raised, a faint smile curling his thin lips.

Rupert gave a shout of laughter, and collapsed on to his pillows.

'Thunder and turf, but I never thought I'd live to be thankful for the sight of you, Justin!' he gasped. 'Stap me if I did!'

Twenty

His Grace of Avon Takes Command of the Game

THE COLOUR CAME FLOODING BACK TO LÉONIE'S CHEEKS.
'Monseigneur!' she gasped, and flew across the room towards
him, laughing and crying at once. 'Oh, Monseigneur, you have
come, you have come!' She landed breathless in his arms, and
clung to him.

'Why, *ma fille!*' said his Grace gently. 'What is all this? Did you
doubt I should come?'

'Take that pistol from her,' recommended Rupert faintly, but
with a smile.

The pistol was pressed to his Grace's heart. He removed it from
Léonie's clutch, and pocketed it. He looked down at the curly
head with a curious smile, and presently stroked it.

'My dear infant, you must not cry. Come, it is in very truth
Monseigneur! There is nothing to frighten you.'

'Oh, I am n–not *frightened!*' said Léonie. 'I am so very glad!'

'Then I beg you will signify your gladness in a more becoming
manner. May I ask what you are doing in those clothes?'

Leonie kissed his hand, and mopped her eyes.

'I like them, Monseigneur,' she said, with a twinkle.

'I doubt it not.' Avon went past her to the bed, and bent over it, laying a cool white hand over Rupert's galloping pulse. 'You are hurt, boy?'

Rupert managed to smile.

'It's naught. A hole in my shoulder, plague take it!'

His Grace produced a flask from one pocket, and put it to Rupert's lips. Rupert drank, and the blue shade went from about his mouth.

'I believe I have to thank you,' said the Duke, and removed a pillow. 'You did well, my child. In fact, you have surprised me. I am in your debt.'

Rupert flushed. 'Pooh, 'twas nothing! I did precious little. 'Twas Léonie got us off. 'Fore Gad, I'm devilish pleased to see you, Justin!'

'Yes, so you remarked.' His Grace put up his quizzing-glass and eyed the coins that lay scattered over the bed. 'What, may I ask, is all this wealth?'

'Oh, that's our money, Monseigneur!' said Léonie. 'We were counting it when you came.'

'*Our* money!' ejaculated Rupert. 'That's rich, 'pon my soul it is! There's some on the floor still.'

'And what,' said his Grace, turning to the broken bowl, 'is this?'

'Rupert did it,' said Léonie. 'It is his broth, but when we heard you coming he threw it on the floor.'

'My appearance seems to have produced a strange effect upon you,' remarked his Grace. 'Can either of you tell me where is my very dear friend Saint-Vire?'

Rupert struggled up on his elbow.

'Tare an' ouns, how did you know 'twas he?'

His Grace put him back on his pillows.

'It is my business always to know, Rupert.'

'Well, I always swore you were at the bottom of it! But how the deuce did you find out that he'd got Léonie? Where were you? How did you guess I was after them?'

'Yes, and how did you know where to find us?' asked Léonie. 'Why did he take me?'

The Duke took off his greatcoat, and smoothed a wrinkle from the velvet sleeve beneath.

'You bewilder me, my children. One question at a time, I beg of you.'

'How did you know who had run off with Léonie?'

The Duke sat down by the bed, and snapped his fingers to Léonie, who came at once to sit at his feet.

'It was really quite simple,' he said.

'Simple, was it, egad! Then for the love of God, Justin, tell us what we've been doing, for I'll be hanged if I know!'

Avon twisted his rings.

'Oh, I think you do!' he said. 'Léonie was abducted by a very pretty rogue, and you rescued her.'

'She rescued herself,' chuckled Rupert.

'Yes. I did,' Léonie nodded. 'When the wheel came off I slipped out of the coach, and ran down the road. *Then* Rupert came.'

'Yes, but there's more to it than that,' interrupted Rupert. 'What did Saint-Vire want with Léonie? Do you know that?'

'I do, my dear boy.'

'Well, *I* think it was a great piece of impudence,' said Léonie. 'Why did he want me?'

'My children, you cannot expect me to tell you all my secrets.'

'But, Monseigneur, I do *not* see that that is fair! We have been on a big adventure, and we have done it all by ourselves, and we do not know what it is about in the very least, and now you will not tell us!'

'I think you might tell us, Justin,' said Rupert. 'We can be discreet, you know.'

'No, my children. My opinion of your discretion is not so great as my opinion of your courage and resource. By the way, what did you do with Mr Manvers's roan?'

Rupert stared. 'Lord, is there anything you don't know? Who told you that?'

'Mr Manvers himself,' replied the Duke. 'I arrived at Avon on the evening of the day you – er – left. Mr Manvers came to retrieve his property.'

'Curse his impudence!' said Rupert. 'I left him a message! Does the fellow think I'm not to be trusted with a horse?'

'That was rather the impression he gave me,' said his Grace. 'What did you do with it?'

'Well, to tell the truth, I sold it,' replied Rupert, grinning.

The Duke lay back in his chair.

'Then I very much fear that Mr Manvers will be satisfied with nothing less than our lives,' he sighed. 'Pray do not imagine that I disapprove of your action, but I should like to know why you disposed of his roan thus speedily?'

'Well, you see, I'd no money,' explained Rupert. 'I forgot I'd my pin to sell. Besides, what else could I do with the animal? I didn't want to bring it to France.'

The Duke looked at him in some amusement.

'Did you set out on this venture penniless?' he inquired.

'No, I'd a couple of crowns in my pocket,' Rupert answered.

'You make me feel incredibly old,' complained his Grace. He smiled down at Léonie. 'What happened to you, my infant?'

'Oh, I was just teasing Rupert!' Léonie replied buoyantly. 'That is why I am in these clothes. I put them on to make him angry. And I ran away from him into the wood, and that pig-person was there –'

'One moment, my infant. You will pardon my ignorance, but I do not know who the – er – pig-person is meant to be.'

'Why, the wicked Comte!' said Léonie. 'He is a pig-person, Monseigneur.'

'I see. I do not think I admire your choice of adjective, though.'

'Well, I think it is a very good name for him,' said Léonie, unabashed. 'He seized me, and threw me into his coach, and I bit him till there was blood.'

'You distress me, child. But proceed.'

'I called to Rupert as loud as I could, and I kicked the pig-person –'

'The Comte de Saint-Vire.'

'Yes, the pig-person – on his legs a great many times. He did not like it at all.'

'That,' said his Grace, 'does not altogether surprise me.'

'No. If I had had my dagger I would have killed him, for I was very angry – oh, but *very* angry! But I had no dagger, so I could only call to Rupert.'

'The Comte de Saint-Vire has yet something to be thankful for,' murmured his Grace. 'He little knows the temper of my ward.'

'Well, but would not you have been angry, Monseigneur?'

'Very, infant; but continue.'

'Oh, you know the rest, Monseigneur! He gave me an evil drink – pig-wash! He called it coffee.'

'Then let us also call it coffee, child, I beg of you. I can support "pig-person," but "pig-wash" I will not endure.'

'But it *was*, Monseigneur! I threw it at him, and he swore.'

His Grace regarded her inscrutably.

'You seem to have been a pleasant travelling companion,' he remarked. 'What then?'

'*Then* he brought more pig – coffee, and he made me drink it. It was drugged, Monseigneur, and it made me go to sleep.'

'Poor infant!' His Grace tweaked one curl. 'But a most indomitable infant withal.'

'There is nothing more to tell you, Monseigneur. I woke up next day at the inn at Le Havre, and I pretended to be asleep. Then the coach broke, and I escaped.'

'And what of Rupert?' The Duke smiled across at his brother.

'Faith, I don't think I stopped running till I came here!' said Rupert. 'I am still something out of breath.'

'Oh, Rupert was very clever!' Léonie struck in. 'Monseigneur, he even sold his diamond to follow me, and he came to France in a dirty old boat, without a hat or a sword!'

'Nonsense, silly chit, Fletcher gave me his Sunday beaver. You talk too much, Léonie. Stop it!'

'I do not talk too much, do I, Monseigneur? And it is as I say. I do not know what would have happened to me but for Rupert.'

'Nor I, ma fille. We owe him a very big debt of gratitude. It is not often that I put my faith in another, but I did so these last two days.'

Rupert blushed and stammered.

'"Twas Léonie did it all. She brought me here, wherever we are. Where are we, Justin?'

'You are at Le Dennier, some ten miles from Le Havre, my children.'

'Well, that's one mystery solved, at all events!' said Rupert. 'Léonie went cross-country till the head turned on my shoulders. Oh, she diddled Saint-Vire finely, I give you my word!'

'But if you had not come I could not have got away,' Léonie pointed out.

'If it comes to that,' said Rupert, 'the Lord alone knows what would have happened if you'd not caught us, Justin.'

'I understand that my bloodthirsty ward would have shot the so dear Comte – er – dead.'

'Yes, I would,' Léonie averred. 'That would have taught him a lesson!'

'It would indeed,' agreed his Grace.

'Will you shoot him for me, please, Monseigneur?'

'Certainly not, infant. I shall be delighted to see the dear Comte.'

Rupert looked at him sharply.

'I've sworn to have his blood, Justin.'

His Grace smiled. 'I am before you, my dear, by some twenty years, but I bide my time.'

'Ay, so I guessed. What's your game, Avon?'

'One day I will tell you, Rupert. Not to-day.'

'Well, I don't envy him if you've your claws on him,' said Rupert frankly.

'No, I think he is not to be envied,' said his Grace. 'He should be here soon now. Infant, a trunk has been carried to your chamber. Oblige me by dressing yourself once more *à la jeune fille*. You will find a package sent by my Lady Fanny, which contains, I believe, a sprigged muslin. Put it on: it should suit you.'

'Why, Monseigneur, did you bring my clothes?' cried Léonie.

'I did, my child.'

'By Gad, you're an efficient devil!' remarked Rupert. 'Come, Justin! Tell us your part in the venture.'

'Yes, Monseigneur, please!' Léonie seconded.

'There is very little to tell,' sighed his Grace. 'My share in the chase is woefully unexciting.'

'Let's have it!' requested Rupert. 'What brought you down to Avon so opportunely? Damme, there's something uncanny about you, Satanas, so there is!'

Léonie fired up at that.

'You shall not call him by that name!' she said fiercely. 'You only dare to do it because you are ill and I cannot fight you!'

'My esteemed ward, what is this lamentable talk of fighting? I trust you are not in the habit of fighting Rupert?'

'Oh no, Monseigneur, I only did it once! He just ran and hid behind a chair. He was afraid!'

'Small wonder!' retorted Rupert. 'She's a wild-cat, Justin. It's Have-at-you! before you know where you are, 'pon my oath it is!'

'It seems I stayed away too long,' said his Grace sternly.

'Yes, Monseigneur, much, much too long! said Léonie, kissing his hand. 'But I was good – oh, many times!'

His Grace's lips twitched. At once the dimple peeped out.

'I knew you were not really angry!' Léonie said. 'Now tell us what you did.'

The Duke flicked her cheek with one finger.

'I came home, my infant, to find my house invaded by the Merivales, your duenna being prostrate with the vapours.'

'Bah, she is a fool!' said Léonie scornfully. 'Why was Milor' Merivale there?'

'I was about to tell you, my dear, when you interrupted me with your stricture upon my cousin. My Lord and Lady Merivale were there to help find you.'

'Faith, it must have been a merry meeting!' put in the irrepressible Rupert.

'It was not without its amusing side. From them I learned of your disappearance.'

'Did you think we had eloped?' Rupert inquired.

'That explanation did present itself to me,' admitted his Grace.

'Eloped?' Léonie echoed. 'With *Rupert*? Ah, bah, I would as soon elope with the old goat in the field!'

'If it comes to that, I'd as soon elope with a tigress!' retorted Rupert. 'Sooner, by Gad!'

'When this interchange of civilities is over,' said his Grace languidly, 'I will continue. But do not let me interrupt you.'

'Ay, go on,' said Rupert. 'What next?'

'Next, my children, Mr Manvers bounced in upon us. I fear that Mr Manvers is not pleased with you, Rupert, or with me, but let that pass. From him I gathered that you, Rupert, had gone off in pursuit of a coach containing a French gentleman. After that it was easy. I journeyed that night to Southampton – you did not think to board the *Queen*, boy?'

'I remembered her, but I was in no mood to waste time riding to Southampton. Go on.'

'For which I thank you. You would undoubtedly have sold her had you taken her to France. I crossed in her yesterday, and came into Le Havre at sundown. There, my children, I made sundry inquiries, and there also I spent the night. From the innkeeper I learned that Saint-Vire had set off with Léonie by coach for Rouen at two in the afternoon, and further that you, Rupert, had hired a horse half an hour or more later – by the way, have you still that horse, or has it already gone the way of its fellow?'

'No, it's here right enough,' chuckled Rupert.

'You amaze me. All this, I say, I learned from the innkeeper. It was rather too late then for me to set out in search of you, and, moreover, I half expected you to arrive at Le Havre. When you did not arrive I feared that you, Rupert, had failed to catch my very dear friend Saint-Vire. So this morning, my children, I took a coach along the road to Rouen, and came upon a derelict.' His Grace produced his snuff-box, and opened it. 'My very dear friend's coach, with his arms blazoned upon the door. It was scarcely wise of my very dear friend to leave his coach lying about for me to find, but it is possible, of course, that he did not expect me.'

'He is a fool, Monseigneur. He did not know even that I was pretending to be asleep.'

'According to you, my infant, the world is peopled by fools. I believe you have reason. To resume. It seemed probable that Léonie had escaped; further, it seemed probable that she had escaped towards Le Havre. But since neither of you had arrived at that port I guessed that you were concealed somewhere on the road to Le Havre. Therefore, *mes enfants*, I drove back along the road until I came to a lane that gave on to it. Down this lane I proceeded.'

'We went across the fields,' Léonie cut in.

'A shorter way, no doubt, but one could hardly expect a coach to take it. At the hamlet I came upon they knew nothing of you. I drove on, and came at length, by devious ways, to this place. The luck, you see, favoured me. Let us hope that my very dear friend will be equally fortunate. Infant, go and change your clothes.'

'Yes, Monseigneur. What are we going to do now?'

'That remains to be seen,' said Avon. 'Away with you!'

Léonie departed. His Grace looked at Rupert.

'My young madman, has a surgeon seen your wound?'

'Ay, he came last night, confound him!'

'What said he?'

'Oh, naught! He'll come again to-day.'

'From your expression I am led to infer that he prophesied some days in bed for you, child.'

'Ten, plague take him! But I shall be well enough by tomorrow.'

'You will remain there, nevertheless, until the worthy surgeon permits you to arise. I must send for Harriet.'

'Lord, must you? Why?'

'To chaperon my ward,' said his Grace calmly. 'I hope my letter will not bring about a fresh attack of the vapours. Gaston had best start for Le Havre at once.' He rose. 'I want pen, ink, and paper. I suppose I shall find them downstairs. You would be the better for an hour's sleep, my dear.'

'But what of Saint-Vire?' Rupert asked.

'The so dear Comte is in all probability scouring the country-side. I hope to see him soon.'

'Ay, but what will you do?'

'I? I shall do precisely nothing.'

'I'd give a pony to see his face when he finds you here!'

'Yes, I do not think he will be pleased,' said his Grace, and went out.

Twenty-One

The Discomfiture of the Comte de Saint-Vire

MINE HOST AND HOSTESS OF THE BLACK BULL AT LE DENNIER HAD never before entertained such quality at their humble inn. Madame sent a serving-man running hot-foot to her neighbour, Madame Tournoise, and presently that lady came hurrying in with her daughter to aid Madame in her preparations. When she heard that no less a personage than an English Duke, with his entourage, had arrived at the inn, she was round-eyed in wonderment, and when his Grace came slowly down the stairs clad in a coat of palest lavender, with lacing of silver, and a silver waistcoat, amethysts in his lace, and on his fingers, she stood staring open-mouthed.

His Grace went to the little parlour, and sent for writing materials. Mine host came bustling with the inkhorn, and desired to know whether Monseigneur would take any refreshment. His Grace bespoke a bottle of canary wine, and three glasses, and sat him down to write to his cousin. A faint smile hovered about his lips.

My Very Dear Cousin, —

I Trust that by the Time you Receive this Missive you will have recovered from the Sad Indisposition which had overtaken

*you when I had the Pleasure of seeing you, three Days
since. I am Desolat'd to be Oblig'd to put you to Added
Inconvenience, but I believe I must Request you to Join me
here as soon as may be. Gaston, who brings this letter, will
Escort you. Pray pack your Trunks for a long stay, for I have
some notion of Proceeding in due Course to Paris. My Ward,
you will be Reliev'd to hear, is with me in this charming
Village, in Company with my Lord Rupert.*

> *I have the Honour, my dear Cousin, to be
> Yr most devot'd, humble, and obedient servant
> Avon.*

His Grace signed his name with a flourish, still smiling. The
door opened, and Léonie came in, all in foaming white muslin,
with a blue sash about her waist, and a blue riband in her hair.

'Monseigneur, is it not kind of Lady Fanny to send me this
pretty dress? I look nice, do you not think?'

The Duke put up his glass.

'My child, you look charming. Lady Fanny's taste is unim-
peachable.' He rose, and picked up a flat velvet case from the
table. 'I beg you will accept this trifling mark of my affection for
you, infant.'

Léonie skipped up to him.

'*Another* present, Monseigneur? I think you are very kind to
me! What is it, I wonder?'

His Grace opened the case. Léonie's lips formed a soundless *Oh!*

'Mon-seigneur!'

The Duke lifted the pearls from their bed of velvet, and clasped
them about her neck.

'Oh, Monseigneur, thank you!' she said in a gasp, and held the
long string between her fingers. 'They are beautiful! I love them,

oh, much! Would you like me to curtsy to you, or may I just kiss your hand?'

His Grace smiled.

'You need do neither, infant.'

'I will do both,' said Léonie, and sank down with skirts outspread and one little foot peeping from beneath the muslin flounces. Then she kissed the Duke's hand, and rose. Lastly she inspected his Grace's clothes.

'That is a nice dress, I think,' she said.

Avon bowed.

'I like it,' Léonie said. 'Monseigneur, I feel very brave now. What will you do to this pig-person when he comes?'

'I shall have the honour of presenting you, my dear,' Avon answered. 'Let him have your haughtiest curtsy. It is a little game we play.'

'Yes? But I do not want to curtsy to him. I want to make him sorry.'

'Believe me, he will be very sorry, but the time is not yet. Bear in mind, *ma fille*, that you have not till now set eyes on my dear friend.'

'Ah, bah, what is this?' she demanded. 'I know him well, and he knows me!'

'Strive to cultivate a little imagination,' sighed his Grace. 'The so dear Comte stole my page, Léon. You are my ward, Mademoiselle de Bonnard.'

'Oh!' said Léonie doubtfully. 'I must be polite, *enfin*?'

'Very polite, child. And remember, you and I are here for our health. We know naught of abductions, or evil drinks, or even – er – pig-persons. Can you play the game of pretence?'

'But yes, Monseigneur! Will he pretend, do you think?'

'I have reason to think, child, that he will follow my lead.'

'Why, Monseigneur?'

'Because, child, he has a secret which he suspects I share. But since it is a highly discreditable secret he would not like me to think that he had any knowledge of it. We fence, you see, but whereas I see my way clearly, he moves in darkness.'

'Oh, I see!' she said. 'He will be surprised to find you, *n'est-ce pas?*'

'I rather think he will,' agreed his Grace. He went to the table and poured out two glasses of canary. One of them he gave to Léonie. 'My dear, I drink to your safe deliverance.'

'Oh, I thank you, Monseigneur! What shall I drink to?' She put her head on one side. '*Voyons*, I will just drink to *mon cher seigneur!*'

'Quite neat,' said the Duke. 'Gaston? *A la bonne heure!* You will journey back to Avon, Gaston, at once.'

Gaston's face fell.

'But yes, Monseigneur.'

'Bearing with you this letter to my cousin. She will accompany you to France again.'

Gaston brightened perceptibly.

'Further, you will go to Milor' Merivale and obtain from him the clothes of Milor' Rupert. It is understood?'

'*All* Milor' Rupert's clothes, Monseigneur?' asked Gaston, aghast.

'All of them. If he is there, bring milor's valet also. I had wellnigh forgot Mademoiselle Léonie's maid. Instruct her to pack the rest of mademoiselle's clothes, and bring her – and them – to me here.'

Gaston blinked rapidly.

'Yes, Monseigneur,' he said with an effort.

'You will board the *Silver Queen*, of course, and you will convey your charges by coach to Portsmouth.' His Grace tossed a fat purse to him. 'At Portsmouth, on your way to Avon, you will seek out a certain roan horse.'

'*Bon Dieu!*' muttered Gaston. 'A roan horse, Monseigneur, yes.'

'A roan horse belonging to one Mr Manvers of Crosby Hall, sold by Milor' Rupert on Monday. You will buy it back.' Another purse followed the first. 'The price is of no moment. You will have the animal conveyed to Crosby Hall, with Milor' Rupert's compliments and – er – thanks. That also is understood?'

'Yes, Monseigneur,' said Gaston dismally.

'*Bien*. This is, I think, Wednesday. You will be here again no later than Monday. Send Meekin to me now. You may go.'

The groom came speedily.

'Your Grace sent for me?'

'I did. You will start for Paris, my friend, within the hour.'

'Ay, your Grace.'

'To apprise the admirable Walker of my coming. You will bring back with you the large berline, the smaller travelling coach, and a light chaise for my Lord Rupert's baggage. You will arrange for change of horses to await me at Rouen, at Tign, and at Pontoise. I shall rest at the Coq d'Or at Rouen for one night.'

'Very good, your Grace. Which day am I to tell the landlord?'

'I have not the least idea,' said the Duke. 'But when I come I shall require four bedchambers, a private parlour, and quarters for my servants. I trust I make myself plain?'

'Yes, your Grace.'

'That is all,' said Avon.

Meekin bowed, and went out.

'*Voyons*,' said Léonie from her seat by the fire. 'It gives me great pleasure to hear you say "Do this – do that!" I like to hear them answer only, 'Yes, Monseigneur,' and go so quickly to do your bidding.'

Avon smiled. 'I have only once in my life had a servant in mine employ who dared to question my commands,' he said.

'Oh?' Léonie looked up in all innocence. 'Who was that, Monseigneur?'

'A page I had, my dear, by name – er – Léon.'

Her eyes sparkled, but she folded her hands demurely.

'*Tiens!* I wonder he dared, Monseigneur.'

'I believe there was nothing he would not dare,' said Avon.

'Truly? Did you like him, Monseigneur?'

'You are a minx, my dear.'

She laughed, blushed, and nodded.

'It is not a compliment,' said his Grace, and came to the fire, and sat down. 'I have sent for your duenna, you hear.'

'Yes.' She grimaced. 'But she will not come till Monday, will she? Why are we going to Paris?'

'As well Paris as anywhere else,' Avon replied. 'Your education is nearly complete. You are going to make your curtsy to the Polite World.'

'Am I, Monseigneur? *Vraiment?* I think it will be *fort amusant*. Shall I go to Vassaud's?'

The Duke's brows twitched together.

'No, *ma fille*, you will not. Vassaud's is one of those places which you will strive to forget.'

Léonie peeped at him.

'And – and the Maison Chourval?'

'Did I take you there?' His Grace was still frowning.

'But yes, Monseigneur, only you sent me to wait for you in the vestibule.'

'I had that much decency left, then. You will most assuredly forget the Maison Chourval. It would be interesting to know what you made of it?'

'Very little, Monseigneur. It is not a nice place, I think.'

'No, infant, you are right. It is not a nice place, nor was I – nice – to take you there. That is not the world you shall enter.'

'Tell me!' begged Léonie. 'Shall I go to balls?'

'Certainly, *ma belle*.'

'And will you dance with me?'

'My dear, there will be gallants enough to claim your hand. You will have no need of me.'

'If you do not dance with me I won't dance at all,' she announced. 'You will, Monseigneur, won't you?'

'Perhaps,' he said.

'I do not like perhaps,' she said. 'Promise!'

'You are really very *exigeante*,' he complained. 'I am past the age of dancing.'

'*Eh bien!*' Léonie tilted her chin. 'Me, I am too young to dance. *Nous voilà!*'

'You, my infant,' said his Grace severely, 'are a very naughty, wilful child. I do not know why I bear with you.'

'No, Monseigneur. And you will dance with me?'

'Quite incorrigible,' he murmured. 'Yes, infant.'

A horse came clattering up the street, and paused at the inn-door.

'Monseigneur – do you think – is it – *he*?' Léonie asked nervously.

'It seems likely, my dear. The game begins.'

'I am not feeling – *quite* so brave, Monseigneur.'

He rose, and spoke softly.

'You will not disgrace yourself, or me, infant. There is naught to fear.'

'N-no, Monseigneur.'

The landlord entered.

'Monseigneur, it is M. le Docteur to see milor'.'

'How disappointing,' said his Grace. 'I will come. Stay here, child, and if my very dear friend should come, remember that you are my ward, and behave with proper courtesy.'

'Yes, Monseigneur,' she faltered. 'You will come back soon, won't you?'

'Assuredly.' His Grace went out with a swish of silken skirts. Léonie sat down again, and regarded her toes. Overhead, in Rupert's chamber, she heard footsteps and the muffled sound of voices. These signs of the Duke's proximity reassured her a little, but when again she heard the clatter of hoofs on the cobbled street some of the delicate colour left her cheeks.

'This time it is in very truth that pig-person,' she thought. 'Monseigneur does not come – he wants me to play the game a little by myself, I think. *Eh bien, Léonie, courage!*'

She could hear Saint-Vire's voice upraised in anger outside. Then came a quick, heavy tread, the door was flung open, and he stood upon the threshold. His boots were caked with mud, and his coat bespattered; he carried a riding-whip and gloves, and his cravat and hair were in disorder. Léonie looked at him in some hauteur, copying Lady Fanny's manner to a nicety. For an instant it seemed that the Comte did not recognise her; then he came striding forward, his face dark with passion.

'You thought you had tricked me, madame page, did you not? I am not so easily worsted. I do not know where you obtained those fine clothes, but they avail you nothing.'

Léonie came to her feet, and let her eyes wander over him.

'M'sieur is in error,' she said. 'This is a private room.'

'Very prettily played,' he sneered, 'but I am no fool to be put off by those airs and graces. Come, where's your cloak? I've no time to waste!'

She stood her ground.

'I do not understand you, m'sieur. This is an intrusion.' She rolled the word off her tongue, and was pardonably pleased with it.

The Comte grasped her arm, and shook it slightly.

'Your cloak! Quickly, now, or it will be the worse for you.'

Much of her icy politeness left Léonie.

'Bah! Take your hand away from my arm!' she said fiercely. 'How dare you touch me?'

He pulled her forward, an arm about her waist.

'Have done! The game is up, my dear. You will do better to submit quietly. I shall not hurt you if you do as I say.'

From the doorway came the faint rustle of silk. A cool, haughty voice spoke.

'You mistake, m'sieur. Have the goodness to unhand my ward.'

The Comte jumped as though he had been shot, and wheeled about, a hand to his sword-hilt. Avon stood just inside the room, quizzing-glass raised.

'*Sacré mille diables,*' swore Saint-Vire. '*You!*'

A slow and singularly unpleasant smile curved his Grace's lips.

'Is it possible?' he purred. 'My very dear friend Saint-Vire!'

Saint-Vire tugged at his cravat as though it choked him.

'You!' he said again. His voice was hardly above a whisper. 'Are you in very truth your namesake? Even – here – I find you!'

Avon came forward. An elusive perfume was wafted from his clothes as he walked; in one hand he held a lace handkerchief.

'Quite an unexpected *rencontre*, is it not, Comte?' he said. 'I have to present my ward, Mademoiselle de Bonnard. I believe she will accept your apologies.'

The Comte flushed dark, but he bowed to Léonie, who swept him a magnificent curtsy, and muttered a few incoherent words.

'No doubt you mistook her for someone else?' said his Grace urbanely. 'I do not think you have met her before?'

'No. As m'sieur says – I mistook her – *Mille pardons, mademoiselle.*'

His Grace took snuff.

'Strange how one may be mistaken,' he said. 'Likenesses are so inexplicable, are they not, Comte?'

Saint-Vire started. 'Likenesses…?'

'You do not find it so?' His Grace drew a fan of lavender silk mounted on silver sticks from his pocket, and waved it languidly. 'One wonders what can have brought the Comte de Saint-Vire to this unsophisticated spot.'

'I came on business, M. le Duc. One also wonders what can have brought the Duc of Avon here.'

'But business, dear Comte, business!' said Avon, gently.

'I come to retrieve some – property – I lost at Le Havre!' said the Comte wildly.

'How singular!' remarked Avon. 'I came on precisely the same errand. Our paths seem fated to – er – cross, my dear Comte.'

Saint-Vire set his teeth.

'Yes, m'sieur? On – on the same errand, you say?' He forced a laugh. 'Singular indeed!'

'Quite remarkable, is it not! But unlike yours, my property was stolen from me. I hold it in – er – trust.'

'Indeed, m'sieur?' The Comte's mouth was unpleasantly dry, and it was evident that he was at a loss to know what to say.

'I trust, dear Comte, that you have found your property?' Avon's tone was silky.

'Not yet,' Saint-Vire answered slowly.

His Grace poured out the third glass of wine, and offered it to him. Mechanically the Comte accepted it.

'Let us hope that I may be able to restore it to you,' said his Grace, and sipped meditatively at his wine.

Saint-Vire choked. 'M'sieur?'

'I shall spare no pains,' continued his Grace. 'The village is not a large hunting-ground, to be sure. You know that it is here, I suppose?'

'Yes – no – I do not know. It is not worth your trouble, m'sieur.'

'Oh, my dear Comte!' protested his Grace, 'if it is worth so much endeavour' – his eyes flickered to those mud-caked boots – 'so much endeavour on your part, I am sure it is also worth my attention.'

The Comte seemed to choose his words carefully.

'I have reason to think, m'sieur, that it is one of those jewels that contain – a flaw.'

'I trust not,' answered Avon. 'So it was a jewel? Now that which was stolen from me is in the nature of a weapon.'

'I hope you have had the good fortune to find it,' said Saint-Vire, goaded, but holding fast to his self-control.

'Yes, my dear Comte, yes. Chance favours me nearly always. Strange. Let me assure you that I shall do my utmost to restore your – jewel, I think you said it was? – your jewel to you.'

'It – is not likely that you will find it,' said Saint-Vire, between his teeth.

'You forget the element of Chance, dear Comte. I am a great believer in my luck.'

'My property can hardly interest you, M. le Duc.'

'On the contrary,' sweetly replied his Grace, 'it would afford me great pleasure to be able to assist you in the matter.' He glanced towards Léonie, who stood by the table, listening with a puzzled frown to the quick give and take of words. 'I have quite a happy – shall we say, knack? – of finding lost – er – property.'

Saint-Vire turned livid. His hand shook as he raised his glass to his lips. Avon regarded him in exaggerated concern.

'My dear Comte, surely you are unwell?' Again his eyes went to Saint-Vire's boots. 'You must have come a long way, dear Comte,' he said solicitously. 'No doubt you are sadly fatigued.'

The Comte spluttered and set down his glass with a snap.

'As you say, I – I am not entirely myself. I have been suffering from a – slight indisposition, which has confined me to my room these last three days.'

'It is really most remarkable,' marvelled his Grace. 'My brother – I think you know him? Yes, quite so, – is at this very moment above-stairs, also suffering from a slight indisposition. I fear there must be something unhealthy in the air of this place. You find it a trifle sultry, perhaps?'

'Not at all, m'sieur!' snarled Saint-Vire.

'No? These annoying disorders, I believe, have a way of over-taking one in any climate.'

'As my Lord Rupert found,' said Saint-Vire harshly. 'I trust his – indisposition has not given him a distaste for my country.'

'Quite the reverse,' said his Grace blandly. 'He is agog to proceed to Paris. He and I, dear Comte, believe firmly in that old remedy: the hair of the dog.'

The veins stood out on Saint-Vire's forehead.

'Indeed? It is to be hoped that my lord does not act rashly.'

'You must not be concerned for him, dear Comte. I stand – as it were – behind him, and I have a wonderfully cool head. So they tell me. But you – ah, that is another matter! You must have a care to yourself, Comte. Let me implore you to relinquish your – search – until you are more yourself.'

Saint-Vire's hand clenched.

'You are too good, m'sieur. My health is not your concern.'

'You mistake, dear Comte. I take a most lively interest in your – er – health.'

'I believe I shall do very well, m'sieur. My complaint is not so serious, I am glad to say.'

'Nevertheless, my dear Comte, it is always well to proceed cautiously, is it not? One never knows when these trifling ailments may not grow suddenly to quite large proportions. I have known a mere chill creep to the lungs, and strike a man down in the very prime of life.' He smiled pleasantly upon the Comte, who sprang suddenly to his feet, overturning his chair.

'Curse you, you've no proof!' he cried.

Up went his Grace's brows. His eyes mocked.

'I assure you, dear Comte, I have known such a case.'

Saint-Vire pulled himself together with an effort.

'It will not happen – to me, I think,' he said thickly.

'Why, we will hope not,' agreed the Duke. 'I believe that no one is – struck down – before the appointed hour.'

The Comte groped for his whip, and stood wrenching the lash between his hands.

'With your permission, m'sieur, I will leave you. I have wasted enough time already. Mademoiselle, your servant!' He spat the words out, snatched up his gloves, and went blindly to the door.

'So soon?' mourned his Grace. 'I shall hope to have the felicity of seeing you in Paris. I must present my ward to your so charming wife.'

Saint-Vire flung open the door, and twisted the handle viciously. He looked back with a sneer.

'You are full of plans, m'sieur. We will hope that none of them go awry.'

'Certainly,' bowed Avon. 'Why should they?'

'There is sometimes – a flaw!' snapped Saint-Vire.

'You bewilder me,' said his Grace. 'Are we speaking of your lost jewel, or my plans – or both? I should warn you that I am something of a judge of precious stones, dear Comte.'

'Yes, m'sieur?' The flush mounted to Saint-Vire's face again. 'It is possible that you are labouring under a delusion, M. le Duc. The game is not played out yet.'

'By no means,' said the Duke. 'Which reminds me that I have not inquired after your so enchanting son. Pray how does he?'

The Comte showed his teeth.

'He is very well, m'sieur. I feel no anxiety on his behalf. Your servant!' The door shut with a slam.

'The so dear Comte!' murmured Avon.

'Monseigneur, you did not do anything to him!' cried Léonie. 'I thought that you would punish him!'

'*Ma fille*, the day comes when I shall punish him,' answered Avon, and threw down his fan. His voice had changed, and sounded harsh in Léonie's ears. 'And there will be no mercy for him at my hands.'

Léonie looked at him in awe and some admiration.

'You look quite angry, Monseigneur!'

His glance came to rest on her face. He went to her, and taking her chin in his hand, looked deep into her eyes. They smiled trustfully up at him. Abruptly he released her.

'I have reason, child. You have seen a villain to-day.'

'Yes, a pig-person,' she nodded. 'You won't let him take me again, will you, Monseigneur?'

'No, my infant. He shall never again have you in his clutches. That I swear.'

She frowned, watching him.

'You seem different, Monseigneur, I think. You are not angry with *me*?'

The grimness left his mouth, and he smiled.

'It would be impossible, my dear. We will go now and solace Rupert's boredom.'

Twenty-Two

The Arrival of Another Player in the Game

MONDAY CAME AND WENT WITH NO SIGN OF GASTON OR HIS charges. His Grace frowned, but Léonie danced with delight, and offered the suggestion that Madame Field had died of agitation.

'It does not seem to worry you over-much,' said Avon dryly.

'No, Monseigneur. I think we are happy without her. What shall we do to-day?'

But the Duke was not pleased. Rupert looked up at him with a grin.

'Never known you so mindful of the proprieties before, Justin, stap me if I have!'

He encountered a cold glance, and was instantly solemn.

'No offence, Avon, no offence! You can be as prudish as you like for aught I care. But she's not.'

'Léonie,' said his Grace crushingly, 'is as feather-brained as you, or nearly so.'

'Egad,' said Rupert irrepressibly. 'I thought we'd not bask much longer in the sunshine of your approval.'

Léonie spoke aggrievedly. 'I am not as feather-brained as Rupert. You are very unkind to say so, Monseigneur.'

Rupert looked at her admiringly.

'That's it, Léonie. Stand up to him, and hit out from the shoulder. It's more than I ever did in my life!'

'I am not afraid of Monseigneur,' said Léonie, elevating her small nose. 'You are just a coward, Rupert.'

'My child' – the Duke turned his head – 'you forget yourself. You owe some gratitude to Rupert.'

'Hey, up I go, and down you go!' said Rupert. 'Ecod, it's a see-saw we're on!'

'Monseigneur, I have been grateful to Rupert all the morning, and now I am not going to be grateful any longer. It makes me cross.'

'So I observe. Your manners leave much to be desired.'

'I think that you are very cross too,' Léonie ventured. '*Voyons*, what does it matter that Gaston does not come? He is silly, and fat, and Madame Field is like a hen. We do not want them.'

'Here's a fine philosophic spirit!' cried Rupert. 'You used to be much the same yourself, Justin. What's come over you?'

Léonie turned to him in triumph.

'I told you he was different, Rupert, and you would only laugh! I never saw him so disagreeable before.'

'Lud, it's easy to see you've not lived with him long!' said Rupert, audaciously.

His Grace came away from the window.

'You're an unseemly pair,' he said. 'Léonie, you were wont to respect me more.'

She saw the smile in his eyes, and twinkled responsively.

'Monseigneur, I was a page then, and you would have punished me. Now I am a lady.'

'And do you think I cannot still punish you, my child?'

'Much she'd care!' chuckled Rupert.

'I should care!' Léonie shot at him. 'I am sorry if Monseigneur only frowns!'

'The Lord preserve us!' Rupert closed his eyes.

'A little more,' said his Grace, 'and you will not get up to-day, my son.'

'Oh, ay! You've the whip-hand!' sighed Rupert. 'I'm silenced!' He shifted his position, and winced a little.

The Duke bent over him to rearrange the pillows.

'I am not sure that you will get up at all to-day, boy,' he said. 'Is it easier?'

'Ay – I mean, I hardly feel it now,' lied his lordship. 'Damme, I won't stay abed any longer, Justin! At this rate we'll never start for Paris!'

'We shall await your convenience,' said Avon.

'Mightily condescending of you,' smiled Rupert.

'You are not to be impertinent to Monseigneur, Rupert,' said Léonie sternly.

'I thank you, infant. It needs for someone to support my declining prestige. If you are to rise to-day you will rest now, Rupert. Léonie, an you wish to ride out I am at your disposal.'

She jumped up.

'I will go and put on my riding-dress at once. *Merci, Monseigneur.*'

'I'd give something to come with you,' said Rupert wistfully, when she had gone.

'Patience, child.' His Grace drew the curtains across the window. 'Neither the doctor nor I keep you in bed for our amusement.'

'Oh, you're a damned good nurse! I'll say that for you,' grimaced Rupert. He smiled rather shyly up at his brother. 'I'd not ask for a better.'

'In truth, I surprise myself sometimes,' said his Grace, and went out.

'Ay, and you surprise me, damme you do!' muttered Rupert. 'I'd give something to know what's come over you. Never was there such a change in anyone!'

And indeed his Grace was unusually kind during these irksome days, and the biting sarcasm which had withered Rupert of yore was gone from his manner. Rupert puzzled over this inexplicable change for some time, and could find no solution to the mystery. But that evening when he reclined on the couch in the parlour, clad in his Grace's clothes, he saw Avon's eyes rest on Léonie for a moment, and was startled by their expression. He pursed his lips in a soundless whistle.

'Thunder an' turf!' he told himself. 'He's fallen in love with the chit!'

Tuesday brought no Gaston, and Avon's frown grew blacker.

'Of a certainty Madame has died,' Léonie said wickedly. '*Tiens, c'est bien drôle!*'

'You have a perverted sense of humour, child,' said his Grace. 'I have often remarked it. We start for Paris on Friday, Gaston or no Gaston.'

But soon after noon on Wednesday there was some bustle in the village street, and Rupert, seated by the parlour window, craned his neck to see if it were Gaston at last.

A hired coach of large dimensions drew up at the door, followed by another, piled high with baggage. From this vehicle Gaston leaped nimbly down, and ran to the door of the first coach. One of the lackeys let down the steps, the door was opened, and a serving-maid climbed out. Behind her came a little lady enveloped in a large travelling cloak. Rupert stared, and burst out laughing.

'Egad, 'tis Fanny! Lord, who'd have thought it?'

Léonie ran to the window.

'It is! It is! *Mon Dieu, que c'est amusant!* Monseigneur, it is Lady Fanny!'

His Grace went in a leisurely fashion to the door.

'So I understand,' he said placidly. 'I fear your unfortunate duenna is indeed dead, infant.' He opened the door. 'Well, Fanny?'

Lady Fanny came briskly in, embraced him, and let fall her
cloak to the ground.

'La, what a journey I have had! My sweetest love, are you safe
indeed?' she embraced Léonie. 'I have been in a fever of curiosity,
I give you my word! I see you are wearing the muslin I sent you.
I knew 'twould be ravishing, but never tie your sash like that,
child! Oh, and there is Rupert! Poor boy, you look quite too
dreadfully pale!'

Rupert held her off.

'Have done, Fan, have done! What in thunder brought you over?'

Lady Fanny stripped off her gloves.

'Since my cousin was nigh dead with the vapours, what would
you?' she protested. 'Besides, 'twas so monstrous exciting I declare
I could not be still!'

The Duke put up his glass.

'May I ask whether the worthy Edward is aware that you have
joined us?' he drawled.

My lady dimpled.

'I am so tired of Edward!' she said. 'He has been most provoking of late. I doubt I have spoiled him. Only fancy, Justin, he said
I must not come to you!'

'You astonish me,' said his Grace. 'Yet I observe that you are here.'

'A pretty thing 'twould be an I let Edward think he could order
me as he chooses!' cried her ladyship. 'Oh, we have had a rare
scene. I left a note for him,' she added naïvely.

'That should console him, no doubt,' said his Grace politely.

'I do not think it will,' she answered. 'I expect he will be prodigiously angry, but I *pine* for gaiety, Justin, and Gaston said you
were bound for Paris!'

'I do not know that I shall take you, Fanny.'

She pouted. 'Indeed and you shall! I won't be sent home. What
would Léonie do for a chaperon if I went? For Harriet is in bed,

my dear, and vows she can no more.' She turned to Léonie. 'My love, you are vastly improved, 'pon rep you are! And that muslin becomes you sweetly. La, who gave you those pearls?'

'Monseigneur gave them to me,' Léonie said. 'They are pretty, n'est-ce pas?'

'I would sell my eyes for them,' said her ladyship frankly, and shot a curious glance at her impassive brother. She sank down into a chair with much fluttering of skirts. 'I implore you, tell me what happened to you, for Harriet is such a fool, and so taken up with her vapours that she can tell me naught but enough to whet my curiosity. I am nigh dead with it, I vow.'

'So,' said his Grace, 'are we. Where do you come from, Fanny, and how have you had speech with Harriet?'

'Speech with her?' cried my lady. 'Oh lud, Justin! "My head, my poor head!" she moans, and: "She was ever a wild piece!" Never a word more could I get from her. I was near to shaking her, I give you my word!'

'Be hanged to you, Fan, for a chatterbox!' exclaimed Rupert. 'How came you to Avon?'

'Avon, Rupert? I protest I've not seen the place for nigh on a twelve-month, though indeed I took some notion to visit my dearest Jennifer the other day. But it came to naught, for there was my Lady Fountain's rout, and I could scarce leave –'

'Devil take Lady Fountain's rout! Where's my cousin?'

'At home, Rupert. Where else?'

'What, not with Edward?'

Fanny nodded vigorously.

'She should suit his humour,' murmured the Duke.

'I doubt she will not,' said Fanny pensively. 'What a rage he will be in, to be sure! Where was I?'

'You were not, my dear. We are breathlessly awaiting your arrival.'

'How disagreeable of you, Justin! Harriet! Of course! Up she came to town in Gaston's charge, and was like to expire in my arms. Some rigmarole she wept down my best taffeta, and at last held out your letter, Justin. She vowed she'd not come to France, do what you would. Then I had more wailings of her sickness did she so much as set eyes on the sea. Oh, I had a pretty time with her, I do assure you! She could but moan of an abduction, and Rupert's hat found in Long Meadow, hard by the wood, and of some man come to find a horse, and you setting off for Southampton, Justin. 'Twas like the threads of a sampler with naught to stitch 'em to. Gaston could tell me little more – la, Justin, why will you have a fool to valet? – and the end of it was that I was determined to come and see for myself and find what 'twas all about. Then, if you please, what says Edward but that I am not to go! 'Pon rep, things have come to a pretty pass between us, thought I! So when he went away to White's – no, it was the Cocoa Tree, I remember, for he was to meet Sir John Cotton there – I set Rachel to pack my trunks, and started off with Gaston to come to you. *Me voici*, as Léonie would say.'

'*Voyons!*' Léonie's eyes sparkled. 'I think it was very well done of you, madame! Will you come to Paris too? I am to make my curtsy to the World, Monseigneur says, and go to balls. Please come, madame!'

'Depend upon it, I shall come, my love. 'Tis the very thing for which I have been pining. My sweetest life, there is a milliner in the Rue Royale who has the most ravishing styles! Oh, I will teach Edward a lesson!'

'Edward,' remarked his Grace, 'is like to follow you demanding my blood. We must await his coming.'

'Dear Edward!' sighed my lady. 'I do hope that he will not come, but I dare swear he will. And now for the love of heaven let me have your story! I shall die of curiosity else.'

So Léonie and Rupert poured forth the tale of their adventures once more into a most sympathetic ear. Fanny interspersed the recital with suitable exclamations, flew up and embraced Rupert before he could save himself when she heard of his narrow escape, and at the end of it all stared in amazement at his Grace, and burst out laughing.

The Duke smiled down at her. 'It makes you feel middle-aged, my dear? Alas!'

'No indeed!' My lady fanned herself. 'I felt an hundred in my boredom, but this adventure – faith, 'tis the maddest ever I heard – throws me back into my teens, 'pon rep it does! Justin, you should have cut him to pieces with your small-sword, the villain!'

'That is what I think,' Léonie struck in. 'I wanted to make him sorry, madame. It was a great impertinence.'

'A very proper spirit, my love, but if you in sooth flung a cup of hot coffee over him I'll wager you made him sorry enough. La, what a hoyden you are, child! But I vow I envy you your courage. Saint-Vire? Ay, I know him well. A head of hair that could set six hayricks ablaze, and the most unpleasant eyes of any I know. What did he want with you, sweet?'

'I do not know,' Léonie answered. 'And Monseigneur will not tell.'

'Oh, so you know, Justin? I might have guessed it! Some fiend-ish game you will be playing.' My lady shut her fan with a click. 'It's time I took a hand indeed! I'll not have this child endangered by your mad tricks, Justin. Poor angel, I shudder to think of what might have befallen you!'

'Your solicitude for my ward's safety is charming, Fanny, but I believe I am able to protect her.'

'Of course he is!' said Léonie. 'Do I not belong to him?' She put her hand on his Grace's arm, and smiled up at him.

My lady looked, and her eyes narrowed. On Rupert's face she surprised a knowing grin, and of a sudden jumped up, saying that she must see to the bestowal of her boxes.

'Faith, the inn won't hold them!' chuckled Rupert. 'Where are you to sleep, Fan?'

'I do not care an I sleep in an attic!' said my lady. ''Deed, I almost expect to sleep in the stables! It would be fitting in such a venture.'

'I believe we need not put that upon you,' said his Grace. 'Gaston shall remove my trunks into Rupert's chamber. Thus you may have my room.'

'My dear, 'twill do excellently well! You shall show me the way, Léonie. 'Pon rep, child, you grow more lovely each day!' She put her arm about Léonie's waist, and went out with her.

'Egad, here's a fine muddle!' said Rupert, when the door was shut behind the ladies. 'Fan's in a mighty good humour, but lord! is she to come with us?'

'I imagine that the worthy Edward will have a word to say to that,' Avon replied.

'How Fan could have chosen such a dull dog, and you abetted her, I don't know!' said Rupert.

'My dear boy, I abetted her because he was dull enough to sober her. And he has money.'

'There's that, of course, but faith, he'd turn the milk sour if he smiled at it! Will you take Fan alone?'

'I almost think that I shall,' said Avon. 'I could find no better hostess.'

Rupert stared. 'Are you going to entertain, Justin?'

'Lavishly, Rupert. It will be most fatiguing, but I have a duty as Léonie's guardian which I must endeavour to perform.'

Rupert sat up in his chair, and spoke briskly.

'You may count on my presence for the season, Justin.'

'I am honoured, of course,' bowed his Grace.

'Ay, but – but will you let me join your party?' Rupert asked.

'You will add quite a *cachet* to my poor house,' Avon drawled. 'Yes, child, you may join us, provided you behave with proper circumspection, and refrain from paying my very dear friend back in his own coin.'

'What, am I not to call him out?' demanded Rupert.

'It is so clumsy,' sighed his Grace. 'You may leave him to my – er – tender mercies – with a clear conscience. The hole in your shoulder is added to the debt he owes me. He shall pay – in full.'

'Poor devil!' said Rupert feelingly. He saw into his brother's eyes, and ceased to smile. 'My God, Justin, do you hate him so?'

'Bah!' said his Grace, '– I borrow the word from my infant's vocabulary – does one hate an adder? Because it is venomous and loathsome one crushes it underfoot, as I shall crush this Comte.'

'Because of what happened twenty years ago – to you?' Rupert asked, greatly daring.

'No, boy. Not that, though it weighs also in the scale.'

'Because of what he did to Léonie, then?'

'Because of what he did to my infant,' softly echoed his Grace. 'Yes, child.'

'There's more to this than meets the eye,' said Rupert with conviction.

'Much more,' agreed his Grace. The unaccustomed harshness went from his face, and left it inscrutable as ever. 'Remind me, boy, that I owe you a diamond pin. It was a single stone, I think, of a peculiar beauty?'

'Ay, you gave it me, years ago.'

'I wonder what can have possessed me?' said his Grace. 'No doubt you were – er – "basking in the sunshine of my approval."'

Twenty-Three

Mr Marling Allows Himself to Be Persuaded

LADY FANNY PARTOOK OF BREAKFAST IN BED NEXT MORNING, AND was sipping her hot chocolate when Léonie scratched on the door. My lady put up her hands to her pretty nightcap and patted her golden curls before she called 'Come in!'

'Oh, 'tis you, child! Mercy, are you riding out so early?'

Léonie was in riding-dress, with polished boots, and leathern gauntlets, tasselled, and a big black beaver on her head with a long feather that swept her shoulder.

'Yes, madame, but only if you do not need me. Monseigneur said that I must ask you.'

Lady Fanny nibbled at a sweet biscuit and regarded the bed-post with rapt interest.

'No, child, no. Why should I need you? Lud, what roses you have; I'd give my best necklet for your complexion. To be sure, I had it once. Go, my love. Don't keep Justin waiting. Is Rupert up?'

'His valet dresses him, madame.'

'I'll bear him company in the parlour,' said her ladyship, and pushed her cup and saucer away. 'Away with you, child! Stay! Send Rachel to me, my love, if you will be so good.'

Léonie went with alacrity. Half an hour later my lady, having bustled exceedingly, came tripping into the parlour dressed in a flowered muslin, and her fair hair unpowdered beneath a becoming cap. Rupert looked up as she entered, and put down the book over which he had been yawning.

'Lord, you're up early, Fan!'

'I came to bear you company,' she cooed, and went to sit by him, at the window.

'Wonders'll never cease,' Rupert said. He felt that this amiability on Fanny's part ought not to go unrewarded. 'You look twenty this morning, Fan, 'pon my soul you do!' he said handsomely.

'Dear Rupert! Do you really think so?'

'Ay – that'll do, though! Léonie has gone riding with his Grace.'

'Rupert,' said my lady.

'Ay, what?'

Fanny looked up.

'I have made up my mind to it Justin shall marry that child.'

Rupert was unperturbed.

'Will he, do you think?'

'My dear boy, he's head over ears in love with her!'

'I know that – I'm not blind, Fan. But he's been in love before.'

'You are most provoking, Rupert! Pray what has that to do with it?'

'He's not married any of 'em,' said my lord.

Fanny affected to be shocked.

'Rupert!'

'Don't be prudish, Fanny! That's Edward's doing, I know.'

'Rupert, if you are minded to be unkind about dear Edward –'

'Devil take Edward!' said Rupert cheerfully.

Fanny eyed him for a moment in silence, and suddenly smiled.

'I am not come to quarrel with you, horrid boy. Justin would not take Léonie as his mistress.'

'No, damme, I believe you're right. He's turned so strict you'd scarce know him. But marriage – ! He'd not be so easily trapped.'

'Trapped?' cried my lady. 'It's no such thing! The child has no notion of wedding him. And that is why he will want her to wife, mark my words!'

'He might,' Rupert said dubiously. 'But – Lord, Fanny, he's turned forty, and she's a babe!'

'She is twenty, my dear, or near it. 'Twould be charming! She will always think him wonderful, and she'll not mind his morals, for she's none herself; and he – oh, he will be the strictest husband in town, and the most delightful! She will always be his infant, I dare swear, and he "Monseigneur." I am determined he shall wed her. Now what do you say?'

'I? I'd be pleased enough, but – egad, Fanny, we don't know who she is! Bonnard? I've never met the name, and it hath a plaguey bourgeois ring to it, damme, so it has! And Justin – well, y'know, he's Alastair of Avon, and it won't do for him to marry a nobody.'

'Pooh!' said my lady. 'I'll wager my reputation she does not come of common stock. There's some mystery, Rupert.'

'Any fool could tell that,' Rupert said frankly. 'And if you asked me, Fan, I'd say she was related to Saint-Vire.' He leaned back in his chair and looked for surprise in his sister. It did not come.

'Where would be my wits if I'd not seen that?' demanded Fanny. 'As soon as I heard that 'twas Saint-Vire who carried her off I felt positive she was a base-born child of his.'

Rupert spluttered. 'Gad, would you have Justin marry any such?'

'I should not mind at all,' said my lady.

'He won't do it,' Rupert said with conviction. 'He's a rake, but he knows what's due to the family, I'll say that for him.'

'Pho!' My lady snapped her fingers. 'If he loves her he'll not trouble his head over the family. Why, what did I care for the family when I married Edward?'

'Steady, steady! Marling has his faults, I'm not saying he hasn't, but there's no bad blood in his family, and you can trace him back to —'

'Stupid creature, could I not have had Fonteroy for the lifting of a finger? Ay, or my Lord Blackwater, or his Grace of Cumming? Yet I chose Edward, who beside them was a nobody.'

'Damn it, he's not base-born!'

'I would not have cared, I give you my word!'

Rupert shook his head.

'It's lax, Fanny, 'fore Gad, it's lax. I don't like it.'

My lady pulled a face at him.

'Oh, tell Justin you do not like it, my dear! Tell him —'

'I'm not meddling in Justin's affairs, I thank you. He'll do as he likes, but I'll lay you a monkey he weds no bastard.'

'Done!' said my lady. 'Oh, Rupert! I lost my big emerald at play last week! I could have cried my eyes out, and Edward could only say that it must be a lesson to me!'

'That's Edward all over,' nodded Rupert. 'Don't I know it!'

'No, you do not, tiresome boy! He will give me another emerald.' She blinked rapidly. 'Indeed, he is very good to me. I wonder if he will come here? I vow I shall be miserable if he does not!'

Rupert's eyes were on the street.

'Well, he has come, and mighty à propos, too.'

'What! Is it really he, Rupert? You're not teasing me?'

'No, it is he, right enough, and in a thundering rage, by the look of him.'

Lady Fanny sighed ecstatically.

'Darling Edward! He will be very angry with me, I am sure.'

Marling came quickly in. He was travel stained, and heavy-eyed from lack of sleep, and his mouth was set in an uncompromising fashion. He looked his pretty wife over in silence.

'That's the last of us,' said Rupert jovially. 'We've all the family now, glory be! Give you good morrow, Edward!'

Lady Fanny rose, and held out her hand.

'Edward, I protest this is foolish of you.'

He ignored the outstretched hand.

'You'll return with me to-day, Fanny. I don't brook your defiance.'

'Whew!' spoke Rupert under his breath. 'Sa-sa – Have at you!'

Lady Fanny tittered.

'Oh, sir, you are ungallant! Pray have you looked at yourself in the mirror? You come to me muddied and in disorder! And I who so love a man to be *point-device*!'

'We'll leave my appearance out of it, if you please. I've borne enough of your whims, Fanny. You'll return with me to England.'

'Indeed, sir, do you think I shall?' The light of battle was in my lady's eyes.

'You are my wife, madam.'

'But not your chattel, sir. Pray take that frown from your face! It likes me not.'

'Ay, do!' Rupert put in. 'How did you leave my cousin, Marling?'

'Yes, sir, and *why* did you leave poor, dear Harriet? It was not well done of you, Edward.'

'Fanny, have you done? I warn you, I am in no mood for these tricks!'

'Now, careful, Fan, careful!' said Rupert, enjoying himself hugely. 'He'll disown you, so he will!'

Marling swung round to face him.

'Your pleasantries are ill-timed, Alastair. I believe we shall do better if you leave us.'

'How dare you, Edward? And the poor boy just out of his bed, with a wound in his shoulder that only escaped the lung by a bare inch!'

'I am not concerned with Rupert's hurts,' said Marling cuttingly. 'He will survive without my sympathy.'

'Ay, but damme, I shall suffer a relapse if I have to look on your gloomy countenance much longer!' retorted Rupert. 'For God's sake, smile, man!'

'Oh yes, Edward, do smile!' begged her ladyship. 'It gives me a headache to see you frowning so.'

'Fanny, you will give me five minutes in private.'

'No, sir, I shall not. You are prodigious ill-natured to talk to me in this vein, and I protest I want no more of it.'

'There's for you, Marling!' Rupert said. 'Go and bespeak some breakfast. You'll be better for it, I swear! 'Tis the emptiness of you makes you feel jaundiced: I know the feeling well. A ham, now, and some pasties, with coffee to wash it down will make a new man of you, stap me if it won't!'

Lady Fanny giggled. Marling's brow grew blacker, his eyes harder.

'You'll regret this, madam. You've trifled with me once too often.'

'Oh, sir, I'm in no mood for your heroics! Pray keep them for Harriet! She has the taste for them, no doubt!'

'Try 'em on Justin,' suggested Rupert. 'Here he is, with Léonie. Lord, what a happy gathering!'

'For the last time, Fanny – I shall not ask again – will you accord me a few minutes alone?'

'Alone?' echoed Rupert. 'Ay, of course she will, as many as you like! Solitude's the thing, so it is! Solitude, and a fat ham –'

'My dear Marling, I hope I see you well?' His Grace had come quietly in.

Marling picked up his hat.

'I am in excellent health, I thank you, Avon.'

'But his spirits!' said Rupert. 'Oh, lud!'

'I confess,' Marling said steadily, 'my spirits are a little – bruised.'

'Never say so!' Rupert feigned astonishment. 'You've had a bad crossing, Edward, and your liver's upside down.'

Avon turned. 'Your conversation is always so edifying, Rupert. Yet I believe we can dispense with it.'

Rupert collapsed promptly. My lady tossed her head. Avon went to the side-table, and poured out a glass of burgundy, and offered it to Marling, who waved it aside.

'I came, sir, to fetch my wife home. As she declines to accompany me there is no more to be said. I'll take my leave of you.'

Avon put up his quizzing-glass, and through it regarded my lady.

'Yes, Justin. I do. I am coming to Paris with you.'

'I am gratified, of course,' said his Grace. 'Nevertheless, my dear, you will go with your husband.'

'I thank you!' Marling laughed harshly. 'I do not take her an she comes at your bidding! She must come at mine.'

'I w-won't go at anyone's b-bidding!' Lady Fanny's face puckered like that of a child about to cry. 'You are very unkind!'

Marling said nothing. She dabbed at her eyes.

'You come – bullying, and – and scowling – I won't go with you! I hate you, Edward!'

'It needed only that,' said Marling, and turned to the door.

There was a rustle of silks as my lady fled across the room.

'Oh, Edward, I didn't meant it, you know I didn't!'

He held her away from him.

'You will return with me?'

She hesitated, then looked up into his face. Two large tears stole down her cheeks. Marling took her hands, and pressed them.

'In truth,' he said gently, 'I cannot bear to see you weep, love. Go with Justin.'

At that she cast herself into his arms, and sobbed.

'Oh Edward, I will come! I truly will! You must f-forgive me!'

'My dear!' He caught her to him.

'I am decidedly *de trop*,' remarked his Grace, and poured out another glass of burgundy.

'I'll come, Edward, but I do – oh, I do want to go to Paris!'

'Then go, sweetheart. I'd not deny you your pleasure.'

'But I c-can't bear to leave you!' sobbed Fanny.

'May I be allowed to make a suggestion?' His Grace came slowly forward. 'There is really no occasion for these heart-burnings. The matter is very simple.' He swept Marling a magnificent leg. 'Pray come with us to Paris, my dear Edward.'

'Oh, I thank you, but –'

'Yes, I know,' said Avon languidly. 'You would prefer not to enter the unhallowed portals of my abode.'

Marling flushed. 'I protest –'

'It is quite unnecessary, believe me. I would not propose such a distasteful plan were it not for the fact that I have need of Fanny.'

'I don't understand why you should need her, Avon.'

His Grace was incredulous.

'My very dear Edward, I should have thought that with your strict sense of propriety the reason must positively leap to your understanding.'

'Léonie! I had forgot.' Marling stood irresolute. 'Can you find no other lady to chaperon her?'

'I could doubtless find an hundred, but I require a hostess.'

'Then Fanny had best stay with you. I will go back to England.'

Fanny sighed. 'Edward, if you will not come to Paris I must return with you. But I do wish that you would come!'

At that moment Léonie appeared, and clapped her hands at the sight of Marling.

'*Parbleu*, it is M. Marling! *Bonjour, m'sieur!*'

He smiled and kissed her hand.

'I hope I see you well, child? Your pretty colour answers me.'

'My infant finds favour in the austere eyes,' murmured his Grace.

'Infant, I am trying to prevail upon Mr Marling to honour my poor house with his presence. Pray add your entreaties to mine.'

'Yes?' Léonie looked from one to the other. 'Please will you come, m'sieur? I shall ask Monseigneur to invite M. Davenant also.'

In spite of himself Avon smiled.

'A happy thought, *ma fille*.'

'Why, child, I believe I must not,' Marling said. 'You shall take her ladyship, and let me go home.'

'Ah, bah!' said Léonie. 'It is because you do not like Monseigneur, is it not?'

'My infant is nothing if not outspoken,' remarked Avon. 'That is the matter in a nutshell, child.'

'You do not think he is enough respectable. But indeed he is very respectable now, *je vous assure!*'

A choking sound came from Rupert; my lady's shoulders shook, and Marling collapsed into helpless laughter. Léonie looked at the convulsed trio in disgust, and turned to the Duke.

'What is the matter with them, Monseigneur? Why do they laugh?'

'I have no idea, infant,' replied Avon gravely.

'They are silly, I think. Very silly.'

But the laughter cleared the air. Marling looked at the Duke, and said unsteadily:

'I confess – it's your lack of – of respectability that sticks – somewhat in my gullet!'

'I am sure it must,' said his Grace. 'But you shall have Davenant to support you. He will be delighted to join you in mourning over my departed morals.'

'The prospect is most alluring,' Marling said. He glanced uncertainly at his wife. 'But I do not think I fit well in this mad venture.'

'My dear Edward, do I fit well in it?' asked his Grace, pained. 'I count upon you to aid me in lending a note of sobriety to the party.'

Marling regarded his Grace's coat of dull crimson velvet quizzically.

'I might lend sobriety, but you, Avon? You supply the magnificence, I think.'

'You flatter me,' Avon bowed. 'I am to understand that you will join us?'

'Yes, Edward, yes! Oh please!'

'*Voyons*, it will be *fort amusant, m'sieur.* You must come.'

Rupert ventured to uplift his voice.

'Ay, join us, Marling. The more the merrier.'

'In face of such kind entreaties what can I say?' Marling took his wife's hand. 'I thank you, Avon. I will come.'

'Gaston, then, had best return to London for your baggage,' said his Grace.

Léonie chuckled. 'He will die, Monseigneur. I know it.'

'As you observe,' remarked his Grace to Marling, 'death and disaster are a source of never-failing amusement to my infant.'

Marling laid his hand on Léonie's head.

'She is a rogue, Avon, is she not? But a pretty rogue.'

Léonie opened wide her eyes.

'*Vraiment?* Am I pretty, Monseigneur? Do you think so?'

'Passable, my infant, passable.'

Her face fell.

'I was afraid you would not think so, Monseigneur.'

Avon pinched her chin.

'Child, do I not call you "*ma belle*"?'

Léonie caught his hand to her lips.

'*Merci*, Monseigneur! You make me very happy, *enfin!*'

Marling looked suddenly at his wife. She smiled, and cast down her eyes. Marling turned to Rupert.

'I think I'll take your excellent – though ill-timed – advice, my boy.'

Rupert grinned.

'What, the ham? Ay, 'twas good advice, stap me it was! But I'll not deny 'twas said to enrage you, Edward.'

'It succeeded in doing so, scamp. Avon, I'll not ask you to send Gaston back to England. I can return there myself, and join you in Paris next week.'

'My dear Edward, it is good for Gaston to bestir himself. He grows fat and lazy. He shall meet us in Paris.'

'You are very good,' Marling bowed.

'That is not my reputation,' said his Grace, and rang the bell.

★★★

On the following morning the whole party set out for Paris. Lady Fanny was flustered, Marling amused, Rupert flippant, Léonie excited, and the Duke leisurely and placid as ever. The entire population of Le Dennier turned out to see the passing of this cavalcade, and marvelled at the chaise piled high with baggage, at the great berline with his Grace's arms blazoned on the door, and at the two smaller coaches that followed it.

The Marlings occupied one of these, while Avon, Léonie and Rupert travelled in the berline. Rupert was propped up with cushions to alleviate the discomfort of the jolting, and whiled away the time by playing cards with Léonie. His Grace lay back in his corner and watched them in some amusement.

Twenty-Four

Hugh Davenant Is Agreeably Surprised

THEY RESTED AT ROUEN OVER THE WEEK-END, AND CAME TO PARIS on Tuesday. Walker awaited them in the hall of the Hôtel Avon, and not by the flicker of an eyelid did he betray that he recognised Léonie. All was in order for his Grace's coming, and Lady Fanny immediately took charge of the establishment. Having seen to the unpacking of her trunks, and scattered her orders broadcast, she repaired to his Grace in the library, what time Léonie went to see Madame Dubois the housekeeper.

'Well, Justin, what now?' said my lady, sitting down opposite him at his desk. 'Are we to make some noise?'

'Decidedly, Fanny. As much noise as possible. I await your suggestions.'

'A ball,' she said briskly. ''Twill do for a beginning.' She bit her finger-tip reflectively. 'I must equip the child first, and myself. I declare I have scarce a rag to my back! A white brocade for Léonie, I think, or a certain shade of green. With that flaming head –'

'My dear, I desire she shall be *poudrée*.'

'As you will, Justin. Yes, it might be pretty. We shall see. I dare swear you have your reasons for wishing it. I shall send the invitations for – a fortnight hence. It's a little enough time, to be sure, but

I don't despair of acceptances. Your name and mine, my dear – !'
Her eyes sparkled. 'I vow I'll have all Paris here! And then?'

'Then, my dear Fanny, Versailles,' he said.

Lady Fanny nodded.

'It's very well. You'll make some stir with her, Justin.'

'It is my intention,' he said. 'Send out your cards, my dear.'

'Expense?' She cocked her head to one side.

'You will not consider it. I think we will have the young
Condé and De Penthièvre. The Duc de Richelieu also.'

'I leave them to you. There must be Madame du Deffand, of
course, and the Duchesse de la Roque.' Lady Fanny half-closed
her eyes. 'My dearest Justin, there is no one who is anyone who
will not come to the ball, I pledge you my word! But la, what
a work I have before me! They'll come out of curiosity, depend
upon it!' She rustled to the door. 'The child's toilettes, Justin?'

'I never quarrel with your taste, Fanny.'

'How droll 'twill be! 'Tis as though I had a daughter, though
thank heaven I have not! She's to be richly clad?'

'As befits my ward, Fanny, but *à la jeune fille.*'

'Oh, never fear! You'll not complain. Dear me, I have not been
so excited since my girlhood, when you took me to Versailles,
Justin. The whole house must be thrown open. I vow some of
the rooms are positively thick with dust. 'Twill need an army to
set all in order. The Ball but starts my activities, I assure you.' She
laughed delightedly. 'We will have *soirées*, and card-parties, a rout,
maybe, and – oh, we shall make some stir!' She hurried away, full
of business-like determination.

His Grace sat down to write a letter to Hugh Davenant.

From then onward the Hôtel Avon was plunged into bustling
activity. Milliners and mantua-makers came and went, dancing
masters and *coiffeurs*; and the servants invaded every shut room, and
threw it open, and swept and garnished it. His Grace was hardly

ever at home. He was at pains to show himself abroad, circulating the news of his return. Rupert he set to promote an ever-ready curiosity, so my lord, as soon as he was well enough, sallied forth to the gaming-houses, and to the abodes of his cronies, and characteristically spread the tale of his brother's latest whim. Léonie's beauty lost nothing in his description of it; he hinted at dark mystery, and assured all and sundry that Avon counted on the presence of the Prince de Condé at his ball, and that also of M. de Richelieu. Paris began to hum, and Fanny sat in her boudoir with notes of acceptance scattered about her.

'Oh, we shall do famously!' she cried. 'Said I not all Paris should come?'

But Léonie slipped away, escaping from dancing-masters and dress-makers alike, and stole into the library, where the Duke was usually to be found. She stood in the doorway regarding him wistfully. He looked up, laid down his quill, and stretched out a hand to her.

'Well, *ma fille?*'

She ran to him, and sank on to her knees beside his chair.

'Monseigneur, it frightens me.'

He stroked her bright curls caressingly.

'What frightens you, child?'

She made a comprehensive gesture.

'This – all of it! There are so many grand people coming, and everyone is so busy. I myself have no time to talk to you, Monseigneur.'

'You do not like it, child?'

She wrinkled her nose.

'*Ah, quant à ça* – ! It excites me, Monseigneur, and – and yes, I like it very well. But it is as it was at Versailles. You remember I lost you. It was so big and brilliant.'

'Child –' He looked down into her eyes. 'I am always here.' He smiled a little. 'I think, infant, it is I shall be in danger of losing you when you are launched into the world. You will no longer wish to sit with me then.'

She shook her head vehemently.

'Always, always! *Voyons*, Monseigneur, I am going round and round in all this gaiety that comes to me and for a little while I like it. But always I want to run away to you. Then I am safe, and – and things do not bewilder me. You see?'

'Perfectly,' said his Grace. 'I shall not fail you, infant.'

'No, Monseigneur,' She nestled her hand in his, and gave a tiny sigh. 'Why do you do all this for me?'

'I have many reasons, infant. You will not bother your head with them.'

'No, Monseigneur,' she said again, obediently. 'It is very far away now, that time with Jean and Charlotte.'

'I desire you will forget it, *ma mie*. It was an evil dream – no more.'

'*Bien,* Monseigneur.' She rested her head against his arm, and stayed so a long time.

That very evening Davenant arrived and was told that the Duke was at dinner. He gave his greatcoat and hat to a lackey and, waving the man aside, went alone to the dining-room, whence a babble of talk came.

The long room was lit by candles that stood in gold clusters on the table. Silver winked, and cut glass, and the mellow light was thrown over all. At the foot of the table my lady Fanny sat, with Marling on her right, hot in argument with Rupert, opposite. Beside Marling was Léonie, dressed in dull yellow gold, and old lace. She was saying something to his Grace, at the head of the table, as Davenant came in, but she looked up at the sound of the opening door and suddenly clapped her hands.

'*Tiens*, it is M. Davenant! He is come, then! See, Monseigneur!'

His Grace rose, and put down his napkin.

'My dear Hugh! You come most opportunely. Jacques, lay for monsieur.'

Davenant clasped his hand a moment, nodding to Rupert, and to Marling.

'I could not resist your invitation – or was it a summons?' he said. He bowed low to Fanny. 'My lady?'

She gave him her hand, in high good-humour.

'I declare I am prodigious glad to see you, Hugh! I vow 'tis an age since I met you last!'

'As beautiful as ever,' he said, kissing her hand. But his eyes were on Léonie.

'Oh!' Lady Fanny pouted. 'I am put in the shade, Hugh, yes, positively I am put in the shade – by this chit! It is so mortifying!' She smiled at Léonie, and beckoned.

Léonie came forward in her best manner, and swept a curtsy. A wicked little smile hovered about her mouth; she fixed Davenant with wide, innocent eyes.

'Is it possible?' he said, and bent over her fingers.

'You are dazzled, in fact?' His Grace came to stand beside his ward.

'Completely! I would not have believed it could be! You are to be congratulated, Alastair.'

'Why, so I think,' said the Duke.

Léonie made a quaint little bow.

'Sometimes, m'sieur, I am still Léon.'

'Ay, that is Léon,' Hugh smiled. 'Do you like being Léonie?'

'At first it did not please me at all,' she answered. 'But now I think it is very agreeable. You have pretty things if you are a girl, and go to balls. There is to be a ball here next week, m'sieur.'

'So I hear,' he said. 'Who comes to it?'

They sat down again at the table, Davenant opposite Léonie. It was Fanny who answered.

'Everyone, Hugh, I give you my word! 'Pon rep, I have worked over this ball!'

'Ay, and made the house a veritable wasps' nest,' grumbled Rupert. 'How are you, Hugh?'

'The same as ever, Rupert. And you?'

'Well enough,' Rupert said. 'We're all of us reformed, as you see. Never was there such a united family, and all of us so amiable one to the other – God knows how long 'twill last!'

Davenant laughed across the table at Marling.

'I learn that I am to bear you company in this disreputable establishment, Marling!'

'We are invited to supply a note of sobriety,' nodded Marling. 'It was Léonie's notion. How did you leave your brother?'

'As long as you did leave him, Hugh, I'm satisfied,' grimaced Rupert.

'Ah yes!' said his Grace. 'The deplorable Frederick! How does he?'

'Oh, there never was a man so tedious as Colehatch!' cried my lady. 'Only fancy, Hugh, he loved me once! The great Lord Colehatch. La! I should be honoured!'

'He is just as deplorable as ever, I fear,' Hugh replied. 'He was not pleased to hear that I intended to visit this house again.'

'Lord, did he want you, Fan?' exclaimed Rupert. 'Well, I always knew the man was a fool.'

'I thank you, my lord!' Davenant made him a mock bow. 'You are all of you vastly complimentary towards my respected brother.'

'Oh, and to me!' said my lady. 'Horrid boy! Do you remember that Colehatch wanted me, Justin?'

'My memory fails me when I try to disentangle your suitors, my dear. Was he the one who demanded you of me with a pistol to my head, as it were? No, I believe that was Fonteroy. Colehatch, I think, wrote me a correct application for your hand which I still cherish. He said that he was willing to overlook such trifling faults in you, my dear, as your levity and your extravagance.'

'Fanny, I make you my apologies on his behalf!' laughed Hugh. Marling helped himself to a peach.

'What an ardent lover!' he remarked, 'I hope I did not say that I would overlook your faults?'

'Dearest Edward, you said that you adored me from my heels to my topmost curl!' sighed her ladyship. 'Lud, what days they were! Cumming – dear soul – fought John Drew because he disparaged my eyebrows, and Vane – do you remember Vane, Justin? – wanted to fly with me!'

Léonie was greatly interested.

'And did you?' she inquired.

'La, child, what will you ask next? He had not a penny, poor darling, and was mad into the bargain.'

'I should like people to fight over me,' Léonie said. 'With swords.'

Davenant was amused.

'Would you, Léon – Léonie!'

'But yes, m'sieur! It would be so exciting. Did you see them fight, madame?'

'Good gracious no, child! Of course I did not. One never does.'

'Oh!' Léonie was disappointed. 'I thought you watched.'

Davenant looked at the Duke.

'The lady would appear to have a taste for bloodshed,' he remarked.

'A veritable passion for it, my dear. Nothing pleases her more.'

'You are not to encourage her, Justin!' said my lady. 'I vow it's scandalous!'

Léonie twinkled merrily.

'There is one thing I made Monseigneur teach me that is very bloodthirsty,' she said. 'You do not know!'

'What is it, puss?'

'Aha, I will not tell!' She shook her head wisely. 'You would say it is unladylike.'

'Oh, Justin, what have you been at? Some hoydenish trick it is, I dare swear!'

'Tell us!' said Marling. 'You've whetted our curiosity, child, and soon we shall begin to guess.'

'Ecod, do you mean –' began Rupert.

Léonie waved agitated hands.

'No, no, *imbécile*! *Tais toi!*' She pursed her mouth primly. 'M. Marling would be shocked, and madame would say it is not at all respectable. Monseigneur, he is not to tell!'

'One would infer that it was some disgraceful secret,' said his Grace. 'I believe I have several times requested you not to call Rupert "*imbécile*," infant.'

'But Monseigneur, he is an *imbécile*!' she protested. 'You know he is!'

'Undoubtedly, *ma fille*, but I do not tell the whole world so.'

'Then I do not know what I am to call him,' said Léonie. 'He calls *me* spitfire, Monseigneur, and wild-cat.'

'And so she is, by Gad!' exclaimed his lordship.

'I am *not*, Rupert. I am a lady. Monseigneur says so.'

'A manifestly false assertion,' said his Grace. 'But I cannot remember ever having said anything of the kind, infant.

She peeped naughtily up at him, through her lashes. It was one of her most captivating little tricks.

'But, Monseigneur, you said only a minute ago that your memory is not at all good.'

There was a shout of laughter; Avon's own eyes were alight with it. He picked up his fan and dealt Léonie a rap across the knuckles. She chuckled, and turned jubilantly to the others.

'*Voyons*, I have made you all laugh!' she said. 'And I *meant* to make you laugh! I am a wit, *enfin*!'

Davenant was looking at Avon, dawning wonder on his face, for Avon's eyes rested on his ward with such tender amusement in them that Davenant could hardly believe it was the Duke that he looked on.

'Oh, lud, what a child it is!' said my lady, dabbing at her eyes. 'I vow I would never have dared speak so to Justin at your age!'

'Nor I!' said Rupert. 'But there's nothing she won't dare, damme, there's not!' He turned to Davenant. 'Never was there such a girl, Hugh! Do you know she's even been abducted?'

'Abducted?' Davenant looked round, half-incredulous. 'What's this?'

'Oh, that pig-person!' said Léonie scornfully.

'My love!' Lady Fanny jumped. '*What* did I hear you say?'

'Well, but, madame, Monseigneur allows me to say pig-person. You do not mind, do you, Monseigneur?'

'My infant, it is not a beautiful expression, nor am I in any way enamoured of it, but I believe that I did say I could support it as long as you refrained from talking of pig – er – wash.'

'Yes, you did,' she said triumphantly.

'But what do you mean?' demanded Davenant. 'Who abducted Léonie? Is it true?'

Marling nodded to him across the table.

'As pretty a piece of villainy as ever I heard.'

'But who did it? Who is the – the pig-person?'

'The bad Comte de Saint-Vire!' said Léonie. 'He gave me an evil drink, and brought me to France, and Rupert saved me!'

Davenant started, and stared at his Grace.

'Saint-Vire!' he said, and again, beneath his breath, 'Saint-Vire.'

His Grace cast a quick look round, but the lackeys had left the room.

'Yes, Hugh, yes. The so dear Comte.'

Davenant opened his mouth to speak, and then shut it again.

'Quite so,' said his Grace.

'But Avon' – it was Marling who spoke – 'Fanny tells me that cards for the ball have been sent to Saint-Vire and his wife. Why did you do that?'

'I believe I had a reason,' said his Grace pensively. 'No doubt it will return to my mind some time or other.'

'If the fellow comes I'll never be able to contain myself!' Rupert said.

'I do not imagine that he will come, my child. Hugh, if you have finished, I suggest we repair to the library. It is the only room that Fanny has left undisturbed.'

Fanny rose, and shook her finger at him.

'I shall throw it open on the night of the ball, never fear! I have a mind to set card-tables there.'

'No,' said Léonie firmly. 'It is our very own room, Monseigneur. You are not to let her!' She laid her finger-tips on his crooked arm, and prepared to go out with him. Hugh heard an urgent whisper. 'Monseigneur, not that room! We always sit there. You brought me to it the very first night.'

Avon turned his head. 'You hear, Fanny?'

'It's most tiresome!' said her ladyship, in a long-suffering manner. 'What odds can it make, child? What's your reason?'

'Madame, I cannot think of the word. It is what Monseigneur says when you ask him why he does a thing.'

Rupert opened the door. 'Faith, I know what she means! A whim!'

'*C'est cela!*' Léonie gave a little skip. 'You are very clever tonight, Rupert, I think.'

The ladies retired early to bed, and as Rupert dragged the unwilling Marling out to Vassaud's, Avon and Hugh were left alone in the quiet library. Hugh looked round with a little smile.

'Egad, it's like old times, Justin!'

'Three months ago, to be precise,' said his Grace. 'I am becoming something of a patriarch, my dear.'

'Are you?' Davenant said, and smiled to himself. 'May I compliment you on your ward?'

'Pray do! You find her to your taste?'

'Infinitely. Paris will be enchanted. She is an original.'

'Something of a rogue,' conceded his Grace.

'Justin, what has Saint-Vire to do with her?'

The thin brows rose.

'I seem to remember, my dear, that your curiosity was always one of the things I deplored in you.'

'I've not forgot the tale you told me – in this very room, Justin. Is Léonie the tool with which you hope to crush Saint Vire?'

His Grace yawned.

'You fatigue me, Hugh. Do you know, I have ever had a fancy to play my game – alone.'

Davenant could make nothing of him, and gave up the attempt. Marling came in presently, and remarked that Rupert was not like to return until the morning.

'Who was there?' Davenant asked.

'The rooms were crowded, but I know so few people,' Marling said. 'I left Rupert dicing with one Lavoulère.' He looked at the Duke. 'The lad's incorrigible, Avon. He will dice his soul away one of these days.'

'Oh, I trust not!' said Avon. 'I suppose he is losing?'

'He is,' Marling replied. 'It is not my affair, Justin, but I think you should strive to check this gambling fever in him.'

'I agree,' Davenant said. 'The boy is too thoughtless.'

Avon strolled to the door.

'Beloved, I leave you to your moralities,' he said softly, and went out.

Hugh laughed, but Marling frowned.

'Impossible Satanas!' said Hugh.

'He seems not to trouble his head over Rupert's welfare,' Marling spoke heavily. 'He should have some hold over the boy.'

'Oh, my dear Marling, Rupert will come to heel whenever Avon chooses to lift his finger.'

'It's very well, Hugh, but I have yet to see him lift it.'

'I have seen it,' Davenant answered. He drew his chair nearer to the fire. 'I see also a vast change in our Satanas.'

'Ay,' Marling admitted. 'It's the child's influence. My lady dreams of a bridal.'

'I would it might be so,' Hugh crossed his legs. 'There is that in Avon's eyes when he looks on Léonie –'

'I do not trust him.'

'Why, I think I do for once.' Hugh laughed a little. 'When last I saw Léonie – Léon she was then – it was "Yes, Monseigneur" and "No, Monseigneur." Now it is "Monseigneur, you must do this," and "Monseigneur, I want that!" She twists him round her little finger, and, by Gad, he likes it!'

'Oh, but there's naught of the lover in his manner, Hugh! You have heard him with her, scolding, correcting.'

'Ay, and I have heard the note in his voice of – faith, of tenderness! This wooing will be no ordinary one, methinks, but there is a bridal in the air.'

'She is twenty years behind him!'

'Do you think it signifies? I would not give Justin a bride his own age. I'd give him this babe who must be cherished and guarded. And I'll swear he'd guard her well!'

'It may be. I do not know. She looks up to him, Davenant! She worships him!'

'Therein I see his salvation,' Hugh said.

Twenty-Five

Léonie Curtsies to the Polite World

LADY FANNY STEPPED BACK TO OBTAIN A BETTER VIEW OF HER handiwork.

'I cannot make up my mind,' she said. 'Shall I put a riband in your hair, or – no, I have it! – a single white rose!' She picked one up from the table at her side. 'You can well spare it from your corsage, my dear. Where is the little buckle Justin gave you?'

Léonie, seated before the mirror, held out the pearl-and-diamond ornament. My lady proceeded to fasten the rose with it above Léonie's left ear, so that it nestled amongst the powdered curls that were skilfully arranged to resemble a coiffure. The *friseur* had worked wonders. The curls clustered thickly about the queenly little head, and just one had been coaxed to fall to the shoulder.

'It could not be better!' said my lady. 'Give me the haresfoot, wench!'

Léonie's maid handed it to her, and stood ready with the various pots.

'Just a touch of rouge, I think,' said Fanny. 'The veriest suspicion – so! The lip-stick, girl!... Keep still, my love, I must not overdo it. There! Powder, girl!' The haresfoot fluttered over Léonie's face. My lady studied the effect intently. 'It's very well.

Now for the patches! Two, I think. Don't wriggle, child!' Expert
fingers pressed the patches on: one below the dimple, one above
the cheekbone. 'Famous!' cried my lady. 'Mercy, look at the time!
I must hurry! Stand up, Léonie, and you, girl, hand me the dress!'

Léonie stood up in her under-dress of lace, ruffle upon ruffle
of it falling over a great hoop to her ankles, and watched my lady
shake out the folds of soft white brocade. Fanny flung it deftly
over her head, so that not a hair was disturbed, pulled it over
the hoop, twitched it into place, and told the maid to lace it up.
Léonie's feet peeped from beneath the lace petticoat in shoes of
white satin with heels that were studded with tiny diamonds.
Buckles flashed on them – yet another present from Avon. Léonie
pointed her toe, and regarded the effect gravely.

Fanny came to arrange a lace fichu about Léonie's shoulders.
Out of the lace they rose, sloping and very white. Fanny shook
out the ruffles, tied the ribbons, and fastened the two other roses
into place over the knot with a pearl pin.

'Why, madame, what is that?' asked Léonie quickly. 'It is not
mine, I know!'

Fanny kissed her lightly.

'Oh, it is naught but a trifle, my love, that I had a mind to give
you! I beg you will not heed it!'

Léonie flushed. 'Madame, you are *very* good to me! Thank
you!'

Someone scratched on the door; the abigail went to open it,
and came back into the room with a small silver tray, on which
were two packages, and white roses in a silver holder.

'For mademoiselle,' smiled the maid.

Léonie ran forward.

'For me? Who sent them?' She bent over the tray to read the
cards. 'Rupert – M. Marling – M. Davenant! But how they are
kind! Why do you all give me presents, madame?'

'My sweet, 'tis your first appearance. I suspect Hugh asked Justin what flowers he should send.' She picked up the bouquet. 'See, child, the holder is so cunningly wrought! What says the card?'

Léonie held it between her fingers.

'"To Léon, from Hugh Davenant." *Voyons*, I am not Léon tonight, but Mademoiselle de Bonnard! What can this be? from M. Marling – oh, the little ring! Madame, look!' She slipped the wrappings from the last package, and disclosed a fan of delicately painted chicken-skin mounted on ivory sticks. 'Oh, this clever Rupert! Madame, how did he know I wanted a fan?'

Fanny shook her head mysteriously.

'La, child, don't ask me! Stop skipping round the room, stupid! Where are Justin's pearls?'

'Oh, the pearls!' Léonie ran to the dressing-table, and extracted the long, milky string from one of the boxes there.

Fanny twisted it twice round her neck, cast another distracted glance at the clock, sprinkled scent on to a handkerchief, and over Léonie, gave a last twitch to the brocade gown, and hurried to the door.

'You will be so late!' Léonie cried. 'All because you dressed me. I will wait for you, madame, shall I?'

'Yes, child, of course! I want to be there when Jus – when they see you. Come and sit with me while I finish my toilette.'

But Léonie was in no mood to sit still. She paraded in front of the mirror, curtsied to herself, fluttered her fan, and sniffed at her roses.

Rachel worked swiftly tonight, and soon my lady stood up in a gown of rose silk, with a petticoat of silver lace, and the most enormous hoop Léonie had ever seen. My lady whisked the haresfoot across her face again, slipped bracelets on to her arms, and fixed nodding feathers into her marvellous coiffure.

'Oh, madame, it is very fine, I think!' said Léonie, pausing in her perambulations to and fro.

My lady pulled a face at her own reflection.

'It matters naught what I look like tonight,' she said. 'Do you like the silver lace, child? And the shoes?' She lifted her skirts and showed a pretty ankle.

'Yes, madame. I like it – oh, much! Now let us go downstairs and show Monseigneur!'

'I am with you in a moment, my sweet life. Rachel, my fan and gloves! Léonie, hold your bouquet in the other hand, and slip the riband of your fan over your wrist. Yes, that is excellent. Now I am ready.'

'I am so excited I feel as though I should burst!' said Léonie.

'Child! Remember you are to put a guard on your tongue! Let me hear no "bursts" or "pig-persons" on your lips tonight, as you love me.'

'No, madame, I will remember. And not "breeches" either!'

'Certainly not!' tittered Fanny, and sailed out to the staircase. At the head of it she paused, and stood aside. 'Go before me, child. Slowly, slowly! Oh dear, you will break hearts, I know!' But this she said to herself.

Léonie went sedately down the broad stairway that was brilliantly lit tonight with branches of tall candles set in the niches of the wall. Below, in the hall, gathered about the fire, the gentlemen were waiting, his Grace with orders glittering on a coat of purple satin; Lord Rupert in pale blue, with much rich lacing, and an elegant flowered waistcoat; Marling in puce; and Davenant in maroon. Léonie paused half-way down the stairs and unfurled her fan.

'But look at me!' she said reprovingly.

They turned quickly at the sound of her voice, and saw her with candles on either side, a little figure, all white, from the ordered curls to the jewelled heels: white brocade cut low across the shoulders, white lace to form a petticoat, white roses at her breast and in her hand. Only her eyes were deep, sparkling blue, and her parted lips like cherries, her cheeks faintly flushed.

'You beauty!' gasped Rupert. 'By – Gad, you beauty!'

His Grace went forward to the foot of the stairs, and held out his hands.

'Come, *ma belle!*'

She ran down to him. He bowed low over her hand, whereat she blushed, and curtsied a little way.

'I am nice, Monseigneur, do you not think? Lady Fanny did it all, and see, Monseigneur, she gave me this pin, and Rupert gave me the flow – no, the fan. It was M. Davenant gave me the flowers, and M. Marling this pretty ring!' She danced over to where they stood, just staring at her. 'Thank you *very* much, all of you! Rupert, you are very grand tonight! I have never seen you so – so tidy, and *tout à fait beau!*'

Lady Fanny came down the stairs.

'Well, Justin? Have I succeeded?'

'My dear, you have surpassed yourself.' His eyes ran over her. 'Your own toilette leaves nothing to be desired.'

'Oh!' she shrugged her shoulders. 'I am naught tonight.'

'You are *très grande dame*, my dear,' he said.

'That, perhaps,' she nodded. 'It was my intention.'

Rupert lifted his quizzing-glass.

'You always look a beauty, Fan; I'll say that for you.'

The lackeys about the great doorway suddenly sprang to attention.

'La, are they arriving already?' cried my lady. 'Come, child!' she led the way into the big ballroom, that ran the length of the house. Léonie looked about her appreciatively.

'*Voyons*, this pleases me!' she said, and went up to one of the great baskets of flowers to inspect the frail blooms. 'We are all very grand, and so is the house. Monseigneur, Rupert is beautiful, is he not?'

Avon surveyed his tall, rakish young brother.

'Would you call him beautiful?' he drawled.

'Devil take you, Justin!' spluttered his lordship.

A footman stood in the wide doorway, and rolled forth names. Rupert effaced himself, and Lady Fanny went forward.

An hour later it seemed to Léonie that the whole house was full of gaily dressed ladies and gentlemen. She had curtsied a hundred times; she still could hear my lady's voice saying: 'I have the honour to present to you Mademoiselle de Bonnard, madame, my brother's ward.'

Very early in the evening Avon had come to her with a young man beside him: a young man dressed in the height of fashion, with orders on his breast, and a marvellous wig upon his head. Avon had said:

'My ward, Prince. Léonie, M. le Prince de Condé desires an introduction.'

She curtsied very low; Condé bent over her hand.

'But mademoiselle is *ravissante!*' he murmured.

Léonie rose from her curtsy, and smiled shyly. M. le Prince laid a hand over his heart.

'Mademoiselle will honour me for this first dance?' he said.

She thought him a charming boy, no more. She put her hand on his arm, and smiled sunnily up at him.

'Yes, please, m'sieur. It is my very own ball! Is it not exciting?'

Condé, accustomed to débutantes who were properly bored, was enchanted with this frank enjoyment. The fiddlers struck up, the couples took their places behind him and Léonie.

'Must we go first?' she asked confidentially.

'But yes, mademoiselle, surely!' he smiled. 'You lead your very own ball.'

Lady Fanny, standing by the door, touched Rupert's arm.

'Who has the child got for partner? It should be a prince of the Blood at least, by the orders! Who is it?'

'Young Condé,' Rupert answered. 'You wouldn't know him, Fan. He's only twenty or so.'

'La, how did Justin get him here so early?' gasped my lady. 'He to lead her out! She's made for life! Look, he's laughing! Oh, she has captivated him, never fret!' She turned her head to find Avon behind her. 'Justin, how did you contrive to get Condé here so early? You're a wizard, I vow.'

'Yes, it was well thought of, was it not?' said his Grace. 'You will present her next to De Brionne. He is just come. Who is that child with the silver roses on her gown?'

'My dear, I don't know! There are so many new faces I protest I cannot remember to whom they all belong! Justin, Condé is enchanted! There's not a man in the room will not hasten to Léonie's side having seen him so enraptured! Ah, madame!' She rustled away to greet a late-comer.

'I think I'll go to the card-room and take charge there,' said Rupert ingenuously, and prepared to depart.

'Quite unnecessary, my child,' said his Grace, barring the way. 'Hugh has it well in hand. You, boy, will lead out Mademoiselle de Vauvallon.'

'Oh, lud!' groaned Rupert, but he moved away to where Mademoiselle was seated.

When next Fanny had leisure to observe Léonie she saw her seated on a couch in an alcove, drinking negus with her partner. The two seemed to be enjoying themselves hugely. Fanny watched, well pleased, and presently, evading the group of young men who were one and all clamouring for an introduction, she took the Comte de Brionne over to the alcove, and presented him. Condé rose, and made a leg.

'Oh, mademoiselle, you must save one little minute for me later!' he said. 'When may it be?'

'We will meet somewhere,' said Léonie. 'I know! Under the

big palm over there, at – at ten minutes past eleven!' She twinkled.
'That is like an adventure!'

'Mademoiselle, I shall be there!' Condé promised, laughing.

Fanny stepped forward.

'My brother's ward, m'sieur. M. de Brionne, Léonie.'

Léonie set down her glass, rose, and curtsied. Her brow was
wrinkled. Inexorably Fanny bore Condé away.

'Mademoiselle looks worried?' De Brionne gave her her glass
again.

She turned to him, and smiled engagingly.

'M'sieur, I am very stupid. I cannot remember who you are!'

De Brionne was taken aback for a moment. It was not thus that
young ladies were wont to address the son of Louis de Lorraine.
But he could not resist the fascination of Léonie's eyes. Moreover,
where Condé had been pleased De Brionne would certainly not
be affronted. He returned the smile.

'You are new come to Paris, mademoiselle?'

She nodded. 'Yes, m'sieur. Now let me think. *I* know! You are
the son of the Comte d'Armagnac – M. le Grand!'

The Comte was much amused. It was probable that he had
never before met a lady who pondered thus naïvely over his
genealogy. He settled down to enjoy himself, and found that he
was required to name most of the people who passed, for Léonie's
edification.

'*Voyons, m'sieur,* you know everybody!' she said presently. 'You
are being very useful to me. Now tell me who it is dancing with
Monseigneur?'

'Monseigneur?'

'Yes, the Duc – my – my guardian.'

'Oh – ! That is Madame du Deffand.'

'Truly?' Léonie regarded the lady intently. 'She amuses him, I
think.'

'She is a very amusing lady,' said De Brionne gravely. 'Did
Condé point our notables out to you?'

'No – no.' Léonie dimpled. 'We found such a lot of other
things to talk about, m'sieur. He told me about duels, and what it
is like to be a royal prince.'

De Brionne began to laugh.

'Did you ask him, mademoiselle?'

'Yes, m'sieur,' said Léonie innocently.

In the doorway Fanny was curtsying low to the Duc de Penthièvre,
who had just arrived. He kissed her hand with pretty gallantry.

'My dear Lady Fanny! One was *bouleversé* when one learned of
the return of the so charming Lady Fanny!'

'Ah, m'sieur!' She smiled, and spread out her fan.

Avon came up with Madame du Deffand on his arm.

'My dear Penthièvre, I am rejoiced to see you.'

'*Mon cher Duc! Madame, votre serviteur!*' He swept a bow. 'Tell
me, Alastair, where is this ward one hears tell of?'

'My ward… Let me see, she was with De Brionne a moment
ago. No, she is dancing now with my brother. In white, with the
rose in her hair.'

De Penthièvre looked across the room to where Léonie was
circling gracefully round Rupert. Their hands were held high, her
foot was pointed, and she was laughing.

'So!' said de Penthièvre. 'Our débutantes will tear their powdered locks, Duc!'

The rooms grew more crowded. Some time later Lady Fanny,
proceeding to the refreshment room, met her husband in the hall,
and said radiantly:

'My dearest love, what a success! Have you seen the child? De
Penthièvre has danced with her, and Condé! Where's Justin?'

'Gone into the little salon. You're satisfied, sweet?'

'Satisfied! Paris will talk of naught but this ball and Léonie for weeks to come! I shall keep them talking, I promise you!' She hurried away to the refreshment room, found it crowded, with Léonie the centre of a delighted and admiring group. Fanny took a forlorn lady under her wing, and bore her off in search of a cavalier.

In the card-room they discussed the Duke's latest whim.

'*Mon Dieu*, Davenant, but what a beauty! What colouring! What wonderful eyes!' cried Lavoulère. 'Who is she?'

The Chevalier d'Anvau cut in before Hugh could reply.

'Ah, he is proud of her, is Satanas! One sees it clearly.'

'He has reason,' remarked Marrignard, toying with a dice-box. 'She has not only beauty, but also *espièglerie*! I was amongst the fortunate who obtained her hand. Condé is greatly *épris*.'

The Chevalier looked at Hugh.

'She is like someone. I cannot think who it may be. I have racked my brains, but it eludes me.'

'Yes, it is true,' nodded Lavoulère. 'When I set eyes on her it came to me in a flash that I had met her before. Is it possible that I have done so, Davenant?'

'Quite impossible,' Hugh said fervently. 'She has but just come from England.'

Madame de Marguéry, playing at lansquenet at an adjacent table, looked up.

'But she is French, surely? Who were her parents?'

'I do not know, madame,' said Hugh with truth. 'As you know, Justin is never communicative.'

'Oh!' Madame cried. 'He loves to make a mystery! It is to intrigue us all! The child is quite charming, and well-born, of course. That naïve innocence should make her success assured. I would my daughters had it.'

Meanwhile Lady Fanny had sent Rupert to extricate Léonie from the refreshment room. She came back on my lord's arm, and chuckled gleefully.

'Madame, M. le Prince says I have eyes like stars, and another man said that a shaft from my eyes had slain him, and –'

'Tie, child!' said my lady. 'Never tell me all that here! I am going to present you to Madame de la Roque. Come!'

But at midnight Léonie escaped from the ballroom, and wandered into the hall. Condé, coming from one of the other salons, met her there.

'The little butterfly! I went to look for you, mademoiselle, and could not find you.'

Léonie smiled upon him.

'Please, have you seen Monseigneur, m'sieur?'

'A dozen monseigneurs, little butterfly! Which one do you want?'

'My own Monseigneur,' said Léonie. 'The Duc of Avon, of course.'

'Oh, he is in the farthest salon, mademoiselle, but shall not I do as well?'

She shook her head.

'But no, m'sieur. I want him.'

Condé took her hand, and smiled down at her.

'You are unkind, Fairy Princess! I thought you liked me just a little?'

'Yes, I do. I like you very much,' Léonie assured him. 'But now I want Monseigneur.'

'Then I'll fetch him for you at once,' Condé said gallantly.

'But no! I will go to him, m'sieur. You take me!'

Condé presented his arm promptly.

'Now you are a little kinder, mademoiselle! Is this monseigneur going to bring you to Versailles, I wonder?'

'Yes, I think so. Will you be there? Please do, m'sieur!'

'Of a certainty I shall be there. Then, at Madame de Longchamps' rout I shall meet you, surely?'

'I do not know,' she said. 'I think I am going to a great many routs, but Monseigneur has not told me which ones yet. Oh, there he is!' She released Condé's arm, and ran forward to where his Grace was standing. 'Monseigneur, I have been looking for you. The Prince brought me. Thank you very much, m'sieur!' She held out a friendly hand. 'Now you will go and dance with – with – oh, with somebody! I do not know the names!'

Condé kissed the small hand.

'You will bring her to court, Duc?'

'To the levee next week,' said his Grace.

'Then I am satisfied,' Condé said, bowed, and left them.

The Duke looked down at his ward in some amusement.

'You dismiss royalty very summarily, Babe.'

'Oh, Monseigneur, he is quite young, and very like Rupert! He did not mind, do you think?'

'He did not appear to mind,' said the Duke. 'What do you want with me, infant?'

'Nothing, Monseigneur. But I thought I would come to find you.'

'You are tired, infant.' He led her to a couch. 'You shall sit quietly with me awhile.'

'Yes, please, Monseigneur. It is a *very* nice dance, I think. I have danced with a great many grand people, and they were all very kind to me indeed.'

'I am glad to hear it, child,' he said gravely. 'How does your Prince please you?'

'Oh, he is *fort amusant*! He told me ever so many things about court, Monseigneur, and he explained who the people were – oh no! It was M. de Brionne who did that. I said "Bah" to the Prince, I am afraid, but he liked it, and he laughed. And I danced with Rupert – and oh, Monseigneur, with M. d'Anvau! He said he was sure he had met me before!' Her eyes danced. 'I wanted to say, "But yes, m'sieur. I brought you wine at Vassaud's one night!"'

'I sincerely trust you did not, infant?'

'Oh no, I was very discreet, Monseigneur. I said "*Tiens!* Me, I do not think I have met m'sieur before." It was not at all true, was it?'

'Never mind, child, it was a very proper reply. And now I am going to present you to a very old friend of mine who desires speech with you. Come, infant!'

'*Qui est-ce?*' she asked.

He walked slowly with her through the salons to the hall.

'It is M. de Richelieu, my child. You will be very polite to him.'

'Yes, Monseigneur,' she said docilely, and nodded her head to a young exquisite who was smiling at her and trying to catch her eye. 'I have been very polite to everyone tonight. Except Rupert, of course.'

'That goes without saying,' said his Grace, and took her back into the ballroom.

A middle-aged exquisite was standing by the fire at one end, holding animated converse with a plump lady of some beauty. Avon waited until others had gathered about his lady, and then he went forward.

Richelieu saw him, and came to meet him.

'Ah, Justin, the promised introduction! Your beautiful ward!'

Léonie took her hand from Avon's arm, and curtsied. Richelieu bowed to her, and took her hand, and patted it.

'Child, I envy Justin. Justin, go away! I shall look after mademoiselle very well without you.'

'I don't doubt it,' said his Grace, and went away to find Lady Fanny.

Armand de Saint-Vire pounced on him as he crossed the hall.

'My friend, who is that girl?' he demanded. 'I craved an introduction. Miladi Fanny was good enough to present me. I talked with the sprite — *mon Dieu, qu'elle est jolie!* — and all the time I asked myself: Who is she? Who is she?'

'And did you obtain an answer from yourself?' inquired his Grace.

'No, Justin, I did not! Therefore I ask you: Who is she?'

'She is my ward, dear Armand,' smiled his Grace, and passed on as Mademoiselle de la Vogue came up.

Fanny was in the refreshment room, with Davenant. She waved to Justin as he entered.

'I have earned a moment's repose!' she said gaily. 'Lud, Justin, I've presented a score of children to each other and never caught one of their names! Where's Léonie?'

'With Richelieu,' he said. 'No, Fanny, you need not to be alarmed. He is under oath to be discreet. Hugh, you have been a godsend to me this night.'

My lady began to fan herself.

'We have all of us worked a little,' she said. 'My poor Edward is with the dowagers, playing at ombre, and Rupert has scarce been inside the card-room.'

'You have worked the hardest of us all,' said Hugh.

'Oh, but I have enjoyed myself so prodigiously!' she said. 'Justin, I don't know how many young beaux have not been making love to Léonie! Condé is ravished, he tells me. Do I not make a famous chaperon? When I present Léonie I feel fifty – yes, Hugh, positively I do! – but when I meet Raoul de Fontanges again – ah, then I am back in my teens!' She cast up her eyes.

But presently people began to take their leave, and at last they were alone again in the hall, tired but triumphant.

Rupert yawned prodigiously.

'Lord, what an evening! Burgundy, Hugh?' He poured out several glasses. 'Fan, you've torn your lace.'

Fanny sank into a chair.

'My dear, I do not care if 'tis in ribbons. Léonie, my pet, you look worn out! Oh, my poor Edward, you did nobly with the dowagers!'

'Ah yes!' said his Grace. 'I have to thank you, Edward. You were quite untiring. Infant, can you still hold your eyes open?'

'Yes, Monseigneur. Oh, madame, M. le Prince said that my dress was ravishing!'

'Ay –' Rupert shook his head at her. 'I'd give something to know what you've been at this night, rogue! Did old Richelieu make love to you?'

'Oh no!' Léonie was surprised. 'Why he is quite an old man!'

'Alas, poor Armand!' said his Grace. 'Don't tell him so, infant, I implore you.'

'Nor anyone, my love,' said her ladyship. 'It would fly round Paris! He would be so chagrined!'

'Well, who did make love to you?' asked Rupert. 'Besides Condé.'

'He didn't, Rupert! No one did.' Léonie looked round innocently. 'He only said I was a Fairy Princess. Yes, and he said that about my eyes.'

'If that's not making –' Rupert encountered a glance from his brother, and broke off. 'Oh ay! I'm dumb, never fear!'

'Monseigneur,' Léonie said. 'I kept thinking it was a dream! If they knew I had been a page I do not think they would have been so kind to me. They would have thought I was not enough respectable!'

Twenty-Six

The Presentation of Léonie

AFTER THE BALL INVITATIONS CAME SWIFTLY TO THE HÔTEL AVON. More than one lady begged that Miladi Fanny would forgive the shortness of the notice and honour her on such-and-such a night, at ball, or rout, or card-party. Fanny went carefully through the pile of little cards, and was triumphant.

'My dearest Justin!' she cried. 'We shall not be above three nights at home, I give you my word! Here is a card from Madame du Deffand, for next month – a soirée. This is from the Comtesse de Meuilly – a ball. And here we have one from my dear Madame de Follermartin, for Saturday! And this one –'

'Spare us, Fanny!' said his Grace. 'Accept and decline as you will, but let us have no lists. Infant, what have you there?'

Léonie had come dancing in with a bouquet in her hand, to which a card was attached.

'Monseigneur, are they not pretty? They come from the Prince de Condé. I think he is very kind to me!'

Fanny looked at her brother.

'So we begin,' she said. 'Where are we like to end, I wonder?'

'I shall end in a debtor's prison, never fear!' said Rupert, from the depths of an arm-chair. 'Two hundred cool guineas last night, and –'

'Rupert, it's wanton!' exclaimed Marling. 'Why do you play so high?'

Rupert deigned no reply, deeming the question beneath contempt. It was Davenant who filled the breach.

'I believe it's in the family,' he said. 'Rupert, of course, is a scamp.'

'Oh no!' said Léonie. 'He is very silly, but he is not a scamp! Monseigneur, tell me what I am to wear at Versailles tomorrow! Madame says blue, but I want to wear my white dress again.'

'No, infant. To wear the same frock twice running would create almost a scandal. You shall wear gold, and dull yellow, and the sapphires I once gave you. And your hair shall be unpowdered.'

'Oh?' said my lady. 'Why, Justin?'

Hugh walked to the fireplace.

'Is it, Justin, because Titian hair has always been one of your ruling passions?'

'Exactly,' bowed his Grace. 'What an excellent memory you have, my dear!'

'I don't understand,' complained Fanny. 'What do you mean?'

'I am not quite sure,' said Avon. 'I suggest you ask Hugh. He is omniscient.'

'Now you are being disagreeable!' Fanny pouted. 'Dull yellow – ay, 'twill do. Léonie, my love, we must order a petticoat of gold net from Cerise; they are quite the rage now, I hear.' She became absorbed in modes and fashions.

She and Avon and Rupert accompanied Léonie to Versailles. Marling and Davenant were alike in their distaste for courts, and they refused to join the party, preferring to spend a quiet evening playing at piquet, and perusing the latest copy of the *Adventurer* which had come that day from London.

So Léonie and her escort left them to their devices, and sped away in the light coach to Versailles. The drive provoked in Léonie

a reminiscent mood. She sat beside Lady Fanny, whose skirts bil-
lowed about her, and addressed herself to the Duke, opposite.

'Monseigneur, do you remember that when we went to
Versailles before you gave me this chain?' She touched the sapphires that lay across her white breast.

'I do, infant. I also remember that on our return you went to
sleep, and would not wake up.'

'Yes, that is true,' she nodded. 'It seems very strange to be
going to Court again, like this!' She indicated her petticoats, and
spread out her fan. 'M. le Prince was at Madame de Cacheron's
party last night, Monseigneur.'

'So I have heard,' said Avon, who had not been present.

'And danced twice with the chit!' said my lady. ''Twas positively unseemly!'

'Ay, so it was,' agreed Rupert. 'If you were to ask me, I should
say he came to see Léonie and none other.'

'Yes, he did,' said Léonie ingenuously. 'He told me so. I like him.'

Rupert looked at her severely.

'Well, you ought not to sit with him talking of God knows
what,' he said magisterially. 'When I wanted to lead you out you
were nowhere to be found.'

Léonie pulled a face at him.

'You are talking like that because you have all your best clothes
on,' she told him. 'They make you feel grand, and very important.
I know!'

Rupert burst out laughing.

'Faith, that's good! But I'll not deny this is a devilish fine coat.'
He regarded his rich claret-coloured sleeve with some affection.

'It is not so – so *distingué* as Monseigneur's gray and pink,' said
Léonie. 'Monseigneur, whom shall I see tonight?'

'Why, child, I thought you had a dozen assignations made!'
remarked her ladyship.

'Yes, madame, but I meant new people.'

'Oh, she's insatiable!' murmured Rupert. 'She'll boast a wonderful collection of hearts before the month's out, mark my words!'

'You will see the King, infant, and the Queen, and possibly the Dauphin,' said his Grace.

'And Madame de Pompadour. I want to see her, because I have heard that she is very beautiful.'

'Very,' said his Grace. 'You will also see her favourite, de Stainville, and Monsieur, and the Comte d'Eu.'

'*Tiens!*' said Léonie.

When they had come to Versailles she went presently up the marble stairway, in Lady Fanny's wake, to the Galerie des Glaces, and looking about her, drew a deep breath.

'*How* I remember!' she said.

'For goodness' sake, child, never say so!' begged Fanny. 'You have never been here before. Let me hear no more of your recollections!'

'No, madame,' said Léonie, abashed. 'Oh, there is M. de la Valaye!'

La Valaye came to talk to them, and stole a curious glance at Léonie's unpowdered head. Rupert slipped away into the crowd, in search of a kindred spirit, and was seen no more for some time.

Many people were turning to look at Léonie.

'*Dis donc,*' said de Stainville, 'who is this beautiful little redhead? I do not recognise her.'

His friend, de Sally, took snuff.

'Have you not heard?' he asked. 'That is the very latest beauty! She is Avon's ward.'

'Oho! Yes, one has heard,' nodded de Stainville. 'It is Condé's new toy, *hein*?'

'No, no, my friend!' De Sally shook his head vehemently. 'Condé's new goddess!'

Léonie was curtsying to the Duchess de la Roque; de Stainville saw my lady Fanny.

'So Alastair has brought his so charming sister! *Madame, votre serviteur!*'

Fanny turned.

'La, so 'tis you, m'sieur.' She held out her hand. 'I declare 'tis an age since I have seen you!'

'Madame, the years fly back when I look upon you,' de Stainville said, kissing her hand. 'But surely it was Etienne once, and not that cold M'sieur?'

My lady hid behind her fan.

'I vow I have no recollection of it!' she said. 'No doubt I was very foolish – so long ago!'

De Stainville drew her apart, and they fell to talking of bygone days. Perceiving that his sister was fully occupied, Avon rescued Léonie from her growing circle of admirers, and bore her off to curtsy to the Comte d'Eu, who was passing down the gallery. Soon Fanny left de Stainville, and came to Avon's side. The Comte bowed to her.

'Madame, I may compliment you upon your charge?' He waved one jewelled hand towards Léonie, who was speaking to a shy débutante who had been present at her ball.

Fanny nodded. 'She pleases you, m'sieur?'

'It could not be otherwise, madame. She is *éclatante*! That hair, and those eyes! I prophesy a *succès énorme*!' He bowed, and moved away on the arm of a friend.

Léonie came back to Avon.

'Monseigneur, I think very young men are silly,' she said flatly.

'Undoubtedly, infant. Who has had the misfortune to incur your disapproval?'

'It was M. de Tanqueville, Monseigneur. He says I am cruel. And I am not, am I?'

'Of course you are, child!' said my lady. 'All young ladies must be cruel. It is *de rigueur*!'

'Ah, bah!' said Léonie. 'Monseigneur, where is the King?'

'By the fire, infant. Fanny, take her to the King.'

My lady furled her fan. 'You arranged, Justin?'

'Certainly, my dear. You are expected.'

So Fanny led Léonie down the room, and curtsied low to Majesty, who was pleased to be gracious. Behind Majesty, with Monsieur, and one or two others, Condé stood. Léonie encountered his gaze, and dimpled mischievously. Majesty was pleased to compliment my Lady Fanny on Mademoiselle de Bonnard; the Queen murmured praise of such beauty, and my lady passed on to make way for the next presentation.

'*Bon!*' said Léonie. 'Now I have spoken to the King.' She turned to Avon, and the twinkle was in her eyes. 'Monseigneur, it is as I said! He is just like the coins.'

Condé made his way to her side, and Lady Fanny withdrew discreetly.

'Oh, Fairy Princess, you flame in our hearts tonight!'

Léonie put her hand to her curls.

'But it is not at all kind of you to speak of my red hair!' she protested.

'Red?' Condé cried. 'It is the colour of copper, Princess, and your eyes are like the violets you wear at your breast. As a white rose you enchanted me, and now as a golden rose you strengthen your spell.'

'M'sieur,' said Léonie severely, 'that is how M. de Tanqueville talks. I do not like it at all.'

'Mademoiselle, I am at your feet! Tell me what I may do to regain your favour!'

Léonie looked at him speculatively. He laughed.

'Oh la, la! It is to be some great venture of chivalry, *enfin?*'

Her eyes danced.

'It is just that I am so very thirsty, m'sieur,' she said plaintively.

A gentleman standing a few paces from them looked at her in astonishment, and turned to a friend.

'*Mon Dieu*, did you hear that, Louis? Who is this beauty who has the audacity to send Condé to fetch her refreshment?'

'Why, do you not know?' exclaimed his friend. 'It is Mademoiselle de Bonnard, the English Duc's ward! She is an original, and Condé is captivated by her so unusual behaviour.'

Condé had given Léonie his arm. Together they passed into an adjoining salon, where he procured a glass of ratafie for her. A quarter of an hour later Lady Fanny found them there, both in high fettle, Condé trying to illustrate for Léonie's benefit a fencing trick, with his quizzing-glass as foil.

'Lud, child, what will you be at?' demanded my lady. She curt-sied low to Condé. 'M'sieur, you will not let her weary you, I beg.'

'Oh, but I am not wearying him, madame, truly!' said Léonie. 'He was thirsty too! Oh, here is Rupert!'

Rupert came in with the Chevalier d'Anvau. When the Chevalier saw Léonie his brow creased.

'Who? Who? *Who? M'sieur, on vous demande.*'

Condé waved him aside. 'Mademoiselle, the promised guerdon?'

Léonie gave him the violets at her breast, and smiled prettily as she did so. Condé kissed her hand, and then the flowers, and went back into the gallery with the fragrant bunch worn on his coat.

'Well!' said Rupert. ''Pon my soul!'

'Come along, Rupert!' said Léonie. 'Take me to find Madame de Pompadour now.'

'No, damme, that I won't!' said my lord gracefully. 'I've but this moment escaped, with d'Anvau here. It's a plaguey dull affair, so it is!'

'Child, I want you,' said Fanny, and took her back to the gal-lery and left her with her very dear friend Madame de Vauvallon, while she herself went in search of Avon.

She found him at length near the Œil de Bœuf, with de Richelieu and the Duc de Noailles. He came to her at once.

'Well, Fanny, where is my infant?'

'With Clothilde de Vauvallon,' she answered. 'Justin, she has given Condé her violets, and he is wearing them! Whither shall this lead?'

'Nowhere, my dear,' said his Grace placidly.

'But, Justin, 'tis not well to ensnare Royalty thus! Too great favour shown spells ruin as surely as too little.'

'I beg you will not distress yourself, my dear. Condé is not in love with the infant, nor she with him.'

'In love! 'Pon rep, I hope not indeed! But all this coquetting and –'

'Fanny, you are sometimes very blind. Condé is amused, no more.'

'Oh, 'tis very well!' shrugged my lady. 'What now?'

His Grace's quizzing-glass swept the gallery.

'Now, my dear, I desire you will take Léonie and present her to Madame de Saint-Vire.'

'Why?' asked my lady, watching him.

'Oh, I think she might be interested!' said his Grace, and smiled.

When Lady Fanny led Léonie to Madame de Saint-Vire, Madame's hand clenched in her fan, and under all her paint she whitened.

'Madame!' Lady Fanny saw the clenched hand, and heard the quick intake of breath. 'It is so long since we met! I trust I see you well?'

'I am very well, madame. You are with – with your brother in – Paris?' Madame spoke with an effort.

'Yes, I am this child's chaperon!' said Fanny. 'Is it not ridiculous? I may present my brother's ward? Mademoiselle de Bonnard, Madame de Saint-Vire!' She stood back.

Madame's hand went out involuntarily.

'Child –' she said, and her voice trembled. 'Sit with me a while, I beg!' She turned to Fanny. 'Madame, I will have a care to her. I should – I should like to talk to her.'

'But certainly!' said Fanny, and walked away at once.

Léonie was left looking into her mother's face. Madame took her hand, and patted it, and stroked it.

'Come, my little one!' she faltered. 'There is a couch by the wall. You will stay with me a few – just a few – minutes?'

'Yes, madame,' said Léonie politely, and wondered why this faded lady should be so agitated. She was not at all pleased at being left with Saint-Vire's wife, but she went with her to the couch, and sat down beside her.

Madame seemed to be at a loss. She held Léonie's hand still, and her eyes devoured the girl.

'Tell me, *chérie*,' she said at last. 'Are you – are you happy?'

Léonie was surprised.

'But yes, madame. Of course I am happy!'

'That man' – Madame pressed her handkerchief to her lips – 'that man – is good to you?'

'You speak of Monseigneur, my guardian, madame?' Léonie spoke stiffly.

'Yes, *petite*, yes. Of him.' Madame's hand trembled.

'*Naturellement* he is good to me,' Léonie answered.

'Ah, you are offended, but indeed, indeed – Child, you are so young! I – I might be – your mother!' She laughed rather wildly. 'So you will not mind what I say to you, will you? He – your guardian – is not a good man, and you – you –'

'Madame' – Léonie drew her hand away – 'I do not want to be rude to you, you understand, but I will not let you speak thus of Monseigneur.'

'You are so fond of him?'

'Yes, madame, I love him *de tout mon coeur* –'

'Ah, *mon Dieu*!' Madame whispered. 'And he – does he love you?'

'Oh no!' said Léonie. 'At least, I do not know, madame. He is just very kind to me.'

Madame's eyes searched her face.

'It is well,' she said, on a sigh. 'Tell me, child, how long have you lived with him?'

'Oh – oh, *depuis longtemps!*' Léonie said vaguely.

'Child, don't tease me! I – I would not tell your secrets! Where did the Duc find you?'

'Pardon, madame. I have forgotten.'

'He told you to forget!' Madame said quickly. 'That is so, is it not?'

Someone came to the couch; Madame shrank a little, and was silent.

'Well met, mademoiselle,' said Saint-Vire. 'I trust I see you in good health?'

Léonie's chin was tilted.

'M'sieur?' she said blankly. 'Ah, *je me souviens!* It is M. de Saint-Vire!' She turned to madame. 'I met m'sieur at – *peste*, I forget! Ah yes! – at Le Dennier, near Le Havre, madame.'

Saint-Vire's brow darkened.

'You have a good memory, mademoiselle.'

Léonie looked him between the eyes.

'Yes, m'sieur. I do not forget people – ever!'

Not ten paces from them Armand de Saint-Vire was standing, as though rooted to the ground.

'*Nom d'un nom d'un nom d'un nom!*' he gasped.

'That,' said a soft voice behind him, 'is an expression which I have never admired. It lacks – er – force.'

Armand swung round to face the Duke.

'My friend, you shall tell me now who is this Mademoiselle de Bonnard!'

'I doubt it,' said his Grace, and took a pinch of snuff.

'But look at her!' said Armand urgently 'It is Henri! Henri to the life now that I see them side by side!'

'Do you think so?' asked his Grace. 'I find her more beautiful than the so dear Comte, and more refined in type.'

Armand shook his arm.

'Who is she?'

'My dear Armand. I have not the slightest intention of telling you, so pray do not grip my arm thus violently.' He removed Armand's hand from his sleeve, and smoothed the satin. 'So. You will do well, my friend, to be blind and dumb concerning my ward.'

'Aha?' Armand looked at him inquisitively. 'I wish I knew what game you are playing. She's his daughter, Justin! I would swear to it!'

'It will be much better if you do no such thing, my dear,' said his Grace. 'Leave me to play this game to a close. You shall not then be disappointed.'

'But I do not understand! I cannot imagine what you think to do with –'

'Then pray do not try, Armand. I have said that you shall not be disappointed.'

'I am to be dumb? But all Paris will be talking of it soon!'

'So I think,' agreed his Grace.

'Henri won't like it,' pondered Armand. 'But I do not see that it can harm him. So why do you –'

'My dear, the game is more intricate than you think. You are better out of it, believe me.'

'Well!' Armand bit his finger. 'I can trust you to deal with Henri, I suppose. You love him as much as I do, *hein*?'

'Less than that,' said his Grace, and went slowly to the couch where Léonie sat. He bowed to Madame de Saint-Vire. 'Your servant, madame. Once again we meet in this exceedingly draughty salon. My very dear Comte!' He bowed to Saint-Vire. 'You renew your acquaintance with my ward?'

'As you see, Duc.'

Léonie had risen, and stood now beside his Grace. He took her hand, and looked mockingly at the Comtesse.

'I had the felicity of meeting my very dear friend in the most unexpected spot only a month ago,' he told her. 'We were both, an I remember rightly, in search of – er – lost property. Quite a curious coincidence, was it not? It seems that there are some sad rogues in this delightful country.' He pulled out his snuff-box, and saw the Comte redden.

Then the Vicomte de Valmé came up, smothering a yawn behind his broad hand.

'Your so charming son,' purred Avon.

Madame rose quickly, and one of the sticks of her fan snapped under her restless fingers. Her lips moved soundlessly; she met her husband's eyes, and stood silent.

The Vicomte bowed to his Grace, and looked admiringly at Léonie.

'Your servant, Duc.' He turned to Saint-Vire. 'Will you present me, sir?'

'My son, Mademoiselle de Bonnard!' Saint-Vire said brusquely.

Léonie curtsied, looking closely at the Vicomte.

'You are ennuyé, Vicomte, as usual?' Avon fobbed his snuff-box. 'You pine for the country, and – a farm, was it not?'

The Vicomte smiled.

'Oh, m'sieur, you must not speak of that foolish wish of mine! In truth, it grieves my parents.'

'But surely a most – ah – praiseworthy ambition?' drawled Avon. 'We will hope that you may one day realise it.' He inclined his head, offered his arm to Léonie, and walked away with her down the long gallery.

Léonie's fingers gripped his sleeve.

'Monseigneur, I have remembered! It came to me in a flash!'

'What, my infant, is "it"?'

'That young man. Monseigneur, we met him before, when I was a page, and I could not think who he was like. But just now it came to me! He is like Jean. It is ridiculous, is it not?'

'Most ridiculous, *ma fille*. I desire you will not repeat that to anyone.'

'No, Monseigneur, of course not. I am very discreet now, you know.'

Avon saw Condé in the distance, with the violets pinned to his coat, and smiled a little.

'I did not know it, infant, nor have I observed any signs of discretion in you, but let that pass. Where, I wonder, is Fanny?'

'She is talking to M. de Penthièvre, Monseigneur. I think he likes her – oh much! Here she is! She looks very pleased, so I expect M. de Penthièvre has told her that she is just as beautiful as she was when she was nineteen.'

Avon put up his glass.

'My infant, you are becoming positively shrewd. Do you know my sister so well?'

'I am very fond of her, Monseigneur,' Léonie hastened to add.

'I do not doubt it, *ma fille*.' He looked towards Fanny, who had paused to speak to Raoul de Fontanges. 'It is most surprising, nevertheless.'

'But she is so kind to me, Monseigneur. Of course, she is sometimes very s –' Léonie stopped, and peeped up at the Duke uncertainly.

'I entirely agree with you, infant. Very silly,' said his Grace imperturbably. 'Well, Fanny, can we now depart?'

'That was exactly what I had a mind to ask you!' said my lady. 'What a crush! Oh, my dear Justin, de Penthièvre has been saying such things to me! I vow I am all one blush! What are you smiling at? My love, what had Madame de Saint-Vire to say to you?'

'She is mad,' said Léonie, with conviction. 'She looked as

though she were going to cry, and I did not like it at all. Oh, here is Rupert! Rupert, where have you been?'

Rupert grinned. 'Faith, asleep, in the little salon over there. What, are we going at last? God be praised!'

'Asleep! Oh, Rupert!' Léonie cried. 'It has been *fort amusant*! Monseigneur, who is that pretty lady over there?'

'La, child, that is La Pompadour!' whispered Fanny. 'Will you present her, Justin?'

'No, Fanny, I will not,' said his Grace gently.

'Here's a haughtiness,' remarked Rupert. 'For the Lord's sake let us be gone before all these young pups crowd round Léonie again.'

'But, Justin, will it serve?' asked my lady. 'She will take offence, belike.'

'I am not a French satellite,' said his Grace. 'And therefore I shall not present my ward to the King's mistress. I believe Léonie can dispense with the lady's smiles or frowns.'

'But, Monseigneur, it would please me to –'

'Infant, you will not argue with me, I think.'

'Oh, won't she!' said Rupert, *sotto voce*.

'No, Monseigneur. But I did want to –'

'Silence, my child.' Avon led her to the door. 'Content yourself with having been presented to their Majesties. They are not, perhaps, so powerful as La Pompadour, but they are infinitely better born.'

'For heaven's sake, Justin!' gasped my lady. 'You'll be heard!'

'Think of us!' Rupert besought him. 'You'll have the lot of us clapped up, if you're not careful, or hounded out of the country.'

Avon turned his head.

'If I thought that there was the smallest chance of getting you clapped up, child, I would shout my remarks to the whole of this very overcrowded room,' he said.

'I think you are not at all in a nice humour, Monseigneur,'

said Léonie reproachfully. 'Why may I not be presented to La Pompadour?'

'Because, infant,' replied his Grace, 'she is not – er – enough respectable.'

Twenty-Seven

The Hand of Madame de Verchoureux

AND PARIS BEGAN TO TALK, IN WHISPERS AT FIRST, THEN GRADU-
ally louder, and more openly. Paris remembered an old, old
scandal, and said that the English Duc had adopted a base-born
daughter of Saint-Vire in revenge for past injuries. Paris thought
that it must irk Saint-Vire considerably to see his offspring in
the hands of his greatest enemy. Then Paris wondered what the
English Duc meant to do with Mademoiselle de Bonnard, and
found no solution to the riddle. Paris shook its head, and thought
that the ways of Avon were inscrutable and probably fiendish.

Meanwhile Lady Fanny swept through the town with Léonie,
and saw to it that her social activities this season should not easily
be forgotten. Léonie enjoyed herself very much, and Paris enjoyed
her even more. In the mornings she rode out with Avon, and two
factions sprang up thereafter amongst her admirers. One faction
held that the divine Léonie was seen at her best in the saddle; the
other faction was firm that in the ballroom she was incomparable.
One excitable young gentleman challenged another on this score,
but Hugh Davenant was present, and he took both young hot-
heads severely to task for bandying Léonie's name about over their
cups, and the affair came to naught.

Others tried to make love to Léonie, whereat she was angry,
and turned a cold shoulder on their enthusiasms. She could be
dignified when she chose, and her admirers were speedily abashed.
Learning of their discomfiture one evening when she was helping
Léonie to dress, Lady Fanny forgot herself, and exclaimed:

'Oh, splendidly done, my love! What a duchess you will make,
to be sure!'

'A duchess, madame?' Léonie said. 'How could I be that?'

Lady Fanny looked at her, and then at a new bracelet that lay
on the table.

'Don't tell me you don't know, puss!'

Léonie was trembling now.

'Madame –'

'Oh, my dear, he's head over ears in love with you, as all the world
must know! I have watched it grow, and – my dearest life, there is
no one I would sooner have for my sister than you, I do assure you!'

'Madame, you – you must be mistaken!'

'Mistaken? I? Trust me to read the signs, my love! I have
known Justin many years, and never have I seen him as he is now.
Silly child, why does he give you all these jewels?'

'I – I am his ward, madame.'

'Pooh!' My lady snapped her fingers. 'A fig for that! Tell me
why he made you his ward?'

'I – I do not know, madame. I – did not think.'

My lady kissed her again.

'You will be a duchess before the year is out, never fear!'

Léonie pushed her away.

'It's not true! You shall not say these things!'

'Why, here's a heat! Is there ever a man you have liked as you
liked "Monseigneur"?'

'Madame –' Léonie pressed her hands together. 'I am very
ignorant, but I know – I have heard what people say when such

as Monseigneur wed – wed ladies of no birth. I am only a tavern-keeper's sister. Monseigneur could not marry me. I – I had not thought of it.'

''Tis I who am a fool to have put the idea into your head!' said Fanny remorsefully.

'Madame, I beg you will not say it to anyone.'

'Not I, child, but everyone knows that you have Avon in your toils.'

'I have not! I hate you when you talk like that!'

'Oh, my dear, we are but two women! What matter? Justin will count no cost, believe me. You may be born as low as you please, but will he care once he looks into your eyes?'

Léonie shook her head stubbornly.

'I know I am not a fool, madame. It would be a disgrace for him to marry me. One must be born.'

'Fiddle, child! If Paris accepts you without question shall not Avon too?'

'Madame, Monseigneur has no love for those who are lowborn. Many, many times I have heard him say so.'

'Never think of it, child.' Lady Fanny wished that she had not allowed her tongue to run away with her. 'Come, let me tie your ribands!' She bustled about Léonie, and presently whispered in her ear: 'My sweet, do you not love him?'

'Oh, madame, madame, I have always loved him, but I did not think – until you made me see –'

'There, child, there! Do not cry, I implore you! You will make your eyes red.'

'I do not care about my eyes!' said Léonie, but she dried her tears, and permitted Lady Fanny to powder her face again.

When they went downstairs together Avon stood in the hall, and the sight of him brought the colour to Léonie's cheeks. He looked at her closely.

'What ails you, infant?'

'Nothing, Monseigneur.'

He pinched her chin caressingly.

'It is the thought of your princely admirer that makes you blush, *ma fille?*'

Léonie recovered herself at this.

'Ah, bah!' she said scornfully.

Condé was not present at Madame de Vauvallon's rout that night, but there were many others who had come to see Léonie, and not a few who had come early in the hope of securing her hand for a dance. Avon arrived late, as ever, and Madame de Vauvallon, who had no daughters of marriageable age, greeted him with a laugh, and a gesture of despair.

'My friend, I have a score of young beaux who give me no peace until I promise to present them to *la petite*! Fanny, Marchérand is back! Let me find – oh, la la! I should say choose – a gallant for Léonie, and I'll tell you the scandal! Come, little one!' She took Léonie's hand, and led her into the room. 'How you have set Paris by the ears! Were my daughters older I should be so jealous! Now child, who will you have to lead you out?'

Léonie looked round the room.

'I do not mind, madame. I will have – Oh, oh, oh!' She let go Madame's hand, and ran forward. 'Milor' Merivale, Milor' Merivale!' she cried joyfully.

Merivale turned quickly.

'Léonie! Well, child, and how do you go on?' He kissed her hand. She was radiant. 'I hoped I might see you here tonight.'

Madame de Vauvallon bore down upon them.

'Fie, what behaviour!' she said indulgently. 'Is this your cavalier? Very well, *petite*. You need no introduction, it seems.' She smiled benignantly upon them, and went back to Fanny's side.

Léonie tucked her hand in Merivale's.

'M'sieur, I am very pleased to see you. Is Madame here too?'

'No, child, I am on one of my periodical visits. Alone. I won't deny that I was drawn hither by certain rumours that reached us in London.'

She put her head on one side.

'What rumours, m'sieur?'

His smile grew.

'Faith, rumours of the *succès fou* that has been achieved by –'

'Me!' she cried, and clapped her hands. 'Milor', I am *le dernier cri*! *Vraiment*, it is so! Lady Fanny says it is. *C'est ridicule, n'est-ce pas?*' She saw Avon coming towards them, and beckoned with pretty imperiousness. 'Monseigneur, see whom I have found!'

'Merivale?' His Grace made a leg. 'Now why?'

'We have heard things in London,' said Merivale. 'Egad, I could not but come!'

'Oh, and we are very glad!' Léonie said enthusiastically.

His Grace offered Merivale snuff.

'Why, I believe my infant speaks for us all,' he said.

'Hey, is it you, Tony, or am I in my cups?' demanded a jovial voice. Lord Rupert came up, and wrung Merivale's hand. 'Where are you staying? When did you come?'

'Last night. I am with De Châtelet. And –' he looked from one to the other – 'I am something anxious to hear what befell you all!'

'Ay, you were in our escapade, weren't you?' said Rupert. 'Gad, what a chase! How does my friend – stap me if I have not forgot his name again! – Manvers! That's the fellow! How does he?'

Merivale flung out a hand.

'I beg you'll not mention that name to me!' he said. 'All three of you fled the country, and faith, it's as well you did!'

'I suggest we repair to the smaller salon,' Avon said, and led the way there. 'I trust you were able to satisfy Mr Manvers?'

Merivale shook his head.

'Nothing less than your blood is like to satisfy him,' he said. 'Tell me all that happened to you.'

'In English,' drawled his Grace, 'and softly.'

So once again the tale was told of Léonie's capture and rescue. Then Madame de Vauvallon came in search of Léonie, and bore her away to dance with an ardent youth. Rupert wandered away to the card-room.

Merivale looked at the Duke.

'And what does Saint-Vire say to Léonie's success?' he inquired.

'Very little,' replied his Grace. 'But he is not pleased, I fear.'

'She does not know?'

'She does not.'

'But the likeness is striking, Alastair. What says Paris?'

'Paris,' said his Grace, 'talks in whispers. Thus my very dear friend Saint-Vire lives in some dread of discovery.'

'When do you intend to strike?'

Avon crossed his legs, and eyed one diamond shoe-buckle pensively.

'That, my dear Merivale, is still on the knees of the gods. Saint-Vire himself must supply the proof to my story.'

'It's awkward, damned awkward!' Merivale commented. 'You've no proof at all?'

'None.'

Merivale laughed. 'It does not seem to worry you!'

'No,' sighed his Grace, 'no. I believe I can trap the Comte through his so charming wife. I play a waiting game, you see.'

'I am glad that I am not Saint-Vire. Your game must be torture to him.'

'Why, so I think,' agreed Avon pleasantly. 'I am not anxious to put an end to his agonies.'

'You're very vindictive!'

There was a moment's silence; then Avon spoke.

'I wonder if you have realised to the full my friend's villainy. Consider for a moment, I beg of you. What mercy would you show to a man who could condemn his own daughter to the life my infant has led?'

Merivale straightened in his chair.

'I know nothing of her life. It was bad?'

'Yes, my dear, it was indeed bad. Until she was twelve years old she, a Saint-Vire, was reared as a peasant. After that she lived among the *canaille* of Paris. Conceive a tavern in a mean street, a bully for master, a shrew for mistress, and Vice, in all its lowest forms, under my infant's very nose.'

'It must have been – hell!' Merivale said.

'Just so,' bowed his Grace. 'It was the very worst kind of hell, as I know.'

'The wonder is that she has come through it unscathed.'

The hazel eyes lifted.

'Not quite unscathed, my dear Anthony. Those years have left their mark.'

'It were inevitable, I suppose. But I confess I have not seen the mark.'

'Possibly not. You see the roguery, and the dauntless spirit.'

'And you?' Merivale watched him curiously.

'Oh, I see beneath, my dear! But then, I have had experience of the sex, as you know.'

'And you see – what?'

'A certain cynicism, born of the life she has led; a streak of strange wisdom; the wistfulness behind the gaiety; sometimes fear; and nearly always the memory of loneliness that hurts the soul.'

Merivale looked down at his snuff-box, and fell to tracing the pattern on it with one finger.

'Do you know,' he said slowly, 'I think that you have grown, Alastair?'

His Grace rose. 'Quite a reformed character, in fact,' he said. 'You can do no wrong in Léonie's eyes.'

'No, it is most amusing, is it not?' Avon smiled, but there was bitterness in his smile, which Merivale saw.

Then they went back into the ballroom, and learned from Lady Fanny that Léonie had disappeared some time ago on Rupert's arm, and had not since been seen.

She had indeed gone out with Rupert to a small salon where he brought her refreshment. Then had come towards them one Madame de Verchoureux, a handsome termagant who had been all things to Avon when Léonie had first come to him. She looked at Léonie with hatred in her eyes, and paused for a moment beside her couch.

Rupert came to his feet, and bowed. Madame swept a curtsy.

'It is – Mademoiselle de Bonnard?' she said.

'Yes, madame.' Léonie got up, and curtsied also. 'I am very stupid, but I cannot at once recall madame's name.'

Rupert, supposing the lady to be one of Fanny's friends, lounged back into the ballroom; Léonie was left looking up at Avon's slighted mistress.

'I felicitate you, mademoiselle,' said the lady sarcastically. 'You are more fortunate than I was, it seems.'

'Madame?' The sparkle was gone from Léonie's eyes. 'Have I the honour of madame's acquaintance?'

'I am one Henriette de Verchoureux. You do not know me.'

'Pardon, madame, but I know of you – much,' Léonie said swiftly. Madame had steered clear of open scandal, but she was somewhat notorious. Léonie remembered the days when Avon had visited her so often.

Madame flushed angrily.

'Indeed, mademoiselle. And of Mademoiselle de Bonnard is also known – much. Mademoiselle is very clever, *sans doute*, but to those who know Avon the so strict chaperon is a poor disguise.'

Léonie raised her eyebrows.

'Is it possible that madame imagines that I have succeeded where she failed?'

'Insolent!' Madame's hand clenched on her fan.

'Madame?'

Madame stared down at Youth, and knew the pangs of jealousy.

'Brazen it out!' she said shrilly. 'You hope to marry in all honour, little fool, but be advised by me, and leave him, for Avon will wed no base-born girl!'

Léonie's eyelids flickered, but she said nothing. Madame changed her tactics suddenly, and stretched out her hand.

'My dear, I protest I pity you! You are so young; you do not know the ways of this world of ours. Avon would not be fool enough to wed with one of your blood, believe me. He were surely lost an he dared!' She laughed, covertly watching Léonie. 'Even an English Duke would not be received were he wedded to such as you,' she said.

'*Tiens*, am I so base?' Léonie said with polite interest. 'I think it is not possible that madame should have known my parents.'

Madame shot her a piercing look.

'Can it be that you do not know?' she asked, and flung back her head, and laughed again. 'Have you not heard the whispers? Have you not seen that Paris watches you, and wonders?'

'But yes, madame, I know that I am quite the rage.'

'Poor child, is that all you know? Why, where is your mirror? Where are your eyes? Have you never looked at that fiery head of yours, never asked whence came your black brows and lashes? All Paris knows, and you are ignorant!'

'*Eh bien!*' Léonie's heart beat fast, but she maintained her outward composure. 'Enlighten me, madame! What does Paris know?'

'That you are a base-born child of the Saint-Vire, my child.
And we – *nous autres* – laugh to see Avon all unconsciously har-
bouring a daughter of his dearest enemy!'

Léonie was as white as her ruffle. 'You lie!'

Madame laughed tauntingly.

'Ask your fine father if I lie!' She gathered her skirts about her,
and made a gesture of disdain. 'Avon must know soon, and then
what comes to you? Little fool, best leave him now while you may
do so of your own choice!' She was gone on the word, leaving
Léonie to stand alone in the salon, her hands clasped together
tightly, her face set and rigid.

Gradually she relaxed her taut muscles, and sank down again
upon the couch, trembling. Her impulse was to seek shelter at
Avon's side, but she restrained herself, and stayed where she
was. At first she was incredulous of Madame de Verchoureux's
pronouncement, but little by little she came to see the probability
of the story's truth. Saint-Vire's attempt to kidnap her was thus
explained, as was also the interest he had always taken in her. Sick
disgust rose in her.

'*Bon Dieu*, what a father I have!' she said viciously. 'Pig-
person! Bah!'

Disgust gave way to a feeling of horror, and of fright. If
Madame de Verchoureux had spoken the truth, Léonie could see
the old loneliness stretching ahead, for it was clearly unthinkable
that such a one as Avon could marry, or even adopt, a girl of her
birth. He came of the nobility; she felt herself to be of mongrel
blood. Lax he might be, but Léonie knew that if he married her he
would disgrace the ancient name he bore. Those who knew him
said that he would count no cost, but Léonie would count the cost
for him, and because she loved him, because he was her *seigneur*,
she would sacrifice everything sooner than drag him down in the
eyes of his world.

She bit hard on her lip; it was better by far to think herself of peasant blood than a bastard daughter of Saint-Vire. Her world was toppling about her ears, but she rose up, and went back into the ballroom.

Avon came to her soon, and gave her his arm.

'I believe you are tired, my infant. We will find Lady Fanny.'

Léonie tucked her hand in his arm, and gave a little sigh.

'Monseigneur, let us go, and leave Lady Fanny, and Rupert. I do not want them.'

'Very well, infant.' Avon beckoned to Rupert across the room, and when he came to them, said languidly: 'I am taking the child home, Rupert. Oblige me by waiting to escort Fanny.'

'I'll take Léonie home,' offered Rupert with alacrity. 'Fanny won't come away for hours!'

'That is why I am leaving you to look to her,' said his Grace. 'Come, *ma fille*.'

He took Léonie home in his light town chaise, and during the short drive she forced herself to talk gaily of the rout they had left, of this man and that, and a thousand other trivialities. Arrived at the Hôtel Avon, she went at once to the library. His Grace followed.

'Well, *ma mie*, what now?'

'Now it is just as it used to be,' Léonie said wistfully, and sat down on a low stool beside the Duke's chair.

His Grace poured out a glass of wine, and looked down at Léonie with a questioning lift to his brows.

Léonie clasped her hands about her knees, and stared deep into the fire.

'Monseigneur, the Duc de Penthièvre was there tonight.'

'As I saw, infant.'

'You do not mind him, Monseigneur?'

'Not at all, infant. Why should I?'

'Well, Monseigneur, he is not – he is not well-born, is he?'

'On the contrary, child, his father was a royal bastard, and his mother a de Noailles.'

'That was what I meant,' said Léonie. 'It does not matter that his father was a bastard prince?'

'*Ma fille*, since the Comte de Toulouse's father was the King, it does not matter at all.'

'It would matter if his father were not the King, would it not? I think it is very strange.'

'It is the way of the world, infant. We forgive the peccadilloes of a king, but look askance on those of a commoner.'

'Even you, Monseigneur. And – and you do not love those who are base-born.'

'I do not, infant. I deplore the modern tendency to flaunt an indiscretion before the eyes of Society.'

Léonie nodded.

'Yes, Monseigneur.' She was silent for a moment. 'M. de Saint-Vire was also there tonight.'

'I trust he did not seek to abduct you again?' His Grace spoke flippantly.

'No, Monseigneur. Why did he try to do it before?'

'Doubtless because of your *beaux yeux*, infant.'

'Bah, that is foolish! What was his real reason, Monseigneur?'

'My child, you make a great mistake in thinking me omniscient. You confuse me with Hugh Davenant.'

Léonie blinked.

'Does that mean that you do not know, Monseigneur?'

'Something of the sort, *ma fille*.'

She raised her head, and looked at him straightly.

'Do you suppose, Monseigneur, that he did it because he does not like you?'

'Quite possibly, infant. His motives need not worry us. May I now be permitted to ask you a question?'

'Yes, Monseigneur?'

'There was at the rout tonight a lady of the name of Verchoureux. Did you have speech with her?'

Léonie was gazing into the fire again.

'Verchoureux?' she said musingly. 'I do not think...'

'It's very well,' said his Grace.

Then Hugh Davenant came into the room, and his Grace, looking at him, did not see the tell-tale blush that crept on Léonie's cheeks.

Twenty-Eight

The Comte de Saint-Vire Discovers an Ace in His Hand

THE COMMENT THAT LÉONIE WAS EXCITING IN THE POLITE WORLD reduced Madame de Saint-Vire to a state of nervous dread. Her mind was in a tumult; she watered her pillow nightly with useless, bitter tears and was smitten alike with fear, and devastating remorse. She tried to hide these sensations from her husband, of whom she was afraid, but she could hardly bring herself to speak to her pseudo-son. Before her eyes, day and night, was Léonie's image, and her poor cowed spirit longed for this daughter, and her arms ached to hold her. Saint-Vire spoke roughly when he saw her red eyes, and wan looks.

'Have done with these lamentations, Marie! You've not seen the girl since she was a day old, so you can have no affection for her.'

'She is *mine*!' Madame said with trembling lips. 'My own daughter! You do not understand, Henri. You cannot understand.'

'How should I understand your foolish megrims? You'll undo me with your sighing and your weeping! Have you thought what discovery would mean?'

She wrung her hands, and her weak eyes filled again with tears.

'Oh, Henri, I know, I know! It's ruin! I – I would not betray you, but I cannot forget my sin. If you would but let me confess to Father Dupré!'

Saint-Vire clicked his tongue impatiently.

'You must be mad!' he said. 'I forbid it! You understand?'

Out came Madame's handkerchief.

'You are so hard!' she wept. 'Do you know that they are saying she is – she is – your base-born child? My little, little daughter.'

'Of course I know it! It's a loophole for escape, but I do not yet see how I can turn it to account. I tell you, Marie, this is not the time for repentance, but for action! Do you want to see our ruin? Do you know how complete it would be?'

She shrank from him.

'Yes, Henri, yes! I – I know, and I am afraid! I scarce dare show my face abroad. Every night I dream that it is all discovered. I shall go mad, I think.'

'Calm yourself, madame. It may be that Avon plays this waiting game to fret my nerves so that I confess. If he had proof he would surely have struck before.' Saint-Vire bit his finger-nail, scowling.

'That man! That horrible, cruel man!' Madame shuddered. 'He has the means to crush you, and I know that he will do it!'

'If he has no proof he cannot. It's possible that Bonnard confessed, or that his wife did. They must both be dead, for I'll swear Bonnard would not have dared let the girl out of his keeping! *Bon Dieu*, why did I not inquire whither they went when they left Champagne?'

'You thought – you thought it would be better not to know,' Madame faltered. 'But where did that man find my little one? How could he know – ?'

'He is the devil himself. I believe there is naught he does not know. But if I can only get the girl out of his hands he can do nothing. I am convinced he has no proof.'

Madame began to pace the room, twisting her hands together.

'I cannot bear to think of her in his power!' she exclaimed. 'Who knows what he will do to her? She's so young, and so beautiful –'

'She's fond enough of Avon,' Saint-Vire said, and laughed shortly. 'And she's well able to care for herself, little vixen!'

Madame stood still, hope dawning in her face.

'Henri, if Avon has no proof how can he know that Léonie is my child? Does he not perhaps think that she is – what they are saying? Is that not possible?'

'It is possible,' Saint-Vire admitted. 'And yet, from things he has said to me, I feel sure that he has guessed.'

'And Armand!' she cried. 'Will he not guess? *Oh mon Dieu, mon Dieu*, what can we do? Was it worth it, Henri? Oh, was it worth it, just to spite Armand?'

'I don't regret it!' snapped Saint-Vire. 'What I have done I have done, and since I cannot now undo it I'll not waste my time wondering if it was worth it! You'll be good enough to show your face abroad, madame. I do not desire to give Avon more cause for suspicion.'

'But what will he do?' Madame asked. 'Why does he wait like this? What is in his mind?'

'*Sangdieu*, madame, if I knew do you suppose that I should stand thus idle?'

'Does – does *she* know, think you?'

'No, I'd stake mine honour she does not know.'

Madame laughed wildly.

'Your honour! Your honour! *Grand Dieu*, you can speak of that?'

He took an angry step towards her; her fingers were about the door-handle.

'It was dead when you made me give up my child!' she cried. 'You will see your name dragged in the mud! And mine! And mine! Oh, can you do nothing?'

'Be silent, madame!' he hissed. 'Do you want the lackeys to hear you?'

She started, and cast a quick, furtive glance round.

'Discovery – will kill me, I think,' she said, quite quietly, and went out.

Saint-Vire flung himself into a chair, and stayed there, frowning. To him came presently a lackey.

'Well?' Saint-Vire shot the word out.

'Monsieur, there is a lady who desires speech with you.'

'A lady?' Saint-Vire was surprised. 'Who?'

'Monsieur, I do not know. She awaits you in the smaller salon, and she says that she will see you.'

'Of what like is she?'

'Monsieur, she is veiled.'

'An intrigue, *enfin*!' Saint-Vire rose. 'In the smaller salon?'

'Yes, monsieur.'

Saint-Vire went out, and crossed the hall to the little withdrawing-room. A lady was standing by the window, enveloped in a cloak, and with a veil hanging down over her face. She turned as Saint-Vire came in, and put back the veil with a small, resolute hand. Saint-Vire looked into his daughter's dark eyes.

'Oho!' he said softly, and looked for the key to the door.

'I have it,' Léonie said calmly. 'And I will tell you, m'sieur, that my maid waits for me in the street. If I do not come to her in half an hour she will go at once to Monseigneur and tell him that I am here.'

'Very clever,' Saint-Vire said smoothly. 'What is it that you want of me? Are you not afraid to put yourself in my power?'

'Bah!' said Léonie, and let him see her little gold-mouthed pistol.

Saint-Vire came further into the room.

'A pretty toy,' he sneered, 'but I know what women are with such playthings.'

'*Quant à ca*,' said Léonie frankly. 'I should like very much to kill you, because you gave me an evil drink, but I won't kill you unless you touch me.'

'Oh, I thank you, mademoiselle! To what am I indebted for this visit?'

Léonie fixed her eyes on his face.

'Monsieur, you shall tell me now if it is true that you are my father.'

Saint-Vire said nothing, but stood very still, waiting.

'Speak you!' Léonie said fiercely. 'Are you my father?'

'My child –' Saint-Vire spoke softly. 'Why do you ask me that?'

'Because they are saying that I am your base-born daughter. Tell me, is it true?' She stamped her foot at him.

'My poor child!' Saint-Vire approached, but was confronted by the nozzle of the pistol. 'You need not fear, *petite*. It has never been mine intention to harm you.'

'Pig-person!' Léonie said. 'I am not afraid of anything, but if you come near me I shall be sick. Is it true what they say?'

'Yes, my child,' he said, and achieved a sigh.

'*How* I hate you!' she said with fervour.

'Will you not be seated?' he asked. 'It grieves me to hear you say that you hate me, but indeed I understand what you must feel. I am very sorry for you, *petite*.'

'I will not be seated,' Léonie said flatly, 'and it makes me feel worse when you call me *petite*, and say you are sorry for me. More than ever I want to kill you.'

Saint-Vire was rather shocked.

'I am your father, child!'

'I do not care at all,' she replied. 'You are an evil person, and if it is true that I am your daughter you are more evil than even I thought.'

'You do not understand the ways of the world we live in,' he sighed. 'A youthful indiscretion — you must not think too hardly of me, child. I will do all in my power to provide for you, and indeed I am greatly exercised over your welfare. I believed you to be in the charge of some worthy people once in mine employ. You may judge of my feelings when I found you in the Duc of Avon's clutches.' Before the look on Léonie's face he recoiled a little.

'If you speak one word against Monseigneur I will shoot you dead,' said Léonie softly.

'I do not speak against him, child. Why should I? He is no worse than any of us, but it grieves me to see you in his toils. I cannot but take an interest in you, and I fear for you when it becomes common knowledge that you are my daughter.'

She said nothing. After a moment he continued.

'In our world, child, we dislike open scandal. That is why I tried to rescue you from Avon a while back. I wish that I had told you then why I carried you off, but I thought to spare you that unpleasant knowledge.'

'How you are kind!' marvelled Léonie. 'Of a truth it is a great thing to be the daughter of M. de Saint-Vire!'

He flushed.

'You thought me brutal, I know, but I acted for the best. You outwitted me, and I saw that it would have been wiser to have told you of your birth. The secret cannot be kept, for you resemble me too greatly. We are like to be plunged in a scandal now that will hurt us all.'

'It seems that most people know who I am,' Léonie answered, 'but I am very well received, *je vous assure.*'

'At the moment you are, but when I openly acknowledge you — what then?'

'*Tiens!*' Léonie stared at him. 'Why should you do that?'

'I have no cause to love your — guardian,' Saint-Vire said, and kept a wary eye on the pistol. 'And I do not think that he would be pleased if the world knew he had adopted a base-born child of mine. His pride would be humbled, I think.'

'What if he knows already?' Léonie asked. 'If others know so must he.'

'Do you think he does?' Saint-Vire said.

She was silent.

'He might suspect,' he went on. 'Perhaps he does; I do not know. Yet I think if he had done so he would hardly have brought you to Paris. He would not like Society to laugh at him as Society will laugh when it learns who you are. I can harm him greatly in this matter.'

'How can you harm him, you – you pig-person?'

Saint-Vire smiled.

'Were you not his page, *ma fille*? It is not *convenable* for young girls to masquerade as boys in the house of an Alastair. Think of the scandal when I tell that tale! Be very sure that I shall take care to set Paris about M. le Duc's ears. His morals are well known, and I do not think that Paris will believe in his innocence, or yours.'

Léonie curled her lip.

'*Voyons*, am I a fool? Paris would not care that Monseigneur had made a bastard his mistress.'

'No, child, but would not Paris care that Avon had had the audacity to take his base-born mistress into Society? You have queened it right royally, and I hear that you even have Condé in your toils. That will not make Paris more lenient. You have been too great a success, my dear. You are a masquerader, and Avon has cheated Society with you. Do you think Society will forgive that? I think we shall not see M. le Duc in France again, and it is possible that scandal might spread to London. His reputation would not aid him to kill the scandal, I assure you.'

'I wonder if it would be better that I kill you now?' Léonie said slowly. 'You shall not harm Monseigneur, pig-person. That I swear!'

'I have no great wish to harm him,' Saint-Vire said indifferently.

'But I cannot see my child in his care. Some paternal feeling you will allow me. Put yourself in my hands, and Avon has nothing to fear from me. All my wish is to see you safely disposed in life. There need be no scandal if you disappear from Society, but if you remain under Avon's roof scandal must come. And since I am like to be involved in it, I prefer to head the cry.'

'And if I go you will say nothing?'

'Not a word. Why should I? Let me make provision for you. I can find a home for you. I will send you money. And perhaps you will –'

'I do not put myself in the hands of a pig-person,' Léonie said crushingly. 'I will disappear, *bien entendu*, but I will go to one who loves me, not to you, who are without doubt a villain.' She swallowed hard, and her hand clutched on the pistol. 'I give you my word that I will disappear.'

He held out his hand.

'Poor child, this is a sad day for you. There is nothing I can say, but that I am sorry. It is for the best, as you will see. Where do you go?'

She held her head high.

'I do not tell you or anyone that,' she said. 'I make just one prayer to the good God that I may never see you again.' Words choked in her throat; she made a gesture of loathing, and went to the door. There she turned. 'I forget. You will swear to me that you will say nothing that may harm Monseigneur. Swear it on the Bible!'

'I swear,' he said. 'But there is no need. Once you are gone there will be no occasion for me to speak. I want no scandal.'

'*Bon!*' she said. 'I do not trust your oath, but I think you are a great coward, and you would not like to make a scandal. I hope you will be punished one day.' She flung the door-key down on the floor, and went quickly out.

Saint-Vire passed his handkerchief across his brow.

'*Mon Dieu*,' he whispered. 'She showed me how to play my ace! Now, Satanas, we shall see who wins!'

Twenty-Nine

The Disappearance of Léonie

LORD RUPERT YAWNED MIGHTILY, AND HEAVED HIMSELF UP IN HIS chair.

'What do we do tonight?' he asked. ''Pon my soul, I've never been to so many balls in my life! It's no wonder I'm worn out.'

'Oh, my dear Rupert, I am nigh dead with fatigue!' Fanny cried. 'At least we have this one evening quiet! Tomorrow there is Madame du Deffand's soirée.' She nodded to Léonie. 'You will enjoy that, my love, I assure you. A few poems to be read, discussion, all the wit of Paris present – oh, 'twill be a most amusing evening, I vow! There is no one who will not be there.'

'What, so we have respite to-day, have we?' said Rupert. 'Now, what shall I do?'

'I thought you said you were worn out?' Marling remarked.

'So I am, but I can't sit at home all the evening. What do you do?'

'Hugh and I are bound for de Châtelet's, to visit Merivale. Will you accompany us?'

Rupert considered for a while.

'No, I believe I'll go to this new gaming-house I hear tell of.'

Avon put up his glass.

'Oh? What, and where, is the novelty?'

'In the Rue Chambéry. It's like to kill Vassaud's if what they say is true. I'm surprised you'd not heard of it.'

'Yes, it is not in keeping with the part,' Avon said. 'I believe I will go with you there this evening, child. It will not do for Paris to think I did not know of it.'

'What, will you all be out?' Fanny asked. 'And I had promised to dine with my dear Julie! Léonie, I am sure that she will be pleased if you come with me.'

'Oh madame, I am so tired!' Léonie protested. 'I would like to go to bed early tonight.'

Rupert stretched his long legs out before him.

'Tired at last!' he said. 'Faith, I thought you'd never be wearied out!'

'My dearest life, I will tell the servants to take a tray to your room,' Fanny said. 'You must not be tired tomorrow, for I am determined you shall come to Madame du Deffand's soirée! Why, Condé is sure to be there!'

Léonie smiled rather wanly, and encountered Avon's scrutiny.

'My infant, what has happened to trouble you?' he asked.

She opened wide her eyes.

'But nothing, Monseigneur! It is just that I have a touch of the *migraine*.'

'To be sure I am not surprised.' My lady shook her head wisely. 'We have been abroad late every night this week. It is I who am at fault to have permitted it.'

'Oh, but madame, it has been *fort amusant*!' Léonie said. 'I have enjoyed myself so much!'

'Egad, and so have I!' Rupert remarked. 'It has been a mad two months, and I scarce know whether I am standing on my head or my heels. Are you off already, Hugh?'

'We are dining with de Châtelet at four,' Hugh explained. 'I'll say good night, Léonie. You'll be abed when we return.'

She gave him her hand; her eyes were downcast. Both he and Marling kissed the slender fingers. Hugh made some joke to Rupert, and they went out.

'Do you dine at home, Justin?' asked my lady. 'I must go change my gown, and order the light chaise to take me to Julie.'

'I will bear my infant company at dinner,' said Avon. 'And then she shall go to bed. Rupert?'

'No, I'm off at once,' said Rupert. 'I've a little matter to talk over with d'Anvau. Come, Fan!'

They went out together. Avon crossed over to the couch where Léonie sat, and tweaked one of her curls.

'Child, you are strangely silent.'

'I was thinking,' she said gravely.

'Of what, *ma mie*?'

'Oh, I shall not tell you that, Monseigneur!' she said, and smiled. 'Let us – let us play at piquet until it is time for dinner!'

So they played at piquet, and presently Lady Fanny came in to say good night, and was gone again in a minute, having adjured Léonie to be sure and retire to bed immediately after dinner. She kissed Léonie, and was surprised to receive a quick hug from her. Rupert went away with Fanny, and Léonie was left alone with the Duke.

'They are gone,' she said in a curious voice.

'Yes, child. What of it?' His Grace dealt the cards with an expert hand.

'Nothing, Monseigneur. I am stupid tonight.'

They played on until dinner was served, and then went into the big dining-room, and sat down together at the table. Avon soon sent the lackeys away, whereat Léonie gave a sigh of relief.

'That is nice,' she remarked. 'I like to be alone again. I wonder whether Rupert will lose much money tonight?'

'We will hope not, infant. You will know by his expression tomorrow.'

She did not reply, but began to eat a sweetmeat, and did not look at his Grace.

'You eat too many sweetmeats, *ma fille*,' he said. 'It's no wonder you are growing pale.'

'You see, Monseigneur, I had never eaten any until you bought me from Jean,' she explained.

'I know, child.'

'So now I eat too many,' she added. 'Monseigneur, I am very glad that we are alone together tonight, like this.'

'You flatter me,' he bowed.

'No. Since we came back to Paris we have hardly ever been alone, and I have wanted – oh, many times! – to thank you for being so very kind to me.'

He frowned down at the walnut he was cracking.

'I pleased myself, infant. I believe I told you once before that I am no hero.'

'Did it please you to make me your ward?' she asked.

'Evidently, *ma fille*, else I had not done so.'

'I have been very happy, Monseigneur.'

'If that is so it is very well,' he said.

She rose, and put down her napkin.

'I am growing more and more tired,' she said. 'I hope Rupert wins tonight. And you.'

'I always win, child.' He opened the door for her, and went with her to the foot of the stairs. 'I wish you a good night's rest, *ma belle*.'

She dropped suddenly on one knee, and pressed his hand to her lips and held it there a moment.

'*Merci*, Monseigneur. *Bonne nuit!*' she said huskily. Then she rose again, and ran up the stairs to her chamber.

Her maid was there, agog with excitement. Léonie shut the door carefully, brushed past the girl, and flung herself on to the

bed, and cried as though her heart would break. The abigail hovered over her, soothing and caressing.

'Oh, mademoiselle, why will you run away like this? Must we
go tonight indeed?'

Downstairs the great front door shut; Léonie clasped her hands
over her eyes.

'Gone! Gone! Ah, Monseigneur, Monseigneur!' She lay bat-
tling with her sobs, and presently rose, quiet and resolute, and
turned to her maid. 'The travelling-coach, Marie?'

'Yes, mademoiselle, I hired one this morning, and 'tis to await
us at the corner of the road in an hour's time. But it has cost you
the best part of six hundred francs, mademoiselle, and the man did
not like to start so late. We shall not reach farther than Chartres
tonight, he says.'

'It's no matter. I have enough money left to pay for everything.
Bring me paper now, and ink. Are you sure – are you *sure* that you
wish to come with me?'

'But yes, mademoiselle!' the girl averred. 'M. le Duc would be
wroth with me an I let you go alone.'

Léonie looked at her drearily.

'I tell you we shall never, never see him again.'

Marie shook her head sceptically, but merely said that she
had quite made up her mind to go with mademoiselle. Then
she fetched ink and paper, and Léonie sat down to write her
farewell.

★★★

Upon her return Lady Fanny peeped into Léonie's room to see
whether she slept. She held her candle high so that the light fell
on the bed, and saw that it was empty. Something white lay upon
the coverlet; she darted forward, and with a trembling hand held

two sealed notes to the candlelight. One was addressed to herself; the other to Avon.

Lady Fanny felt suddenly faint, and sank down into a chair, staring numbly at the folded papers. Then she set her candle down upon the table, and tore open the note that was for her.

My Dear Madame, (she read), –

I write this to say Fare Well, and Because I want to Thank you for your Kindness to me. I have told Monseigneur why I must go. You have been so very Good to me, and I Love you, and indeed, indeed I am sorry thatt I can only write to you. I shall never forget you.

Léonie.

Lady Fanny flew up out of her chair.

'Oh, good God!' she cried. 'Léonie! Justin! Rupert! Oh, is *no* one here? Heavens, what shall I do?' Down the stairs she ran, and seeing a lackey by the door, hurried up to him. 'Where's mademoiselle? When did she go out? Answer me, dolt!'

'Madame? Mademoiselle is abed.'

'Fool! Imbecile! Where's her maid?'

'Why, madame, she went out just before six, with – Rachel, I think it was.'

'Rachel is in my chambers!' snapped her ladyship. 'Oh, what in God's name shall I do? Is his Grace returned?'

'No, Madame, not yet.'

'Send him to me in the library as soon as he comes in!' Lady Fanny commanded, and went there herself, and read Léonie's note again.

Twenty minutes later his Grace entered.

'Fanny? What's to do?'

'Oh, Justin, Justin!' she said on a sob. 'Why did we leave her? She's gone! Gone, I tell you!'

His Grace strode forward.

'Léonie?' he said sharply.

'Who else?' demanded my lady. 'Poor, poor child! She left this for me, and one for you. Take it!'

His Grace broke the seal of his note, and spread out the thin sheet. Lady Fanny watched him while he read, and saw his mouth set hard.

'Well?' she said. 'What does she write to you? For heaven's sake, tell me!'

The Duke handed the note to her, and went to the fire, and stared down into it.

Monseigneur, –

I have run away from you because I have discovered thatt I am not what you Think me. I told you a Lie when I said that Madame de Verchoureux had not Spoken to me the other Night. She told me thatt Every One knows I am a Base-born daughter of Saint-Vire. It is Quite True, Monseigneur, for on Thursday I slipped out with my Maid, and went to his House, and asked him if it were indeed so. Monseigneur, it is not convenable thatt I stay with you. I cannot bear thatt I should bring Scandal to you, and I know thatt I must do this if I stay with you, for M. de Saint-Vire will say thatt I am his Bastard, and your Mistress. I do not want to go, Monseigneur, but it is best thatt I should. I tried to Thank you Tonight, but you would not let me. Please, you must not be anxious for me. I wanted at first to Kill myself, but then I saw thatt thatt is Cowardly. I am Quite Safe, and I am going very far away to Some One who will be good to me, I know. I have left all my Things, except the Money you gave me, which I must take to pay my journey, and the Sapphire Chain which you gave me when I was your Page. I thought you would not Mind if I took thatt, because it is the only thing I have kept which you gave me. Marie goes with me, and Please you must not be Angry with the lackeys for letting me go, for they thought I was Rachel. I leave for Rupert, and M. Davenant, and M. Marling, and Milor' Merivale my so Great Love for them. And for you, Monseigneur. I cannot write it. I am Glad thatt we were Alone tonight.

A Dieu

Infant.

Lady Fanny's face worked for a minute, then she whisked out her handkerchief and cried into it, regardless of paint and powder. His Grace picked up the note, and read it through again.

'Poor little infant!' he said softly.

'Oh, Justin, we must find her!' sniffed her ladyship.

'We shall find her,' he answered. 'I think I know where she has gone.'

'Where? Can you go after her? Now? She is such a babe, and she has only a foolish abigail with her.'

'I believe that she has gone to – Anjou.' His Grace folded the note and put it into his pocket. 'She has left me because she fears to endanger my – reputation. It is somewhat ironic, is it not?'

Lady Fanny blew her nose vigorously, and gave yet another watery sniff.

'She loves you, Justin.'

He was silent.

'Oh, Justin, do you not care? I felt so certain that you loved her!'

'I love her – too well to marry her, my dear,' said his Grace.

'Why?' Lady Fanny put away her handkerchief.

'There are so many reasons,' sighed his Grace. 'I am too old for her!'

'Oh, fiddle!' said my lady. 'I thought that maybe 'twas her birth you cavilled at.'

'Her birth, Fanny, is as good as yours. She is Saint-Vire's legitimate daughter.'

Lady Fanny gaped at him.

'In her place he has put that clod you know as de Valmé. His name is Bonnard. I have waited too long, but I strike now.' He picked up a hand-bell, and rang it. To the lackey who came he said: 'You will go at once to the Hôtel de Châtelet, and request M. Marling and M. Davenant to return at once. Ask Milor' Merivale to accompany them. You may go.' He turned again to his sister. 'What did the child write to you?'

'Only farewell!' Lady Fanny bit her lip. 'And I wondered why she kissed me so sweetly tonight! Oh dear, oh dear!'

'She kissed my hand,' Avon said. 'We have all been fools this day. Do not distress yourself, Fanny. I shall bring her back if I have to search the world for her. And when she comes she will come as Mademoiselle de Saint-Vire.'

'But I don't understand how – oh, here is Rupert! Yes, Rupert, I have been crying, and I do not care. Tell him, Justin.'

Avon showed his young brother Léonie's letter. Rupert read it, exclaiming at intervals. When he came to the end he snatched his wig from his head, threw it upon the floor, and stamped on it, saying various things beneath his breath that made Lady Fanny clap her hands over her ears.

'If you don't have his blood for this, Justin, I shall!' he said at last, picked up his wig, and put it on his head again. 'May he rot in hell for a black scoundrel! Is she his bastard?'

'She is not,' said Avon. 'She is his legitimate daughter. I have sent for Hugh and Marling. It is time that you all knew my infant's story.'

'Left her love for me, bless her!' choked Rupert. 'Where is she? Are we to set off at once? Only give the word, Justin, and I'm ready!'

'I do not doubt it, child, but we do not start to-day. I believe I know whither she has gone; she will be safe enough. Before I bring her back she shall be righted in the eyes of the world.'

Rupert glanced down at the letter in his hand.

'*I cannot bear thatt I should bring Scandal to you,*' he read. 'Burn it, your life's one long scandal! And she – Devil take it, I could cry like a woman, so I could!' He gave the letter back to the Duke. 'She's made a cursed idol of you, Justin, and you're not fit to kiss her little feet!' he said.

Avon looked at him.

'That I know,' he said. 'My part ends when I bring her back to Paris. It is better so.'

'So you do love her.' Rupert nodded to his sister.

'I have loved her for a long time. And you, my son?'

'No, no, I'm no suitor of hers, I thank you! She's a darling, but I'd have none of her to wife. It's you she wants, and it's you she'll have, mark my words!'

'I am "Monseigneur,"' Avon replied with a crooked smile. 'There is glamour attached to me, but I am too old for her.'

Then the others came in in a state of liveliest curiosity.

'What's to do, Justin?' asked Hugh. 'Has there been a death in the house?'

'No, my dear. Not a death.'

Lady Fanny sprang up.

'Justin – she – she would not have killed herself, and – and said that in her letter so that you should not guess her intention? I never thought of that! Oh, Edward, Edward, I am so unhappy!'

'She?' Marling put an arm about Fanny. 'Do you mean – Léonie?'

'She has not killed herself, Fanny. You forget that she has her maid with her,' Avon said reassuringly.

Davenant shook him by the arm.

'Speak out, man, for God's sake! What has happened to the child?'

'She has left me,' Avon said, and put Léonie's note in his hand.

With one accord Merivale and Marling went to look over Hugh's shoulder.

'God's truth!' exploded Merivale, and clapped a hand to his sword-hilt as he read: 'Oh, what a villain! *Now*, Justin, you shall have at him, and I'm with you to the death!'

'But –' Marling looked up with puckered brows. 'Poor, poor child, is it true?'

Hugh came to the end, and said huskily: 'Little Léon! 'Fore God, it's pathetic!'

Rupert, at this juncture, relieved his feelings by throwing his snuff-box at the opposite wall.

'Oh, we'll send him to hell between us, never fear!' he stormed. 'Cur! Dastardly cur! Here, give me some burgundy, Fan! I'm in such a heat – Swords are too good for the rogue, damme they are!'

'Much too good,' agreed his Grace.

'Swords!' Merivale exclaimed. 'It's too quick. You or I, Justin, could kill him in less than three minutes.'

'Too quick, and too clumsy. There is more poetry in the vengeance I take.'

Hugh looked up. 'But explain?' he begged. 'Where is the child? What are you talking about? You have found a way to pay your debt in full, I suppose, but how have you found it?'

'Curiously enough,' said his Grace, 'I had forgotten that old quarrel. You remind me most opportunely. The scales weigh heavily against M. de Saint-Vire. Give me your attention for one minute, and you shall know Léonie's story.' Briefly, and with none of his accustomed suavity, he told them the truth. They listened in thunderstruck silence, and for some time after he finished, could find no words to speak. It was Marling who broke the silence.

'If that is true the man is the biggest scoundrel unhung!' he said. 'Are you sure, Avon?'

'Perfectly, my friend.'

Rupert shook his fist, and muttered darkly.

'Good God, do we live in the Dark Ages?' cried Hugh. 'It's almost incredible!'

'But the proof!' Fanny cut in. 'What can you do, Justin?'

'I can stake everything on the last round, Fanny. I am going to do that. And I think — yes, I really think that I shall win.' He smiled unpleasantly. 'For the present my infant is safe, and I believe I may put my hand on her when I wish.'

'What do you intend to do?' shouted Rupert.

'Oh yes, Justin, please tell us!' besought my lady. 'It is so dreadful to know nothing. To have to sit idle!'

'I know, Fanny, but once more I must ask you all to be patient. I play my games best alone. One thing I may promise you: You shall be in at the death.'

'But when will it be?' Rupert poured out another glass of burgundy. 'You're too devilish tricky for me, Justin. I want a hand in the affair.'

'No.' Hugh shook his head. 'Let Avon play his game to a close. There are too many of us to join with him, and there's a proverb that says "too many cooks spoil the broth." I'm not usually bloodthirsty, but I do not want Saint-Vire's broth to be spoiled.'

'I want to see him crushed,' said Merivale. 'And that soon!'

'You shall, my dear Anthony. But for the present we will behave as ever. If any ask for Léonie she is indisposed. Fanny, did you say that Madame du Deffand gives a soirée tomorrow?'

'Yes, but I've not the heart to go,' sighed my lady. 'It will be so brilliant too, and I did want Léonie to be there!'

'Nevertheless, my dear, you will go, with us all. Calm yourself, Rupert. Your part was played, and played well, at Le Havre. Now it is my turn. Fanny, you are tired out. Go to bed now; you cannot do anything yet.'

'I must go back to de Châtelet,' said Merivale. He gripped Avon's hand. 'Act up to your name now, Satanas, if ever you did! We are all with you.'

'Even I,' said Marling with a smile. 'You may be as devilish as you please, for Saint-Vire is the worst kind of villain I have had the ill-luck to meet.'

Rupert, hearing, choked in the act of drinking his third glass of burgundy.

'Damme, I boil with rage when I think of him!' he swore. 'Léonie called him pig-person, but 'fore Gad he's worse than that! He's – !'

Fanny fled incontinently from the room.

Thirty

His Grace of Avon Trumps the Comte's Ace

THE MARLINGS CAME EARLY TO MADAME DU DEFFAND'S HOUSE, and were followed shortly by Merivale and Hugh Davenant. Madame du Deffand wanted to know what had become of Léonie, and was informed that she was indisposed, and had remained at home. Rupert presently arrived in company with d'Anvau and Lavoulère, and was twitted by several people, Madame du Deffand included, on his appearance at such a function.

'Doubtless you are come to read us a madrigal or a rondeau,' Madame teased him. '*Faites voir*, milor', *faites voir!*'

'I? No, b'Gad!' Rupert said. 'I've never written a verse in my life! I'm come to listen, madame.'

She laughed at him. 'You will be so bored, my poor friend! Bear with us!' She moved away to greet a fresh arrival.

Under the wail of the violins which played at one end of the room, Merivale spoke to Davenant. 'Where's Avon?'

Hugh shrugged. 'I've scarce set eyes on him all day. He starts for Anjou immediately after this party.'

'Then he means to strike tonight.' Merivale looked round. 'I saw Armand de Saint-Vire a moment ago. Is the Comte here?'

'Not yet, I think, but I am told that both he and his wife are coming. Justin will have a large audience.'

The rooms were filling speedily. Merivale presently heard a footman announce Condé. Behind the Prince came the Saint-Vires, and the Marchérands, and the Duc and the Duchesse de la Roque. A young exquisite approached Fanny and demanded Mademoiselle de Bonnard. On being told that she was not present his face fell considerably, and he confided mournfully to my lady that he had written a madrigal to Léonie's eyes which he had intended to read tonight. My lady commiserated him, and turned to find Condé at her elbow.

'Madame!' he bowed. 'But where is *la petite*?'

Lady Fanny repeated Léonie's excuses, and was requested to bear a graceful message to her charge. Then Condé moved away to join in a game of *bouts-rhymés*, and the wail of the violins died down to a murmur.

It was just as Madame du Deffand had called upon M. de la Douaye to read his latest poems that some slight stir arose by the door, and his Grace of Avon came in. He wore the dress he had once worn in Versailles, cloth of gold, shimmering in the candle-light. A great emerald in the lace at his throat gleamed balefully, another flashed on his finger. At his side was a light dress sword; in one hand he carried his scented handkerchief, and a snuff-box studded with tiny emeralds, and from one wrist hung a fan of painted chicken-skin mounted upon gold sticks.

Those who were near the door drew back to let him pass, and for a moment he stood alone, a tall, haughty figure, dwarfing the Frenchmen about him. He was completely at his ease, even a little disdainful. He raised his quizzing-glass, and swept a glance round the room.

'By Gad, he's a magnificent devil, 'pon my soul he is!' said Rupert to Merivale. 'Damme if I've ever seen him look more regal!'

'What a dress!' said Fanny, in her husband's ear. 'You cannot deny, Edward, that he is truly handsome.'

'He has a presence,' conceded Marling.

Avon went forward across the room, and bowed over his hostess's hand.

'Late as usual!' she scolded him. 'Oh, and you still have a fan, I see! *Poseur!* You are just in time to hear M. de la Douaye read to us his poems.'

'The luck always favours me, madame,' he said, and inclined his head to the young poet. 'May we beg m'sieur to read us his lines addressed to the Flower in her Hair?'

La Douaye flushed with pleasure, and bowed.

'I am honoured that that so poor trifle should still be remembered,' he said, and went to stand before the fireplace with a roll of papers in his hand.

His Grace crossed slowly to the Duchesse de la Roque's couch, and sat down beside her. His eyes flickered to Merivale's face, and from thence to the door. Unostentatiously Merivale linked his arm in Davenant's and moved with him to a sofa that stood by the door.

'Avon makes me feel nervous,' murmured Davenant. 'An impressive entrance, a striking dress, and that in his manner that sends a chill down one's back. You feel it?'

'I do. He means to hold the stage tonight.' Merivale spoke lower still, for La Douaye's liquid voice sounded in the first line of his poem. 'He sent me to sit here. If you can catch Rupert's eye signal to him to go to the other door.' He crossed his legs, and fixed his attention on La Douaye.

A storm of applause greeted the verses. Davenant craned his neck to see where Saint-Vire was, and caught a glimpse of him by the window. Madame de Saint-Vire was at some distance from him, and several times she looked across at him with wide apprehensive eyes.

'If Saint-Vire's seen that Léonie's not here he'll be feeling that chill down his back too, methinks,' said Merivale. 'I wish I knew what Avon means to do. Look at Fanny! Egad, Avon's the only one of us who's at his ease!'

La Douaye began to read again; followed praise, and elegant discussion. Avon complimented the poet, and moved away to the adjoining salon where some were still playing at *bouts-rhymés*. In the doorway he met Rupert. Merivale saw him pause for an instant, and say something. Rupert nodded, and lounged over to the two by the main door. He leaned over the back of the couch, and chuckled gleefully.

'Mysterious devil, an't he?' he said. 'I've orders to watch the other door. I'm agog with excitement, stap me if I'm not! Tony, I'll lay you a monkey Justin wins this last round!'

Merivale shook his head.

'I'll not bet against a certainty, Rupert,' he said. 'Before he came I was assailed by doubts, but faith, the sight of him is enough to end them! The sheer force of his personality should carry the day. Even I feel something nervous. Saint-Vire, with the knowledge of his own guilt, must feel a thousand times more so. Rupert, have you any idea what he means to do?'

'Devil a bit!' answered Rupert cheerfully. He lowered his voice. 'I'll tell you something, though. This is the last soirée I'll attend. Did you hear that fellow mouthing out his rhymes?' He shook his head severely. 'Y'know it ought not to be allowed. An under-sized little worm like that!'

'You'll agree that he is something of a poet nevertheless?' smiled Hugh.

'Poet be damned!' said Rupert. 'He's walking about with a rose in his hand! A rose, Tony!' He snorted indignantly, and saw to his horror that a portly gentleman was preparing to read an essay on Love. 'God save us all, who's this old Turnip-Top?' he demanded irreverently.

'Hush, child!' whispered Lavoulère, who was standing nearby. 'It is the great M. de Foquemalle!'

M. de Foquemalle began to roll forth impressive periods. Rupert edged along the wall towards the smaller salon, with a look of comical dismay on his face. He came upon the Chevalier d'Anvau, who pretended to bar his passage.

'What, Rupert?' The Chevalier's shoulders shook. 'Whither away, *mon vieux?*'

'Here, let me pass!' whispered Rupert. 'Damme if I can stand this! The last one kept snuffing at a rose, and this old ruffian's got a nasty look in his eye which I don't like. I'm off!' He winked broadly at Fanny, who was sitting with two or three ladies in the middle of the room, soulfully regarding M. de Foquemalle.

In the other salon Rupert found an animated party gathered about the fire. Condé was reading his stanza amid laughter, and mock applause. A lady beckoned to Rupert.

'Come, milor', and join us! Oh, is it my turn to read?' She picked up her paper and read out her lines. 'There! It goes not well when one has heard M. le Duc's verse, I fear. Do you leave us, Duc?'

Avon kissed her hand.

'My inspiration fails, madame. I believe I must go speak with Madame du Deffand.'

Rupert found a seat beside a lively brunette.

'Take my advice, Justin, and keep away from the other room. There's an ill-favoured old rascal reading an essay on Love, or some such nonsense.'

'De Foquemalle, I'll lay a pony!' cried Condé, and went to peep through the doorway. 'Shall you brave it, Duc?'

M. de Foquemalle came at last to his peroration; Madame du Deffand headed the compliments that showered upon him; de Marchérand started a discussion on M. de Foquemalle's opinions. A lull fell presently, and lackeys came in with refreshments.

Learned arguments gave way to idle chatter. Ladies, sipping negus and ratafie, talked of toilettes, and the new mode of dressing the hair; Rupert, near the door he guarded, produced a dice-box, and began surreptitiously to play with a few intimates. His Grace strolled over to where Merivale stood.

'More commands?' inquired my lord. 'I see Fanny has Madame de Saint-Vire in close conversation.'

His Grace waved his fan languidly to and fro.

'But one more command,' he sighed. 'Just keep our amiable friend away from his wife, my dear.' He passed on to speak to Madame de Vauvallon, and was presently lost in the crowd.

Lady Fanny was complimenting Madame de Saint-Vire on her gown.

'I declare, that shade of blue is positively ravishing!' she said. 'I searched the town for just such a taffeta not so long ago. La, there is that lady in puce again! Pray who may she be?'

'It is – I believe it is Mademoiselle de Cloué,' Madame replied. The Vicomte de Valmé came up. 'Henri, you have seen your father?'

'Yes, madame, he is with de Châtalet and another, over there.' He bowed to Fanny. 'It is Milor' Merivale, I think. Madame, may I be permitted to fetch you a glass of ratafie?'

'No, I thank you,' said my lady. 'Madame, my husband!'

Madame gave her hand to Marling. Up came Madame du Deffand.

'Now, where is your brother, Lady Fanny? I have asked him to entertain us with some of his so amusing verses, and he says that he has another form of entertainment for us!' She rustled on, looking for Avon.

'Is Avon to read us his verses?' asked someone nearby. 'He is always so witty! Do you remember the one he read at Madame de Marchérand's rout last year?'

A gentleman turned his head.

'No, not verse this time, d'Orlay. I heard d'Aiguillon say that it was to be some kind of story.'

'*Tiens!* What will he be at next, I wonder?'

Young de Chantourelle came up with Mademoiselle de Beaucour on his arm.

'What's this I hear of Avon? Is it a fairy tale he means to tell us?'

'An allegory, perhaps,' suggested d'Anvau. 'Though they are not now in fashion.'

Madame de la Roque gave him her wine-glass to take away. 'It is so strange to tell us a story,' she remarked. 'If it were not Avon one would go away, but since it is he one stays, full of curiosity. Here he comes!'

His Grace made his way across the room with Madame du Deffand. People began to seat themselves, and those gentlemen who could find no chairs ranged themselves along the wall, or stood in small groups by the doors. Out of the tail of her eye Lady Fanny saw Saint-Vire seated in a small alcove near the window, with Merivale perched on the edge of a table beside him. Madame de Saint-Vire made a movement as though to get to him. Lady Fanny took her arm affectionately.

'My dear, do sit with me! Now where shall we go?' Avon was at her side.

'You lack a chair, Fanny? Madame, your most devoted servant!' He raised his eyeglass, and beckoned to a lackey. 'Two chairs for mesdames.'

'There is not the need,' said Madame hurriedly. 'My husband will give me his —'

'Oh no, madame, you must not leave me thus alone!' said Fanny gaily. 'Ah, here are chairs! I vow we have the best place in the room!' She whisked Madame into a spindle-legged chair that had been brought by the lackey, so that she sat by the fireplace, to one side, able to see the room, and to be seen by nearly everyone.

On the same side, but withdrawn a little into the alcove, her husband sat, and could only see her profile. She turned to look at him imploringly; he sent her a warning glance, and set his teeth. Merivale swung one leg gently, and smiled across at Davenant, leaning against the doorpost.

Madame du Deffand settled herself beside a small table, and laughed up at Avon.

'Now, my friend, let us hear your fairy tale! I hope it is exciting?'

'Of that, madame, I shall leave you to judge,' Avon replied. He took up his stand before the fire, and opened his snuff-box, and helped himself delicately to a pinch of snuff. The firelight and the candlelight played upon him; his face was inscrutable, except that the strange eyes held a mocking gleam.

'There's something afoot, I'll swear!' d'Anvau confided to his neighbour. 'I mislike that look on our friend's face.'

His Grace shut his snuff-box, and flicked a speck of snuff from one great cuff.

'My story, madame, begins as all good stories should,' he said, and though he spoke softly his voice carried through the room. 'Once upon a time – there were two brothers. I have forgotten their names, but since they detested each other, I will call them Cain and – er – Abel. I have no idea whether the original Abel detested the original Cain, and I beg that no one will enlighten me. I like to think that he did. If you ask me whence sprang this hatred between the brothers I can only suggest that it may have originated in the heads of each. Their hair was so fiery that I fear some of the fire must have entered into the brain.' His Grace spread open his fan, and looked serenely down into Armand de Saint-Vire's face of dawning wonderment. 'Quite so. The hatred grew and flourished until I believe there was nothing one brother would not do to spite the other. It became a veritable obsession with Cain, a madness that recoiled on him in the most disastrous manner, as I shall show you. My tale is not without a moral, you will be relieved to hear.'

'What in the world does all this mean?' whispered Lavoulère to a friend. 'Is it a fairy tale, or does something lie behind?'

'I don't know. How does he manage to hold his audience so still, I wonder?'

His Grace went on, speaking very slowly and dispassionately.

'Cain, being the elder of these two brothers, succeeded in due course to his father, who was a Comte and went the way of all flesh. If you imagine that the enmity now subsided between him and Abel, I beg you will permit me to disabuse your minds of so commonplace a thought. Cain's succession but added fuel to the fire of hatred, and whereas our friend Abel was consumed of a desire to stand in his brother's shoes, Cain was consumed of a like desire to keep him out of them. A situation fraught with possibilities, you perceive.' He paused to survey his audience; they watched him in mingled bewilderment and curiosity. 'With this life-ambition in view, then, our single-minded friend Cain took a wife unto himself, and doubtless thought himself secure. But Fate, capricious jade, evidently disliked him, for the years went by, and still there came no son to gladden Cain's heart. You conceive the chagrin of Cain? Abel, however, grew more and more jubilant, and I fear he did not hesitate to make – er – a jest of his brother's ill-luck. It was perhaps unwise of him.' His Grace glanced at Madame de Saint-Vire, who sat rigid, and very pale, beside Lady Fanny. His Grace began to wave his fan rhythmically to and fro. 'I believe Cain's wife presented him once with a still-born child. It began to seem unlikely that Cain would realise his ambition, but contrary to Abel's expectations, Madame le Comtesse raised her husband's hopes once more. This time Cain determined that there should be no mistake. Possibly he had learned to mistrust his luck. When madame's time was upon her he carried her off to his estates, where she was delivered of – a daughter.' Again he paused, and looked across the room at Saint-Vire. He saw the Comte cast a furtive glance towards the door, and colour angrily at sight of Rupert lounging there. His Grace smiled, and swung his eyeglass on its riband. 'Of a daughter. Now observe the cunning of Cain. On his estate, possibly in his employ, there dwelt a farm-labourer, as I judge, whose wife had just presented him with a second son. Fate, or Chance, thus set a trap for Cain, into which he walked. He bribed this peasant to give him his lusty son in exchange for his daughter.'

'But what infamy!' exclaimed Madame de Vauvallon comfortably. 'You shock me, Duc!'

'Strive to bear with me, madame. There is always the moral. This exchange, then, was effected, none being the wiser save the parents of each child, and of course the midwife who attended Madame la Comtesse. What became of her I do not know.'

'*Mon Dieu*, what a tale!' remarked Madame du Deffand. 'I so dislike these villains!'

'Go on, Justin!' said Armand sharply. 'You interest me extraordinarily!'

'Yes, I thought that I should,' nodded his Grace pensively.

'What became of – Cain's daughter?'

'Patience, Armand. Let us first dispose of Cain and his supposed son. Cain presently brought his family back to Paris – did I tell you that this tale takes place in France? – leaving instructions that his daughter's foster-father was to leave his estates for some remote spot, unknown to anyone, including himself. In Cain's place I think I should not have desired so ardently to lose all trace of the child, but no doubt he acted as he thought wisest.'

'Duc,' interposed Madame de la Roque, 'it is inconceivable that any mother could consent to such a wicked plan!'

Madame de Saint-Vire held her handkerchief to her mouth with one shaking hand.

'Al-most inconceivable,' Avon said gently. 'Probably the lady feared her husband. He was a most unpleasant person, believe me.'

'We can easily believe that,' Madame smiled. 'A villainous creature! Go on!'

From under his heavy lids Avon watched Saint-Vire tug at his cravat; his eyes travelled on to Merivale's intent countenance, and he smiled faintly.

'Cain, and his wife, and his pretended son, returned to Paris, as I have said, and greatly discomposed poor Abel. When Abel watched his nephew grow up with no trace of his family's characteristics either in face or nature, he was more than ever enraged, but although he wondered at the boy, the truth never occurred to him. Why should it?' Avon shook out his ruffles. 'Having disposed of Cain for the moment, we will return to Cain's daughter. For twelve years she remained in the heart of the country, with her foster-parents, and was reared as their own child. But at end of those years Fate once more turned her attention to Cain's affairs, and sent a plague to sweep the neighbourhood where his daughter was. This plague struck down both foster-father and mother, but my heroine escaped as did also her foster-brother, of whom more anon. She was sent to the Curé of the village, who housed her, and cared for her. I beg you will not forget the Curé. He plays a small but important part in my story.'

'Will it serve?' Davenant muttered.

'Look at Saint-Vire!' Marling answered. 'The Curé was an inspiration! It has taken him completely by surprise.'

'We shall remember the Curé,' said Armand grimly. 'When does he play his part?'

'He plays it now, Armand, for it was into his hands that my heroine's foster-mother, before she died, placed her – written – confession.'

'Oh, she could write, then, this peasant woman?' said Condé, who had been listening with knit brows.

'I imagine, Prince, that she had once been tire-woman to some lady, for certainly she could write.' Avon saw Madame de Saint-Vire's hands grip together in her lap, and was satisfied. 'That confession lay for many years in a locked drawer in the Curé's house.'

'But he should have published it abroad!' Madame de Vauvallon said quickly.

'So I think, madame, but he was a singularly conscientious priest and he held that the seal of the confessional could never be broken.'

'What of the girl?' asked Armand.

His grace twisted his rings.

'She, my dear Armand, was taken to Paris by her foster-brother, a youth many years her senior. His name was Jean, and he bought a tavern in one of the meanest and most noisome of your streets. And since it was inconvenient for him to have a girl of my heroine's tender years upon his hands, he dressed her as a boy.' The gentle voice grew harder. 'As a boy. I shall not discompose you by telling you of her life in this guise.'

Something like a sob broke from Madame de Saint-Vire.

'*Ah, mon Dieu!*'

Avon's lips sneered.

'It is a harrowing tale, is it not, madame?' he purred.

Saint-Vire half rose from his chair, and sank back again. People were beginning to look questioningly at one another.

'Further,' continued the Duke, 'he married a slut whose care was to ill-use my heroine in every conceivable way. At this woman's hands she suffered for seven long years.' His eyes wandered round the room. 'Until she was nineteen,' he said. 'During those years she learned to know Vice, to Fear, and to know the meaning of that ugly word Hunger. I do not know how she survived.'

'Duc, you tell us a ghastly tale!' said Condé. 'What happened then?'

'Then, Prince, Fate stepped in again, and cast my heroine across the path of a man who had never had cause to love our friend Cain. Into this man's life came my heroine. He was struck by her likeness to Cain, and of impulse he bought her from her foster-brother. He had waited for many years to pay in full a debt he owed Cain; in this child he saw a possible means to do so, for he too had remarked the plebeian manners and person of Cain's supposed son. Chance favoured him, and when he flaunted my heroine before Cain's eyes he saw Cain's consternation, and slowly pieced the tale together. Cain sent an envoy to buy his daughter from this man whom he knew to be his enemy. Thus the suspicion that this new player in the game fostered grew to be a conviction.'

'Good God, d'Anvau,' murmured de Sally, 'can it be – ?'

'H'sh!' d'Anvau answered. 'Listen! This grows very interesting.'

'From Jean,' Avon continued, 'Cain's enemy learned of my heroine's old home, and of the Curé who lived there. I trust you have not forgotten the Curé?'

All eyes were on the Duke; one or two men had begun to see daylight. Condé nodded impatiently.

'No. Go on, I beg of you!'

The emerald on the Duke's finger glinted evilly.

'I am relieved. This man journeyed to the remote village, and – er – wrought with the Curé. When he returned to Paris he brought with him – that.' From his pocket Avon drew a dirty and crumpled sheet of paper. He looked mockingly at Saint-Vire, who sat as though carved in stone. 'That,' repeated his Grace, and laid the paper down on the mantelpiece behind him.

The tension could be felt. Davenant drew a deep breath.

'For a moment – I almost believed it *was* a confession!' he whispered. 'They're beginning to guess, Marling.'

His Grace studied the painting on his fan.

'You may wonder, perhaps, why he did not expose Cain at once. I admit that was his first thought. But he remembered, messieurs, the years that Cain's daughter had spent in hell, and he determined that Cain too should know hell – a little, a very little.' His voice had grown stern; the smile was gone from his lips. Madame du Deffand was watching him with horror in her face. 'And therefore, messieurs, he held his hand, and played – a waiting game. That was his way of justice.' Again he swept a glance round the room; he held his audience silent and expectant, dominated by his personality. Into the silence his words fell slowly, quite softly. 'I think he felt it,' he said. 'From one day to the next he knew not when the blow would fall; he lived in dread; he was torn this way and that by hope, and – fear, messieurs. Even he was cheated into the belief that his enemy had no proof, and for a while thought himself secure.' Avon laughed soundlessly, and saw Saint-Vire wince. 'But the old doubts came back, messieurs; he could not be sure that there was no proof. Thus he lived in an agony of uncertainty.' Avon shut his fan. 'My heroine was taken by her guardian to England, and taught to be a girl again. She was left on her guardian's estates in the care of one of his kinswomen. Little by little, messieurs, she learned to like her girlhood, and to forget, in part, the horrors that lay in the past. Then, messieurs, Cain came to England.' His Grace took snuff. 'Like a thief,' he said gently. 'He stole my heroine, he drugged her, and carried her to his yacht that awaited him at Portsmouth.'

'Good God!' gasped Madame de Vauvallon.

'He'll fail!' whispered Davenant suddenly. 'Saint-Vire has himself well in hand.'

'Watch his wife!' Marling retorted.

His Grace flicked another speck of snuff from his golden sleeve.

'I will not weary you with the tale of my heroine's escape,' he said. 'There was another player in the game who followed hot-foot to the rescue. She contrived to escape with him, but not before Cain had sent a bullet into his shoulder. Whether the shot was meant for him or for her I know not.'

Saint-Vire made a hasty movement, and was quiet again.

'That such villains live!' gasped de Châtelet.

'The wound, messieurs, was severe, and compelled the fugitives to put up at a small inn not many miles from Le Havre. Happily my heroine's guardian found her there, some two hours before the indefatigable Cain arrived.'

'He did arrive, then?' said de Sally.

'But could you doubt it?' smiled his Grace. 'He arrived *bien sûr*, to find that Fate had foiled him once again. He said then, messieurs, that the game was not played out yet. Then he – er – retreated.'

'*Scélérat!*' snapped Condé, and cast one glance at Madame de Saint-Vire, who seemed to cower in her chair, and fixed his eyes on the Duke again.

'Exactly, Prince,' said his Grace smoothly. 'We return now to Paris, where her guardian presented my heroine to Polite Society. Be silent, Armand, I am nearing the end of my story. She made no little stir, I assure you, for she was not an ordinary débutante. She was sometimes, messieurs, just a babe, but withal she had great wisdom, and greater spirit. I might talk to you of her for hours, but I will only say that she was something of an imp, very outspoken, full of *espièglerie*, and very beautiful.'

'And true!' Condé interjected swiftly.

His Grace inclined his head.

'And true, Prince, as I know. To resume: Paris began presently to remark her likeness to Cain. He must have been afraid then, messieurs. But one day it came to the child's ears that the world thought her a base-born daughter of Cain.' He paused, and raised his handkerchief to his lips. 'Messieurs, she loved the man who

complete. Condé was leaning forward in his chair, his face grim and anxious.

'But continue!' he said harshly. 'She – went back?'

'No, Prince,' Avon answered.

'What then?' Condé had risen.

'Prince, for those who are desperate, for the unwanted, for the broken-hearted, there is always a way out.'

Madame du Deffand shuddered, and covered her eyes with her hand.

'You mean?'

Avon pointed to the window.

'Outside, Prince, not so very far away, runs the river. It has hidden many secrets, many tragedies. This child is just one more tragedy that has ended in its tide.'

A choked scream rang out, piercing and shrill. Madame de Saint-Vire came to her feet as though forced, and stumbled forward like one distraught.

'Ah, no, no, no!' she gasped. 'Not that! Not that! Oh, my little, little one! God, have you no mercy? She is not *dead*!' Her voice rose, and was strangled in her throat. She flung up her arm, and collapsed at Avon's feet, and lay there, sobbing wildly.

Lady Fanny sprang up.

'Oh, poor thing! No, no, madame, she is alive. I swear! Help me, someone! Madame, madame, calm yourself!'

There was a sudden uproar; Davenant wiped the sweat from his brow.

'My God!' he said huskily. 'What a night's work! Clever, clever devil!'

In the confusion a woman's voice sounded, bewildered.

'I don't understand! Why? – What? – Is that the end of the story?'

Avon did not turn his head.

'No, mademoiselle. I am still awaiting the end.'

A sudden scuffle in the alcove drew all attention from Madame de Saint-Vire to the Comte. He had sprung up as Madame's control left her, knowing that her outburst had betrayed him completely, and now he was struggling madly with Merivale, one hand at his hip. Even as several men rushed forward he wrenched free, livid and panting, and they saw that he held a small pistol.

Condé leaped suddenly in front of the Duke, and faced that pistol.

It was over in a few seconds. They heard Saint-Vire's voice rise on a note almost of insanity:

'Devil! Devil!'

Then there was a deafening report, a woman screamed, and Rupert strode forward, and flung his handkerchief over Saint-Vire's shattered head. He and Merivale bent over the Comte's body, and his Grace came slowly up to them, and stood for a moment looking down at that which had been Saint-Vire. At the far end of the room a woman was in hysterics. His Grace met Davenant's eyes.

'I said that it should be poetic, did I not, Hugh?' he remarked, and went back to the fireplace. 'Mademoiselle' – he bowed to the frightened girl who had asked him for the story's end – 'M. de Saint-Vire has provided the end to my tale.' He took the soiled paper from the mantelshelf where he had left it, and threw it into the fire, and laughed.

Thirty-One

His Grace of Avon Wins All

INTO THE VILLAGE OF BASSINCOURT ONCE AGAIN RODE HIS GRACE of Avon, upon a hired horse. He was dressed in breeches of buff cloth, and a coat of dull purple velvet, laced with gold. His high spurred boots were dusty; he carried his gloves in one hand, with his long riding crop. Into the market-place he came, from the Saumur road, and reined in as he met the uneven cobble-stones. The villagers, and the farmers' wives who had come into Bassincourt for the market, gaped at him, as they had gaped before, and whispered, one to the other.

The horse picked its way towards the Curé's house, and there stopped. His Grace looked round and, seeing a small boy stand-ing near to him, beckoned, and swung himself lightly down from the saddle.

The boy came running.

'Be so good as to take my horse to the inn, and see it safely housed and watered,' said his Grace, and tossed the boy a louis. 'You may tell the landlord that I shall come to pay the reckoning later.'

'Yes, milor'! Thank you, milor'!' stammered the boy, and clutched his louis.

His Grace opened the little gate that led into the Curé's garden,

and walked up the neat path to the front door. As before the
rosy-cheeked housekeeper admitted him. She recognised him, and
dropped a curtsy.

'*Bonjour, m'sieur!* M. le Curé is in his room.'

'Thank you,' said his Grace. He followed her along the passage
to de Beaupré's study, and stood for a moment on the threshold,
point-edged hat in hand.

The Curé rose politely.

'M'sieur?' Then, as Avon smiled, he hurried forward. '*Eh, mon fils!*'

Avon took his hand.

'My ward, father?'

The Curé beamed.

'The poor little one! Yes, my son, I have her safe.'

Avon seemed to sigh.

'You have relieved my mind of a load that was – almost too
great for it to bear,' he said.

The Curé smiled. 'My son, in a little while I think I should have
broken my promise to her and sent a message to you. She suffers – ah,
but how she suffers. And that villain – that Saint-Vire?'

'Dead, *mon père*, by his own hand.'

De Beaupré made the sign of the Cross.

'By his own hand you say, my son?'

'And by contrivance,' bowed his Grace. 'I come now to
fetch – Mademoiselle de Saint-Vire.'

'It is really so?' De Beaupré spoke anxiously. 'You are sure, Duc?'

'I am sure. All Paris knows. I saw to that.'

De Beaupré caught his hands and pressed them.

'M'sieur, you bring the child happiness, then. God will forgive
you much for your kindness to her. She has told me.' He smiled
benevolently. 'I see that I have no cause to regret my alliance
with – with Satanas. You have given her life, and more than that.'

'My father, I advise you not to credit all that my infant says of me,' said Avon dryly. 'She has seen fit to place me upon a pedestal. I do not sit well there.'

De Beaupré opened the door.

'No, my son, she knows what "Monseigneur's" life has been,' he said. 'Now come to her.' He led the way to the sunny parlour at the back of the house, and opening the door, spoke almost gleefully. '*Petite*, I bring you a visitor.' Then he stood back so that Avon might pass in, and went out quietly, and quietly shut the door.

'Of a surety God is very good,' he said wisely, and went back to his study.

In the parlour Léonie was seated by the window, with a book open upon her lap. And since she had been crying she did not at once turn her head. She heard a light, firm tread, and then a beloved voice.

'*Ma fille*, what does all this mean?'

She flew up out of her chair then, and cried out in joy and astonishment.

'Monseigneur!' She was at his feet, laughing and weeping, his hand to her lips. 'You have come! You have come to me!'

He bent over her, his fingers on her curls.

'Did I not say, *ma fille*, that I should not lose you very easily. You should have trusted me, child. There was no need for your flight.'

She rose to her feet, and swallowed hard.

'Monseigneur, I – I *know*! I could not – you do not understand! It was not possible – Oh, Monseigneur, Monseigneur, why have you come?'

'To take you back, my infant. What else?'

She shook her head.

'Never, never! I c-can't! I know so well that –'

'Sit down, child. There is so much that I must tell you. Crying, *ma mie*?' He raised her hand to his lips, and his voice was very tender. 'There's naught now to distress you, *mignonne*, I swear.'

He made her sit down on the couch, and placed himself beside her, still holding her hand. 'Child, you are not base-born, you are not even peasant-born. You are, as I have known from the first, Léonie de Saint-Vire, daughter of the Comte and his wife, Marie de Lespinasse.'

Léonie blinked at him.

'Mon-monseigneur?' she gasped.

'Yes, my child, just that,' said his Grace, and told her briefly what was her history. She stared at him, round-eyed and with parted lips, and when he finished could find no words for a long minute.

'Then – then I am – noble!' she said at last. 'I – Oh, is it true, Monseigneur? Is it really true?'

'I should not else have told you, *mignonne.*'

She sprang up, flushed and excited.

'I am *well*-born! I am – I am Mademoiselle de Saint-Vire! I can – I can come back to Paris! Monseigneur, I think I am going to cry!'

'I beg you will not, *ma fille.* Spare your tears for my next news.'

She paused in her dance across the room, and looked at him anxiously.

'I have to inform you, infant, that your father is dead.'

The colour returned to her cheeks.

'*Vraiment?*' she said eagerly. 'Did you kill him, Monseigneur?'

'I am very sorry, infant, but I did not actually kill him. I induced him to kill himself.'

She came back to the couch, and sat down again.

'But tell me!' she said. 'Please tell me quickly, Monseigneur! When did he kill himself?'

'On Tuesday, my child, at Madame du Deffand's soirée.'

'*Tiens!*' She was entirely unperturbed. 'Why, *enfin?*'

'I thought that the earth had harboured him too long,' Avon replied.

'You did it! I know you did it!' she said exultantly. 'You meant him to die that night!'

'I did, child.'

'Was Rupert there? And Lady Fanny? *How* Rupert must have been pleased!'

'Moderately, child. He did not display any signs of the unholy ecstasy you appear to feel.'

She tucked her hand in his, and smiled trustingly up at him.

'Monseigneur, he was a pig-person. Now tell me how it happened. Who was there?'

'We were all of us there, babe, even M. Marling, and Milor' Merivale. For the rest there was Condé, the de la Roques, the d'Aiguillons, the Saint-Vires, including Armand; Lavoulère, d'Anvau – in fact, infant, all the world.'

'Did Lady Fanny and the others know that you were going to kill the pig-person, Monseigneur?'

'Infant, pray do not go through the world saying that I killed him.'

'No, Monseigneur. But did they know?'

'They knew that I meant to strike that night. They were all very bloodthirsty.'

'*Vraiment?* Even M. Marling?'

'Even he,' nodded Avon. 'You see, *ma fille*, they all love you.'

She blushed. 'Oh...! What did you wear, Monseigneur?'

'Thus the female mind,' murmured his Grace. 'I wore gold, infant, and emeralds.'

'*I* know. It is a very fine dress, that one. Go on, please, Monseigneur.'

'Rupert and Hugh stood by the doors,' said his Grace, 'and Merivale engaged Saint-Vire in pleasant converse. Lady Fanny had your mother in hand. I told them your story, child. That is all.'

'*Voyons!*' she exclaimed. 'It is nothing! When you had told them what happened?'

'Your mother collapsed. You see, my child, I let them think that you had drowned yourself. She cried out then, and Saint-Vire, since she had thus betrayed him, shot himself.'

'It must have been very exciting,' she remarked. 'I wish I had been there. I am sorry for Madame de Saint-Vire, a little, but I am glad that the pig-person is dead. What will the Vicomte do? I think it is very sad for him.'

'I believe he will not be sorry,' replied Avon. 'No doubt your uncle will make provision for him.'

Her eyes sparkled.

'*Voyons*, I have a family, it seems! How many uncles have I, Monseigneur?'

'I am not quite sure, infant. On your father's side you have one uncle, and an aunt, who is married. On your mother's side you have several uncles, I think, and probably many aunts and cousins.'

She shook her head.

'I find it very hard to understand it all, Monseigneur. And you knew? How did you know? Why did you not tell me?'

His Grace looked down at his snuff-box.

'My child, when I bought you from the estimable Jean it was because I saw your likeness to the Saint-Vire.' He paused. 'I thought to use you as a weapon to – er – punish him for something – he had once done to me.'

'Is – is that why – why you made me your ward, and gave me so many, many things?' she asked in a small voice.

He rose, and went to the window, and stood looking out.

'Not entirely,' he said, and forgot to drawl.

She looked at him wistfully.

'Was it a little because you liked me, Monseigneur?'

'Afterwards. When I came to know you, child.'

She twisted her handkerchief.

'Am I – will you – still let me be your ward?'

He was silent for a moment.

'My dear, you have a mother now, and an uncle, who will care for you.'

'Yes?' she said.

His Grace's profile was stern.

'They will be very good to you, *ma fille*,' he said evenly. 'Having them – you cannot still be my ward.'

'N-need I have them?' she asked, a pathetic catch in her voice.

His Grace did not smile.

'I am afraid so, infant. They want you, you see.'

'Do they?' She rose also, and the sparkle was gone from her eyes. 'They do not know me, Monseigneur.'

'They are your family, child.'

'I do not want them.'

At that he turned, and came to her, and took her hands.

'My dear,' he said, 'it will be best for you to go to them, believe me. One day I think you will meet a younger man than I who will make you happy.'

Two great tears welled up. Léonie's eyes looked piteously into the Duke's.

'Monseigneur – please – do not talk to me of marriage!' she whispered.

'Child –' His clasp on her hands tightened. 'I want you to forget me. I am no proper man for you. You will be wiser not to think of me.'

'Monseigneur, I never thought that you would marry me,' she said simply. 'But if – you wanted me – I thought perhaps you would – take me – until I wearied you.'

There was a moment's silence. Then his Grace spoke, so harshly that Léonie was startled.

'You are not to talk in that fashion, Léonie. You understand me?'

'I – I am sorry!' she faltered. 'I – I did not mean to make you angry, Monseigneur.'

'I am not angry,' he answered. 'Even were it possible, Léonie, I would not take you as my mistress. That is not how I think of you.'

'You do not love me?' she said, like a child.

'Too – well to marry you,' he said, and released her hands. 'It is not possible.'

She stayed quite still, looking down at the marks of his fingers about her wrists with a little wise smile.

'You will take me to this mother and uncle whom I do not know?'

'Yes,' he said curtly.

'Monseigneur, I would rather stay here,' she said. 'Since you do not want me I will not go back. *C'est fini, tout cela.*' A sob rose in her throat. 'You bought me, Monseigneur, and I am yours till I die. I told you – once – that it was so. You do not remember?'

'I remember every word you have spoken to me.'

'Monseigneur, I – I do not want to be a burden to you. You are tired of – of having a ward, and – and I would rather leave you than stay to weary you. But I cannot go back to Paris. I *cannot*! I shall be quite – happy – here with M. de Beaupré, but I cannot bear to go back alone – to the world I have lived in with you.'

He looked across at her. She saw his hand clenched hard on his snuff-box.

'Child, you do not know me. You have created a mythical being in my likeness whom you have set up as a god. It is not I. Many times, infant, I have told you that I am no hero, but I think you have not believed me. I tell you now that I am no fit mate for you. There are twenty years between us, and those years have not been well spent by me. My reputation is damaged beyond repair, child. I come of vicious stock, and I have brought no honour to the name I bear. Do you know what men call me?

I earned that nickname, child; I have even been proud of it. To no women have I been faithful; behind me lies scandal upon sordid scandal. I have wealth, but I squandered one fortune in my youth, and won my present fortune at play. You have seen perhaps the best of me; you have not seen the worst. Infant, you are worthy of a better husband. I would give you a boy who might come to you with a clean heart, not one who was bred up in vice from his cradle.'

One large tear glistened on the end of her lashes.

'Ah, Monseigneur, you need not have told me this! I know – I have always known, and still I love you. I do not want a boy. I want only – Monseigneur.'

'Léonie, you will do well to consider. You are not the first woman in my life.'

She smiled through her tears.

'Monseigneur, I would so much rather be the last woman than the first,' she said.

'Infant, it's madness!'

She came to him, and put her hand on his arm.

'Monseigneur, I do not think that I can live without you; I must have you to take care of me, and to love me, and to scold me when I am *maladroite*.'

Involuntarily his hand went to hers.

'Rupert would be a more fitting bridegroom,' he said bitterly.

Her eyes flashed.

'Ah, bah!' she said scornfully. 'Rupert is a silly boy, like the Prince de Condé! If you do not marry me, Monseigneur, I will not marry anyone!'

'That would be a pity,' he said. '*Mignonne*, are you – sure?'

She nodded; a tremulous smile curved her lips.

'Oh, Monseigneur, I never thought that *you* would be so very blind!' she said.

His Grace looked deep into her eyes, and then went down on one knee, and raised her hand to his lips.

'Little one,' he said, very low, 'since you will stoop to wed me, I pledge you my word that you shall not in the future have cause to regret it.'

An insistent hand tugged at his shoulder. He rose, and opened wide his arms. Léonie flung herself into them, and they closed about her, and her lips met his.

M. de Beaupré entered softly, and seeing, prepared to depart in haste. But they had heard the opening of the door, and they fell apart.

He beamed upon them.

'*Eh bien, mes enfants?*'

His Grace took Léonie's hand in his, and led her forward.

'*Mon père,*' he said, 'I want you to wed us.'

'Of a surety, *mon fils,*' said De Beaupré calmly, and stroked Léonie's cheek. 'I am waiting to do so.'

Thirty-Two

His Grace of Avon Astonishes
Everyone for the Last Time

'MY DEAR COMTE,' SAID FANNY, IN A VOICE OF LONG-SUFFERING, 'I have not seen Justin since that terrible night.'

Armand threw out his hands.

'But it is over a week ago!' he cried. 'Where is he? Where is the child?'

Lady Fanny cast up her eyes. Davenant it was who answered.

'If we knew, Armand, we should be more at ease, I assure you. The last we saw of Avon was at Madame du Deffand's.'

'Where did he go?' demanded Armand. 'Did he not return here at all?'

Marling shook his head.

'He vanished,' he said. 'We knew that he meant to set out for Anjou after the soirée, in search of Léonie, but he did not tell us exactly where he was bound. His valet is with him, and he has taken the light chaise. That is all we know.'

Armand sat down weakly.

'But – but did he set out in his ball-dress?' he said. 'He must surely have returned here first to change it for something more *convenable*!'

'He didn't,' Fanny replied positively. 'That gold dress is not in his room. We looked.'

'*Fi, donc!*' cried Armand. 'Is he travelling through France in it?'

'I should hardly think so.' Davenant was amused. 'He will have halted somewhere for the night, and if I know aught of Justin he did not set out without some baggage.'

Armand looked round helplessly.

'And not one of you in his confidence!' he said. 'It becomes serious! Three times have I come to see –'

'Four,' said my lady wearily.

'Is it so, madame? Four times, then, I have come to see if you have news of him, and of my niece! What can have happened, think you?'

Davenant looked at him.

'We try not to think, Armand. Believe me, our anxiety is as great as yours. We do not know whether Léonie be alive or dead.'

Lady Fanny blew her nose, and cleared her throat.

'And we can't *do* anything!' she said. 'We must just sit idle, waiting!'

Marling patted her hand.

'You at least have not been idle, my love.'

'No, indeed!' Armand turned to her. 'Madame, your kindness to my unfortunate sister overwhelms me! I can find no words! That you should have brought her here, and housed her – Madame, I can only thank –'

'Oh, fiddle!' said Fanny, reviving. 'What else could I do? She is in no fit case to be alone, I do assure you. At one time I feared she was like to die of her hysterics, pour soul! She has seen a priest, and since she wrote her confession I do think she is easier. If only Justin would send us word! I cannot sleep o' nights for thinking of what may have befallen that poor, poor child!'

Davenant stirred the fire to a blaze.

'In truth,' he said, 'there can be no ease for any of us, until we know her to be safe.' His smile went awry. 'The house is like a tomb since she left it.'

No one answered him. Rupert walked in, to an uncomfortable silence.

'Hey, in the dumps again?' he said breezily. 'What, Armand here again? You'd best come and live with us, and ha' done with it!'

'I don't know how you can find the heart to laugh, Rupert!' said my lady.

'Why not?' replied the graceless Rupert, coming to the fire. 'Justin told us that he knew where Léonie had gone, and I don't see him failing now, Fan, damme, I don't! I'll lay a monkey he'll bring her back before the week's out, safe and sound.'

'If he finds her,' Marling said quietly. 'It's more than a week now, Rupert.'

'That's right, Edward,' retorted his lordship. 'Look on the cheerful side! Stap me if ever I met such a gloomy fellow! We don't know how far Justin may have had to go.'

'But he's sent us no word, Rupert!' Fanny said anxiously. 'This silence frightens me!'

Rupert regarded her in some surprise.

'Lord, and did you ever know Justin to send word of what he would be at?' he demanded. 'He'll play his own game, mark my words! He's not one to take others into his confidence, and he don't need any help.' He chuckled. 'We saw that on Tuesday last, so we did! The man likes to keep us in the dark, and that's all there is to it.'

A lackey announced my Lord Merivale, and Anthony came in.

'No news?' he asked, bowing over Fanny's hand.

'No, alas!'

Rupert made room for my lord on the couch.

'Fan's in the dumps over it,' he said. 'I'm telling her she should have more faith in Justin.' He wagged his finger at her. 'He's won every trick in the game, Fan, and he wouldn't be Justin an he lost the last.'

'Faith, I believe Rupert is right,' Merivale agreed. 'I am fast coming to think Avon omnipotent.'

Marling spoke gravely. 'He is a very dangerous man,' he said. 'It will be long before I forget the happenings at that soirée.'

Rupert was disgusted.

'Y'know, Edward, you're a kill-joy,' he said.

Fanny shuddered.

'Oh, Edward, pray do not speak of it! It was horrible, horrible!'

'I do not wish to speak ill of the dead,' Davenant said, 'but it was – justice.'

'Ay, and he did it well, by Gad!' said Rupert. 'I can see him now, standing there like – damme, like an executioner! But he was devilish, oh, he was devilish! He had me fascinated, I give you my word!'

The door opened.

'*Madame est servie*,' bowed a lackey.

Fanny rose. 'You'll dine with us, Comte? And you, Anthony?'

'I trespass upon your hospitality!' Armand protested.

'Devil a bit, man!' said Rupert. 'It's Avon's hospitality you trespass on, and our patience.'

Fanny laughed. 'Disagreeable boy! Comte, will you give me your arm? I protest I am shy amongst so many of you men!'

'What of Madame?' Marling asked, as she passed him.

'She has a tray in her room,' Fanny replied. 'I cannot induce her to join us yet, and indeed, I think she is better alone.'

So they went into the dining-room, and seated themselves round the long table, Fanny at one end, and Marling at the other.

'Y'know I scarce dare venture abroad nowadays,' remarked Rupert, shaking out his napkin. 'Wherever I go I'm pounced on for news.'

'Ay, no one seems able to believe that we know no more than the rest of the world,' said Davenant.

'And the people who flock to the house to inquire if Léonie

is safe!' said my lady. 'This very day I have received Condé, and
de Richelieu, and the de la Roques! The child will have a great
welcome when   if   if she returns.'

'Plague take your "ifs," Fan!' said Rupert. 'Will you have claret,
Tony?'

'Burgundy, I thank you, scamp.'

'I have ceased to answer the letters,' said Fanny. 'People have
been very kind, but in truth I cannot hope to reply to all.'

'Kind?' snorted Rupert. 'Damned inquisitive, is what I say!'

'Armand, what becomes of de Valmé – I mean, Bonnard?'

Armand laid down his fork.

'If you will believe me, the boy is almost glad!' he said. 'He
understood not in the least what was toward at Madame du
Deffand's that night, but when I explained the matter to him –
what do you think he said?'

'We don't know,' said Rupert. 'We've enough mystery without you trying to start a fresh one, stap me if we've not!'

'Rupert!' My lady frowned upon him. 'Rude boy!'

'He said,' Armand went on, '"At last, at last I may have a farm!"'
He looked round impressively. 'Did you ever hear the like of it?'

'Never,' said Davenant gravely. 'And so?'

'I shall buy him a farm, of course, and settle money upon him.
I suggested that he might wish to remain in Paris, and assured him
of my protection, but no! He hates town-life, if you please!'

'Mad,' said Rupert with conviction.

Merivale started up.

'Listen!' he said sharply.

Outside in the hall was some stir, as of an arrival. Those in the
dining-room sprang up, looking half shamefacedly at each other.

'A – a caller,' Fanny said. 'I'm sure it's only –'

The door was flung open, and his Grace of Avon stood upon
the threshold, booted and spurred, and greatcoated. Beside him,

her hand in his, was Léonie, flushed and radiant. She had shed her cloak and hat, and her bright curls were tumbled.

There was an outcry. Fanny ran forward, exclaiming incoherently; Rupert waved his napkin over his head.

'What did I tell you?' he shouted. 'Mademoiselle de Saint-Vire!'

His Grace raised one white hand, holding them in check. A curiously proud smile hovered above his mouth.

'No, Rupert,' he said, and bowed slightly. 'I have the honour to present to you all – my Duchess.'

'Thunder an' turf!' gasped Rupert, and surged forward.

Fanny reached Léonie first.

'Oh, my sweet life! I am so glad – I can hardly believe – where did you find her, Justin? Silly, silly child! We have been in such a taking – Kiss me again, my love!'

Rupert pushed her aside.

'Hey, you little madcap!' he said, and kissed her soundly. 'What a sister you have given me, Justin! *I* knew you'd find her! But married already, egad! It beats all, so it does!'

Merivale thrust him away.

'My dear little Léonie!' he said. 'Justin, I felicitate you!'

Then Marling and Davenant in their turn pushed forward. Armand grasped Avon's hand.

'And my permission?' he asked with mock dignity.

Avon snapped his fingers.

'So much for your permission, my dear Armand,' he said, and looked across at Léonie, surrounded by the vociferous family.

'Where was she?' Armand tugged at his sleeve.

His Grace was still watching Léonie.

'Where was she? Where I had expected her to be. In Anjou, with the Curé I spoke of,' he said. 'Well, Fanny? Have I your approval?'

She embraced him.

'My dear, 'tis what I planned for you months ago. But to be married thus secretly when I had dreamed of a truly magnificent wedding! It's too bad, I declare! Dear, dear child! I could weep for joy!'

A hush fell. In the doorway, shrinking, Madame de Saint-Vire stood, her eyes fixed on Léonie. There was a moment's uncomfortable silence. Then Léonie went forward, and put out her hand with pretty hesitancy.

'*Ma – mère?*' she said.

Madame gave a shattering sob, and clung to her. Léonie put an arm about her waist, and led her quietly out.

Fanny's handkerchief appeared.

'The dear, sweet child!' she said huskily.

Davenant took Avon's hand, and wrung it.

'Justin, I cannot find words to tell you how glad I am!'

'My dear Hugh, this is most unexpected,' drawled his Grace. 'I made sure of a despondent head shake.'

Hugh laughed. 'No, no, my friend, not this time! You have learned to love another better than yourself at last, and I believe that you will make your Duchess a good husband.'

'It is mine intention,' said his Grace, and struggled out of his coat. There was a tinge of colour in his cheeks, but he put up his glass in the old manner, and surveyed the room. 'My house seems to be remarkably full of people,' he observed. 'Is it possible we were expected?'

'Expected?' echoed Rupert. 'Stap me, but that's rich! We've done naught but expect you for the past ten days, I'll have you know! It's very well for you to go careering off to Anjou, but it's mighty poor sport for us. What with Armand hopping in and out like a jack-in-the-box, and Madame upstairs with the vapours, and half Paris forcing its way in to nose out the mystery, the house is a veritable ants' nest. I believe Merivale still sleeps with de Châtelet, for I don't see him here at breakfast, thank the Lord!'

'What I want to know,' said Merivale, ignoring his lordship, 'is this: Did you journey all the way to Anjou in that preposterous gold dress?'

'Faith, he must have startled the countryside!' chuckled Rupert.

'No, my friend, no,' sighed his Grace. 'I changed it for more sober garments at the first halt. Armand, is all well?'

'Completely, Justin! My sister wrote her confession as soon as she was able, and mine erstwhile nephew is to have a farm, and retire from Society. I owe you a debt of gratitude which I can never hope to repay.'

His Grace poured himself out a glass of burgundy.

'I have taken payment, my dear, in the person of your niece,' he said, and smiled.

Then Léonie came in, and went at once to Avon's side.

'My mother desires to be left alone,' she said gravely. The sparkle came into her eyes again. 'Oh, I am so *very* pleased to see you all again!'

Rupert nudged Davenant.

'Look at Justin's face!' he whispered. 'Did you ever see aught to equal the pride of him? Léonie, I'm devilish hungry, and with your permission I'll go on with my capon.'

'I am very hungry too,' she nodded. 'Madame, you have no idea how nice it is to be a married lady!'

'Oh, have I not indeed?' cried my lady. 'How am I to take that?' She led Léonie to her own place at the foot of the table. 'Sit down, my love!'

'Madame, that is where you sit!' Léonie said.

'My sweet, I am a guest in your house now,' said Fanny, and curtsied.

Léonie looked at Avon inquiringly.

'Yes, infant. Sit down.'

'*Voyons*, I feel very important!' Léonie said, settling herself in the high-backed chair. 'Rupert shall sit beside me on one side, and – and –' she debated – 'M. de Saint-Vire – I mean, my uncle, on the other.'

'Very prettily done, my dear,' nodded her ladyship, and went to a seat on Avon's right.

'And since I am now a Duchess,' said Léonie, twinkling, 'Rupert must treat me with respect, *n'est-ce pas*, Monseigneur?'

Avon smiled at her across the table.

'You have only to say the word, *mignonne*, and he shall be cast forth.'

'Respect be damned!' said Rupert. 'I'll have you remember you're my sister now, child! Lord, where are my wits!' He sprang up, wine-glass in hand. 'I give you all a toast!' he said. 'The Duchess of Avon!'

They rose as one.

'The Duchess!' Davenant bowed.

'My dearest sister!' Fanny cried.

'My wife!' said his Grace softly.

Léonie stood up, blushing, and taking Rupert's hand, jumped on to her chair.

'Thank you very much!' she said. 'May I give a toast, please?'

'Ay, bless you!' said Rupert.

'Monseigneur!' Léonie said, and made him a quaint little bow. 'Oh, where is my glass? Rupert, hand it up to me quickly!'

The Duke's health was duly drunk.

'And now,' said Léonie, 'I drink to Rupert, because he has been very good, and useful to me!'

'Here's to you, brave lad!' said his lordship gravely 'What now, minx?'

Still perched upon the chair, Léonie said gleefully:

'*Voyons*, I get higher and higher in the world!'

'You'll fall off the chair if you jump like that, silly chit!' Rupert warned her.

'Do not interrupt me,' said Léonie reprovingly. 'I am making a speech.'

'Lord save us, what next will you be at?' Rupert said, unrepentant.

'*Tais-toi, imbécile!*... First I was a peasant, and then I became a page. Then I was made Monseigneur's ward, and now I am a Duchess! I am become very respectable, *n'est-ce pas?*'

His Grace was at her side, and lifted her down from the chair.

'My infant,' he said, 'duchesses do not dance on chairs, nor do they call their brothers "*imbécile.*"'

Léonie twinkled irrepressibly.

'I do,' she said firmly.

Rupert shook his head at her.

'Justin's in the right of it,' he said. 'You'll have to mend your ways, spitfire. No more bouquets from Princes of the Blood, eh, Justin? Dignity! That's the thing! You must let your hair grow too, and speak to me politely. I'll be pinked an I'll have a sister who tells all my friends I'm an imbecile! Politeness, my lady, and some of your husband's haughtiness! That's what you must have, isn't it, Fan?'

'Ah, bah!' said the Duchess of Avon.

Afterword

by Jennifer Kloester,
Georgette Heyer's official biographer

Though it was first published in 1926, Georgette Heyer actually wrote *These Old Shades* in 1922. She was nineteen when she began it and just twenty when she told her agent, Leonard Moore, that she was writing a sequel to her first novel, *The Black Moth*. Heyer was enthusiastic about the new book, describing it as "naturally a much better book than *The Moth* itself, and designed to catch the public's taste. I have also tried to arrange it that anyone who reads it need not first read *The Moth*. It deals with my priceless villain, and ends awfully happily." By the time she finished it, *These Old Shades* was not so much a sequel as a new story with enough elements of *The Black Moth* to tantalize her readers. The first edition included a poem by Austin Dobson, which explains why he (and later, Heyer) liked the era of "fans and masks, periwigs and patches":

Whereas with these old Shades of mine,
Their ways and dress delight me;
And should I trip by word or line,
They cannot well indict me.

But—should I fail to render clear
Their title, rank, or station—
I still may sleep secure, nor fear
A suit for defamation.

Heyer thoroughly enjoyed writing *These Old Shades* and told Moore, "I've packed it full of incident and adventure, and have made my heroine masquerade as a boy for the first few chapters. This, I find, always attracts people!" She was not wrong. When it was finally published in 1926, the book was an instant success, selling 30,000 copies in its first few months and winning her an enthusiastic international audience, with one Australian reader writing to tell Heyer that she was "a bonzer woman" and that "all the girls who read the *filthiest* books like yours." With its glorious cast of memorable characters, including "Satanas," Duke of Avon, Léonie, Rupert, Lady Fanny, and the wicked Comte de Saint-Vire, it is not surprising that, nearly a hundred years after its debut, many readers still cite *These Old Shades* as their favourite Georgette Heyer novel.

Glossary of Regency Slang

Excerpted from

Georgette Heyer's Regency World

by Jennifer Kloester

The definitive guide for all fans of Georgette Heyer,
Jane Austen, and the glittering Regency period.

Glossary of Regency Slang

CANT

During the Regency it became the fashion for upper-class men to integrate into their everyday speech the language of certain of the lower classes. Mainly as a result of the rising interest in sport and the predominance of the horse in this period, many well-born males used boxing cant, racing cant, and the vocabulary of the stable hand and the coachman as part of their daily talk. In addition, forays by bored young men into the seedier parts of town saw the inclusion of phrases culled from the extraordinary and colourful slang used in London's underworld. The famous Regency writer and journalist, Pierce Egan, was undoubtedly one of the foremost exponents of sporting cant during the period, and Georgette Heyer enjoyed and made great use of the language in his lively tale of Jerry Hawthorn and his friend Corinthian Tom in Egan's book *Life in London*.

BOXING

a bit of the home-brewed: punching or hitting done by an untrained boxer

bone box: mouth

bottom: courage, guts, stability—in pugilism one who can endure a beating

a bruiser: a boxer

claret: blood

displays to advantage: boxes well, looks good in the ring or in a fight

to draw his cork: to make him bleed—particularly by punching him in the nose

fib him: to beat or hit someone

a mill: a fight, usually a boxing match or fist fight

a milling cove: a pugilist or boxer

milling a canister: break someone's head

plant a facer: punch someone in the face

HORSES

beautiful stepper: a good horse with a fine easy gait

blood cattle: well-bred horses, thoroughbreds

bone-setters: ill-bred horses, inferior horses

bottom: a strong horse with good temperament and endurance

cattle: horses

hunt the squirrel: the often dangerous sport of following closely behind a carriage and then passing it so closely as to brush the wheel. Considered an amusing pastime by stagecoachmen and some sporting gentlemen, the practice often resulted in the victim's carriage being overturned.

neck-or-nothing: a rider who will try anything, a bold daring sportsman or sportswoman

part company: to fall off a horse

prime bits of blood: top quality horses

a screw: a very poor quality horse

a sweetgoer: a horse with an easy action

throwing out a splint: become lame as a result of swelling in the ligament next to the splint bone

DRINKING

a ball of fire: a glass of brandy

blood and thunder: a mixture of port wine and brandy

blue ruin: gin

boosey: drunk

boozing-ken: a tavern or alehouse

bosky: drunk

a bumper: a full glass

daffy: gin

dipping too deep: drinking too much

disguised: drunk

drunk as a wheelbarrow: inebriated

eaten Hull cheese: drunk

an elbow-crooker: a drinker

a flash of lightning: strong spirits, a glass of gin

foxed: intoxicated

fuddled: drunk

half-sprung: tipsy, mellow with drink

heavy wet: porter or stout, malt liquor

in his altitudes: drunk

in your cups: drunk

jug-bitten: tipsy
making indentures: drinking
on the cut: to go on a spree; to get drunk
shoot the cat: to vomit
to cast up one's accounts: to vomit
too ripe and ready: drunk
top-heavy: drunk

FEELINGS AND BEHAVIOUR

a bear-garden jaw: rude, vulgar language; a real talking to
be on the high ropes: to stand on one's dignity; to become very
    angry; to be excited
blue as megrim: depressed, sad, unhappy
break-teeth words: difficult words, hard to pronounce
buffle-headed: confused, stupid, foolish
corky. lively, merry, playful, restless
cry rope: to cry out a warning
cut one's eye teeth: to become knowing, to understand the
    world
dicked in the nob: silly, crazy
done to a cow's thumb: exhausted
fagged to death: exhausted
fit of the blue-devils: sad, miserable, depressed, in low spirits
fly up into the boughs: fly into a passion, lose one's temper
Friday-faced: a sad or miserable countenance—derived from the
    tradition of Friday abstinence which prohibited publicans from
    dressing dinners on Fridays
high in the instep: arrogant, haughty, proud
a honey-fall: good fortune
in a dudgeon: angry, in a bad mood

in high ropes: ecstatic, elated, in high spirits

kick over the traces: to go the pace; kick up larks; behave in a headstrong or disobedient manner

knocked-up: exhausted

make a mull of it: to mismanage a situation; to fail; to make a muddle of something

mawkish: falsely sentimental, insipid or nauseating

more than seven: to be knowing or wide-awake, experienced in the ways of the world

mutton-headed: stupid

napping her bib: to cry; to get one's way by weeping

ring a peal over one: to admonish or scold someone

set up one's bristles: to irritate or annoy; to offend or make someone angry

spleen: anger

to catch cold: advice to cease or desist; a suggestion that one should cease making threats

to pull caps with someone: to argue

to swallow one's spleen: to curb one's temper

within ames-ace: nearly, or very near

LYING

bag of moonshine: nonsense, a lot of nothing

bamboozle: to deceive, hoax or make a fool of a person; to humbug or impose on someone

Banbury stories: a long-winded nonsense tale, a cock-and-bull story

bouncer: a big lie

Canterbury Tales: a long, tedious story

a clanker: a huge lie

cut a sham: to deliberately trick, cheat or deceive

cut a wheedle: to deliberately lead astray or decoy by flattery and insinuation

doing it much too brown: to go over the top in telling a lie; to lie or cheat thoroughly

faradiddles: a petty lie; originally 'taradiddle'

flummery: false compliments

fudge: nonsense

fustian or fustian nonsense: pompous rubbish

gammon: nonsense, lies; to pretend, lie or deceive

gulled: duped, fooled, tricked

a hum: a falsehood, a deceit, a made-up story

pitching the gammon: to talk plausibly; to hoax someone; to flatter without restraint; to tell grand stories; to deceive merrily

plumper: an arrant lie—possibly from the false cheeks worn in previous centuries

shamming it: to pretend or make things up

slum: to speak cant or talk nonsense

to offer Spanish coin: to flatter with fair words and compliments

toad-eat: to pay compliments or to flatter in the hope of winning a person's favour or approval

whiskers: lies

MONEY

at a stand or a standstill: run out of money and in financial difficulty

blunt: money

brass: money

brought to point non plus: backed into a financial corner with few options for recovery

cheeseparing: miserly, niggardly, mean with money

dibs not in tune: not enough money; in a parlous financial state

dished: financially ruined

drawing the bustle: spending too much money

a dun: a persistent creditor

flush in the pocket or flush with funds: having plenty of ready money

full of juice: wealthy

gingerbread: money

grease someone in the fist: to put money into a person's hand; to bribe someone or give them a monetary incentive

gullgropers: a professional moneylender, especially one who does business with gamblers

hang on someone's sleeve: to rely on someone financially

haven't a sixpence to scratch with: flat broke

high water with him: wealthy; he has lots of money

in deep: in serious debt

in dun territory: in debt

in the basket: to be in financial difficulty—from the practice of putting those who could not pay their gambling debts at a cock-fight into a basket suspended above the pit. The term also relates to those purse-pinched stagecoach travellers who could only afford to travel in the boot—originally a large basket strapped to the back of the carriage.

low ebb or at ebb-water: a lack of money

low water: lack of money

nip-cheese or nip-farthing: a miser

not a feather to fly with: no money, dead broke

note of hand: an IOU

on the rocks: financially ruined, bankrupt

outrun the constable: to overspend; to live beyond one's means

plump in the pocket: to have plenty of ready cash

pockets to let: no money, penniless
purse-pinched: short of money
raise the wind: borrow money
the ready: money, particularly money in hand
recruits: money, often money that is expected
the rhino: money
the River Tick: standing debts
rolled-up: no money and in serious financial trouble
run off one's legs: to have spent all one's money
run on tick: to buy on credit
swallow a spider: to go bankrupt
swimming in lard: very wealthy
tip over the dibs: to lend or give money to someone
to bleed: to extort money either openly or in an underhand way
to fleece: to swindle
to frank someone: to pay their way
to stand huff: to pay the bill in a tavern; to pay for everyone
under the hatches: in debt
vowels: IOUs
well-breeched: having plenty of money in your pockets—a
　prime target for robbery
well-inlaid: plenty of money

NOT THE THING

a bridle cull: a highwayman
a cursed rum touch: a strange person; an odd or eccentric man
　who is also annoying
a flat: an honest man; a fool, one who is easily tricked; a greenhorn
fulhams: loaded dice

half flash and half foolish: having a small knowledge of cant and a limited experience of the world

an ivory-turner: one who cheats in dice games

a peep-o-day boy: an unsteady young man always involved in pranks or larks

a rattle: one who talks too much

a rum 'un: a strange person, an odd or eccentric man

a sharp: a cheat who lives by his skill at manipulating the cards or dice

smoky: suspicious, curious

uphills: loaded dice; false dice made to roll to the higher or upper numbers—as opposed to downhills which fall to the lower numbers

PEOPLE

all the crack: in the mode, the height of fashion

an ape leader: a woman beyond marriageable age; an old maid—so-called because of a proverb that says their failure to increase and multiply dooms them to lead apes in hell. Also used by Shakespeare in *Much Ado About Nothing* II.i.41 and *The Taming of the Shrew* II.i.34

awake on every suit: knowing what's going on, understanding the business

a bang-up cove: a dashing man who spends money easily; a good-natured splendid fellow

bang up to the knocker: first-rate; well dressed, turned out in prime style

bang up to the mark: first-rate

bird-witted: thoughtless, brainless, easily imposed upon, gullible, inconsiderate

a bit of muslin: a girl; an attractive female—though usually one who is ready to be seduced or taken as a mistress

bracket-faced: ugly, hard-featured

bran-faced: freckled

a chawbacon: a country bumpkin; a stupid man

a chit: a young girl

a cicisbeo: a married woman's lover or escort

clunch: a clownish person, awkward, foolish

complete to a shade: superbly dressed, dressed in the height of fashion

a diamond of the first water: a remarkably beautiful woman

a dowdy: a plain, ill-dressed female

a downy one: aware, a knowing intelligent person

a doxy: a whore

a green girl: a naive, inexperienced young woman

a hoyden: an active, tomboyish romp of a girl

a hussy: a forward, badly behaved female

a jade: a disreputable woman

a jilt: a woman who cries off from an engagement not long before the wedding

a Johnny raw: a novice, an inexperienced or untried youth

a loose fish: an unreliable person; a person of dissipated habits; a lecher or a drunk

a mort: a woman or wench; but could sometimes mean a harlot

an out and outer: one who is first-rate; a perfect person; excellent in every way

a prime article: a handsome woman, a beautiful female

a romp: a forward girl

a swell mort: an upper-class woman

a tabby: an old maid

a vixen: a shrewish woman

a vulgar mushroom: a pushing, pretentious member of the new rich—the reference being to mushrooms as a kind of fungus which comes up suddenly in the night

a wet goose: a simple or stupid person

SEX AND SOCIETY

an abbess: a procuress of prostitutes, a female keeper of a brothel

barque of frailty: a woman of easy virtue

base-born child: an illegitimate child, a bastard

bird of paradise: a showy prostitute

by-blow: an illegitimate child, a bastard

carte-blanche: monetary support and protection offered to a man's mistress in place of marriage

chère-amie: a mistress—literally 'darling beloved'

crim. con.: short for criminal conversations—a euphemism for adultery

a game-pullet: a young prostitute or a girl likely to become a whore

Haymarket ware: a prostitute

an impure: a woman of easy virtue

incognitas: a masked or disguised prostitute

lady-bird: a lewd or light woman, a prostitute

light o' love: a mistress

lightskirt: a prostitute

loose in the haft: a man of easy virtue and few morals

on-dit: gossip—literally 'one says'

one of the muslin company: a prostitute; a female ready to be set up as a mistress

Paphian: a woman of easy virtue; relating to sexual love

a petticoat-pensioner: one who lives off a woman's ill-gotten earnings, a whoremonger

a rake: a man of great sexual appetite and few morals

side-slips: illegitimate children, bastards

a slip on the shoulder: to seduce a woman, seduction

trollop: a sluttish woman

MARRIAGE

become a tenant for life: get married off, get married

cry off: to change one's mind and call off the wedding

an eligible parti: a suitable marriage partner

leg-shackled: married

make an offer: propose marriage

on the shelf: unmarried and beyond the usual age of marrying

puff it off: announce one's engagement in the papers

riveted: married

set your cap at a man: to try to win a man's favour and a proposal of marriage

smelling of April and May: madly in love

Reading Group Guide

1. When the Duke of Avon first meets Léon, he thinks one thing but quickly changes his opinion. Léon instantly adores the Duke. How important do you think first impressions are? Tell about a time you were right about your first impressions and a time you were wrong about someone.

2. The Duke's friends are puzzled by his relationship with Léon. How long did it take you to figure out what was really going on? Have you ever had a situation in your life that looked like one thing and turned out to be something completely different? What happened?

3. The Duke has a terrible reputation, but Léon won't hear a word against him. Have you ever been in a situation where you could see someone's good side when no one else did? Did your confidence in this person make them a better person?

4. Georgette Heyer is known for her historical research. What is your favorite time period to read about? Is there any historical time period that you wish you could visit or live in? What

attracts you to that time period? What are your favorite things about living in today's world?

5. What did you think of the gentlemen in the story? Did you find the Duke of Avon a sympathetic hero or difficult to warm up to? Are there any qualities in the Duke that you would like to see more of in people today?

6. Were there any scenes in the book that made you laugh out loud? Were there any that made you cringe? Describe your reactions.

7. Describe the family dynamics of the Alistairs and of the Saint-Vires. Do you have colorful characters in your family? What is the best thing about your own family dynamics?

8. The Duke of Avon has been waiting for nearly twenty years for an opportunity to take his revenge. Have you ever waited a long time and then gotten revenge on someone? What was that like? Would you do it again?

9. Have you read any other books by Georgette Heyer? Which are your favorites? Which are your least favorites, and why?

About the Author

Georgette Heyer is an international bestseller with over twenty million copies sold worldwide. A natural-born storyteller, she composed her first novel, *The Black Moth*, at the age of seventeen to amuse her brother while he was ill. She got her first publishing contract when she was eighteen. *The Black Moth* was published when she was nineteen and became an instant success.

Heyer was very close to her father, who supported her writing and encouraged her to pursue publication. His sudden death in 1925 when she was twenty-two was devastating. She missed him terribly—but she kept writing for the rest of her life.

She wrote country-house mysteries, historical novels, and the romances for which she became most famous. In her romances, Heyer skewers human nature with shrewd insight, razor-sharp wit, and a genius for sheer delightful romantic comedy. She brings to life a kaleidoscope of unforgettable characters: quirky, resourceful heroines, irresistible heroes, chilling foes, enchanting urchins, overbearing aunts, long-suffering husbands, rapscallion friends, and more.

Georgette Heyer was a very private woman and refused all media attempts to discuss her works or personal life. She was married to George Ronald Rougier, an engineer and later a barrister, with whom she had one son, Richard. Despite her reluctance to be a public figure during her lifetime, the brilliant Georgette Heyer is beloved by millions of readers and has inspired generations of authors. Her work lives on to inspire millions more.